IRISH SCIENCE

Liverpool Science Fiction Texts and Studies

Recent titles in the series

IRISH SCIENCE FICTION

JACK FENNELL

LIVERPOOL UNIVERSITY PRESS

First published 2014 by
Liverpool University Press
4 Cambridge Street
Liverpool
L69 7ZU

This paperback edition published 2022

British Library Cataloguing-in-Publication data
A British Library CIP record is available

ISBN 978-1-78138-119-9 cased
ISBN 978-1-80207-693-6 paperback

Typeset by Carnegie Book Production, Lancaster
Printed and bound by CPI Group (UK) Ltd, Croydon CR0 4YY

Contents

Acknowledgements

This book owes its existence to the generosity of a great many people.

First and foremost, I want to thank Prof. Tom Moylan and Dr. Michael J. Griffin. Thanks also to Dr. Mark Bould and to Prof. Margaret Harper for their kind words, encouragement and constructive criticism. I would also like to thank all those who offered feedback on my work, in particular Prof. Anthony McElligott, Prof. Peadar Kirby, Prof. Tom Lodge, Dr. Joachim Fischer, Prof. Antonis Balasopoulos, Kim Stanley Robinson, Darko Suvin, Anthony Cond, Sue Barnes, Sebastian Manley and Prof. Philip O'Leary.

The whole undertaking would have been practically impossible without the generous support of the Irish Research Council for the Humanities and Social Sciences (now known simply as the Irish Research Council). Huge thanks also to Prof. Bríona Nic Dhiarmada, without whose help this book would probably not exist at all.

In my experience, it seemed that while no comprehensive bibliography of Irish science fiction exists, everyone I spoke to was aware of at least one such work. This project would have been significantly shorter if not for people suggesting texts for me to look at. Much thanks to Dr. Michael G. Kelly, John and Mary Fitzgerald and countless others.

Thanks are also due to the University of Limerick's Glucksman Library, the library of Mary Immaculate College, the National Library of Ireland and Cork City Library, whose staff were all very helpful and gracious in allowing me access to odd and hard-to-trace materials. Here I would especially thank Éadaoin Ní Chléirigh for her extraordinary kindness in granting me access to her late father's personal library.

I would also like to thank those whose friendship and support kept me sane through the past number of years, namely David Smart, John "Donny" Rowe, Aaron Smart, Ciara Williams, Jana Bedaňová, Claire Crowley, Pádraig Baggott, Alan Collins, Shane and Jason Sibbel, Gary, Aidan and Ryan O'Doherty, Aoife Harney, Eoghan O'Brien, Barry Cronin, Rory Devane, Jean Cronin, Trish and Roberto, Liam and Finola, Tom and Joan, Mark Fennell, Johnny and Anna, Martin and Liz (and the rest of the Hamburg crew). My apologies to anyone I may have omitted; I know there must be some...

Last but most certainly not least, I want to thank my parents, who have put up with my fascination for the bizarre since I was old enough to talk.

Introduction

Science *knows* it doesn't know everything – otherwise, it would stop. Just because science doesn't know everything doesn't mean you can fill in the gaps with whatever fairytale most appeals to you.

– Dara Ó Briain, *Dara Ó Briain Talks Funny* (2008)

This book is not an encyclopaedia. I began with the expectation that the area I had chosen to scrutinise would be small and manageable. Little did I know that there were many more Irish SF works than I suspected, in English and in Irish, going back at least as far as the 1850s. Everyone I spoke to knew of one or two books or short stories and assumed that was the extent of it, but the one or two examples given were different every time. There was a general awareness of this stuff, but nobody had pulled it together systematically. With every week that went past, more and more novels and short works were brought to my attention. The project expanded far beyond what I originally expected, until I was forced to abandon my ambition to cover every single Irish SF text.

To begin with, I have omitted films, firstly because film studies is not my forte, and secondly because the few Irish films that could have been included – *The Boy from Mercury* and *Zonad*, for example – make tongue-in-cheek use of the genre while keeping it at arm's length (in the former, the science-fictional elements occur only in the imagination of the daydreaming young protagonist, while in the latter, an escaped criminal cons the moronic inhabitants of a small village into believing that he is an extraterrestrial). Other productions, such as *Éireville*, parody known SF works in order to poke fun at aspects of Irish society, but the SF is never more than exotic window-dressing for an over-the-top satire. For the most part, Irish films have not engaged with the genre on its own terms, though this is starting to change, as evidenced by the genetic-engineering horror *Isolation* and the alien-invasion comedy *Grabbers*.

When it comes to deciding what to omit from a strictly literary study, the most obvious question is who exactly gets included under the label

"Irish"? Is such a distinction meaningful at all? There are political concerns to take into account, for a start: the island of Ireland contains two different countries, though the name "Ireland" is colloquially assumed to refer only to the twenty-six county Republic. I devote an entire chapter of this book to analysing the work of Bob Shaw and James White, and another to the SF of Ian McDonald; C.S. Lewis is briefly mentioned as well, along with the many anonymous and pseudonymous authors of nineteenth-century "future war" fiction, all of whom were/are Northern Irish.

My get-out-of-jail-free card here is that when I say "Ireland" I am referring to the island as a whole, both territories included, and I am not attempting to construct any single, overarching definition of "Irishness." This gives rise to a host of other problems, though: when I say "Irish SF," am I simply referring to SF produced on the island of Ireland? If so, this survey ought to include the work of writers such as Harry Harrison and Anne McCaffrey, who had established their careers as SF authors in the USA long before moving to take advantage of the Republic's tax exemption for writers and artists. For some reason their inclusion would seem odd, and yet their exclusion seems quite unfair – both were of Irish descent (Harrison had one Irish grandparent on his father's side, while the surname "McCaffrey" quite clearly demonstrates an Irish heritage), both of them became Irish citizens, and both of them resided in Ireland from the 1970s onwards. As I have explained, the present study is not intended to be encyclopaedic, but it looks suspicious when I conveniently omit any mention of authors who might complicate my terms of reference.

Here too, I have an escape hatch: among my plans for the future is a study of the SF, fantasy and horror of the Irish Diaspora, under which Harrison and McCaffrey would certainly be included, along with authors such as Anne Rice, Caitlín R. Kiernan and M.P. Shiel. My working definition of "Diaspora" will doubtlessly prove as problematic as any definition advanced in these pages, not least because some of the authors considered here could be categorised under it.

To abuse one of Carl Freedman's terms, my choice of subjects is largely "pre-critical": that is, instinctive or emotive rather than logical. On the one hand, adopting a too-stringent set of criteria for "Irishness" comes close to nativism and auto-exoticism; on the other hand, lax criteria would result in blatant absurdities and a book of unmanageable size. Hard as it may be to put into words, there is no way I could accept a definition under which Frank Herbert would be included for writing *The White Plague*, or Ian McDonald excluded for living in Belfast.

My final excuse in this regard is that this book is not intended to be both the start and the end of the discussion. A *discussion* implies a dialogue. The terms and definitions I rely on for this book will of course have aspects that others will find problematic – my readings of the texts are subjective and the conclusions I reach are opinionated. I have no interest in building bulwarks against all potential criticisms; if there is an argument to be had, I look forward to it.

Yes, It Does Exist

To many people, the very idea of "Irish science fiction" is inherently ridiculous. Firstly, there are the laughs to be had from inserting science-fictional tropes into an Irish setting, as in the old joke about the Irish astronauts planning to blast off in a turf-powered rocket.[1] Secondly, there is comic value in placing Irish characters in science-fictional settings, as in "Cork People in Space," a recurring sketch on the Irish television comedy programme *Nighthawks* (1988–1992). Like oil and water, Ireland and science fiction are commonly imagined to be incompatible things. Though it may be difficult, however, it is in fact possible to mix oil and water, whereupon the real difficulty lies in trying to separate them again. Ireland's relationship with SF is somewhat similar – it is difficult to imagine any compatibility between them, but once they are mixed, it is nearly impossible to conceive of an Ireland that is *not* science-fictional to some extent. The aim of this study is not to prove the existence of an Irish science-fictional imagination. It is a matter of fact that SF has been written by Irish authors for at least a hundred and fifty years (or longer, depending on the rigidity of one's definition of the genre).[2]

I will argue that SF, fantasy, horror and the other "ahistorical" genres (nomenclature coined by Darko Suvin) have a common root in myth, the dominant cultural logic of traditional or "premodern" societies. Originally, they were not differentiated – this only occurred when the emergence of political and economic modernity in Europe brought about changes in the way history was conceived, and "tradition" was recast as something that had to be overcome. Originally characterised as "savagery" and "superstition," it was later dismissed as "ideology." *Gulliver's Travels*, discussed in more detail below, is the perfect example of this, demonstrating that in the eighteenth century, genres were still being mixed and matched according to the author's intentions, and that secular modernity did not defeat mythological tradition overnight.

With political modernity came the rise of imperialism, which drew its self-justification from a pejorative view of tradition. Colonisers (and present-day apologists for imperialism) emphasise colonisation as a process of "modernisation," while at the same time emphasising colonised people's exoticism (or premodern otherness). Ironies abound in modernisation discourse, the most obvious of which is that traditional belief systems are no more ridiculous than the imperial colonisers" belief in the resurrection of Jesus (Langer 127), or modern SF tropes such as faster-than-light travel (137). In other words, colonies were places in which tradition and modernity existed side by side – myth is stronger in these places than in the imperial centre, and as a consequence, generic tendencies may not be as clearly defined.

The reason for this is that the process of "modernisation" necessarily involves the popularisation of science, to a greater or lesser degree. This in turn was often undertaken according to the colonisers' economic needs – in many cases, extending only to the creation of a productive economic base.[3] Additionally, Joe Cleary notes that in contrast to the generations-long modernisation process undergone by the nations that would become imperial centres, "One of the distinguishing character-istics of the colonial outposts of [the] Atlantic economy is the velocity of their transition from various forms of pre-capitalist society to mercantile capitalist modernity, without experiencing [...] the long conditioning of other medieval European societies" (Cleary 33).

Rudimentary science education, along with the speed with which colonies were modernised, create the conditions that Tatiana Chernyshova argues (outlined in greater detail below) allow for the emergence of modern myths, as incomplete scientific knowledge is supplemented by "projection from oneself": in other words, from the residual tradition or mythology of the colonised. Different means of technological education in different colonies, received according to different cultural logics, will thus produce different scientific myths from which parochial pseudo-sciences will arise. In addition, there are postcolonial SF texts, in which indigenous traditions and Western science are intentionally hybridised (Langer 127) to criticise the latter's dominance (131–2) and demonstrate that the former has not been eradicated (136).

The problem with studying "national science fictions" in terms of tradition is that one runs the risk of taking for granted the existence of a stable, unchanging national identity, or a single tradition. Tradition means different things to different people – some will retain tradition purely because it is familiar, while others may abandon it and actively try to distance themselves from it, and others still may return to it as a means of reclaiming an "authentic" identity. In Ireland, the latter created an urge to turn back time completely and start again from the middle ages with an intact Gaelic culture: this can be seen in the twentieth-century Catholic fascination with antiquity and mediaevalism, and in specific texts such as Charlotte ("L") McManus's *The Professor in Erin* and

Micheál Mac Craith's "Cuairt ar an nGealaigh," both of which will be discussed in the following chapters.

Definitions of Science Fiction

Freedman notes that "[it] is symptomatic of the complexity of SF as a generic category that critical discussion of it tends to devote considerable attention to the problem of definition" (13). Within SF criticism, there are a number of differing (sometimes mutually antagonistic) schools of thought regarding this problem, divided, as in the case of so many intractable differences, along historical lines.

A number of critics maintain that the genre's history begins at the point when it was first called "science fiction," and thus hold that Hugo Gernsback was the pre-eminent force behind its emergence. Debates surrounding this "Gernsback School" are almost invariably heated, as exemplified by the work of Gary Westfahl, who begins his historical analysis by declaring: "If critics are free to ignore contemporary criticism in a genre and look only at texts, then the door is open for them to define the genre in any way they choose, select as exemplars any works they choose, and reach any conclusions they choose" (3). In pursuing "The *True* History of Science Fiction" (my italics), he thus feels it necessary to accuse critics such as Brian Aldiss and Darko Suvin of distortion (3–5) and prevarication (13–16), and even goes so far as to equate literary criticism with bullying (8). There is much that is objectionable in Westfahl's analysis, but his arguments are predicated on quite a reasonable assertion: "Literary genres appear in history for one reason: someone declares that a genre exists and persuades writers, publishers, readers and critics that she is correct" (12). In other words, the existence of a genre is indicated and confirmed at the level of production and reception, as is the case for SF (6).

A major difficulty emerges, however, when this observation is taken to be the sole investigative paradigm. Edward James, in surveying nineteenth-century SF, notes that Verne referred to his works as *voyages extraordinaires*, while "scientific romances" was the preferred label in Britain (though Wells referred to his less plausible texts as "scientific fantasies"). In America, the terms used were more varied, including "romance," "scientific fiction," "invention stories," "off-trail stories," "impossible stories," "different stories" and "pseudo-scientific studies" (James 28–9). James concludes from this that "[no one] before 1929, therefore, was writing within a self-conscious genre, or had begun to formulate any kind of definition of the type of fiction which they were writing" (29), a conclusion as reductive as it is astonishing. Though different authors used different terms to describe what they were writing, it does not follow that they were blind to the obvious similarities between their respective bodies of work.

Outside the "Gernsback School," analyses and historical inquiry into SF tend to rely more on aesthetic and textual issues, with historical context accounted for in terms of literary and cultural influences. Probably the most oft-cited origin point for the genre apart from Gernsback is Mary Shelley's *Frankenstein*, acknowledged as a progenitor text by John Clute, Brian Aldiss and many others. To take just one example, author Brian Stableford cites *Frankenstein* as a work of SF because, as he sees it, the narrative contains no stereotypically "gothic" tropes: "sinister ancient edifices, evil conspiracies, hideous apparitions [...] the threat of sexual violation, and intimations of incest" (Stableford 1995b, 47). Stableford makes a convincing case against the charge that the narrative is anti-scientific, pointing out that Victor Frankenstein renounces sorcery in favour of scientific inquiry (47–8), and interpreting the novel's subtitle, "The Modern Prometheus," in light of the atheism of Mary Shelley's husband, Percy Bysshe Shelley, to whom the legendary Prometheus was "a great hero whose condemnation [...] was firm proof of the horrid unreasonableness and downright wickedness of godly tyrants" (49).[4]

Along with these reasonable arguments, though, one must take into account Stableford's implied definition of SF narratives. *Gulliver's Travels* must be disqualified, he argues, "on the grounds that its vitriolic parody of the activity and ambitions of scientists alienates it completely from the kind of proto-scientific world-view which Mary Shelley is ready to embrace" (48). Though he admits that Victor Frankenstein is a scientist rather than a wizard simply because Shelley wanted "to do something different" with her horror story (53), it appears as though, in Stableford's view, an uncritical view of science is the necessary defining characteristic of SF.

Another critical tendency, somewhat less pronounced, is the differentiation of SF from fantasy as the offspring of different religious cultures: SF is intrinsically "Protestant," while fantasy is inherently "Catholic," a binary framework with an obvious Irish resonance. The most recent scholar to advance this point of view is Adam Roberts, whose reading of James Blish's classic novel *A Case of Conscience* (in which a Jesuit priest destroys an extraterrestrial race that has no concept of God, sin or an afterlife) highlights the ideological underpinnings of this binary framework: "Under the logic of [Catholicism], the novel is an interesting exploration of a theological conundrum; under the logic of

[Protestantism], a heartbreaking story of human arrogance and short-sightedness" (Roberts 2007, xiii–xiv). The equation of Catholicism with fantasy and vice versa is not politically innocent, since it is inextricably bound to a conception of Catholicism as a tyrannical, anti-intellectual monoculture and of fantasy as a conservative, reactionary genre. It also fails to account for the fact that SF's future worlds tend overwhelmingly to be either atheist or passively non-religious, and that many of the genre's greatest writers come from cultural backgrounds other than Protestantism. It seems self-evident to me that while religiosity may be a defining characteristic of individual texts, it can by no means be considered a driving force for genres as a whole.

The emphasis on finding a single progenitor (be it an editor, a novel or a philosophy) seems to be linked to the idea that "science" is the operative word in "science fiction," and implies that the philosophy of scientific inquiry appeared suddenly, out of nowhere, thus making it possible to identify a discrete origin point for the genre. The fact is, though, that science in itself is not integral to SF. In fact, most of the best works in this genre are derived from "science" that is distinctly muddled and unreliable. As for the notion that science and modernity appeared suddenly, everywhere, causing massive cultural upheaval, it must be noted that they arrived more suddenly in some places than they did in others. If a comparative historical analysis is applied to this idea, with due attention to the imperial realities of the age, it can be said to be false. Modernisation did not happen instantaneously in imperial centres, but rather occurred over a number of generations; it was in fact colonised territories that experienced modernisation as a sudden and traumatic process.

Another issue is that, for many critics, a fondness for one particular genre of the ahistorical literature family seems to necessitate a disparaging attitude towards the others: choosing to make a particular genre the focus of one's study obliges the analyst to argue for that genre's uniqueness, and thus to frame that genre in terms that distance it from the others. Likewise, the identification of a single progenitor requires a series of arguments outlining the ways in which other theorists' exemplars fall short of a definition constructed in terms of that progenitor's influence. A related tendency, especially pronounced in the work of Darko Suvin, is to make the case for a genre's literary superiority in terms of an assumed innate political character – as if it were as impossible for an SF text to be reactionary as for a fantasy or a horror to be progressive.[5] Edward James's point that "It would be dangerous to start excluding works because they did not correspond to the accepted wisdom of late twentieth-century readers" (James 31) applies as much to works that are morally or politically repugnant as it does to texts with questionable scientific content.

Understandable though they may be, these impulses obfuscate the kinship between the genres. In my opinion, the non-realist or estranged genres have far more similarities than differences, and readers and producers recognise these similarities, even as they mark the distinctions. As China Miéville says, the "atom" of these genres' estrangement is an "unreality function," or an explicit articulation of alterity (Miéville 243–4), and for this reason, I assert that the definition debate may be most usefully informed by considering them in the context of an ur-category: myth.

Definitions of Myth

Invoking myth is problematic. Firstly, the term itself can cause confusion: on the one hand, in the West it is often understood only in the classical sense, whereby the generic term "myth" is taken to refer exclusively to the mythology of Greece and Rome, to the exclusion of all others.[6] On the other hand, it has a rather vague vernacular usage referring to misconceptions, rumours and urban legends. The overall major problem with the term is that, because it seems so expansive and yet so vague, invoking it can seem somewhat glib. Freedman points out that "The very ease with which the broadest definition of science fiction can be justified may itself arouse suspicion" (Freedman 16). It is fortuitous, then, that SF's relationship to myth has been subject to a number of contrasting interpretations that preclude any easy definition.

To begin with, most SF criticism is hostile to myth: Suvin encapsulates this position in saying, "myth is re-enactment, eternal return, and the opposite of creative human freedom" (Suvin 2010, 89). Where criticism is not antagonistic to myth, it is often indifferent, regarding myth as an irrelevance or treating it as a handy resource for authors, rather than a constitutive element of the genre itself. For example, there is Robert Scholes's and Eric S. Rabkin's brief 1977 analysis, wherein they relate various SF tropes to particular myths, with a strong emphasis on religiosity: for example, the "personality tape" (in modern sci-fi parlance, "uploaded mind"), unnatural life extension, and the artificial creation of life all invoke archetypal stories dealing with the anxieties of life and death (Scholes and Rabkin 165–7). Alongside those who borrow from Judaeo-Christian myth, there are other authors, such as Roger Zelazny, who consciously use non-Western myths in their writing (168), and others, such as Frank Herbert and H.P. Lovecraft, who set out to create their own mythological systems (169).

Among literary critics with a more sympathetic view of myth, there is no broad consensus as to what the relationship between myth and SF actually is. In 1957, Northrop Frye suggested that the then-increasing popularity of SF was symptomatic of "a return" from irony to myth as a means of re-appraising modern society's distance from the condition of "savagery" (Frye 48–9). He does not elaborate upon this idea, but in noting that SF was displacing the murder mystery's central place in the popular literature of the mid-twentieth century, he allows us to infer that this return to myth was a consequence of the emergence of the police state, for which "melodramatic" literary forms such as the murder mystery were "advance propaganda" (47). In this conception, myth is nostalgia for a supposed age of greater moral certitude.

Rather than seeing SF as a "return" to myth, Robert M. Philmus proposed in 1970 that the genre is in itself mythopoetic, "taking literally, and dramatizing, the metaphors expressive of those ideas that define, at least in part, the beliefs and nature of the social order" (Philmus 21). The purpose of this, whatever the politics of a given text, is to "[interpret] sectors of historical actuality through mythic displacement" (30). Philmus's reading is opposed to Frye's, with myth essentially described as a vehicle of ironic exaggeration, but it also resonates with Walter Benjamin's use of "mythic" as an "approximate term" for the substance of the sphere of the "poetized" (*das Gedichtete*), "the transition from the functional unity of life to that of the poem," from which successful art draws life, in contrast to weak art that refers only to "the immediate feeling of life" (Benjamin 1996, 19–20).

Neither a consolatory return nor a generative force in and of itself, SF emerges from Tatiana Chernyshova's 1972 analysis as an expression of humanity's myth-making urge, and I find this particular analysis to be the most useful. The human mind, Chernyshova argues, is capable of drawing conclusions from incomplete information, and it does so by supplementing "true information" with "false information," drawing upon "inner resources" of consciousness (Chernyshova 348). Myths originate as explanatory models of reality, and they gradually become more complex as more "true information" comes to light; this is also, Chernyshova points out, precisely how scientific knowledge evolves (346), and this similarity logically leads to the use of analogy in the popularisation of science. While science cannot be strictly equated with analogy, at the same time it could not exist without analogical frames of reference (349), and every so often, these analogies escape from the lab to gain wider social currency, giving rise to a new myth (351).[7] The

difference between "proper science" and scientific myth is the difference
between "exact knowledge" and "approximate knowledge"; because
everyday thought is based on images rather than calculations, popular
scientific knowledge is *approximate* rather than *exact*, and the gaps in
that knowledge are filled by the mythopoetic impulse, or "projection
from oneself" (352).

This "projection from oneself," or substitution of "false information" for
"true information," is precisely what the author Abe Kôbô alludes to in his
1962 assessment of pseudoscience's role in popular culture.[8] Both "pro"-
and "anti"-SF critics are united, in Abe's view, in their hostility towards
the "absurdities" of pseudoscience; Abe himself, on the other hand, saw
pseudoscience as "the very foundation of science fiction," and argued
that "as long as it clings naively to that word 'science,' science fiction will
never venture off the sight-seeing trails printed in guidebooks" (Abe 343):

> We must not forget that the concept of realism is no more than a
> literary technique, with no relation to the facts of science, let alone
> to "realness" in the conventional sense. For example, there are
> critics who will praise a work by saying that the author's predictions
> have become reality: not only does this have nothing to do with
> the criticism of literature, it does literature a disservice. (344)

The notion that SF must have some predictive element, in other words,
is so transparently false that the task of dispelling it is a waste of time:
it turns out that the operative word in "science fiction" is "fiction," after
all. Science fiction, despite all the implications of that name, is a genre
in which *approximate* knowledge and "false information" – the basis of
pseudoscience in the popular imagination – are of greater importance to
the reading process than scientific literacy. Science fiction is a literature
of *gaps*.

The truth of this manifests itself in the science-fictional reading
process. Marc Angenot's seminal 1978/79 essay "The Absent Paradigm:
An Introduction to the Semiotics of Science Fiction" outlines how the
strategic withholding of information on the part of the author triggers
"projection from oneself": when the author presents the reader with
a Martian word, the absent paradigm implied is a Martian *language*,
with its own syntax; the notion of a Martian language presupposes the
existence of a Martian *culture*, with its own history, art forms, and so
on. While the full context of the hypothetical Martian society will more
than likely never be revealed in the story, this lack of information does
not prevent the reader from presupposing the existence of that context,
and so the reader becomes an active participant in the construction of

the fictional world (Agenot, 9–19). This process of "filling in the gaps" provides us with a means to examine non-Western pseudoscience, and thus, non-Western SF: Dick Roughsey (birth name Goobalathaldin), an Australian Aboriginal, gives a perfect example of this process in his autobiography, *Moon and Rainbow* (1971).

In a chapter discussing *puri-puri*, or magic intended to harm another, once practised by Aboriginal tribes around the Gulf of Carpentaria, Roughsey tells us, "I once asked an old man why he couldn't kill a white man with his puri-puri. He said, 'We can't puri-puri white men because they've got too much salt in their bodies.' I told him that I would be eating plenty of salt from then on and would be safe from his puri-puri" (Roughsey 79). Clearly, this magic only does harm to those who believe in it, but the unidentified practitioner, who accepts *puri-puri* as an objectively real phenomenon, chooses to explain the white man's immunity in material, physical terms that reveal a distinct cultural logic. Doubtlessly as a result of observing the bleaching effects of salt water, the old man has concluded that salt is the cause of white skin. White people's bodies contain "too much" salt, and from this line of reasoning, we might conclude that without this excessive amount of salt, their skins would naturally be black. White men's immunity to magic, or lack of belief in it, is a consequence of the same condition that makes them divergent from the black norm, reversing the colonial discourse that has always presented indigenous traditions as proof of the racial inferiority of dark-skinned people. The emergence of a pseudoscientific myth is confirmed by the author when he says he will increase his salt intake to build up his own immunity to magic, which seems like a reasonable and practical precaution for a believer to take.

The description of SF as a variant form of myth-making, however, returns us to the circular debates on the distinction between SF and fantasy: both genres are manifestly non-realist (often distinctly *anti*-realist), and they generally appeal to the same readers. Readers recognise a distinction between them, but that distinction can be quite difficult to describe.

Cognition

Currently, the dominant definition of the SF genre is that proposed by Suvin – that it is a literature of "cognitive estrangement," the necessary condition for which is the presence of a *novum* or "cognitive innovation" within the text: "*a totalizing phenomenon or relationship deviating from the author's and implied reader's norm of reality* [...] a mediating category whose explicative potency springs from its rare bridging of literary and extraliterary, fictional and empirical, formal and ideological domains, in brief from its unalienable historicity" (Suvin 2010, 68; my italics). These traits distinguish it from fantasy, which Suvin initially described as "a proto-Fascist revulsion against modern civilization, material rationalism, and such" (73). It should be noted here that Suvin has since changed his stance on fantasy somewhat, conceding that "[if] all estranged genres aspire to be read as parables, then each Fantasy text also has a tenor and cannot be simply dismissed because of its vehicle" (Suvin 2000, 211). As China Miéville notes, this "grudging open-mindedness" reflects a critical necessity rather than a Damascene conversion, and is to be taken as Suvin's response to the current erosion of boundaries between SF and fantasy (Miéville 232).

Within an SF story, the novum is hegemonic – it permeates every aspect of the fictional world and necessitates new human relationships and norms estranged from our own. Within the story-world, these altered social structures are unremarkable in themselves and operate according to an internal logic that the characters usually take for granted (Suvin 2010, 74–6). The implied reader is brought into this estranged world, and must navigate it by drawing upon his or her capacity for problem-solving and pattern recognition (i.e., *cognitively*), with reference to prior knowledge of logic and scientific fact:

> The novum is postulated on and validated by the post-Baconian scientific method [...] what differentiates SF from the "ahistorical" literary genres [...] is the presence of scientific cognition as the sign or correlative of a method [...] identical to that of a modern philosophy of science [...] [however] a proper analysis of SF cannot focus on its ostensible scientific content or scientific data. (69)

Here Suvin presents a concise answer to the question of how SF differs from fantasy: reliance on a rationalist discourse defined by the "non-supernatural explanation of realities," making use of logical principles such as Occam's razor, falsifiability, and so on (72). This is not an admission that scientific plausibility is a genre prerequisite:

> Though such cognition obviously cannot, in a work of verbal fiction, be empirically tested either in laboratory or by observation in nature, it can be methodically developed against the background of a body of already existing cognitions, or at the very least as a "mental experiment" following accepted scientific, that is, cognitive, logic. (70)

Returning to Abe's observation that SF is more about "pseudoscience" than actual science, the *portrayed method* matters more than the result: one can have a vessel capable of travelling faster than light (contradicting all that is currently understood about the physical universe), provided that the supernatural is not invoked to acquire it. The sensibility of cognition, even as it pertains to the presentation of a world different to our own, thus requires consistent adherence to both the internal logic of that invented world and the social or physical norms of the implied reader's empirical environment:

> [The] novelty has to be convincingly explained in concrete, even if imaginary, terms [...] the particular essential novum of any SF tale must in its turn be judged by how much new insight into imaginary but coherent and this-worldly, that is, *historical,* relationships it affords and could afford. (85–6)

Freedman, for whom "cognition" is necessarily linked to both science and critical thought (Freedman 3–4, 8), finds the term's application to SF problematic: "the category of cognition," he says, "appears to commit the literary critic to making generic distinctions on the basis of matters far removed from literature and genre," precisely because the science in SF is not always "real science," and some texts do not easily fit into just one category. "Must we wait for a scientific consensus on the matter before deciding whether the text is science fiction or fantasy?" (17). Freedman's second difficulty with the Suvin definition is that a lot of SF texts do not produce meaningful estrangements or cognitive moments, and enforcing this criterion produces odd results: "Can we really accept a definition by the logic of which [*Star Trek*] is not science fiction at all but the plays of Brecht – to take the obvious instance – are?" (19). Freedman's solution is to fine-tune the definition of "cognition":

> What is rather at stake is what we might term [...] the *cognition effect.* The crucial issue for generic discrimination is not any episte-mological judgement external to the text itself on the rationality or irrationality of the latter's imaginings, but rather [...] the attitude *of the text itself* to the kind of estrangements being performed. (18)

The distinction between "cognition" and Freedman's "cognition effect" must be consciously noted, otherwise "patent absurdities" would ensue – such as reclassifying older SF texts as fantasy because scientific advance has since ruled out the plausibility of their *nova*. The shift in emphasis from "cognition" to "cognition effect" certainly allows for greater critical emphasis on the pseudoscience Abe determines to be fundamental to the genre, but this potential was already implicit in Suvin's formulation. Freedman's re-phrasing of Suvin continues in his dialectical reading of "cognitive estrangement," which affirms the hierarchical relationship Suvin proposes between SF and its notional antagonist, fantasy:

> If the dialectic is flattened out to mere cognition, then the result is "realistic" or mundane fiction [...] if the dialectic is flattened out to mere estrangement (or, it might be argued, pseudo-estrangement), then the result is fantasy, which estranges, or appears to estrange, but in an irrationalist, theoretically illegitimate way. (17)

By contrast, Miéville complicates both Suvinian "cognition" and Freedman's "cognition effect" by focusing on literature's necessarily hierarchical relationship between author and reader – they are not equal partners in the enterprise, he argues, because literature (especially in an "ahistorical" genre such as SF) is a process of *something being done with language by someone to someone,*" meaning that "the question, then, becomes, *whose* cognition effect? More pertinently, whose cognition? And whose effect?" (Miéville 235). Miéville argues that, rather than the product of a "scientific register," the cognition effect, which is a form of *persuasion,* is "a function of (textual) *charismatic authority.* The reader surrenders to the cognition effect to the extent that he or she surrenders to the authority of the text and its author function" (238).

This resonates with the analysis of author and critic Samuel R. Delany, who points out that individual words convey no information unless they are placed in a formal relationship with each other: "The idea of *meaning, information* or *content* as something contained by words is a misleading visualization" (Delany 2). In this light, the act of reading reveals itself to be intensively cognitive and "rational," regardless of the text being read: "The process as we move our eyes from word to word is corrective and revisionary rather than progressive. Each new word revises the complex picture we had a moment before" (4).

The reader's socio-cultural context, Delany argues, determines what kinds of revisions are accepted as legitimate. Taking the word "dog" as an example, he demonstrates that it has a limited number of modifiers that make logical sense within everyday speech or naturalistic fiction: one can naturalistically describe a *collie dog* or a *big and shaggy dog*, but not a *Chevrolet dog*, an *oxymoronic dog* or "a *turgidly cardiac dog*" (5). At the time of writing, none of the latter examples make logical or grammatical sense as naturalistic word-combinations. The difference between the two registers presented here, the naturalistic and the nonsensical, is described by Delany as a difference in "subjunctivity," "the tension on the thread of meaning that runs between (to borrow Saussure's term for 'word':) sound-image and sound-image": the subjunctive register of reportage, Delany says, permeates the text with the sentiment *this happened*; each genre has a subjunctive level that determines its reception by the reader, so naturalistic fiction has a subjunctive level of *this could have happened*, while fantasy has one of *this could not have happened* (10–11).

These descriptors are strictly true only at the beginning of a fictive text. During the process of reading, providing that the story is sufficiently well-written and internally consistent, the natural tendency of a text's subjunctive level is to "drop" to that of straightforward reportage (*this happened*) or at the very least, the *could have happened* of naturalistic fiction. In Delany's opinion, this re-processing – synonymous in his argument with "escape value" or a "sense of adventure" – is achieved through "the intensity with which the real actions of the story impinge on the protagonist's [and therefore the reader's] consciousness" (7–8), which is dependent upon the implied "expertise" of the author, as represented by one or more characters in the story (18).

For Miéville, this implied expertise has a sinister political significance. Science fiction's cognition is not truly cognition at all, but a process whereby the reader "surrenders the terrain of supposed conceptual logic and rigour to the whims and diktats of a cadre of 'expert' author-functions," which Miéville maintains is "a translation into meta-literary and aggrandising terms of the very layer of technocrats often envisaged in SF and its cultures as society's best hope" (Miéville 239). Furthermore, "neither writer nor reader finds cognitive logic in the text's claims. Instead, they *read/write as if they do*" (239; original italics). This invites questions as to how exactly the author-function persuades the reader to surrender his or her cognition. For Miéville (as for Delany), the ideological nature of the "cognition effect," relative to a charismatic author-function, is sufficient to explain this, since "[in] ideology, charisma and authority become autotelic – that is their point. In mediated microcosm, this is how SF can easily and with some justification end up being defined as that which is written by an SF writer" (241–2). As for Suvin's "post-Baconian scientific method," Miéville stridently asserts:

> To the extent that SF claims to be based on "science," and indeed on what is deemed "rationality," it is based on capitalist modernity's ideologically projected self-justification: not some abstract/ideal "science," but capitalist science's bullshit about itself. This is not, of course, to argue in favour of some (perhaps lumpen-postmodernist)

irrationalism, but that the "rationalism" that capitalism has traditionally had on offer is highly partial and ideological. (240–1)

Returning once again to the issue of pseudoscience in SF, Robert Philmus argues that "The locus of credibility, as it were, must be extended from the scientific rationale to the entire fictive situation – or, precisely, to its signification" (Philmus 19). In other words, SF is less about the cognitive side of Suvin's equation than it is about the estrangement itself (19–20). This idea is important to Miéville's conception of how SF may be distinguished from fantasy "as different ideological iterations of the 'estrangement' that, even in high Suvinianism, both sub-genres share" (Miéville 243).

This foreshadows my own argument by referring to SF and fantasy as "sub-genres," or to put it another way, different manifestations of the same over-arching category. However, I must disagree with Miéville on one point – in my opinion, the subject at hand is not a "dyad," but, at the very least, a "triad": there are forms of estrangement fundamental to the modern horror genre that are not necessary to either fantasy or SF, and vice versa. While these are not central to the present book, by briefly considering them and taking note of their similarities and differences we can enhance our understanding of the subject at hand. Taking Suvin's umbrella category of "ahistorical literatures" as our starting point, and with reference to the subjunctivity levels proposed by Delany, we can start to distinguish between the genres by examining their non-normative relationships to history.

Estrangement

For Suvin, estrangement (which, as he points out, is a necessary function of any work of fiction) is best characterised as a "feedback oscillation" between the page and the mind, as the reader uses the norms of his or her own world to understand the story's novum, and uses that understanding to reflect back on those norms, thus seeing them in a different light: key to this is "a narrative reality sufficiently autonomous and intransitive to be explored at length as to its own properties and the human relationships it implies" (Suvin 2010, 76). Some genres are "ahistorical" because the quality of their estrangements arises from non-normative relationships to history – "history" encompassing not just the chronological record, but also the ideological/hegemonic definitions of what is historically possible.

Miéville and Delany implicitly place the genre nowadays recognised as "horror" within the sphere of fantasy, while Suvin does so explicitly with the compound term "horror-fantasy," the better to emphasise the pejorative character he once ascribed to the fantasy genre. While I admit that the distinction is often quite weak, especially in the case of supernatural horror, the fact remains that there is (in Gary Westfahl's terms) a consensus of fans, critics and authors (or, as phrased by Miéville, a sociological phenomenon of production and consumption) that SF, fantasy and horror are to a large extent separate genres, even though they belong to the same literary family.

H.P. Lovecraft advances what seems to be a perfectly straightforward observation when he argues that the supernatural horror tale must contain "a certain atmosphere of breathless and unexplainable dread of outer, unknown forces" (Lovecraft 144). Thus, I would argue, its parent modes are what we might provisionally term the "incongruous modes": the Fantastic as defined by Tzvetan Todorov, the Grotesque according to Wolfgang Kayser, and the Absurd as outlined by Neil Cornwell (the capitalisation of each term is my own).

Todorov's Fantastic emerges from a narrative situation typical of estranged literature: "In a world which is indeed our world, the one we know, a world without devils, sylphides, or vampires, there occurs an event which cannot be explained by the laws of this same familiar world," an event to which the reader responds with confusion and hesitation (Todorov 25). Wolfgang Kayser's definition of "the Grotesque," on the other hand, is threefold: firstly the Grotesque depicts "the estranged world," where the mundane practices and artefacts of lived experience take on a sinister, altered aspect (Kayser 184–5); secondly, the Grotesque is "a play with the absurd," in which "the possibility of a deeper meaning" is suggested, but never confirmed (185–6); and finally, it represents "an attempt to invoke and subdue the demonic aspects of the world," representing the triumph of art over alienation (188). This in turn invites comparisons with Neil Cornwell's appraisal of the Absurd as an existentialist mode whose defining traits are futility, irrationality, ambiguity and nihilism, and whose operational paradigms are incongruity and paradox (Cornwell 3–5). The defining characteristic of the Absurd is its capacity to remove apparent meaning and purpose from the world as we understand it (13).

As outlined in the citations above, both Kayser's Grotesque and Todorov's Fantastic arise in an ephemeral moment prior to critical analysis, while the Absurd as defined by Cornwell denies the possibility of critical thought: to put it bluntly, they are all estrangement, and no cognition. Thus, the estrangement engendered by horror and its parent modes is that of the world breaking down, an ontological disaster that most closely corresponds to the subjunctive level Delany assigns to fantasy as a whole: *this could not happen*. In the context of ahistorical literature, those modes and genres that foreground estrangement while eschewing cognition depict the end of temporality. They are ahistorical because, in causing the accepted models of our reality to break down, they *end* history.

These "incongruous" modes do not provide a satisfactory context for discussing *fantasy* as it is understood today. Again, there is a sociological consensus that a fantasy genre exists, and that it has certain recognisable characteristics distinct from those of the other ahistorical literatures. There are in fact many sub-genres of fantasy, which critic Farah Mendlesohn has organised into a number of over-arching categories: the Portal-Quest fantasy (Mendlesohn 2008, 1–58); the Immersive fantasy, which "to make itself real, seems to demand that it is all there is" (89); the Intrusion fantasy (114–81), which depicts an incursion of the marvellous into the "real world"; and the Liminal fantasy (182–245). Simple incongruity is not the driving force behind any of these narrative forms, because the fantastic elements are deployed according to the texts' own logics, which have an internal consistency that must be appraised cognitively. To take into account the stubborn traces of cognition within the various fantasy sub-genres, Delany's proposed fantasy-subjunctive, *this could not have happened*, must be extended and refined to read: *this could not have happened in the world as we know it*. In fantasy, "the world as we know it" (i.e. the sum total of our knowledge and ideology) is of no importance – thus, fantasy is ahistorical because it treats our history as being irrelevant or incomplete.

I would argue, then, that SF is ahistorical in that *it pretends to be history*. The estrangements on offer are always presented as being historically possible or inevitable: futuristic settings obviously come with histories that have not yet happened, "alternative worlds" posit histories that supposedly *could have* happened, and time-travel stories allow for all kinds of reinterpretations or re-contextualisations of history. More than either of the other ahistorical genres, SF tries hard to persuade us that *this happened*. Occasionally, the media will proclaim that "science *fiction* has become science *fact*," usually in connection with the invention or market launch of a consumer gadget reminiscent of technology seen in SF television or film.[9]

Kathleen L. Spencer describes the concept of *genre* as an "unwritten contract" between author and reader – having identified the genre of a text, the reader's interpretation of it will be guided by certain expectations, which the author has implicitly agreed to satisfy (Spencer 35). "Reader expectations" may seem like a reductive basis for describing genres, and it carries an unwholesome implication of market-mandated mediocrity. To a large extent, this is correct, as there is a large market for derivative ahistorical works, endless reiterations of *The Lord of the Rings* and *Star Wars*. In a broader sense, though, I would argue that reader expectations correspond closely to these non-normative approaches to history, though these expectations may not be entirely conscious and may possibly resist articulation. They read horror, in my opinion, because they wish to experience the suspension of historical causality; they read fantasy to experience a history completely removed from their own; and SF allows them to experience history in an altered context. This desire for different kinds of ahistoricity is a product of the emergence of modernity.

It is my intention to argue not that there is no qualitative difference between SF and the other ahistorical genres – the differences between them are obvious and manifold, even when they are considered not as discrete "genres" but as coexistent "generic tendencies" (see Freedman, below) – but that, at one point, they were undifferentiated. Indeed, one could even argue that this separation did not occur until the early twentieth century, when, as Mark Bould and Sherryl Vint point out, there was no overall consensus about the importance of science in SF, and magazines printed a wide variety of ahistorical texts (Bould and Vint 2011, 41). Though the various qualities of estrangement outlined above appear distinctly different with regard to their respective attitudes to history, these differences are neither immutable nor universal. For all their historical contrasts, there is considerable overlap between the different estrangements and more than one variety may pop up within the same text. Miéville notes that "[at] the same sociological level at which SF and fantasy continue to be distinguished, the boundaries between them also – if anything at an accelerating pace – continue to erode" (244), and Victoria De Zwaan sees the emergence of "slipstream" fiction as a possible indication of SF's movement towards "anti-realism" (De Zwaan 502). Freedman, examining the problem of fluid genre boundaries dialectically, comes to the conclusion that "a text is not filed under a generic category; instead, a generic tendency is something that happens within a text" (Freedman 20). This comes perilously close to redefining genre out of existence, but it highlights an important point: the various ahistorical genres work particularly well together, which explains how the author-fan-critic consensus is currently changing as to how different they really are.

In my opinion, this erosion (or perhaps reconfiguration) of the distinctions between the genres is only possible because of their common ancestry in myth, and the various proposed links between SF and myth can be detected in the other genres, too. Frye's reading of SF as a "return to myth" also resonates with reactionary fantasy texts (most obviously, Tolkien's *The Lord of the Rings*, in which myth is invoked in an attempt to reverse the process of industrialisation), and the notion of this return being "from the age of irony" has informed a great deal of modern horror (as in John Landis's film *An American Werewolf in London*, in which the protagonists' twentieth-century insouciance is violently shattered by actual contact with a legend from the Dark Ages). By the same token, Philmus's proposed "deflection of history into myth" is explicitly true in the case of much postmodern "intrusion fantasy," which co-opts conspiracy theory and the machinery of *realpolitik* into its narrative logic: witness the growing number of texts in which a shadowy police force, government department or corporate concern exerts bureaucratic control over the supernatural, while keeping its own existence secret from the general public.

In my opinion, the most convincing analysis of myth's connection to SF is that advanced by Chernyshova, by virtue of the fact that it can be applied more successfully to SF than to the other estranged genres. If myths are formed by analogising what is "known," and filling in the gaps with "projection from oneself" (or from "a body of previously-existing cognitions," to use Suvin's words) (Suvin 2010, 70) with the purpose of building an explanatory model of reality, myth formation will necessarily reflect hegemonic understandings of what is "known" or held to be possible, and this model is applicable only to the generic tendency of SF. Neither the return-to-myth of Tolkien's Middle-earth nor John Landis's werewolf present any explanatory model of the world we live in, and the paranoia of *The X-Files* and similar texts in fact foregrounds the *impossibility* of knowing the world. The mythic readings of Frye and Philmus can be applied to all of the estranged genres to one extent or another, whereas Chernyshova's fits SF, and SF only. The reason for this is apparent in the following excerpt from Wolfe: "Scientific rationalism has apparently 'worked' so often in the past that we are led to believe that it can be applied to almost any situation" (Wolfe 4). Expanding on this, Wolfe points out that there is no real "evil" in SF stories except forces "that prevent man from realizing his true technological potential [...] from accepting the utopia that automation promises" (Wolfe 13). As I asserted earlier, SF is "a literature of *gaps*," and those gaps are filled in with suppositions derived from the assumptions of a dominant cultural logic or ideology – in other words, whatever logic has been shown to "work" in the past.

The Problem with Myth: Tradition and Modernity

In contrast to his earlier rhapsodising about the Mythic as *das Gedichtete*, in "Critique of Violence," Benjamin later came to see "violence as a manifestation" (i.e. as in a blind rage, rather than violence as a means to an end) as constitutive of myth. The gods do not smite mortals in order to accomplish a particular goal, and yet for humanity this divine punishment constitutes "lawgiving violence" (Benjamin 1986, 294–5). When Benjamin states that mythical violence is "fundamentally identical with all legal violence" (296), it is to charge the latter with arbitrariness, irrationality and unaccountability. The reading of myth as a manifestation of lawgiving violence, and as Suvin puts it, "the opposite of creative human freedom" (Suvin 2010, 89), is reflected across a large swathe of academic inquiry and in popular culture, to the point where it has become an apparent truism.[10]

Thus far, an apparent contradiction has already presented itself. If myth is indeed a "model" for reality, how can it then simultaneously be the source of an *"unreality* function," as Miéville puts it? The answer to this is that these aspects of myth do not represent the opposing sides of a binary relationship: myth presents a model for reality at the same time that it produces narratives and images that are indisputably unreal. One can believe in the Judaeo-Christian God, for example, without believing in the historical veracity of the Judaeo-Christian creation myth. It is also worth remembering that to premodern cultures, especially oral ones, the distinction between truth and "unreality" is often not important in the specific context of the act of storytelling. As Angela Bourke explains:

> Oral cultures have [...] developed elaborate verbal art-forms through which to arrange knowledge and ideas into patterns, partly in order to conserve and transmit them with maximum efficiency; partly for the intellectual and aesthetic pleasure of such patterning. Much of what an oral culture has to teach is packaged and conveyed in stories. (Bourke 81)

Chernyshova agrees with most commentators in saying that myth is simultaneously narrative and ideology, and thus legitimates social hierarchies to a certain extent, but she argues that "such definitions often identify one or another of myth's functions, and absolutize them. They consequently lean too far in one direction, and the whole picture is necessarily distorted" (Chernyshova 345). Far from being static, mythology can and does change: "It preserves one or another world-view only as long as it believes it is true" (346). According to her model, mythology was not exactly killed off by rationalism, but changed naturally by degrees until it gave rise to the ideology that succeeded it. While disagreeing with the implication that this was a peaceful transition, I find this model satisfying in that it allows for the discussion of modernity as an *emergent* paradigm, rather than a fully formed hegemony that appeared suddenly, almost out of nowhere.

Philip E. Wegner's differentiation between myth and utopian literature is paralleled by a distinction between the practices of traditional societies and modern ones:

> [While] the inhabitants of traditional societies reflect on already established norms with the aim of clarifying their applicability to current problems, thereby emphasizing the essential continuity of present cultural forms with the past, in modernity, social and cultural institutions and practices are continuously re-examined, and then ultimately reformed, in the light of new incoming information. The consequence of this process is to open up the possibility of imagining a disjuncture between what now have become differentiated temporal locales: the past, the present, and the potentiality of the future. (Wegner 24)

This concurs with Suvin's definition of SF. The novum, being a "cognitive innovation," necessarily communicates strangeness and *newness*. As such, it can only exist in the context of what Wegner refers to in the above statement as "differentiated temporal locales," particularly "the potentiality of the future," which distinguishes the modern society from the traditional one. This argument implicitly defines the "traditional society" as one in which the mythological world-model allows for no level of subjunctivity other than *this happened* or *this could have happened*. Central to it is the assumption of *literal belief* in the mythological, in turn implying a childlike inability to distinguish between the actual and the fictional. The unsavoury political implications of this construction of traditional societies are immediately obvious. As Chernyshova reminds us, "no matter how underdeveloped the consciousness of the myth-creators might have been, it was already human consciousness" (Chernyshova 346), and the usefulness of this negative conception of traditional society to the colonial project is apparent when one bears in mind that narrative is an essential element of cultural memory and identity formation: "erasure of [indigenous] narratives," as Jessica Langer says, "is a central function of colonial power" (Langer 129).

Fredric Jameson argues that the first use of the term "modern" in its particular historical sense can be traced back to the sixth-century

Roman writer Cassiodorus, who saw the Goths' conquest of the Western Roman Empire as "a fundamental dividing line between a henceforth classical culture and a present whose historic task lies in reinventing that culture" (Jameson 2002b, 17). Reinvention (or remaking, or progress) would later become central to the project of modernity, eventually giving rise to the very conception of human *development*, described by Raymond Williams as a belief in "the progressive establishment of more rational and therefore more civilized systems" (Williams 1977, 16).

This progress was less an organic development than a consciously pursued ideal, a vehicle whose means of propulsion was the abjection of that which had come before, with each great leap forward punctuated by, as Jameson puts it,

> a unique moment, in which the past is created by way of its energetic dissociation from the present; by way of a powerful act of dissociation whereby the present seals off its past from itself and expels and ejects it; an act without which neither present nor past truly exist, the past not yet fully constituted, the present still a living on within the force field of a past not yet over and done with. (Jameson 2002b, 25)

The need to expel the past and dissociate it from the present became all the more pronounced with the rise of capitalism, a stage of societal development in which "time becomes finally the equivalent of money and thus of all things" (Suvin 2010, 78). Suvin argues that by privileging the depiction of the passage of time, the bourgeoisie "[reduced] the universe to individuals," with narrative form changing as a necessary consequence – whereas mythology frequently pitted individuals against impersonal forces (such as Nature or the supernatural), narratives of modernity set individuals against other individuals, "who are reachable and perhaps removable by other people" (Suvin 2010, 79). Thus, along with an awareness of the possibility of revolution, modernity developed what Langer calls a "colonial ideology of progress," in which time is linear, with "technologically progressive societies pushing forward and leaving others behind" (130). It seems inevitable to me that this emphasis on the passage of time would give rise to a desire for ahistorical narrative: after all, the range of possible artistic responses to a dominant cultural theme includes repudiation, contradiction and reinterpretation.

If the "modern" society was one in which history was a democratic process of individual and social reinvention, new learning and economic progress, it logically follows that the "traditional" past it sought to transcend had to be constructed as oppressively communal, static, superstitious and barbaric. This construction of the past was, according to Theodor Adorno and Max Horkheimer, central to the Enlightenment project, which presents scientific knowledge as being open to everyone, the privilege of no one individual or class. However, the manifestation of this knowledge, technology, is productive of nothing but capital, and creates "neither concepts nor images, nor the joy of understanding" (Adorno and Horkheimer 2). In essence, Adorno and Horkheimer argue that actual knowledge (understanding, comprehension) of scientific principles remains the privilege of a particular class functionally no different from the shamans or magicians of a traditional society. The *qualitative* difference is that traditional magic acknowledges limits to its power: "The magician imitates demons [...] Although his task was impersonation he did not claim to be made in the image of the invisible power, as does civilized man, whose modest hunting ground then shrinks to the unified cosmos, in which nothing exists but prey" (6).

Karl Popper has, with some justification, criticised Adorno and Horkheimer for denying the possibility of social change for the better, saying that social critique is "vacuous and irresponsible" if it does not allow for "the promise of a better future" (Popper 80). However, their reading of enlightenment and modernity is useful in the present context in that it foregrounds the notion of a conflict between two ideologies. Enlightenment not only "recognizes itself in the old myths" (Adorno and Horkheimer 3), but is also predicated on a "horror of myth," seeing traces of the ideological system it displaced "in any human utterance which has no place in the functional context of self-preservation" (22). Here is the paranoia inherent in the act of abjection or expulsion: that the jettisoned thing might come back. Enlightenment only feels safe from the possible return of myth when it identifies "the thoroughly mathematized world" with objective truth (18), meaning that "anything which does not conform to the standard of calculability and utility must be viewed with suspicion" (3); thus, "Enlightenment is mythical fear radicalized. The pure immanence of positivism, its ultimate product, is nothing other than a form of universal taboo" (11).

Adorno and Horkheimer identify Francis Bacon as the originator of this particular ideology of modernity, arguing that he combined two "enlightening" trends that have been seen as inextricably linked ever since – the liberation of human beings from fear, and "the disenchantment of the world" (1). Suvin echoes this with his referencing of the "post-Baconian" scientific method, and Denise Albanese concurs, pointing out that it was not until Bacon that the Classical world came to be regarded as the "infant stage" rather than the "wise parent" of the present (Albanese 34–5). Even so, his impact does not constitute the clean break with tradition that his legacy suggests – almost four and a half centuries after his death, his arguments had still not quite given rise to a dominant ideology, as evidenced by the publication of Jonathan Swift's *Travels into Several Remote Nations of the World, in Four Parts. By Lemuel Gulliver, First a Surgeon, and Then a Captain of Several Ships* (1727), hereafter referred to by its commonplace shorthand, *Gulliver's Travels*.

Case in Point: Jonathan Swift and *Gulliver's Travels*

Gulliver's Travels fits rather uneasily into any notional SF canon, for a number of reasons. The most obvious among these relates to the various countries and peoples encountered by the eponymous mariner: the six-inch-tall Lilliputians; the seventy-two-foot Brobdingnagians (and the proportionately colossal wildlife of their island); the floating island of Laputa; the necromancer and the ghosts of Glubbdubdrib; the immortals of Luggnagg; and the Houyhnhnms, sapient horses with a highly developed culture and a corresponding sense of superiority. Swift does not make any attempt to rationalise these anomalies: he gives no account of the Lilliputians, the Brobdingnagians or the Houyhnhnms that might give them origins in material reality, nor does he advance any pseudoscientific theory that might allow for the actual existence of ghosts or immortality. This is the substance of Aldiss's assertion that *Gulliver's Travels* does not count as SF, because Swift's satirical or moral intent takes precedence over any speculative development of the world described (Aldiss and Wingrove 81). A far thornier issue for other critics is the Academy of Lagado on the flying island of Laputa, where learned men engage in a variety of nonsensical projects – such as extracting sunbeams from cucumbers, turning human waste back into food, making gunpowder from ice and teaching mathematics by having students ingest written formulae. To many, this is a clear indication of an anti-science bias in Swift's writing; combined with the present-day conception of science – that is, "science" or "truth" conceived as a *thing* with an independent, objective existence of its own – this notional bias is sufficient reason for commentators such as Stableford to place *Gulliver's Travels* not just outside SF, but in an almost diametrically opposed position (Stableford 1995b, 48).

There are also, however, many scholars who maintain that, even if *Gulliver's Travels* is not SF per se, science does inform the narrative to a greater extent than others would allow. Philmus sees the influence of Isaac Newton and William Gilbert in Swift's depiction of the mechanics of the floating island, which draws upon Gilbert's research into magnetic forces and Newton's *Principia Mathematica* (Philmus 10–12). Paul Baines emphasises that Gulliver is "the apostle of science and technology," and during his stay in Lilliput, he exhibits a compulsion towards measurement that leads him to admire Lilliputian science and mathematics. Thus, the comical scientists of Laputa are not in fact representative of Swift's attitude to science in general (Baines 9–10). Adam Roberts in turn argues that Swift, along with Voltaire, "[re-wrote] the rules of imaginative speculation, freeing it from both the choking literalism of 'science poetry' and the deadening constraints of conventional religious thought" (Roberts 2007, 68). He goes on to make a very good case for appreciating *Gulliver's Travels* as SF, pointing out that the first two parts (describing Lilliput and Brobdingnag) "embody mathematics" in their presentation of worlds divided or multiplied by a factor of twelve – as well as the fact that naval navigation was the pre-eminent science of the age (70). This reading of the novel leads Roberts to conclude that *Gulliver's Travels* is not about Gulliver at all, but about travel.

Though these readings of *Gulliver's Travels* are oppositional and contradictory, each of them is convincing in its own way: Swift appears to be paradoxically anti-science and scientifically minded at the same time, and *Gulliver's Travels* is as obviously fantastical as it is grounded in the material reality of exploration and colonisation. In my opinion, all of these points of view can be considered equally valid by virtue of the historical moment in which Swift lived: one important piece of evidence for this is that in *A Modest Proposal*, Swift attributes his "knowledge" of the pros and cons of cannibalism to conversations with several experienced foreigners, among whom is listed one George Psalmanaazaar (c. 1679–1763).

"Psalmanaazaar" was almost certainly French, but the exact place of his birth – along with his birth date and birth name – have never been ascertained (Knowlson 871). He became famous in the courts of early eighteenth-century Europe by presenting himself initially as a visitor from Japan, and later (to avoid exposure) as a native of Formosa who had been kidnapped from his homeland by Jesuits (872–3); the longer he remained in the public eye, the more detailed his deception became, until eventually he had fabricated an entire civilisation: he invented a "Formosan" language, and an alphabet in which to write it (871–2, 876), a religion based around the worship of a demonic "Arch-Fiend" (873), a currency (874) and myriad other customs and rituals. His downfall came when he claimed, despite the complete lack of contact between "Formosa" and Europe prior to his arrival, that Greek was taught at

Formosan academies (876). Psalmanaazaar admitted his fraud, and until he died at (approximately) the age of eighty-four in 1763, he was "esteemed by all who knew him, and had become the excellent friend of Dr. Johnson, who, though acquainted with his earlier waywardness, praised him as if he were a saint" (871–2).

Psalmanaazaar was not in fact an atypical citizen of his age. The eighteenth century was something of a golden age for tellers of tall tales, among them the celebrated Baron von Münchhausen (1720–1797). That these men were quite often believed to be telling the truth was yet another consequence of the bourgeois preoccupations with time, progress and the onward development of man, preoccupations John Rieder explicitly links to colonialism: "The way colonialism made space into time gave the globe a geography not just of climates and cultures but of stages of human development that could confront and evaluate one another" (Rieder 6). To be a citizen of a "modern" nation was to imagine premodern ones beyond the horizon, from where it was conceivable that a person such as Psalmanaazaar might come. It is also worth noting, as Neil Cornwell does, that the period stretching from the end of the Elizabethan era to the eighteenth century was something of a boom time for literary absurdity, particularly "violent farce" and English nonsense poetry (Cornwell 41). At the very least, this vibrant cultural trend might account for the affection shown to charlatans like Psalmanaazaar by those whom they had hoodwinked.

The most important observation of all, however, belongs to Freedman: "In 1726, *it was still possible* [my italics] for a serious mind [...] to refuse to take science seriously, to lampoon it as a series of frivolous, self-referential games in which no authentic intellectual activity was taking place and no practical consequences were at issue" (Freedman 4–5).

Even if the society of the time could no longer be called "traditional" by the standards of the ideological tradition/modernity divide, neither was it wholly given over to rational inquiry. Thus, Swift was not "anti-science" per se. What Stableford and others see as a bias against science is in fact the expression of a hegemony that was mostly Enlightened (in which knowledge was judged by its utility) but not yet Technocratic (in which the potential utility of *all* knowledge is taken for granted). Within this context, however, there is the wizard of Glubbdubdrib, who can summon ghosts at will, and the immortal Struldbrugs – both of them representative of a past that will not go away, and only rationalised in the sense that they are geographically situated in a hitherto-undiscovered country. The modern has not yet been differentiated from the traditional, because outside the European sphere of influence, magic has not yet been extirpated by rationality. This introduces an air of poignancy into the narrative: as Roberts says,

> it requires a sort of blindness of imperial ideological logic to argue, as Swift ironically has Gulliver do, that "the Lilliputians, I think, are hardly worth the charge of a fleet and army to reduce them," or to imply that the Brobdingnagians and Houyhnhnms would be too formidable as opponents, despite having already established that neither people possess the destructive technologies of artillery or explosives. (Roberts 2007, 71–2)

Gulliver, however, is not blind to imperial logic – he tells us he has visited both the East and the West Indies, at a moment in history when African slaves were traded in the Caribbean for commodities such as sugar and lumber, and the East India Company still exerted political clout through a trading monopoly in South-East Asia. Gulliver's journeys to these places are facilitated by imperialism, which indicates that his arguments against colonisation of the "remote regions" are not intended to be ironic: they are in fact his way of mitigating the danger he is placing these tribes in by telling the world about them, a disguised plea to leave them alone. Reading Lemuel Gulliver in this light, it is hard not to see specific correspondences between the world of the text and the empirical world of the author.

Declan Kiberd places Lemuel Gulliver at the centre of his analysis of the novel, and interprets *Gulliver's Travels* as an allegory of Anglo-Irish relations. He presents a number of texts and incidents that may very well have inspired the novel: a visit to Swift's friend Thomas Sheridan in County Cavan, during which Swift was greatly amused by the difference in size between Sheridan's labourers and those on the neighbouring farm (Kiberd 2001, 80); the folktale *Imtheachta Tuaithe Luchra* [The Deeds of the People of Luchra], in which humans venture into the leprechaun kingdom, and a leprechaun visits the human world (88); and the traditions of rural Ireland that may have provided a template for those of the Lilliputians (89) – and in the immortal but continually aging Struldbrugs, Kiberd sees echoes of the Celtic hero Oisín and the elderly Irish speakers of County Cavan (96).[11] Ireland was fundamental to Swift's work: "Without it, there would have been no Drapier, no Gulliver, no Modest Proposer" (106). The relationship between Ireland and England is most obviously discussed in Book Three of *Gulliver's Travels*, in the relationship between the flying island of Laputa and its colony, Balnibarbi. Like Ireland, Balnibarbi is a victim of Laputan economic theory (87, 93); it is ruled by absentee nobles and landlords

(93); and it has an agricultural landscape, onto which rationalists project demented hypotheses (94), much as Ireland had become "an open-air experimental laboratory" (95).[12] More importantly, Kiberd outlines Ireland's influence on Swift in terms of national and individual identity. Swift, he argues, was both "a frustrated loyalist and a precursor nationalist," who sought an Irish identity for himself after despairing of the inefficient Anglicisation of the Irish (73). While this new self-identification was "understood and welcomed" (80), Swift's "Hibernianisation" was as incomplete as the Anglicisation he had reacted against, and thus he would always have a liminal identity – in Swift's writing, Kiberd notes a certain "homelessness of mind" (81), "[existing] fully only on the hyphen between two secure codes" (88).

Thus, Kiberd reads Gulliver as a metaphor for Swift himself, articulating the frustrations of life "on the hyphen." Gulliver "becomes more and more decentred as the tale proceeds" (103), seeming to lose fragments of his own identity with every voyage (indeed, Kiberd notes that he begins each voyage as a *tabula rasa*, regardless of all that has happened to him – 90); he embodies the conflation of individual and national identity, and because for most of the narrative he is a man without a country, he cannot be a stable subject. His liminality reaches a crisis point in the land of the Houyhnhnms, whose rationalism urges them to categorise him: he must become either a Houyhnhnm or a Yahoo (read: "modern subject" or "traditional subject"), reflecting the "[colonialist] illusion that such binary choices were inevitable" (97). The distinction between the modern and traditional subjects was therefore coded in scientific, economic and cultural terms, with the result that anything beyond the limits of the emerging Western capitalist hegemony could be considered "traditional" automatically. Gulliver (Swift) exists "on the hyphen" not just ethnically, but temporally, as a combination of the past and present. Thus, he is a typical character of Irish SF.

Parochialism and Science Fiction

Paul Campbell, in a light-hearted piece for the *Linen Hall Review*, gives a brief run-through of notional SF texts by Irish writers, in an effort to publicise the existence of a native SF tradition. However, having listed a great many Irish authors of SF works – from seemingly unlikely personages such as Æ (George William Russell) and Brian Moore, to "possibles" like J.F. Maguire and Bram Stoker, to recognised (and renowned) SF authors such as Bob Shaw and James White – Campbell concludes that [there is] no such thing as *Irish* science fiction, since science fiction, as a prerequisite to being itself, must transcend the parochial [...] This is not to say that science fiction could not deal with present issues – the best does – but that it cannot deal with present issues from a narrow – provincial or local – viewpoint without the flaws being immediately and glaringly apparent. (Campbell 5)

Campbell's "brief look at the Irish in science fiction" (4) is not an in-depth survey, and as mentioned above, it is light-hearted in tone. Thus, to take serious issue with his assertions would be an over-reaction. On the other hand, to ignore the argument he makes in his closing paragraphs would be just as foolhardy, because it precisely delineates a problem for researchers of "national" science fictions: at what point does "transcending the parochial" necessitate denying the validity of different cultural logics? Which issues are "parochial" (and therefore, not appropriate for an SF story), and which ones are "universal"? If one does manage to accurately define "universal issues," how does one then respond to those issues from a "universal" viewpoint? Unfortunately, Campbell does not give us a working definition for "parochial" in the context of his argument, so there is no way to be sure.

Patrick Kavanagh's dichotomy between provincialism and parochialism holds that "the provincial has no mind of his own" because his attitudes are constantly swayed by the fashions of "the metropolis"; the "parochial," on the other hand, "is never in any doubt about the social and artistic validity of his parish" (Kavanagh 2). To the provincial mindset, he attributes ineffectual handwringing about the state of the wider world, while the parochial, by contrast, is courageously insular: "There is always that element of bravado which takes pleasure in the notion that the potato-patch is the ultimate."[13] While Kavanagh's view of parochialism can be interpreted as auto-exoticism, his mention of "social and artistic validity" points to an important issue that one sees echoed in criticism of "parochial" science fictions throughout the world.

In surveying the post-World War II production of SF in Japan, Kôichi Yamano finds that the main flaw in all of the works surveyed is "a forced connection between Japanese subjectivity and Western political objects" (Yamano 72); this is a consequence of authors writing in a genre that was every bit as alien to Japanese society as the pre-fabricated houses that appeared during the American occupation (70). Yamano is careful to point out that national identity is not significant in itself – the historically determined *subjectivity* of a people, on the other hand, gives rise to specific literary personalities. Yamano characterises British SF as a literature of "rational idealism," while Polish authors such as

Stanisław Lem combine this rational idealism with materialism, and German authors produce works of "pure ideology" (74). Japanese SF, according to Yamano, became imitative of the American genre as a consequence of the drive to secure economic prosperity (75–6), and will develop its own style "only when it can cope with various forms of Japanese civilization" (74). The way to achieve this authenticity is to appropriate Western SF tropes into the author's subjectivity (79): in other words, to re-decorate the pre-fabricated house. The idea that SF, as a genre, is suited only to "universal" issues implies that it exists beyond cultural subjectivities and that there are a limited number of "correct" forms it can take; this view is as short-sighted as the modernist/colonialist ideology of "progress" that it imitates. This is the essence of the present study of Irish SF, and in the following chapters, I will try to outline the qualities of what I believe to be Irish SF's distinct literary personality.

1. Mad Science and the Empire: Fitz-James O'Brien and Robert Cromie

In the first half of the nineteenth century, the growth of a new middle-class reading public undermined long-standing systems of literary patronage, giving rise to subscription networks, instituting the beginnings of commercial publishing, and altering the relationship between the reader and the author, who became, as Raymond Williams describes it, "a fully-fledged 'professional man'." This in turn led to the emergence of a new attitude towards "the public" (a dissatisfied or scornful one) which, combined with the stubborn realities of literary commercialism, in turn led to the figuration of art as "imaginative truth," and the artist as "a special kind of person" capable of making that truth visible (Williams 1960, 35–8). The transcendent, imaginative truth of the world, codified as "the sublime" by romantic artists and poets, contributed to the emergence of modern SF by figuring "a material realm of incomprehensible vastness and complexity [...] reaching back through history to a much longer prehistory before the evolution of mankind, and positing a similar post-historic future after mankind" (Bould and Vint 7).

This cultural milieu gave rise to the "mad scientist," a new variation on the Promethean or Faustian archetype invested with all the qualities of the Romantic artist. He is definitely "a special kind of person" whose function is to expose hidden truths, and his pursuit of scientific knowledge is a profession at the very least, if not a vocation; in addition, he derides those who do not appreciate the value of his work, be they members of an uneducated public, or unimaginative ignoramuses within the scientific community. If the mad scientist is a "special person," it is because he belongs to a learned class whose privilege is true understanding of scientific principles; if he is not appreciated or understood by his peers, it is because his comprehension of the world exceeds theirs to the extent that he is, for all intents and purposes, a shaman or a wizard. The mad scientist acknowledges no limit to either his ambitions or his intellectual power, and sees the universe as his own "cosmic hunting ground." Even though his methods may seem obscure, narrative cues imply (or rather, direct the reader to accept on faith) that the mad scientist derives his dangerous knowledge logically from an understanding of a "fully mathematized world." These are all attributes that Adorno and Horkheimer attribute to modern subjects in general. The usefulness of his work is not always apparent (its utility often being inversely proportional to the destruction it causes), and it rarely conforms to the post-Baconian calculability invoked by Suvin.

In outlining the material circumstances that led to the emergence of the Romantic "genius," Williams refers particularly to the case of nineteenth-century England. As Kiberd makes clear, the influence of these trends was certainly felt in Ireland, even though the material circumstances were quite different:

> Those Irish who were literate in English were not great buyers of books and so Irish artists wrote with one eye cocked on the English audience. They were, for the most part, painfully imitative of English literary modes, which they practiced with the kind of excess possible only to the insecure [...] Cultural colonies are much more susceptible to the literature of the parent country than are the inhabitants of that country itself [...] A colonised people soon comes to believe that approved fictions are to be imitated in life, and this notion in due time proves vitally useful to the exponents of resistance literature. (Kiberd 1996, 115)

In the case of Ireland, Kiberd explains, "What fell with Hugh O'Neill was not a Gaelic civilization so much as an aristocratic order," in which the *filí* (bards) "had always been unapologetically aristocratic, with certain families serving as hereditary poets to the Gaelic leaders" (Kiberd 2001, 3–4). Following the fall of this order, these poets lamented the loss of their patronage as "the defeat of Ireland itself" (9–10), and were obliged by market forces to abandon the elitist jargon in which they had previously composed (15). Obliquely comparing themselves to prostitutes in their verse, the *filí* "must have been among the first poets in the world to seek an originality that was market-oriented," and consequently developed an ambivalent attitude to their new audiences: "They tried to sell their wares to the crowd and at the same time they voiced patrician contempt for that crowd" (19–20). The similarities to the Romantic poets as described by Williams are obvious thus far, but the two groups differ in that instead of becoming soothsayers, interpreting the world via "imaginative truth," the *filí* became necromancers, conversing with ghosts and prophesying doom:

> Gaelic Ireland always seemed to be dying – if not at the funeral of a lord, then on the deathbed of a poet, if not in the loss of native

speakers to death or emigration, then in sheer impoverishment of the words in the spoken language [...] the dead in Ireland clearly had a secure place in the privileged classes. (21)

Thus, between the Gaelic "death cult" and the Ascendancy gothic novel (discussed below), Ireland's fictional mad scientists were often more explicitly wizardly than their English brethren. In 1818, Victor Frankenstein described his conscious decision to abandon the "chimerical" teachings of Agrippa, Magnus and Paracelsus in favour of the "real and practical" systems of modern science (Shelley 38–9). In Ireland, it was not always clear that there was such a distinction to be made. Just as market forces had given rise to the romantic genius/mad scientist, there were also a number of economic reasons why genre differentiation did not take root in nineteenth-century Ireland.

Surveying the fortunes of the Irish publishing industry from 1650 to 1900, Rolf and Magda Loeber present a history of repeated decline and resurgence. The decline had begun in the 1790s, due to a number of factors (including difficulties with the paper supply), but it was to be compounded by the Act of Union in 1801 and the introduction of the Copyright Act in the same year, which effectively ended the lucrative "Grub Street" end of the Irish publishing industry. With the market for pirated books erased, Irish publishers were forced to depend on original works for their survival. However, the rate of production of original Irish fiction declined steadily from the late eighteenth century to the 1820s. There was a three-decade resurgence from the 1830s to the 1860s, after which original Irish fiction declined once more, probably in the face of competition from London publishers (Loeber and Loeber xci). At the same time, the dominance and expense of the "three-decker" form gave rise to travelling libraries, which in turn dominated the distribution of popular literature, fixed prices and caused authors to self-censor to ensure publication. Edward James maintains that under this system, explicitly science-fictional material had only a marginal appeal, existing in the form of "novelettes [...] pamphlets, or as single-volume publications intended for boys" (James 39–40).[1] In Ireland, the traditional existed alongside the modern in everyday life, and because of the various market forces shaping the publishing industry, there was as yet no widespread cultural trend that challenged that juxtaposition.

The fiction of Fitz-James O'Brien, for example, combines the paranoia of the Ascendancy gothic with an imperial drive towards bureaucracy, making no distinction between rationalism and superstition. This cross-fertilisation of ideologies is mirrored in O'Brien's protagonists, who, like Lemuel Gulliver, Swift and O'Brien himself, exist "on the hyphen" between discrete national or ethnic identities. His heroes often suffer from split personalities, displaying an urge for imperial/quasi-religious apotheosis while wishing to maintain a distinct Irish identity. Belfast author Robert Cromie, by contrast, was a self-identified British citizen, and he framed this identity in terms of being under siege: his works contain undisguised hostility towards feminism, science and socialism; frequently, the villains of his novels are secret societies bent on either the advancement or destruction of society (for Cromie, these terms were synonymous, unless the proposed advancement was to be achieved by a feat of engineering). Tellingly, his two best-known novels are partially set in industrial enclaves in isolated wildernesses, surrounded by hordes of superstitious natives.

The Lost World

One of the problems with the conception of Ireland as a colony, as outlined by Joe Cleary, is that the Irish appear to have been, "like the Scots, enthusiastic co-partners and beneficiaries in the British imperial enterprise" (Cleary 21). Elsewhere, Ralph Pordzik summarises other objections from a variety of different theorists: principally that the word "postcolonial" encourages insubstantial comparisons between Ireland and African or Asian colonies, and that the components of race and slavery do not appear in the colonisation of European nations (Pordzik 331).

It is true that there was little outright racism towards the Irish at an administrative level during the nineteenth century: for example, MPs who opposed the 1886 Home Rule Bill went to great lengths to avoid appearing racist, and even argued that there were no racial differences at all between the English, the Irish, the Welsh and the Scots (Bew 2007, 348–9). This does not mean, however, that the Irish were not generally perceived as Other. As for Irish enthusiasm for the imperial project, this is certainly borne out by the number of Irish personnel who joined expeditions to as-yet-unconquered regions of the globe.[2] Luke Gibbons explains this as the imperial utilisation of a colonial resource rather than the enthusiastic cooperation Cleary describes: in Gibbons's terms, "genocide was never really on the cards, for, despite the revulsion towards 'popery,' the Gaelic language, and clan society, the able-bodied male was too valuable as a foot-soldier, or as menial labourer, in strengthening the sinews of empire" (Gibbons 21). Thus, the Celt was re-figured as a "fighting machine," best kept at a safe remove from the imperial centre and utilised for the ideological and material gain of the Empire (21–2).

The question of whether or not Ireland "qualifies" as a colonised territory is not straightforward, but this complexity highlights the fact that there can be no such thing as a one-size-fits-all definition of colonisation.

The consideration of nineteenth-century Ireland as a colonised territory has political implications for the study of its ahistorical literature. The degree to which Ireland was colonised, or participated in the colonial project, is of interest to the present study because colonialism was, as John Rieder argues, one of the factors that energised the SF genre: "science fiction exposes something that colonialism imposes" (Rieder 15). This point is taken up by Jessica Langer, who points out that the two predominant motifs of SF – "The Stranger and the Strange Land" – were also the dominant themes of colonial discourse; postcolonial SF "hybridizes them, parodies them and/or mimics them against the grain" (Langer 3–4). For others, the study of Ireland's ahistorical literature has political connotations in itself. Cleary, for example, appears to be of the opinion that by emphasising non-naturalist trends in Irish literature, one runs the risk of constructing "a renovated version of the obdurate Arnoldian distinction between the orderly and empirical Saxon and the more flighty but imaginative Celtic characters," especially when such a reading is construed as a "nationalized realist/anti-realist dichotomy" wherein realism is particularly English and "anti-realism" Irish (Cleary 49). This sensitivity and ambivalence to ahistorical Irish literature, as Philip O'Leary points out, is a persistent feature of twentieth-century Irish culture: while on the one hand, folklore was held to be constitutive of an authentically Irish psyche (O'Leary 2010, 89), on the other, intellectuals and authors tried to distance themselves from it, due both to its misuse by English authors and to "the impression of ignorance" they believed it gave (114).

Jameson describes two traditional approaches to genre criticism, the "semantic" (which aims to describe an over-arching "essence" or "spirit" for each genre) and the "syntactic" (which concentrates on the "mechanisms and structure" of a genre), the distinction between them basically boiling down to "what it means" versus "how it works"; Jameson argues that to find a dialectical synthesis between these approaches, one must historicize them, since every universalising approach to a given topic conceals its own contradictions (Jameson 2002a, 93–6). The "third term," Jameson argues, is "history itself, as an absent cause" (132). This reveals that the "what it means"/"how it works" dichotomy of traditional genre criticism relates only to "form," whereas an awareness of the historicity of genres allows for a complementary analysis of "substance," in which we find "social and historical raw material" expressed as "ideologemes and narrative paradigms" (134).

Thus, to ignore the weird and unnatural side of Irish literature because of some vague anxiety that to speak of it would validate colonial discourse is nonsensical, because every genre has a particular historical significance. To this, we might add that the quintessential genre of nineteenth-century Ireland was not naturalism, but the Ascendancy gothic. To downplay or dismiss ahistorical literature for fear of what the neighbours might think is a sign not of maturity, but of insecurity and timidity.

The proliferation of the Ascendancy gothic is attributed to the perceived threats of Irish nationalism and Catholic emancipation – ranging from hypothesised loss of power and privilege, to the undeniably real possibility of injury or even murder. Kiberd argues that this anxiety was an indelible element of Irish Protestantism, dating back to the time of the Plantations: "The English planters who had occupied Ireland were, in a sense, the first Provisionals, by no means certain of their tenure in a land where they would always be outnumbered by those whom they had extirpated" (Kiberd 1996, 366–7). Cleary echoes this analysis, and explicitly links Irish Protestant anxiety to the gothic mode:

> Much more immediately threatened by Catholicism, Irish Protestantism was situationally prone to be darker in temper, more fundamentalist and less optimistically liberal than its English counterpart. Hence it was the gothic novel – with its character-istically paranoid atmospherics, its sense of historical guilt, its climate of degeneration and impending collapse – and not classical realism that would become the most successfully realised form of the Ascendancy novel in nineteenth-century Ireland. (Cleary 63)

Though religious concerns undoubtedly constituted an animating force for the gothic, Gibbons argues that they were not the genre's defining characteristics. The legitimacy of the post-Glorious Revolution monarchy was another motivational anxiety, as was the notion that liberty could only be preserved in Britain through the administration of colonialism and despotism abroad, starting with the Celtic periphery (Gibbons 18–19). Racial anxieties were just as important to the gothic as religious ones, articulating fears of the possible contamination of modernity by the "savagery" of the past (23), or of the imperial centre by "a restless, insurgent culture" (42) composed of "invisible" racial enemies, such as Jews or the Irish, who could "pass" as white long enough to contaminate the classes in which they circulated (61). To a certain extent, these fears were realised by the increasing number of Irish labourers in the industrial centres of Britain, one effect of which was an increasing militancy and political organisation among the working classes (67).

Jarlath Killeen, in turn, summarises a number of the Ascendancy gothic's characteristics: Protestantism, a colonial history, a fear of (rather than actual) marginalisation, and a paradoxical simultaneous revulsion towards and eroticisation of Catholicism. Of principal importance to the subject at hand, however, is a tendency arising out of the same colonial discourse that would later prove to be one of the driving forces behind nineteenth-century SF:

> What is peculiarly "Irish" about the gothic tradition is that it emerged from a geographical zone which was defined as weird and bizarre. Indeed, Ireland as a whole was defined as a gothic space [...] the Celtic fringes were not only configured as repositories of all that which England wished to deny and banish (the irrational, the superstitious, the perverse, the Catholic, the cannibal), they also became a kind of zone of atemporality, a place of the primitive and the atavistic which the modern world had not yet touched. If the gothic is often seen as the return of the repressed, the past that will not stay past, Ireland was usually read as a place where the past had never in fact disappeared, a place where the past was still present. (Killeen 2006)

Gibbons echoes this point to a certain extent, noting that in the mediaeval imagination, Purgatory could be visited physically via special portals and passageways; this made Ireland "a liminal zone between the natural and the supernatural" (Gibbons 25–6), which had been synonymous since at least the late twelfth century with cannibalism, incest, famine and bloodshed (12). This conforms to the central tenet of colonial ideology, as described by Rieder – that of anachronism, most obviously seen in the sub-genre of the "lost world" or "lost race" adventure story, in which "the living anthropological traces of the past that are thought to remain visible in colonial settings bring to life the geological ones as well," highlighting the primitiveness of indigenous populations through the use of tropes such as human-dinosaur coexistence (Rieder 52–3).

Explicit lost-world texts are largely absent from nineteenth-century Irish literature, with only a couple of examples on record. This is perhaps not surprising given that at the time, as Kiberd asserts, the popular literature of Ireland was imitative of that of the imperial centre, and, as Edward James notes, lost-world stories were far more popular in America than in Britain (James 35), as were utopian narratives (37) and "invention stories" (39).[3] On the other hand, though there are no nineteenth-century texts that depict dinosaurs grazing in Connemara, the colonial image of Ireland was a synthesis of the gothic and lost-world narratives. The resonance between Rieder's description of these narratives and Killeen's of the Ascendancy gothic is too striking to be ignored.

One possible reason for the lost-world perception of Ireland is that the Ascendancy gothic was complemented almost perfectly by Irish mythology. Most, if not all, of Irish fairy lore (as distinct from the heroic myths and the *immrama* or "fantastic voyage" tales) is macabre – Ireland's supernatural denizens are not "fairies" in the popular conception, but murderous, child-stealing monsters.[4] As explained in a rather ominous tone by W.B. Yeats, "The visible world is merely their skin" (Yeats 11). This tension was heightened by the fact that most of rural Ireland had not yet transitioned from "tradition" to "modernity," and belief in the actual existence of these beings was commonplace among the rural Irish. This was just one facet of a premodern tradition which had persisted in Ireland, exerting considerable influence on Irish culture.

Until her death in 1873, the wise woman Biddy Early, from the parish of Feakle in County Clare, was emblematic of the enduring power of tradition. According to the folklorist Diarmuid Mac Manus, her popularity with the people of East Clare led to an adversarial relationship between Biddy and the Catholic Church: "When people urgently wanted themselves or their dear ones or their animals to be saved, it was to Biddy they turned, knowing that she alone could do so if she wished" (MacManus 157). The antagonism between Biddy Early and the Catholic hierarchy is indicative of an incomplete process of modernisation – as Langer puts it, "magic" is not simply indicative of ignorance, "but rather a different way of understanding, a different cultural logic" (Langer 128–9), and it had been seen to work in the past. It is important to note that this particular instance was not a contest between tradition and modernity, but between two different kinds of tradition, the Catholic and the pagan. Irish fairy lore persisted because it conveyed information related to everyday life, instructing believers on social norms as well as providing entertainment and "narrative maps" of the physical and social landscape (Bourke 87–8).

This is not to say that modernity had no impact at all. The historian Enda Leaney, for example, suggests that Irish interest in scientific and technological innovation at the time was much higher than is commonly believed, as indicated by the popularity of public scientific lectures. Initially conceived of by English radicals as a means by which the common people could be introduced to a rationalist discourse that would enable them to question the legitimacy of hierarchical rule, these lectures, staged by travelling scientists, "blurred the distinction between education and entertainment" (Leaney 160), while at the same time stressing the notion that study of the natural world led one to a more perfect understanding of the magnificence of God's creation (162, 175). In the non-industrial countryside of Ireland, this religiosity was doubly important, since many of the scientific principles demonstrated at these lectures had no practical application in the everyday lives of the audiences. Rather, Leaney argues, "Most members of the Irish lecture-going public appreciated science primarily because it validated religion" (174). The teaching of science was not politically or culturally innocent, and neither was the manner in which it was received:

> This call for the extension of science education was heard across the political spectrum, with its votaries embracing O'Connell's Repeal Association, the Young Irelanders, and members of the Catholic hierarchy. Unionists saw science and technology as forces for generating industrial development and thus serving as a much-wanted distraction from political and sectarian animosities. (171–2)

Here, we see the necessary conditions for the emergence of popular pseudoscience. The popular science lectures exposed country people to knowledge they would otherwise never have encountered, but this was done with a specific political agenda in mind, and science was carefully presented as being compatible with pre-existing ideologies. The progress of scientific endeavour was also often written into Ireland's material being, and onto its gothic landscape. Perhaps the most famous example of this is the story of how Sir William Rowan Hamilton, a native of Dublin, was struck by a flash of inspiration while out walking with his wife in 1843, and carved a formula into Brougham Bridge, on the Royal Canal. This formula provided the basis for the use of quaternion numbers in mathematical equations, and helped give birth to the scientific field of quantum mechanics. Another example was Birr Castle in County Offaly, a centre of scientific experimentation thanks to the efforts of the Parsons family, and home of the world's largest telescope from 1845 to 1917.[5]

Nineteenth-century Ireland, then, was a zone in which the traditional and the modern were almost equally matched in strength. This is not a particularly unusual occurrence, because, as Langer points out, to many colonised people "science and spirituality are intertwined and inseparable" (Langer 129). However, the tug-of-war between them was happening against the backdrop of one of the most dramatic transitions from tradition to modernity in the history of Western Europe.

The summer of 1845 was marked by atrocious weather, affecting harvests all over Britain and driving up the price of wheat and other crops. Even basic foodstuffs such as bread became prohibitively expensive, and food became scarcer for almost the entire population of the United Kingdom. Ireland was worst hit, given that potatoes were the staple diet of the rural poor and potato blight had suddenly overtaken the country. Land given over to potato cultivation was rendered useless by the disease, thus compounding rural poverty. Advocates for the Repeal of the Act of Union were enraged by the situation, and public anger was stoked by reports from a *Times* correspondent, Mr. T.C. Foster, whose dispatches described the abject misery of the Irish poor in graphic and disturbing detail (Archer 87).

As a result of the combined effects of starvation and emigration, the population of Ireland was drastically reduced between the years of 1845 and 1850. In addition to this, those who struggled to survive afterwards were under economic pressure to abandon Irish culture (regarded at the time as a bar to employment), and with it, a sizeable portion of the Gaelic culture, which was largely composed of oral traditions. Another major contributing factor to the dismemberment of this culture was the post-Famine "Devotional Revolution," through which Irish Catholicism "sought to distance itself as much as possible from the 'primitive' vernacular base which had sustained it during the Penal Laws" (Gibbons 13). This base was more than just an embarrassing throwback: when some of the Penal Laws were relaxed in the latter half of the eighteenth century, Emmet Larkin says, "hierarchical authority had been so weakened that the attempt to reassert episcopal control was met with a fierce and sustained resistance on the part of the lower clergy." To combat this, the Bishops pointed to the "the anti-clericalism of a disgusted laity" and corruption in the local Church, and used Rome's power over episcopal appointments to force the Irish clergy to submit. This task, which Larkin refers to as a "pacification," was begun by John Thomas Troy, Archbishop of Dublin, in 1786, and was continued by Patrick Curtis, Archbishop of Armagh (301). By the second half of the nineteenth century, this mission was undertaken by Cardinal Cullen, a man of nationalist convictions but opposed to revolutionary action, who was occasionally obliged to chastise turbulent priests given to insulting bishops from the pulpit (Steele 244–6). Henceforth, there could be no dissent among the ranks, and the authority of the Pope was restored as a central tenet of the Irish Catholic faith. Tradition was losing ground to modernity, and the Irish Church with its new ultramontanist zeal had decided that it was not going to share this shrinking ideological territory with the likes of Biddy Early.

The holes left in Gaelic culture were filled by what Chris Morash terms "dislocated, isolated emblems of suffering": cannibalism, hunger as "a stalking skeleton," the corpse with the grass-stained mouth, a landscape full of emaciated wraiths – representations of atrocity "made up of static, iconic tableaux, each existing in a single timeless moment" (Morash 114). These images survive in all their vividness because they are disconnected from time:

> Because atrocity upsets our sense of cause and effect, it hampers our ability to construct sequential narratives which follow the conventions of mimetic literary representation. It may well be as a consequence of this breakdown of literary convention that the literature of the Famine is constructed as an archive of free-floating signs, capable of incorporation in any number of sequential semiotic systems, including the constructive cultural memory which seeks to unite past, present and future in the creation of an individual identity. (117)

The Famine is, in effect, a horror narrative. In estranging the country from the passage of time, it effectively *ended history*, in more ways than one – it ruptured not only the Gaelic way of life, but also the projected future-history envisioned in the economic policies that led to the disaster. It is not surprising, therefore, that the Irish culture of the time had a strong tendency towards the macabre that could not be squeezed out by the various incoherent and incomplete attempts to modernise the country.

First published anonymously in *Dublin University Magazine* in 1851, Joseph Sheridan Le Fanu's "Ghost Stories of Chapelizod" begins by arguing for the appreciation of the folklorist as a public servant:

> You might as well expect to find a decayed cheese without mites or an old house without rats as an antique and dilapidated town without an authentic population of goblins. Now, although this class of inhabitants are in nowise amenable to the police authorities, yet as their demeanour directly affects the comforts of her Majesty's subjects, I cannot but regard it as a grave omission that the public have hitherto been left without any statistical returns of their numbers, activity, etc., etc. And I am persuaded that a Commission to inquire into and report upon the numerical strength, habits, haunts, etc., etc., of supernatural agents resident in Ireland would be a great deal more innocent and entertaining than half the Commissions for which the country pays, and at least as instructive. (Byrne 1)

Though this "deflection of history into myth" is clearly meant as a tongue-in-cheek defence of ghost stories, here Le Fanu subconsciously betrays the anxieties of the social class to which he belonged. In the context of the years prior to the publication of "Ghost Stories of Chapelizod," Le Fanu's exasperation with the seemingly endless series of "Commissions" is perhaps understandable. Among them were the Irish Poor Law Commissions of 1835, 1838 and 1847, and a Commission for the sale and transfer of encumbered estates, established in 1848. More unsettling than the bureaucracy and expense incurred by the establishment of these Commissions were the implied accusations that their very existence levelled against the landowning class to which Le Fanu belonged. The Commission of 1847 concluded that the Irish peasantry were "the worst housed, the worst fed, and the worst clothed of any in Europe" (Archer 117). Le Fanu's proposed Commission for the study of Ireland's supernatural denizens would certainly be much more entertaining than the variously pessimistic and bureaucratic foregoing examples, but more telling is the hypothetical Commission's proposed function. There are creatures abroad, Le Fanu tells us, whose activities are detrimental to the Queen's peace; it would be wise to learn how many of them there are, how they can be identified, and where they can be found. As Gibbons puts it, "the gothic spread out into the recesses of everyday life, giving rise to a phantom public sphere haunted by fear, terror, and the dark side of civility" (Gibbons 10). Science and bureaucracy were the means by which it was to be kept at bay or exorcised, but, as demonstrated by Irish popular fiction of the time, this was not an easy task in a place where genre boundaries were not clearly defined.

"Glittering with green and silver and gold": Fitz-James O'Brien (1828–1862)

Fitz-James O'Brien's biographical data is riddled with contradictions. A short biography in an anthology originally published by Hammond and Hammond in 1947 notes that he was born in 1828, and emigrated to the United States in 1852 after "taking part in the revolts that followed the Great Famine." When the American Civil War broke out, he joined the Seventh Regiment of the National Guard of New York, and was soon appointed to the staff of General Lander. He was wounded in a skirmish in February 1862 and died a month later (Wise and Fraser 323). A more thorough biography is presented by Rolf and Magda Loeber, and the contrast gives an interesting insight into the man's character.

Michael Fitz-James O'Brien was probably born in Cork, and was the son of a wealthy family. His father, James O'Brien, was a lawyer, and his mother was Eliza O'Driscoll of Baltimore, West Cork. Following the death of James, Eliza remarried and the family moved to Castleconnell, County Limerick, where Michael was educated privately. Loeber and Loeber note that some dispute the claim that he later attended Trinity College Dublin, and others hypothesise that he spent some time in France, since he spoke French fluently. Witnessing the suffering of the peasantry during the Great Famine, he wrote poetry calling for relief programmes, and advocated emigration to America. In 1849, he came into a large inheritance, and used it to move to London. Within two years, he had squandered it all, thereafter emigrating to New York and becoming a leading member of a group of artists (among whose other members was the poet Walt Whitman). In addition to his short fiction, he contributed poetry, columns and articles to various journals and newspapers in New York (Loeber and Loeber 992–3).

These biographies hint at a fascinating and contradictory personality. Though it is stated in the lean Hammond biography that he "took part in" the post-Famine revolts, the Loeber biography makes it clear that he had no actual involvement in the uprisings at all. The source of this confusion could very well have been O'Brien himself, playing the part of the exiled Irish revolutionary for the entertainment of his bohemian companions in New York, despite the fact that he hailed from the same landowning class as Le Fanu (economically speaking), and that his short fiction exhibits both the paranoia of the Ascendancy gothic and the colonial ideology of early imperial SF. Whether he was conscious of it or not, O'Brien himself was a mixture of New and Old World. His protagonists are knowledgeable and courageous, scientific of mind and yet superstitious in their souls. O'Brien apparently has no problem juxtaposing scientific fact with mysticism, and makes no distinction between them in terms of value.

In "The Diamond Lens" (first published in 1858), the protagonist is one Mr. Linley, who lashes out with scorn against the scientific community that has judged him insane, and remarks, "Every great genius is mad upon the subject in which he is greatest. The unsuccessful madman is disgraced and called a lunatic" (O'Brien 1887, 8). If we are to accept his claims, Linley is indeed a gifted microscopist:

> It was I who destroyed [Christian Gottfried] Ehrenberg's theory that the *Volcox globator* was an animal, and proved that his "monads" with stomachs and eyes were merely phases of the formation of a vegetable cell [...] It was I who resolved the singular problem

of rotation in the cells and hairs of plants into ciliary attraction, in spite of the assertions of Mr. Wenham and others, that my explanation was the result of an optical illusion. (9)

His ambitions are continually thwarted by the inadequacy of the commercially available microscopes he uses. Linley resolves to construct his own, superior apparatus, and he seeks advice from the supernatural realm to do it. He visits a spiritualist named Madame Vulpes, who contacts the spirit of the Dutch scientist Leeuwenhoek, who pioneered many techniques for the study of microscopic life. When Linley asks how the microscope can be perfected, the ghost gives him a routine, matter-of-fact answer: "A diamond of one hundred and forty carats, submitted to electromagnetic currents for a long period, will experience a rearrangement of its atoms *inter se*, and from that stone you will form the universal lens" (15).

Happily for Linley, his neighbour Simon happens to be a diamond prospector and slave-trader, and happens to have a diamond of exactly the required dimensions in his possession. Linley has no qualms about killing Simon for the greater good: "[after] all, what is the life of a little peddling Jew, in comparison with the interests of science? Human beings are taken every day from the condemned prisons to be experimented on by surgeons" (21).

Linley's eventual acquisition of the diamond lens enables him to observe an ecosystem beyond the merely microscopic (25–6), and he falls in love with an inhabitant of a subatomic universe suspended in a single droplet of water. The beautiful woman, whom he names Animula, lives in an Arcadian world:

> Animula [...] had approached the wondrous forest, and was gazing earnestly upwards. Presently one of the trees – as I must call them – unfolded a long ciliary process, with which it seized one of the gleaming fruits that glittered on its summit, and sweeping slowly down, held it within reach of Animula. The sylph took it in her delicate hand, and began to eat. (28)

The love-struck scientist pines over Animula for days, tormented by the fact that he cannot communicate with her. His torment is brought to a tragic conclusion when the water droplet starts to evaporate, and Animula's universe dies (33–4).

Linley's own descriptions of his forays into the microscopic realm are of particular interest from a colonial standpoint. On two occasions, he describes the act of peering through a microscope as "penetration": "I penetrated beyond the external portal of things, and roamed through the sanctuaries" (4); "I had penetrated beyond the grosser particles of aqueous matter, beyond the realms of infusoria and protozoa, down to the original gaseous globule, into whose luminous interior I was gazing, as into an almost boundless dome filled with a supernatural radiance" (25–6). Of even greater significance are his comparisons to Earthly ecosystems, and the implication that Linley's "penetrations" into the unknown have revealed new territories, begging to be explored:

> In the common spots of mould, which my mother, good housekeeper that she was, fiercely scooped away from her jam pots, there abode for me, under the name of mildew, enchanted gardens, filled with dells and avenues of the densest foliage and most astonishing verdure, while from the fantastic boughs of these microscopic trees hung strange fruits glittering with green and silver and gold [...] I was like one who, having discovered the ancient Eden still existing in all its primitive glory, should resolve to enjoy it in solitude, and never betray to mortal men the secret of its locality. (5)

In laying bare these "enchanted gardens," and resolving to keep them for himself, Linley reveals the seeming motivation behind his interest in the microscopic – a kind of apotheosis into something between an emperor and a god, assuming both the imperial privilege of exploration and conquest, and godlike omnipotence over all that he surveys. Upon discovering Animula's world, he proclaims, "What cared I, if I had waded to the portal of this wonder through another's blood?" (28).

According to Rieder, the late nineteenth-/early twentieth-century trend towards stories of interplanetary or subterranean exploration could be seen as a reaction to the comprehensive mapping of planet Earth:

> Having no place on Earth left for the radical exoticism of unexplored territory, the writers invented places elsewhere. But this compensatory reflex is only the beginning of the story. For colonialism is not merely an opening up of new possibilities, a "new world" becoming available to the "old" one [...] The exotic, once it had been scrutinized, analyzed, theorized, catalogued and displayed, showed a tendency to turn back upon and re-evaluate those who had thus appropriated and appraised it. (Rieder 4)

The attraction behind finding new "colonies" at the other end of the microscope is that it represents absolute imperial/divine power. The object is, in fact, completely unaware of the subject's gaze, and thus can do nothing to prevent or protest its appropriation, or to evaluate its coloniser. If we view Linley's metaphor of "penetration" with a prurient eye, we might conclude that the diamond lens serves as a kind of prophylactic, allowing him to colonise Arcadia without the risk of contamination. In Linley's case, this insulation results in a diminution of power – he is unable to interact with his microscopic paradise in any meaningful way, and even the destruction of Animula and her universe occurs contrary to his will. It would take over a century for another viewer to achieve what Linley could not, with the protagonist of Lord Dunsany's *The Pleasures of a Futuroscope* (published posthumously in 2005) benevolently influencing the lives of a family seen through the lens of the titular instrument. The interplay between science and magic, meanwhile, appears to have been a theme dear to O'Brien's heart.

"What Was It?" (first published 1859), perhaps O'Brien's best-known short story, could be one of the earliest known examples in modern fiction of a story involving an invisible predator. In this story, the creature in question attacks the narrator in the middle of the night. Fortunately, the other inhabitants of the house are alerted by their friend's cries for help, and they arrive in time to save him. They incapacitate the creature in the dark, only to discover, once the lamps have been lit, that it is invisible to the human eye.

The lamplight ambience of the story, along with the nocturnal habits of the creature depicted and the "big house" setting (albeit in the urban milieu of nineteenth-century New York), appear at first glance to characterise this as a purely gothic tale – indeed, the house in which the characters are staying has a reputation for being haunted (O'Brien 1887, 251), and the purpose of their staying there is to find the truth of the matter. This ambience is reinforced by a conversation between Harry (the narrator) and his friend, Doctor Hammond, in which they discuss the nature of terror:

> "The calling of voices in Brockden Brown's novel of 'Wieland' is awful; so is the picture of the Dweller of the Threshold, in Bulwer's [sic] 'Zanoni'; but," he added, shaking his head gloomily, "there is something more horrible still than these [...] my brain is running upon all sorts of weird and awful thoughts. I feel as if I could write a story like [E.T.A.] Hoffman to night, if I were only master of a literary style." (254)

On closer inspection, however, the generic tendency of the story is not so easily settled. This tale is indeed about a predator very much like a ghost, but what distinguishes it from the gothic tradition is its insistence that the creature is not supernatural at all – having caught the thing, the characters each try to classify it with recourse to knowledge and rational inquiry. In trying to explain how an animal could be invisible, Hammond posits the existence of a kind of matter that allows light to pass through it:

> "Let us reason a little, Harry. Here is a solid body which we can touch, but which we cannot see. The fact is so unusual that it strikes us with terror. Is there no parallel, though, for such a phenomenon? Take a piece of pure glass. It is tangible and transparent. A certain chemical coarseness is all that prevents its being so entirely transparent as to be totally invisible. It is not theoretically impossible, mind you, to make a glass which shall not reflect a single ray of light [...] We do not see the air, and yet we feel it." (261)

So far, so plausible. When Harry replies that these properties are not usually seen in living creatures, however, Hammond makes reference to a phenomenon that would seem completely at odds with the laws of physics and chemistry:

> "You forget the strange phenomena of which we have so often heard of late," answered the Doctor, gravely. "At the meetings called 'spirit circles,' invisible hands have been thrust into the hands of those persons round the table – warm, fleshly hands that seemed to pulsate with mortal life." (261–2)

We cannot dismiss Hammond's supposition on the grounds that modern science does not allow for such things: this is the mistake made by Aldiss in his appraisal of "The Diamond Lens" as "callow" and "risible," because the analogy central to its plot – that the structure of the atom is similar to that of the solar system – has been "long discarded" (Aldiss and Wingrove, 88). In this instance, Hammond is not rationalising the existence of the invisible predator with reference to "spirit hands" (if such rationalisation is necessary, it is the job of the author-function, not the characters) but rather re-appraising the latter in light of the revealed existence of the former: in the fictional world of the story, an invisible predator has been discovered, thus allowing for the possibility that spiritualist phenomena may have some basis in material reality as well. Thus assured that their nocturnal visitor has corporeal form despite its invisibility, the protagonists are overwhelmed with curiosity about what it actually looks like:

As well as we could make out by passing our hands over the creature's form, its outlines and lineaments were human. There was a mouth; a round, smooth head without hair; a nose, which, however, was a little elevated above the cheeks; and its hands and feet felt like those of a boy. (O'Brien 1887, 262–3)

The other attributes of the creature are recorded throughout the narrative – it weighs about the same as a fourteen-year-old boy (260); it breathes, and its skin is smooth (258); and it is described as being muscular and having talons ("bony hands") (256). Taking advantage of the knowledge that the thing needs to respire, Hammond suggests that they dose it with chloroform, and then make a plaster cast of it:

It was shaped like a man, – distorted, uncouth and horrible, but still a man. It was small, not over four feet and some inches in height, and its limbs revealed a muscular development that was unparalleled. Its face surpassed in hideousness anything I had ever seen. Gustave Doré, or Callot, or Tony Johannot, never conceived anything so horrible. There is a face in one of the latter's illustrations to *"Un Voyage où il vous plaira,"* which somewhat approaches the countenance of this creature, but does not equal it. It was the physiognomy of what I should have fancied a ghoul to be. It looked as if it was capable of feeding on human flesh. (263)

Harry and his companions have evidently made a discovery that would make the work of Le Fanu's Ghost Commission considerably easier – they have uncovered a creature that could be called a ghost, a ghoul, a vampire or even a succubus (since the creature's modus operandi appears to be to attack people in their beds; 255–6). It is implied (through the references to "spirit hands" and the reputation of the house for being haunted) that this creature, a categorically non-supernatural one, is the basis of all human folklore regarding spiritual predators – the first step has been taken in the eventual conquest of the gothic by the scientific. Once the questions of its nature and appearance have been settled, the process of integrating it into the human world begins: the landlady threatens Harry et al. with legal action if they do not remove the creature from the house (264), prompting amusing speculation on the reader's part as to how such a case would look played out if it were ever taken to a court of law.

In both "The Diamond Lens" and "What Was It?" we can see a pronounced degree of intertextuality, employed in a manner suggestive of a sort of inferiority complex: respected members of the scientific and literary communities are referenced by name, only to have their achievements compared unfavourably to the narrator's. This tendency is more pronounced in "The Diamond Lens," most evidently in the previously quoted passage where Linley fairly snarls, "It was I who *destroyed* Ehrenberg's theory" (emphasis mine),[6] and it recurs in "What Was It?" in a subtler but no less provocative form, when Harry and Hammond invoke the names of Brockden Brown, Bulwer Lytton and others, only to demonstrate the inferiority of the products of these creators' imaginations to the creature they trap and analyse. Also significant is Doctor Hammond's assertion, "I feel as if I could write a story like Hoffman to night, if I were only master of a literary style," especially since Harry has informed us that he himself has written a ghost story for *Harper's Monthly* (251). This audacity seems to be a compensatory reflex masking a deep insecurity of identity.

O'Brien campaigned on behalf of the poor of Ireland through his early poetry, and yet he seized the opportunity to emigrate to London as soon as he came into his inheritance, never to return to the country of his birth. After arriving in New York, it is probable that he represented himself as an exiled Irish revolutionary and exaggerated the extent of his involvement in the post-Famine uprisings. I would argue, however, that the plot and execution of "The Diamond Lens" betray a longing for imperial power. Most obvious of all is the dissonance between his assumed identity of the New World bohemian and the residual influence of his native land, a place where the gothic and the science-fictional were competing for dominance.

Ulster, at first blush, appears to be the exception that contradicts the above description of Ireland. One could be forgiven for assuming that Ulster, the most thoroughly industrialised province on the island, with its shipyards and foundries, was one place in which the science-fictional and the modern had triumphed and the gothic and traditional had been displaced. However, the work of Robert Cromie indicates that this was not the case: his most famous novels, *A Plunge into Space* and *The Crack of Doom*, exhibit the central paranoia of modernity (that the jettisoned, superstitious past might return), localised in such a manner as to portray the industrial north-east as an Ascendancy "Big House" writ large. If Ulster had expelled its ghouls and embraced modernisation, it now had much more to lose, should those ghouls find a way to get back in.

Robert Cromie (1856–1907)

A journalist by trade, Cromie was educated at the Royal Belfast Academic Institution and worked on the staff of *The Northern Whig*. He was unashamed of writing futuristic fiction (which he called "histories of the future"), declaring "this method has already many students; and certainly some advantages over writing the history of the past. It can hardly be so full of error" (Loeber and Loeber 329). His life and work present a pertinent contrast to those of Fitz-James O'Brien. O'Brien was born in County Cork and grew up in County Limerick, the son of a landowning family based in the gothic "lost world" of the Irish countryside, and consequently matured into a writer tormented by his hybrid identity. Cromie, on the other hand, was born in County Down, and later he lived and worked in Belfast – thus, he lived in an Ireland where the gothic had been banished; his was a world of industry and progress, and he happily regarded himself as a subject of the British Empire.

Cromie's most famous work is, without a doubt, *A Plunge into Space*, originally published in 1890. Following the discovery of a means to circumvent the law of gravity, a team of seven adventurers take off from Alaska and travel to Mars. There, they discover a quasi-anarchist society (Cromie 1890, 145), with unchanging laws (153); with no disease, money (154) or conflict (147–8); where there is (for all practical intents and purposes) no material scarcity; and where it only rains at night-time (173). The Martians are depicted as beautiful, wise and resplendently dressed (since the eradication of want and need has left them with nothing else to do besides dress themselves; 112), observing total equality between the sexes (128) and a two-hour working day (139).

Each member of the expedition has his own reason for embarking upon this momentous voyage, all of which resonate rather obviously with Rieder's observation that there were no "blank spaces" left on the map of Earth, and betray a subconscious imperial anxiety that the world has been "used up." The tough, pragmatic Scot, MacGregor, has explored every corner of the Earth, and lives in dread of living the rest of his life in "ignoble ease" (14). Sir George Sterling is "[a] financier in search of a new speculation"; Walter Durand is "a literary man in search of a plot"; Victor Graves is "an artist in search of a new subject"; Charles Blake, an Irishman, is "a politician in search of a post"; and Frederick Gordon is "a special correspondent in search of copy" (23). There is another (perhaps more honest) reason for their taking part in the experiment in Sir George's remark that "[there] is not a man in the lot good for fifty pounds" (29).

The foundry established to build the vessel by which the voyage will

be made is situated in Alaska, for the readily accessible steel and coal, and
"the absence of public opinion" (47). It is difficult not to interpret this
hive of industry as a Belfast shipyard, transplanted to the New World:

> Terrible furnaces seethed and raged. Great streams of molten metal
> gurgled and sparkled and shot up showers of hissing spangles as
> it filled huge ladles [...] Swarthy smiths were at work hammering
> and fashioning strange devices, some familiar, some fantastic,
> some fiendish [...] Mighty cranes were swaying to and fro. Giant
> hammers crashed and smote on yielding bars of red hot steel. And
> fierce fanged saws, with demoniac shriek, tore riotously through
> the massive metal plates. (30–1)

This breathless description is that of an admiring layman, conveying
the wonder that Cromie might have felt at the heavy industry that
surrounded him, and yet from which he was separated, being a
mere newspaperman. However, industry has one major drawback: not
even this marvellous foundry, out of sight of civilisation, can escape
the omnipresent scourge of the Industrial Revolution – the workers
themselves, who are "loafing about making speeches on your tremendous
wealth, their hard work, poor pay and so on" (35). The prospect of
industrial action is not all that the enterprise has to deal with. There is
also the matter of the indigenous population – "Blackfeet Indians" (sic)
who have been displaced in order to make room for the foundry. These
superstitious troublemakers are initially repelled by a show of electric
fireworks (36–7), and are later defeated utterly when the scientist,
Barnett, uses the principle of gravitation to dissolve their chief into "a
shapeless mass of pulp" (41), a rather forceful image of modern ingenuity
destroying premodern tradition.

While it would be foolish in the extreme to interpret this incident
as a metaphor for any single real-world occurrence of the time (e.g. for
"Indian chief," read "Charles Stuart Parnell"; for "gravitational device,"
read "Kitty O'Shea Affair"), it seems safe to assume that the image of
an industrial enclave under siege from superstitious heathens speaks
directly to Cromie's socio-economic position as a loyal subject of the
British Empire, a political entity Cromie depicts as having a mandate
from the physical universe itself. After arriving on Mars, the voyagers
eventually learn from their hosts that the dominant planetary power is
almost a mirror image of the Empire of their origin:

> Much of the peninsula of Lagrange lies between the degrees of
> North latitude upon the Earth which enclose the British Isles. It is

the seat of what slight government obtains in Mars. Its people are not, indeed, more civilised or more scientific than those of other lands of Mars [...] And when the soldiers of Lagrange had purchased with their lives a highway for its thankless colonists, missionaries, merchants and mechanics, from it, too, had proceeded all those insidious influences whereby the work of conquest is completed, and the ground is cleared for more useful races. (162–3)

This state of affairs has led to the eventual establishment of a Martian utopia, not through popular revolution, but by individual effort and "the slow evolution of solid truth" (178–9). Robert Philmus interprets Cromie's depiction of the Martian state as a prophecy of post-millennial decline (Philmus 16–17); Cromie's clumsy transposition of the British Empire to Mars contradicts this reading to a large extent. The Martian facsimile of the British Empire has flourished because it did not restrain itself, as Cromie implies the British Empire has, from doing what needs to be done: the Martians won their utopia because they simply annihilated the peoples that would not submit. The main problem with Martian society, rather, is that its prosperity precludes any kind of adventure or excitement. Succumbing to boredom due to the lack of conflict in Martian society, culture, literature and art, the banker and politician reach the conclusion that this utopia can be improved upon:

> Sir George soon discovered that he had a mission. The terrible financial ignorance of the Martians must not continue. There was neither a court of bankruptcy nor a company promoter on the planet. Against such dense stupidity the soul of the financier rose within him. And Blake, appalled by the want of an executive Government, or the want of an executive Government to denounce, was ripe for any scheme which promised excitement. (Cromie 1976, 201)

The schemes of Sterling and Blake anger the Martian senate, and the Earthmen are ordered to go home. By the time this happens, the sensitive writer Durand has fallen in love with a Martian woman named Mignonette, with tragic consequences. On the return journey to Earth, the protagonists are alarmed to discover that their carefully rationed air supply is running out. A search of the ship reveals that Mignonette has stowed away with them, and that her presence is to blame for their predicament (231). MacGregor has already stated that he will, as captain of the expedition, throw the expendable members of the group out of the ship if need be (68), and so it seems that Mignonette's fate is sealed. In the face of a slow death by suffocation, chivalry quickly disappears:

> There was not a man amongst them who would not have stood, revolver in hand, by the gangway of a sinking ship to see the women first into the boats. There was not a heart amongst them that would have quailed had duty bid them charge an army. But this thing of horror that was before them was more than a man might dare. (232)

They are brought to this horrible moment of truth by the actions of a romantic author; had it not been for Durand's interactions with Mignonette, she would not have fallen in love with him and so sealed her own fate. This apportioning of blame may seem argumentative and baseless, but in Cromie's next SF novel, it becomes abundantly clear that the romantic genius is a force for chaos and destruction, however well-intentioned he may be.

The Crack of Doom (1895) features Herbert Brande, an insane scientist *par excellence* who wants to destroy the Earth in order to end the hardship of the material world. The hero of the story is "an active, athletic Englishman, Arthur Marcel by name" (Cromie 1895, 3), who joins the mysterious *Cui Bono?* Society (sic) in order to be close to Brande's beautiful sister, Natalie (7), only to discover that he cannot leave, and that he has become embroiled in a plot to reduce the planet to pure "ether." There follows an expedition to a remote Pacific island, where the stiff-upper-lipped Marcel manages to foil Brande's dastardly plot and rescue not one, but two damsels in distress. Once again, the narrative is saturated in imperial ideology, articulated in opposition to the beliefs of the villainous *Cui Bono?* Society.

First of all, an early description of one of Brande's more harmless experiments provides an explicit link to O'Brien's murderous lunatic, Linley. When Marcel peers into a strange instrument not unlike a microscope, he is shocked at how powerful it is:

> I looked through the upper lens, and saw a tiny globe suspended in the middle of a tiny chamber filled with soft blue light, or transparent material. Circling round this globe four other spheres revolved in orbits, some almost circular, some elliptical, some parabolic. As I looked, Brande touched a key, and the little globules began to fly more rapidly round their primary, and make wider sweeps in their revolutions. (17)

Marcel is incredulous when Brande tells him that he has just witnessed the destruction of a molecule of swamp gas; Brande further proves himself as Linley's heir when he says: "'This is a scientific victory which dwarfs the work of Hermholz, Avogadro, or Mendelejeff. The immortal Dalton himself' (the word 'immortal' was spoken with a sneer) 'might rise from his grave to witness it'" (18).

The core principle of the Society is the pursuit of science for science's own sake, as it was for O'Brien's Linley: "No man can say to science 'thus far and no further.' No man has ever been able to do so. No man ever shall!" (20). Brande's discoveries go even further than Marcel can imagine; the scientist later reveals that he has financed the Society's activities with the secret of the Philosopher's Stone (119). Near to the novel's climax, Brande lets slip the true extent of his faith in science and rationality when he swears "by the living god – Science incarnate" (177). Cromie evidently had greater faith in engineering than he did in science.

The second warning Marcel receives about the diabolical nature of the Society comes when he meets Natalie Brande, and her friend Edith Metford, dressed in men's clothing and smoking cigarettes. When he demands to know the meaning of this unseemly transvestism, he is bewildered by the answer he receives:

> "Our dress! Surely you have seen women rationally dressed before!" Miss Brande answered complacently, while the other girl watched my astonishment with evident amusement [...]
> "Rationally dressed! Oh yes. I know the divided skirt, but –"
> Miss Metford interrupted me. "Do you call the divided skirt monstrosity rational dress?" she asked pointedly.
> "Upon my honour, I do not," I answered. (24)

The strange behaviour of the two women includes their smoking, a distinct lack of "hysterical fear" (29) and even "manly" handwriting (21). These qualities deliberately invoke the figure of the "New Woman" of the late nineteenth and early twentieth centuries – the term, coined by Irish-born author Sarah Grand, described a woman who was strong, assertive and intelligent, and, in a revolutionary innovation for the time, attractive to both men and women in spite of these qualities (O'Toole 126). In feminist fiction of the time (and in the caricatures printed by the suffrage movement's detractors), cigarettes, bicycles and divided skirts were among the typical accoutrements of this character (128); Miss Metford's dismissal of the divided skirt in favour of trousers thus serves as a warning of more extreme feminist politics to come. Indeed, she even goes so far as to say, "The conventional New Woman is a grandmotherly old fossil" (Cromie 1895, 27).

> Woman no longer wanted man's protection ("Enslavement" they called it). Why should she, when in the evolution of society there was not now, or presently would not be, anything from which to protect her? ("Competing slaveowners" was what they said) [...] All this was new to me, most of my thinking life having been passed in distant lands, where the science of ethics is codified into a simple statute – the will of the strongest. (34)

He confronts Herbert Brande about Natalie's behaviour, saying that as her brother, Herbert has a responsibility to set her straight. Brande disagrees, and makes a mockery of Marcel's chauvinism: "Very well, I am her brother. She has no right to think for herself; no right to live save by my permission. Then I graciously permit her to think, and I allow her to live" (37).

Complementing the "manly" women are "unmanly" men, most notably a young man named Halley, who is transparently coded as homosexual: "His face was as handsome and refined as that of a pretty girl. His figure, too, was slight and his voice effeminate" (66); Halley is shown to be unable to fight for himself, and thus Marcel categorises him as "unselfish coward" (113). The young man is later presumed to be a rival for Natalie's affections (131), but his unswerving devotion to the young woman is revealed to be nothing more than friendship (161). In addition to this feminism and gender confusion, the villains of the novel also seem to exhibit socialist political leanings. Further conversations with Natalie and Miss Metford reveal a worrying concern for the plight of the disadvantaged:

> On every [subject] Miss Brande took the part of the weak against the strong, oblivious of every consideration of policy and even ethics, careful only that she championed the weak because of their weakness. Miss Metford abetted her in this, and went further in their joint revolt against common sense. (33)

Finally, as if all of this were not bad enough, Brande reveals in a public lecture that the *Cui Bono?* Society is based upon a frustrated utopian impulse:

> "That 'Nature is made better by no mean but Nature makes that mean,' is true enough. It is inevitably true. The question remains,

in making that mean, has she really made anything that tends toward the final achievement of universal happiness? I say she has not." (84)

Having realised that the "universal happiness" they long for is not possible in nature, the Society's feminism, scientism and socialism bring them to one logical conclusion – that the only way to prevent the material universe's endless cycle of inequality, suffering, death and rebirth is to destroy it utterly: "Back, then, from this ill-balanced and unfair long-suffering, this insufficient existence. Back to Nirvana – the ether! And I will lead the way" (121). Marcel eventually defeats Brande by administering a poison to the scientist and altering his equations while he lies insensible (139–40). The altered equations lead to an adverse reaction, and the resultant explosion decimates the Pacific island, wiping out the primitive natives (188–97). In the course of escaping the island, Marcel rescues Miss Metford and Natalie – he attempts to rescue a third woman, the wife of one of the Society members, but she dies tragically in the earthquake (194). Marcel and Miss Metford return home to England, and planet Earth endures.

All's well that ends well, but where did these outlandish theories of evolution, socialism, feminism and utopia come from in the first place? Throughout *The Crack of Doom*, Cromie makes several references to the telepathic powers of Herbert and Natalie Brande, as well as a handful of members of the *Cui Bono?* Society. They are evidently powerful enough, under normal conditions, to send a mental signal over a radius of a thousand miles (170), and the Society uses these powers to will the death of anyone who attempts to leave it (49). Following the escape from the island, Natalie Brande dies, having been telepathically linked to her brother at the moment of his death (207). These abilities are not elaborated upon in any detailed manner, and the reader might even assume that the Society acquired them through training and experimentation, until he or she arrives at this announcement by Herbert:

"This time we shall not fail!"
A low murmur rose from the audience as the lecturer concluded, and a hushed whisper asked:
"Where was that other effort made?"
Brande faced round momentarily, and said quietly but distinctly:
"On the planet which was where the Asteroids are now." (122)[7]

This could be taken as nothing more than a mad scientist's flight of fancy, but for his use of the word "we." Later, Brande informs Marcel that Grey, another member of the Society, has led a similar expedition to Labrador: "If we fail to act before the 31st December, in the year 2000, he will proceed" (151). Brande has already informed us that the secret of eternal life is of no interest to him (119), and the story takes place in 1895 – therefore, we must assume that though he and his companions are not immortal, they are extraordinarily long-lived. Given their longevity, their telepathy and their knowledge of previous scientific experiments conducted on other planets, it seems reasonable to conclude that Herbert and Natalie Brande are in fact extraterrestrials.

To Marcel, the stereotype of steadfast Britishness, this conclusion would undoubtedly make sense (in the course of the text, however, he does not seem to reach it himself). As far as he is concerned, there are clearly defined social constants, such as the moral authority of the strong, and the behaviour expected of males and females in a "civilized" society. Feminism, socialism and utopianism are so estranged from these norms that they contravene the natural order of things. These strange ideas must have originated *elsewhere*. It is notable that in both of the novels described above, the site of scientific breakthrough is isolated from any urban centre, especially when one bears in mind O'Toole's observation that much New Woman fiction made use of urban settings (O'Toole 129), and Luke Gibbons' accounts of the moral panics surrounding immigration in nineteenth-century Britain, whereby Irish immigrants particularly were seen to be "spreading physical and moral contamination round them," in the words of one commentator of the time (Gibbons 43–4). The urban landscape has been taken over by unnatural creatures, and thus, industrial progress is paradoxically possible only in the wilderness.

The essential correctness of the British way of life is evident from the manner in which Miss Metford, originally the "manlier" of the two female protagonists, eventually repents of her behaviour. When Marcel remarks that she is not a man, she responds, "Right! And what's more, I am glad of it" (132), thereafter abandoning her "rational" clothing. Before she dies, Natalie also expresses sorrow at her wicked behaviour:

> "I was mesmerised. I have been so for two years. But for that I would have been happy in your love – for I was a woman before this hideous influence benumbed me. They told me it was only a fool's paradise that I missed. But I only know that I have missed it. Missed it – and the darkness of death is upon me." (206–7)

As Tina O'Toole points out, the "New Woman" figure was repeatedly represented as "a sexless monster and an anarchist" (O'Toole 127), a notion which, when tackled via SF's capability to literalise ideas, casts this character either as a non-human or as the victim of a terrible enchantment. To reinforce Marcel's role as a gallant, chivalrous Englishman, it is necessary that the female characters fall into the latter category, and thus Natalie's radical feminism, socialism and scientific rationality must be revealed as the results of her brother's telepathic influence, suggesting that regular Britons might be indoctrinated into those beliefs by malignant exterior agencies.

The *Cui Bono* are, in the end, qualitatively no different from the supernatural antagonists of the Ascendancy gothic. It makes little difference if the beast scratching at the door is from outer space or from out of the grave, because in this case they pose the same threat: contamination. Cromie's protagonists are as horrified at the idea of being turned into a socialist or a feminist as the heroes of supernatural novels are at the prospect of becoming a werewolf or a vampire; Cromie's innovation in this regard is to re-orient the external threat temporally. The traditional supernatural foes of folklore and the gothic are remnants of a past that won't die, but Cromie's villains are harbingers of an unwelcome future – this would prove to be an important, recurring theme in Irish SF.

The End

Both O'Brien and Cromie exhibit ambiguous attitudes to modernity, a consequence of the ongoing ideological struggle between modernity and tradition in the land of their birth. O'Brien moved from Ireland to New York, from an environment that was still largely traditional to one that was industrialised and modern, and his hybrid identity became all the more pronounced for it. Cromie, on the other hand, professed to be modern – his narratives move in the opposite direction, from modernity to tradition, on a mission of conquest. His relationship with modernity is no less ambiguous than O'Brien's. Cromie's characters do not sweep tradition away to make room for science, which is a dangerous pursuit when it challenges the status quo. Rather, Cromie wants tradition to yield to a modernity characterised by engineering, and he seems to perceive the ancient and modern worlds as being equally dangerous.

On 15 March 1895, the cultural logic that had sustained the reputation of Biddy Early's cures was dealt a severe blow when it was shown, in a most horrific manner, not to "work" any more, with the murder of Bridget Cleary in the townland of Ballyvadlea in northern Tipperary. Michael Cleary, Bridget's husband, accompanied by onlookers and a local man who proclaimed himself to be an expert on the occult, tortured Bridget to death, under the impression that they were exorcising a changeling.[8] The subsequent police investigation revealed that Bridget was afflicted with nothing more severe than a bronchial infection.

The cultural significance of this atrocity lies in the application of folklore to a situation that clearly contradicted it. When kidnapping a human child, fairies were held to have very specific criteria, and chief among these in Catholic Ireland was that the child should not be baptised (since the sacrament of baptism prevents travel between the earthly and fairy realms).[9] At the time that she died, Bridget Cleary was twenty-six years old, and it is hardly likely that she was not baptised. Read in this light, the incident represents a desperate grasp at rural, pre-Christian tradition, by people who were willing to contradict that tradition's own internal logic in order to ensure its survival. The incident occurred two years after the second Home Rule Bill, providing ammunition for those who opposed Irish nationalism at a time when violent land agitation seemed to have waned. Bridget Cleary's tragic story was the disturbing counterpoint to the legend of Biddy Early, and occurrences like the Ballyvadlea incident provided moral justification for the processes of colonisation and modernisation. Towards the end of the century, this moral certitude was increasingly encoded as a set of legal, medical and psychological norms: "Under the disciplinary regimes of this zealous [Puritan, 'Teutonic'] modernity, those who persisted in the delusions of the pre-modern [...] were removed to the new 'houses of confinement' that sprung up [at] the edges of cities, as if to ward off the evils of outlying, primitive regions" (Gibbons 87).

This could be viewed as hyperbole on Gibbons's part were it not for the demographic research of Thomas McCarthy, whose analysis of census data between the years of 1861 and 1901 revealed that the number of registered insane in Ireland during that time was increasing at a steady rate, despite a significant decline in population (McCarthy 559). McCarthy's research also outlines a phenomenal increase in the material power of the Roman Catholic Church during the same period – for one thing, the Church directly controlled most of the insane asylums in Ireland at this time. In addition to this, the total number of priests, monks and nuns increased by 137 per cent, even though the total Roman Catholic population of Ireland had decreased by 27 per cent (x), and of over eight thousand national schools open in the year 1899, almost six thousand of them were exclusively Catholic in their ethos and administration (552). Following the Famine, the mostly illiterate, mostly Irish-speaking rural poor vacated huge swathes of the countryside, to be replaced by middle-class, English-speaking landowners; the hovels in which the poor had lived were swept aside by sturdier labourers' cottages, and oral traditions gave way to print (Bourke 1998, 79). The storytellers, healers and poets who had serviced the old rural communities were "given short shrift" by the institutions of this changed society (80–1).

Catholicism had cemented its place as Ireland's dominant tradition, but the body of indigenous myth it displaced did not disappear: Philip O'Leary's research demonstrates that the tradition of the *seanchaí* storyteller continued up until the 1950s, around which time it was superseded by academic folklore-collectors (O'Leary 2010, 90–2). Though literal belief in Gaelic (or "pagan") myth was dying out,[10] it was simultaneously being reinvigorated by revolutionary rhetoric, in which context its literal "unreality" was of little importance compared to its usefulness as a reservoir of potent metaphors and imagery. In addition, this nationalist/ethnocentric reinvigoration was occurring while the popular fiction authors of Europe were projecting nationalist and ethnic animosities into the future.

2. "Future War" and Gender in Nineteenth-Century Ireland

By the latter half of the nineteenth century, the anxieties articulated by the Ascendancy gothic showed signs of coming true. The Fenian Brotherhood, while regarded as a very real threat to the security of Britain, behaved as though they had escaped from the pages of one of Cromie's novels, their plans for obtaining Irish freedom characterised by ostentation and insufficient planning. Romanticism, "New Departure" nationalism, and a growing awareness of the possibilities offered by new technology led to a sense that Irish independence was imminent. All that was required was the right "magic ingredient" at the right time, and this idea seems to have been so compelling in itself that nobody was prepared to entertain more than one hypothetical tactic at a time.

This romantic idea emerged in Irish nationalism just as a new literary form emerged across Europe, offering the perfect means to express it. Popular culture seemed suffused with a general expectation of war, which manifested itself in all kinds of literature: Richard Astle, for example, reads the vampire hunt in *Dracula* as "an allegorical rehearsal for World War I" (Astle 103). It was therefore hardly surprising that a literary form would emerge to service this cultural trend. The belligerent patriotism of nineteenth-century "future-war" novels was undoubtedly born of a sense of vulnerability or insecurity, arising from increased media coverage of the contest between the Big Powers. The defining characteristic of this new form was a fascination with shiny new weapons, without any consideration of the ways in which these things would change the very nature of combat.

Irish authors of the time were keen observers of developments in international politics, and directly reference those developments in their fiction – for example, the British defeat by the Boers at Majuba Hill in 1881 is discussed in almost every late nineteenth-century Irish future-war text, from both nationalist and unionist perspectives. Thus, we can say with a degree of certainty that the philosophical father of Irish nationalist future-war narratives was none other than Daniel O'Connell, whose aphorism "England's difficulty is Ireland's opportunity" allowed nationalists to engage with British future-war novels in ways that those novels' authors could never have intended. British anxieties regarding the state of the Fleet, and Continental outbreaks of sabre-rattling, were transformed into windows of opportunity during which a rebellion could succeed. Alas for O'Connell, those authors inspired by his rhetoric did not respond with as much enthusiasm to his assertion that "The freedom of Ireland is not worth the shedding of one drop of blood." Before discussing the future-war novel, however, we must briefly consider the short-lived sub-genre that appeared in Ireland before it and appeared sporadically alongside it: a sub-genre that I will for convenience's sake refer to as the "future-marriage" novel.

Prince Charming and the Frontier

Discussing the 1801 Act of Union between Britain and Ireland, Jane Elizabeth Dougherty writes:

> From the moment [the Act] was proposed [...] it was seen in the popular imagination as a marriage between Great Britain and Ireland, with Britain as the groom and Ireland as the bride. In part, this metaphor gained wide currency because the Act of Union had so many of the hallmarks of the classic marriage contract. The Irish Parliament became in 1800 the only parliament in history to freely vote for its own abolition; likewise, the classic marriage contract has been defined as a vehicle through which, by their own consent, women give up their civil rights, specifically their right to make any future contracts. (Dougherty 134)

The theme of a marriage between the two countries became prominent in middle-class drama and melodrama, and some writers even projected this domestic solution to Anglo-Irish difficulties into the future. John Francis Maguire, for example, a Cork-born barrister and Irish Independent Party MP for Dungarvan, Co. Waterford, from 1852 to 1865, produced a future-marriage novel that provides justification for the Empire even as it preaches equality between all peoples and advocates Home Rule. *The Next Generation* (1871), set in the year 1892, depicts a middle-class utopia, where Ireland and Britain exist in a federal union (Maguire 181), passports no longer exist (96), and Dublin has its own parliament (124) and is "now [London's] rival in gaiety" (112). Following the Emancipation Acts (64), women are free to serve as MPs for their respective constituencies, and are capable of succeeding to some of the highest posts in the Federation, though they are expected to give up their political careers once they become mothers (326). Female doctors are also becoming more common. Though Ireland is depicted as being slightly more conservative than Britain (249), we are told that there are around fifty female surgeons at work throughout the country (238–9). One could venture to say that this narrative world is only mildly futuristic: as O'Toole outlines in her overview of Irish contributions to "New Woman" literature, the latter half of the nineteenth century saw more and more women entering the public sphere (O'Toole 129), and the literature they produced was politically engaged, challenging patriarchal power and highlighting inequality, abuse and exploitation (127).

The Ireland depicted in *The Next Generation* is a pastoral utopia, where violence and sectarian hatred are things of the past (Maguire 115). A young Irish maid is described as coming from "Gentle Tipperary" (56), and the change in Ireland's political temperament has been mirrored in the very landscape: the crops are good, the blight is gone, the rains are "soft" and refreshing, there is no land agitation, and overall, the state of things is "prosaic, but pleasant" (126). There is even an uncanny foreshadowing of twentieth-century Irish political discourse, in a throwaway description of the "comely young maidens" that inhabit this amiable country (143).[1]

A number of reasons are given for the emergence of this happy state of affairs. The parish priest makes reference to "the growth of confidence in the mind of a people" (130), while the rector cites much more specific causes, such as the granting of Home Rule (154–5) and the disestablishment of the Church of Ireland (158). In addition to this, he continues, the absence of racism in the media has in turn eliminated racism from public life (173–4). Most importantly, there has been a matrimonial union between England and Ireland:

> We Irish are not Republicans in spirit – we are Monarchists at heart. But the former policy starved the feeling down almost to the very roots. Much more delay, and possibly it was gone – killed out altogether. It was a wise thing that the young Prince was allowed to marry the daughter of a great Irish house; and it was still wiser to render him, as a Viceroy, independent of Parliamentary change and Party conflict. (182–3)

It seems that not everyone is happy with the new, peaceful union between Britain and Ireland. In the Imperial Parliament, this dissatisfaction is voiced by an MP who opines that "namby-pambyism, Sir, is the greatest vice of our age" (15). In Ireland, Sir Martin worries, "I fear me you Irish are in a fair way to lose all your romance" (127), and this sentiment is echoed by an irascible carriage driver who grumbles that "all the sperrit is clane gone out of the counthry" (223). As in Cromie's *A Plunge into Space*, the biggest drawback to utopia is boredom, and this is certainly reflected in *The Next Generation*'s narrative: the plot unfolds in an atmosphere so amiable and lacking in conflict that it almost lacks a plot entirely. At the time, however, not even boredom was politically innocent, and this kind of insipid domesticity was a very serious issue.

Imperialist ideology, according to Anne M. Windholz, maintained that the genders of both the coloniser and the colonised benefited from the process of colonisation – the benefit for the coloniser was experience of the "real world" outside of an easy and sometimes degenerate "civili-sation," and this experience was held to imbue a young man with virtues appropriate to his gender: "British manhood would bring civilisation to the hinterlands of the world; in turn, the hinterlands of the world would save British manhood from civilization" (Windholz 631). In other words, the complacent, gentle utopia of *The Next Generation* was precisely what the Empire strived to avoid, and gender in itself was constructed as a convenient justification for expansion: as the colonies were "civilised," the masculinising "frontier" moved further and further away.

As well as a place where "degenerate" specimens could be sent to become real men, the imperial frontier was also a handy dumping ground for men who were considered dangerous to British society. The problem with this was that, in an ever-expanding empire, frontiers are not an inexhaustible resource. As there came to be less and less space outside of the Empire, effeminate men such as *The Crack of Doom*'s Halley would become increasingly common, and this threat was foreshadowed in "The Diamond Lens," by Linley's failure to penetrate Animula's world – a failure of both his manhood and his attempt to appropriate the position of imperialism. This issue could only have become more vexed within the context of the Act of Union's marriage metaphor.

Without any blank spaces on the map, British manhood and society in general were at risk of atrophying into insipid degeneracy. Indeed, this is the primary reason for MacGregor, the commander of the expedition to Mars in *A Plunge into Space*, to leave Earth. When the expedition gets there, they are given a vision of the future of the British Empire: with nowhere left to conquer, the Martian Empire has become a boring and decidedly queer place to live. Initially, the Earthmen express concern at the apparent lack of women on Mars (Cromie 1976, 121); this observation is demolished when their Martian host shows them a holographic image of his daughter Mignonette, "the vision of a young girl enshrined in a strange halo of light [...] a face of exquisite loveliness, undimmed by a shadow of that soft melancholy which clings to everything of perfect beauty upon the earth" (123). The Earthmen are understandably excited to meet Mignonette in the flesh, but Durand and the artist Graves seem more than happy to ogle the androgynous beauty of a young Martian boy in the meantime (126–8). After this momentary homoerotic gaze (no pun intended), the natural order of things is quickly set to rights once more – it turns out that the "boy" the two men have been gushing over is in fact Mignonette, dressed in unisex travelling garb (128). Later in the narrative, however, when Durand finds himself isolated from Mignonette, he takes comfort in the companionship of her younger brother: "Besides, he resembled Mignonette very much" (135).

As if to re-assert his masculinity, Durand later assumes the mantle of a kind of enforcer of gender roles. Upon hearing that Mignonette's fiancé has quietly abdicated all claim to the girl's affections, having witnessed the blossoming romance between her and the Earthman, Durand fumes that back on Earth, "we would dress him in petticoats" for behaving in such a manner (199). Mignonette argues that her former beau's behaviour was perfectly sensible, an attitude that Durand finds appalling:

> "Sensible! Mignonette we shall never understand each other. In our world, two or three hundred years ago, we used to fight for our sweethearts –"
>
> "I know," Mignonette interrupted; "we have all sorts of queer specimens of the early ages in our museums." (198–9)

Durand's conception of masculinity is based on traditional assumptions of ownership, and the combat necessary to protect that ownership. In the sexually egalitarian society of Mars, where these old assumptions are frowned upon and the distinctions between the sexes are not always apparent, this masculine identity comes under threat – and it certainly does not help that Blake, a stereotypically rakish Irishman, has also set his sights on Mignonette.

Durand need not worry. It later transpires that Blake finds Martian women to be boring in the extreme, as they have "lost the instinct of flirtation" (141). He has only been flirting with Mignonette in order to annoy Durand, and in presenting his reasons for doing so, he utters a Freudian slip that hints (rather bizarrely for a Cromie story) at a nuanced understanding of gender politics: "You seemed to think you had a peasant proprietorship – oh, bother it, I mean a personal proprietorship over the girl. I did not see the justice of your claim. Therefore I disputed it" (158). Blake thereafter abandons his pursuit of Mignonette, and instead spends his spare time teaching another Martian girl to "murmur simple commonplaces seductively" (187). Durand and Mignonette are thus allowed to proclaim their love for one another (200), only for their romance to be cut short by the Earthmen's expulsion from Mars.

The last future-marriage novel to be produced in the nineteenth century was Alice Milligan's *A Royal Democrat*. Prince Cormac Arthur, heir to the British throne, has always been too clever for his own good – so much so that his family and tutors spend his entire childhood trying to dull his intelligence so that he will be a suitable, "orthodoxly empty-headed" monarch (Milligan 7–9). In 1939, at the age of twenty-one, the Prince causes a scandal by publicly cheering for a radical socialist MP (31); to avoid further disgrace to the royal family, he is dispatched on a tour of the world to keep him out of the public eye until such time as he learns to behave himself. During his travels, the royal ship sinks, and the Prince is shipwrecked on Innishowen; knowing that he will be presumed to be dead, he seizes his chance to escape his royal destiny, and pretends to be an American citizen (39–49). The locals of Innishowen accept him into their community, where he eventually falls in love with a local girl, and Ireland and Britain live happily ever after. The Union between Britain and Ireland is apparently not an intrinsically bad thing, so long as Mister Right can be found. This state of domestic bliss, however, was only one side of an ambivalent and often dysfunctional relationship.

War Breaks Out

The most important factor in the rise of future-war stories in the late nineteenth century, according to I.F. Clarke, is the Franco-German War of 1870, which shocked European onlookers by unseating France as the dominant Continental military power, and elevating Germany to a position of military strength it had never previously held (Clarke 2–3). This upheaval occurred at a time of rising nationalism (11, 79, 86), in a milieu where there were very real antagonisms between the different European nations and alliances, and it produced a literature that expressed the then-commonplace anxiety that what happened to France could just as easily (and suddenly) happen elsewhere (30–63). The stories themselves owed their popularity to an increase in literacy levels among the general populace, which allowed authors to appeal directly to the masses, left readers susceptible to demagoguery, and made the conduct of war a matter for popular discussion, rather than the sole preserve of generals and statesmen (113). The prevalent themes of future-war narratives were hope and fear (29), and the intent of the author was usually to terrify the reader (38), and as a consequence such stories usually appeared in response to political crises (24). As the sub-genre "matured," the stories often came to be narrated in the first person by a "volunteer" (33), and sometimes by a citizen of the enemy power who defects to fight on the side of righteousness (7). The fictional wars became out-and-out fights to the finish, wars of either total destruction or total victory between two powers representing either spotless virtue or evil incarnate (122).

Perhaps the most important characteristic described by Clarke is the Victorian attitude to science and warfare: in short, they expected future wars to proceed exactly as wars always had, not imagining that the new weaponry would actually change the manner in which war was conducted, and they believed that the faster a war could be fought, the more humane it would be (69). It is to this lack of foresight that Clarke attributes the unprecedented slaughter of World War I (133). Clarke also presents a list of geopolitical conditions necessary for the emergence of the future-war narrative:

> The conditions were that a nation should be actively concerned in the international manoeuvring of the time. Big power – or nearly big power – status alone qualified for entry into the new club. Spain and Serbia, for instance, are innocent of the new fiction; and Ireland only appears when Irish patriots are involved in the internal power struggles of their great power neighbour. (44)

It is my opinion that Clarke's assertions are to an extent trammelled by the focus of his research (i.e. texts depicting future wars between two distinct European powers) and thus he overlooks imaginary conflicts between ethnic groups. He is factually correct in maintaining that Ireland's future wars were "internal" to the United Kingdom; from within the island's opposing political/cultural traditions, however, the anticipated combat was always clearly against a foreign or alien enemy.

To nationalists, who did not acknowledge the legitimacy of the Act of Union, that enemy was Britain, which they continued to characterise as a foreign invader. To unionists, the Other was a secret network of rebels bent on the total destruction of their community, aided by foreign ideologies and materiel, and the perpetual threat that Home Rule might be granted served to undermine the credibility of the Act of Union. In addition, Gibbons notes that the Celts were excluded from the category of "Caucasian" through a quasi-scientific discourse that originally arose to distinguish between different races of white people, via the use of phrenology and philology (Gibbons 38–9). Thus, when

Clarke notes that, as future-war narratives depart from political reality, "The element of fantasy increases and the stories turn into a species of nationalistic utopia in which the superior virtues, intelligence and vigour of the fatherland defeat an enemy without honour, without honesty, and without intelligence" (Clarke 121), we need not discount his observations on semantic grounds. To unionist authors, after all, Britain might be the "fatherland," but British citizenship and loyalty to the Crown are just one element of a complex identity encompassing a specific history, religion and culture, and the term "fatherland" could just as easily be applied to the soil their ancestors had lived on for generations. Thus, I argue that both nationalists and unionists produced "nationalistic utopias" of the kind Clarke describes, if we read "nationalistic" as "ethnocentric."

Those Magnificent Fenians in Their Flying Machines

In the latter half of the nineteenth century, the drive towards Irish independence underwent a quantum leap. For much of Irish history, nationalist rhetoric had been dominated by two distinct modes – on the one hand, the drive towards parliamentary reform championed by Daniel O'Connell, and on the other, the tactics of agrarian violence perpetuated by secret societies. From the mid-nineteenth century, this would change into the form of Irish republicanism familiar to us in the twentieth – parliamentary debate, combined with covert paramilitary operations: "a bullet in one hand, and a ballot in the other." The two historical prime causes of this were the Fenian Brotherhood and Charles Stuart Parnell.

The Fenian Brotherhood was founded in New York by James Stephens and John O'Mahoney on Saint Patrick's Day, 1858. Originally intended as an American extension of the Irish Republican Brotherhood, the Fenians eventually came to be seen as the principal driving force behind the republican cause (a notion that persists, in a linguistic sense, to this day – the word "Fenian" is used as a pejorative term for Catholics by Northern Ireland's unionist community), and the group's name was taken from mythology, "Fenian" being a corruption of *Fianna*, the name of the warrior sect to which the legendary hero Fionn Mac Cumhail belonged. The adoption of this name was a transparent assumption of a sense of historical legitimacy, with Stephens and O'Mahoney metaphorically positioning themselves as Fionn's contemporary descendants. This quasi-mystical link to a pre-Christian Irish warrior society may go some way to explaining the attitude with which the Fenian Brotherhood pursued the ideal of Irish freedom.

At first glance, it seems that the Fenians believed that anything was possible, as though they were capable, like the original Fianna, of miraculous victories against seemingly insurmountable odds. This sense of fantastic possibility allowed them to consider truly outrageous plans for achieving Irish independence, none of which had the slightest hope of actually succeeding, one example being the attempted invasion of Canada in June 1866 with a force of just eight hundred men.[2] The following year saw a Fenian uprising in Ireland, the anticipated success of which depended upon the entire British army and the police force deserting Dublin to catch the rebels, leaving the capital undefended (Bew 2007, 260–1). Interpreting these plots and their execution charitably, one could argue that these were not serious attempts to end British rule in Ireland, but rather a series of romantic gestures designed to fire the imagination of the Irish people and foster popular support for the cause of independence. In this respect, they succeeded, and in so doing they completely changed the modus operandi of Irish republicanism. Following the hanging of the Fenians Allen, Larkin and O'Brien on 23 November 1867 (for the killing of a Manchester policeman in the course of attempting to rescue other Fenians from a prison van), there was an enormous swell of popular support for the republican cause, enabling the election of Charles Stuart Parnell as MP for County Meath seven years later. An astute political animal, Parnell in 1877 had initiated a series of discussions with the Fenian leader John Devoy, seeking a means to use the Brotherhood's popular support to make advances towards Irish independence in Westminster. The coming together of these political traditions, which had demonstrated mutual animosity in the past, was so unprecedented in Irish history that it was popularly labelled "The New Departure" (Kee 72).

This blend of physical-force nationalism and parliamentary debate had a tremendous impact on Irish political culture, an impact that science could not match, despite the best intentions of the radicals who had organised public scientific lectures earlier in the century. In hindsight, this is hardly surprising, given that the most strident justifications of imperial ideology often concerned, as Langer puts it, the "lionization – indeed, the reification at the expense of all others – of the discourse and methods of Western science" (Langer 129). While this was not a common criticism at the time, it seems that something of science education's ideological tenor was apparent to the public:

> Although the diffusion of science was seen by nationalists as a necessary preliminary to economic independence, science was perceived by the majority of the Irish public as a socially

conservative agency, inculcating the values of sobriety, civic virtue, and theological orthodoxy [...] Unlike Britain, Ireland did not produce a "low scientific culture," especially not one in which science was appropriated by the working classes as a device for legitimizing social revolution. (Leaney 172)

According to Gibbons, the outbreak of "Fenian Fever" in the 1860s transformed British fears of Irish infiltration into "a fully fledged political gothic" (Gibbons 69). Closely linked to Fenian paranoia was the perceived propensity of the Irish to join trade unions and secret societies, as well as the impenetrable and necessarily clannish social milieu in which they interacted, a transplanted population with their own beliefs, customs and language: "the gothic element is imparted through the persistent alarms over the Celtic aptitude for conspiracy and violence, aided and abetted by the Jesuit cunning of the Catholic Church" (68). With the advent of the New Departure, this conspiracy seemed to have reached the House of Commons at a time when the incumbent Prime Minister seemed set on appeasing the Irish, and this perception is reflected in the future-conflict literature of the time.

The Re-conquest of Ireland, AD 1895 (Anonymous 1881), for example, is a short future-history pamphlet detailing the consequences of Gladstone's Second Land Act of 1881. The establishment of Land Courts to fix fair rents for impoverished tenants leads to a flood of spurious claims against decent, hardworking landlords, who are beaten or assassinated if they dare to defend their income. The Land League and the Fenians continue to preach revolution and rent defaulting, and the situation is made worse by a second famine from 1892 to 1895 (14–19). American Fenians finally stage an uprising of ten thousand men on the banks of the Shannon, and only after three days of pitched battle is the rebellion quelled (25–7). A couple of recurring late-imperial obsessions are mentioned in the text: firstly, a successful Boer uprising (24), and secondly, the Russian advance into Afghanistan – as in other future-war texts of the time, from this the author extrapolates an attempted Russian conquest of the Indian subcontinent, which diverts the fleet to the other side of the world (23–4). The publication of this pamphlet also coincided with the imprisonment of Charles Stuart Parnell and the defeat of the British armed forces at the Battle of Majuba Hill.

The Battle of the Moy; or, How Ireland Gained Her Independence, 1892–1894 (Anonymous 1883) follows a similar pattern, though from the opposite perspective. It opens with a run-through of the state of the world, in which we learn that Poland, Norway and Canada have gained their independence and become republics; the Turks have withdrawn across the Bosporus, allowing the Greeks to reclaim Constantinople; Bosnia, Herzegovina and Albania have united into a single entity known as the Dalmatian League; and an independence movement has started in India, diverting large numbers of British troops (1). Due to massive savings held in offshore bank accounts, accruing interest since the end of the Famine, Ireland is able to boycott Britain and import foodstuffs from America, refusing to raise crops or livestock for export to Britain. Panicking, the British government gives in to Irish demands for Home Rule in 1892 (2–3). Two years later, Britain finds itself engaged in war on the continent, as Germany and Austria join forces to conquer the Netherlands and Belgium, thus threatening Britain's mastery over the seas (6–9). Nationalist parties in the Irish Parliament seize the opportunity to declare Ireland's full independence (10) and sign a treaty with the Austro-German forces (13). This triggers a three-month war in Ireland, the key battle of which is fought on the banks of the river Moy in County Sligo, and Ireland is finally transformed into an independent nation.

The depiction of the Irish victory is sheer fantasy: Austro-German and Irish-American soldiers are able to land in Ireland without any hindrance from the British, the conflict is conducted without any recourse to guerrilla warfare, cavalry forces clash head-on, and numerous references are made to "the hatred of centuries" carrying the day for the Irish, in the absence of any military training. Equally unbelievable is the description of the Irish march on Belfast, where they are received with open arms by the local populace (66). The only futuristic weapon mentioned is a nitro-glycerine gun, used to break through barriers and blockades (58, 65). The text includes a map of the Moy region of Sligo, and exhaustive lists of the officers on each side (21–5), as well as "reprinted" texts of proclamations and casualty figures numbering in the thousands. In a perhaps unfortunate twist of fate for the author, the publication of this pamphlet coincided with the 1883 London Underground bombings.

Despite the obvious political differences between them, the anonymous authors of *The Re-conquest of Ireland* and *The Battle of the Moy* agreed on one thing – all that was needed to achieve the total independence of Ireland was British acquiescence, something that both authors seemed to regard as likely under a Liberal government. When Gladstone proposed his first Home Rule Bill in 1886, it appeared as though that acquiescence was about to be given.

The object of the Bill was to create an Irish legislature, though matters considered to be of imperial importance would be reserved for Westminster. In the political climate of nineteenth-century Ulster, however, no consideration could be given to such niceties. The unionist "siege culture" came to be tempered, now more than ever before, with the understanding that the weakest link in its defences was the Westminster government to which it pledged allegiance. Writing about the proliferation of anti-Home Rule texts in the late nineteenth century, Edward James notes:

> There is little political imagination here; the Unionist authors can think of no alternative to the continuation of the status quo, and display almost no sympathy with what we might regard as the legitimate grievances of the majority of the Irish people. All of these works stem from a crucial period in the development of Protestant identity in Ulster [...] one can well imagine that if an Orangeman sat down today to express his views in science-fictional terms, the results would not, *mutatis mutandis*, look markedly different. (James 1986, 8)

If Britain's resolve ever faltered, Ulster unionists would be outnumbered. Before the spectre of Home Rule could return to haunt Irish unionists in reality, a new fable for physical-force nationalists appeared at a time when the Fenians seemed to be considering the use of scientific means to achieve their ends. If, as Declan Kiberd argues, colonised peoples sooner or later come to believe that popular fiction is to be imitated (Kiberd 1996, 115), the story of *The Fenian Ram* indicates that at least a handful of nationalist revolutionaries were reading Jules Verne.

John Philip Holland (1841–1914) of Liscannor, County Clare, is credited with the invention of the first reliable submarine. A former Christian Brother, in 1872 he left the order and travelled to the United States. In 1875, he approached the United States Navy with his plans for a submarine, only for the Secretary of the Navy to reject the idea as unworkable. Holland continued to work towards making his submarine a reality, and pursued this end with private funding. Among the financiers were friends and family, but he also received a substantial amount of money from nationalist political organisations such as Clan na nGael and the Fenian Brotherhood. In the submarine, the Fenians saw an opportunity to land a decisive strike against the British Navy, and thus to achieve independence for Ireland. With their funding, the finished vehicle, christened the *Fenian Ram*, was constructed by the Delameter Iron Company and launched in New York in 1881, the same year in which Charles Stuart Parnell was imprisoned. Four years later, Thomas Greer's novel *A Modern Daedalus* was published.

Born in County Down, Greer was a physician by trade, educated at Queen's College Belfast, who practised medicine at Cambridge. He unsuccessfully contested North Derry as a Liberal Home Rule candidate in 1892 (Loeber and Loeber 510). He elaborates upon his political views in the preface to his novel:

> Let no reader suppose that this book is the work of an enemy of England. On the contrary, though a native of Ireland, I am a lover of England, and a firm believer in the necessity of a firm and lasting union between the two countries. Nobody more deeply deplores the disunion at present so apparent between them. For the objects, and still more for the methods of the so-called "dynamite party," I have the deepest abhorrence. (Greer 1885, v)

This abhorrence is shared by the novel's protagonist, John O'Halloran from County Donegal, who invents a pair of mechanical wings with which a man might fly as a bird. So consumed is he by the perfection of this apparatus, that he fails to notice the change in temperament taking place in the Irish countryside. Since the departure from politics of a British prime minister friendly to Irish concerns, advances in Anglo-Irish solidarity have started to backslide: land courts have been abolished, and their rulings reversed, "disloyal" newspapers have been suppressed, public gatherings have been banned, rents have skyrocketed, and the villages of Ireland are full of policemen and soldiers (8–9). In the face of this worsening situation, men such as the young inventor's father and brothers are becoming increasingly militant:

> My father and brothers – staunch supporters of the English connection as long as they hoped for justice at the hands of an English Parliament – now threw themselves with stern energy into the popular movement, and for some months their house had been the scene of secret meetings, and the storehouse for an immense armoury of modern weapons, including dynamite bombs of New York manufacture. (9–10)

After going on a secret nocturnal excursion in the sky, and thus witnessing the assassination of a landlord's agent (21–3), John returns home and argues with his family about the political value of violence (29–31), and with stunning naïveté he then reveals his invention to them. His father is the first to see the obvious application of John's apparatus:

> This will ensure the triumph of Old Ireland. You must keep it a secret; you must set yourself to train your brothers and other young men, till we have a flying brigade that can go anywhere and do

anything! Nothing will be able to stand against it, and you will have the glory of delivering your country and striking the chains from her hands! (35–6)

When the pacifist John reacts with horror to this suggestion, refusing to allow his work to be used for such a purpose, his father confiscates the machine and banishes him from the family home (50–2). Downhearted but not defeated, John travels to Letterkenny, where he finds shelter with two old college friends, and builds himself a second, improved flying machine. He then flies to London to publicly announce his achievement (75), with the intention of making it available to the general public, not anticipating the calamitous impact his appearance has on the population of London – he causes a stampede in which several people are injured (77–8), creates a bomb scare in St. Paul's Cathedral (82) and triggers a parliamentary debate in which the House of Commons calls for the immediate arrest of all Irish MPs (89–92).

Desperate to allay British fears of a conspiracy of flying Irish assassins, John presents himself to the Home Secretary, explaining his actions and intentions (109–113). This backfires when the Home Secretary orders John's arrest, and imprisons him until such time as he agrees to produce flying machines for the British military (161). During his imprisonment, John reads newspaper accounts of a massive uprising in Ireland (136–59), and his ill treatment at the hands of the British authorities causes him to sympathise more and more with the Irish nationalist cause (167). Some time later, John's brother Dick aids his escape, bringing with him the prototype flying machine from their father's cottage (175–88). During this escape, Dick informs John that the main driving force behind the rebellion is their eldest brother Dan, who has proved himself to be something of a military genius and "a born leader of men" (181). Flying to Dublin, John meets the first President of the Irish Republic, and sets about creating an Irish Flying Brigade, which ensures the ultimate triumph of the Irish rebellion with a series of crushing aerial attacks on Dublin Castle (200–2), the British navy (206–11) and British garrisons in the north (236–7, 242–4). When news of these defeats reaches the English public, initial outrage and calls for vengeance soon turn to acquiescence and acceptance of the independent Ireland (248–51).

A Modern Daedalus brings together many of the literary themes discussed thus far. Most obviously, there is the figure of the mad scientist, albeit a much more sympathetic variant of the trope than O'Brien's Linley or Cromie's Brande. John O'Halloran's particular brand of "madness" is his naïveté, or his unwillingness to perceive the warmongering potential of his discovery – a naïveté reflecting the contemporary zeitgeist. On several occasions, he outlines his utopian vision of a world in which everyone is capable of flight: "What additions to the sum of human pleasure; what an extension of mutual knowledge and brotherhood among nations; what new and higher forms of civilisation; what a revolution in the social and political conditions of the race seemed now about to be inaugurated!" (17).

At the very beginning of the text, O'Halloran warns us not to expect any detailed descriptions of how the apparatus works (xi), and even though he admits to jealously guarding the secret of his discovery (2), he tells us that the machine is no more difficult to use than a bicycle (67). The initial description of what the machine looks like reflects the inventor's utopian visions for its use: "I stood before [my friends] in a form almost exactly that which the popular mythology extends to angels" (66). Having become involved in the uprising, O'Halloran reflects upon the conflict between this utopian longing and the situation in which he finds himself:

> That the necessity [of my involvement in warfare] arose as an almost direct consequence of the peaceful scientific labours to which I had devoted myself [...] is one of those moral paradoxes which perplex alike the reason and the conscience, and lead almost irresistibly to the conclusion that the evils of life result from the machinations of a capricious and malignant personality, rather than the ordered sequence of cause and effect. (234)

This notion of a satanic influence is echoed by a later observation, as O'Halloran and his flying brigade attack an English camp with fire-bombs:

> Even at such a moment I remember remarking with a certain feeling of amusement how like huge bats were the figures that flitted around me in the gloom, and remembering that the wings they used were of the form attributed by superstition to devils, rather than to angels. (238–9)

Forced by circumstance to become a man of war, O'Halloran's personal pacifism is transmuted into its mirror opposite:

> To say that they may make war, indeed, but that they must not make it too effectively; that to kill a man with a solid bullet is legitimate, but to wound him with an explosive one is atrocious;

that to blow your enemy to fragments with gunpowder is civilised warfare, but to employ dynamite for the same purpose is worthy only of savages; is a species of cant born of the idea that war is a magnificent game for kings and nobles, and it must be carried on under rules that disguise its essentially revolting nature, and prevent it from being too dangerous or disagreeable to them. (247)

For an individual who regards all violence as morally bankrupt, there is no reason to conduct it in a "civilised" manner – this is in marked contrast to the attitude of his brother Dan, who ironically proclaims with the stereotypical heartiness of a British gentleman-officer, "We must breakfast in Belfast this morning" (242). In this instance, it seems that pacifists make the most terrible warlords. It is also noteworthy that not once in the text does O'Halloran re-examine his view of science as inherently peaceful in the light of at least one exemplary piece of evidence to the contrary – his brother's rifle, referred to by Dan as "my dark Rosaleen" (41), one of many "advanced" weapons used by the rebels.

These rifles, along with the dynamite, have been imported from New York, which characterises the uprising as an operation of the Fenian Brotherhood. "Americans" are also suspected of carrying out many of the killings of local landlords (62, 194), but they are not the only dangerous foreign influence. When O'Halloran returns home to Donegal at the novel's beginning, he finds that his father and brothers have been immersed in cryptic political literature: "The whole history of Russian Nihilism, of German Socialism, of the Italian Carbonari, of the French Commune, was at their fingers' ends" (7). In addition to these seditious histories, the O'Halloran family has drawn inspiration from a motley assortment of international revolutionaries, such as Washington and Garibaldi (30–1), and service with the British army has prepared a whole generation for guerrilla warfare: "The Boers taught us a lesson at Majuba Hill that hasn't been thrown away, and there are a thousand lads in Ireland who could hit an officer between the eyes at a thousand yards, and never throw away an ounce of lead" (31–2).

A Modern Daedalus refers back to the work of Fitz-James O'Brien in more ways than one. Firstly, as has already been mentioned, O'Halloran keeps his scientific discoveries to himself, just as Linley the microscopist guards the knowledge of the subatomic realms he discovers, even though the principle behind the former's discovery is allegedly quite simple, and the latter's achievements are open to anyone with a microscope. Secondly, though O'Halloran is a much more sympathetic character than Linley, while flying over Downing Street during his first escape attempt, he does give in to Linley's megalomania, perhaps betraying a similar inferiority complex:

> "That is where a dozen crawling wingless insects are sitting at this moment," I soliloquised, "to determine whether they will allow me to give these powers to men, or even to exercise them myself. Why should I hold myself at their beck and call? They have forfeited all claim to courtesy at my hands; let them come to me if they want to see what I can do. I will trust them no longer; I laugh at their puny authority ..." (131)

Thirdly, O'Halloran displays a trait previously observed among O'Brien's protagonists, a combination of hyperbole and intertextuality. After witnessing a demonstration of his flying machine, O'Halloran's friends remark that "One would fancy that we were in the 'Arabian Nights,' or that Munchausen had come to life again" (69). Later, while describing the destruction that he has wrought on a British camp, O'Halloran describes it as "a scene such as even the author of the 'Inferno' could not have painted" (237). Later, when the conflict has ended, O'Halloran says, "I heard myself compared at one time to Timour, to Robespierre, to O'Donovan Rossa; at another to Wallace, to Washington, to Garibaldi; and one side aroused my resentment as the other tickled my vanity" (254).[3]

The contrast between these references – to the *Arabian Nights*, Baron von Münchhausen and Dante Alighieri on the one hand, and to a string of warlords and revolutionaries on the other – perhaps indicates a hybrid identity similar to Fitz-James O'Brien's. However, whereas O'Brien's identity crisis arose from his origins in the landed gentry of the Celtic periphery, and manifested itself in his heroes' unsuccessful attempts to exert imperial power, Greer's anxieties of origin have their roots in his socio-economic position as a middle-class professional Irishman, financially secure in a time when most of his countrymen were not, schooled by a British education system, a would-be participant in the British political establishment, and yet trying to retain an Irish identity. Like Fitz-James O'Brien, Greer expressed his hybrid identity through the changing moods and opinions of his protagonist. While flying over the Donegal countryside, surveying the misery wrought by the landlords' "crowbar brigades" (eviction squads), O'Halloran reflects that the evicted paupers have nobody to blame but themselves (14–15).

Later on his flight, however, when he spies the agent responsible for this eviction, he swears that if he saw an ambush lying in wait for this contemptible man, he would "not stoop to utter a single word of warning!" (21). Back at the family home, following his final refusal to allow his invention to be used in an uprising, his brother Dan levels the following, telling accusation at him: "'so,' he said, 'he refuses, does he? Didn't I tell you he was English at heart? The spawn of those cursed Government colleges always are'" (52).

It is difficult not to assume that Greer himself, educated at Queen's College Belfast and later employed as a physician at Cambridge, heard similar charges directed against him. O'Halloran could thus be seen as a form of overcompensation for Greer's anxieties about being perceived as "English at heart," waging uncompromising war against the British armed forces in spite of the character's abhorrence of bloodshed.

In Robert Cromie's terms, O'Halloran is an "unselfish coward" who tries to become a "man of action" like his brothers, especially after internalising their view of his pacifism as effeminacy: traits such as curiosity, fear and avoidance of bloodshed are seen as "womanish," and his father remarks, "we will soon teach you to sing a more manly tune" (43); later, having bombed Dublin Castle and the British navy, his brother Dick admonishes him for his regret over such action by saying, "Don't spoil it by whining over it like a woman" (213). As in Robert Cromie's works, masculinity is here linked to patriotism, ruthlessness and violence, and it is difficult to place this construction of masculinity at any kind of remove from the matrimonial construction of the act of union. If Britain had established itself as the "male" head of the household, then to be feminine or ambiguously gendered was a mark of treachery or collaboration with the enemy.

In *Newry Bridge; or, Ireland in 1887* (Anonymous 1886), the unionist nightmare of abandonment by Westminster comes true: the Home Rule Bill passes (Anonymous 1886, 4–5), and Ireland is transformed into a single-party state dominated by the Land League and their puppet ministers. Ulster refuses to recognise the Dublin government, and, after its pleas to England to be taken back into the Union are ignored by the ineffectual Liberals, establishes a provisional government of its own (19). This state of affairs leads to a civil war in 1887, the key battle of which happens at Newry, a railway hub providing access to the entire island. After Newry is secured by the Ulstermen, the rest of the country falls, and Ireland is delivered back into the British Empire (68–9). The story is told by a gentleman in late middle age, to his children, and it includes a sub-plot of star-crossed love between him and a Catholic woman. The depiction of an independent Ireland conforms to a couple of typical patterns – after an initial period of lawlessness and anarchy, the government introduces martial law and Ireland becomes a police state, ruled by incompetent demagogues, once again with the help of the Irish-American Diaspora. Even after Ireland is re-conquered, violence and rioting continues all around the world, in any colony or territory where Irishmen and Englishmen live in close proximity (69–70).

Unionist future-war narratives are steeped in gendered ideology. As can be seen from the few examples I've given here, unionist authors often supplemented their military fantasies with matrimonial themes or sub-plots: by defeating the enemy, the hero proves his worth to lead a family, and he usually wins over a "Fenian" girl in the process, reaffirming the marriage of the Act of Union by re-enacting it in miniature, placing their cultural tradition on the masculine side of the equation. In fact, at a time when the vice of "namby-pambyism" appeared to have emasculated the British government, Ulster was a reservoir of proper manliness, especially since the shipyards of the North-East were intrinsically linked to the imperialist project. Robert Wyndham Bourke, the Earl of Mayo, affirms this link with his novel *War Cruise of the Aries*, in which British dominance is asserted over the Mediterranean, North Africa and the Middle East by means of a war ship with a battering ram designed to penetrate the hulls of enemy vessels. The shipyards of Belfast are thus instrumental in equipping the Royal Navy with what is, in effect, a magical phallus against which there is no defence (Wyndham Bourke 1894).

In *London's Peril* (1900, Edmund Downey writing as "F.M. Allen"), a "big power" future-war rather than a conflict internal to Ireland, Mr. Treherne, assistant to the British State Secretary for Foreign Affairs, is informed by a French traitor of a plot to invade London, via a secret tunnel under the channel. Along with a Russian invasion of India and Majuba Hill, invasion via a secret tunnel was another recurring obsession of future-war authors, and it is difficult not to interpret it sexually, as an act of feminisation and penetration, given the degree to which this genre was gendered by Irish authors.

In *The Red-Leaguers* (1904), James Shaw, an upstanding Protestant with military experience in Cuba, the Philippines and South Africa (11), joins a revolutionary movement distributed over the whole of Ireland, and assumes command of the Armoy Commando in County Fermanagh. Ireland is liberated in a single night, and a Republic is declared (147).

It is tempting to read this novel as a sort of autobiography. The son of a unionist Presbyterian minister, John William Bullock rebelled against his domineering father by adopting the Irish name "Shan Fadh" (*Seán Fada*, or "Long John") upon leaving home, and he retained "Shan F. Bullock" as a pseudonym after beginning his writing career (Loeber and Loeber 199). Similarly, the character of James Shaw turns his back on his own people for ambiguous reasons. Despite his fondness and sympathy for the Catholics, however, he is soon forced to admit that the Protestant bigots he despises were right all along – the Irish cannot govern themselves, and his motivations for leading their doomed bid for independence were, at root, personal. The parallels between this realisation and Bullock's biography – that of a young unionist man who adopted a Gaelic identity out of anger, only to write a pro-unionist novel when he came of age – are striking enough to give the reader pause.

A genuine hatred of anti-Catholic bigotry (36–7), combined with unrequited love for Leah Hynes, who is betrothed to a "clodhopper" named Jan Farmer (8), drives Shaw to join forces with Christy Muldoon, the local commander of the Red League. The Red League's interest in Shaw is based upon his service record in South Africa, and once again the Battle of Majuba Hill is invoked. Muldoon's summary of Britain's position in international politics summarises many of the recurring nightmares of British future-war narratives:

> "Look at her there with only the ships between her an' perdition. Russia waitin' to grab up India; the States hungry for Canada; Germany ready with her new navy to spear the whale; France ready with her armies on the cliffs an' her submarines in the harbours only waitin' for the word. All the world against her. Not a friend under the stars of heaven. An ould image of a statesman guidin' her. Her government gone to pot. Credit broken, trade goin'; herself bankrupt a'most an' rotten to the heart. Oh, be the eternal King, she's done for. Limb be limb she'll drop away, colony be colony into the ocean, till only the carcase is left; an' then ..."
> With a significant gesture Christy snapped his fingers at the floor and stamped England into the clay; then, to the sound of shuffling feet and creaking stools and the applause of the company, sat back in his chair and mopped his face. (12–13)

Assured that Protestants will not be specifically targeted (18), Shaw agrees to lend his military experience to the Red League's cause. His martial expertise carries the Armoy Commando to swift victory, and soon he finds himself laying siege to a castle occupied by Leah's father and the hated enemy, Jan Farmer. At this point, the glorious military adventure starts to fall apart. The Armoy volunteers get drunk on whiskey (142), the great Christy Muldoon turns out to be a feckless, workshy daydreamer (146), the Protestants refuse to surrender (154), and Shaw reveals himself to be a bully, keen to use his new power to force Leah to return his affections (157–8). An assault on the castle is easily repealed, with massive losses for the Red League (164–9), and an attempt to bombard the castle with cannon fails spectacularly, further humiliating the rebels (239–42). These failures to *penetrate* the castle, and thereby to prove himself a real man (as he has previously done on the imperial frontier), provoke a crisis of character in Shaw that hearkens back to that of *A Modern Daedalus*'s John O'Halloran, and the comparison is hammered home when one of the Red Leaguers tells him that he is "as full of whims as a woman" (134). Shaw and O'Halloran share a fear of "unmanliness," and in Shaw's case this dread is all the more pronounced for the fact that his primary goal – entering into a heterosexual relationship – is taken for granted by the "real" men surrounding him, and yet he is incapable of attaining it.

The "gender trouble" to which the protagonists of both novels are subjected highlights the degree to which the imperialist construction of Irish masculinity had been internalised. In John O'Halloran's case, third-level education disqualifies him from being Irish, and pacifism disqualifies him from being properly male; James Shaw, on the other hand, is contaminated by nationalism and as a result loses his ability to function as a heterosexual man. Intelligence, education and pacifism are alien to this particular conception of Irish masculinity. Nationalist men were expected to play up to the violent ape-man stereotype established in the now-infamous *Punch* cartoons, and were considered neither Irish nor properly male if they could not. Nationalist masculinity in Ireland was thus always figured as being defective.

After the lengthy siege, Shaw decides to take the captive Leah to Dublin, purely to confound Jan Farmer. As they proceed through the country, warning signs start to present themselves:

> On the crest of a hill that overlooked a lake, diversion was in full swing. There were foot races on the programme, jumping and wrestling competitions, contests between local athletes at throwing the hammer and putting the weight, obstacle races, sack races, egg and spoon races, a football match, a match at hurley for the championship of Glann, and all the rest. The hubbub was great. Sporting gentlemen were shouting the odds. Ballad-singers swelled the din. Gipsies and Jews yelled by their shooting galleries and roulette tables. Fortune-tellers, thimble-riggers, card-sharpers, trick o' the loops, had each their noisy following. Glib simpletons with hooked noses sold purses of sovereigns for half-crowns. On the stalls and standings were displays of cheap jewellery, ginger-bread and sugar-sticks, oranges and mineral waters. The shebeen tents were crowded. Round a score of carts men and women were drinking porter and whiskey and poteen, laughing, shouting, quarrelling.

> Already many were drunk, many glorious. Fights were common. Blackthorns whirled and fell. (288)

The full horror of the situation becomes clearer the further the Protestants travel. Education, infrastructure and law and order have all gone to pot (294), a village mayor arrests the travellers as Protestant enemies of the Republic (296), Dublin is dilapidated (288–9) and the price of everyday foodstuffs has skyrocketed (301). Faced with this squalor, Shaw is finally forced to say, "Let the Celt go. Let the Saxon come" (303), and when the British army comes to save Ireland from itself, he escapes to France (315).

Bullock's novel serves to demonstrate how narratives of imaginary war had largely run their course by 1904. Most of the plot of *The Red-Leaguers* is composed of direct reversals and subversions of the usual future-war clichés: for example, the main character is an "enemy citizen" whose perfect grasp of right and wrong leads him to join the opposing side, but here, that moral sense is exposed as a sham. The "secret weapon" trope appears not in the form of a fantastic new invention, but in the retrograde shape of rusty old cannons that cannot shoot straight; the war is fast and mostly humane, but the aftermath is a bloody, drawn-out nightmare; and the protagonist discovers too late that he is not the hero of this story at all, but a villain doomed to defeat at the hands of a band of stalwart unionists, the perennial heroes of Home Rule war fantasies.

A survey of the Irish rebellion fantasies reveals that the super-weapons so beloved of future-war authors in other territories are nowhere near as popular in Ireland. There is the spectacular exception of Thomas Greer's flying machine, as well as the nitro-glycerine gun in *The Battle of the Moy*, but for the most part, the protagonists of these future-wars do not seek aid from mad scientists. Rather, the external catalyst that makes victory (for either side) possible more often takes the form of foreign or overseas aid: nationalists depend on guns, money and volunteers from America, and on occasion from Continental Europe, not to mention foreign incidents to distract the British military. Unionists, of course, count on the British armed forces. Occasionally, the magic ingredient needed for a successful rebellion is the right strategy (hence the nationalist interest in Majuba Hill), or the right man to lead the nationalist forces (as in *A Modern Daedalus* and *The Red-Leaguers*). Technology does not have a significant role to play in this imaginary warfare, and I would argue that this is due to Ireland's position as an island, paradoxically on the periphery of the Empire despite its close proximity to the imperial centre. Bould and Vint note that in the final years of the nineteenth century, Britain was undergoing a massive cultural change, brought about by technological development, "the commodification of innovation" and increasing scientific literacy (Bould and Vint 36). This cultural sea change bypassed Ireland, and that loss or lack could account for the absence of fictional technology, but there is another, pragmatic factor to consider.

The principal difference between Irish writers of future war and their British counterparts is that Irish writers did not need to imagine a means by which the enemy would arrive. While stories of invasion proliferated in Britain, exploiting anxieties about the Channel Tunnel or the hypothetical absence of the Fleet (Clarke 29, 107, 109–114), the belligerent parties in Ireland knew not only that the enemy was already here, but that the enemy was omnipresent, whether in the guise of the army and police, or as hordes of Fenians who plotted in hidey-holes scattered throughout the countryside.

The prospect of all-out war was much closer, both in time and in distance, and this did not allow much time for scientific endeavour. The stories of nationalist authors were clearly meant to inspire, and thus they could not allow their fictional rebellions to depend on hypothetical super-weapons, which in any case could only be manufactured in unionist-controlled industrial strongholds such as Belfast. Unionist authors, by contrast, knew that they were under siege, and that the hypothetical uprising could come at any time. When that uprising happened, they would be obliged to defend themselves until such time as the British armed forces arrived in sufficient numbers to restore order. The defence of their way of life would require practical action and preparation – imaginary weapons were of no practical value whatsoever.

3. Nationalist Fantasies
of the Early Twentieth Century

The removal of *terra incognita* from the map of the world had as profound a consequence for Irish culture as it did for the British Empire. Through the early modern period, when there were still "blank spaces" left on the map, the unexplored frontier was figured as a zone in which traditional societies continued to flourish, and where a *file* might once again find an aristocratic patron. Once the world had been fully mapped, this longing for tradition had to be re-oriented away from the geographical and towards the temporal, and just as the *filí* had made a profession of hearkening back to a golden age, lamenting, as Kiberd puts it, "not so much a lost community as a seigneurial life of cattle raids, warrior feuds, high culture and immense wealth" (2001, 38), the imaginations of twentieth-century Irish revolutionaries and artists were oriented towards the past. This kind of poetic sensibility, combined with the fact of literal belief in folk magic in certain parts of Ireland, created a cultural milieu in which (up to the late 1840s, at any rate) tradition, magic and myth had not been "proven wrong" by modernity, science and positivism, but rather had been pushed aside or suppressed, and were still accessible.

Thus, to a certain degree, nationalist claims for political legitimacy necessitated a supposed continuity with the "golden age" of the *filí*, emphasising the premodern, pre-Christian past as a foundation for ethnic identity: one possible origin point was presented in the *Lebor Gabála* [Book of Invasions], in which the island was settled by a number of civilisations (of which the Gaels were the last), each of which contributed to the genealogy of Ireland's greatest heroes and to the ancestry of the present-day Irish; this historical scheme carried a great deal of emotive power, and was still being entertained by historians in the mid-twentieth century (O'Leary 2010, 180).[1] This historical continuity with a mythological age was further emphasised by a latter-day *Fianna*, the Fenian Brotherhood. In the aftermath of the Famine, however, as this politicisation of Celtic mythology was progressing, literal belief in it was declining, and what was once a three-way contest between modernity, Catholicism and quasi-pagan tradition became a one-on-one conflict between Catholicism and the encroaching modern world – Catholicism having successfully positioned itself as the only legitimate traditional cultural logic.

Due to its increasing utilisation as a political and artistic resource, as well as its usurpation by the Catholic Church, myth in nationalist culture of the time no longer occupied a place on the tradition–modernity continuum, but still exerted a powerful ideological influence. This is particularly notable in the mystical patriotism of Pádraig Pearse and the utopian nationalist visions of a de-Anglicised Ireland, but its spectre looms over those who rejected it in favour of "realism," be it the fundamentalist "social truth" of the Catholic bourgeoisie or the historical materialism of James Connolly. Irish nationalism at the beginning of the twentieth century was not politically or ideologically homogenous, and these diverse ideologies were set to collide once independence was achieved.

Which Ireland Do We Dream of?

In 1892, Douglas Hyde presented a lecture to the newly formed National Literary Society entitled, "The Necessity for De-Anglicising Ireland." It would be inaccurate to credit this lecture as the historical moment that inaugurated the late nineteenth-century Gaelic Revival, but it is useful as a starting point for any discussion of the Revival in that it sums up the concerns that energised that movement: in addition to aspirations of independence, this lecture highlights an increasing anxiety regarding the possible loss of Ireland's cultural distinctiveness, which would render that independence a moot point. Hyde argued that without a national sense of *self*, the sought-after right to self-determination would be worthless:

> We have at last broken the continuity of Irish life, and just at the moment when the Celtic race is presumably about to largely recover possession of its own country, it finds itself deprived and stript of its Celtic characteristics, cut off from the past, yet scarcely in touch with the present [...] Just when we should be starting to build up anew the Irish race and the Gaelic nation – as within our own recollection Greece has been built up anew – we find ourselves despoiled of the bricks of nationality. (Hyde 84–5)

Tomás Mac Donagh argued that the end of the Gaelic kinship system was a necessary step towards literary innovation and maturity, since the Gaelic aristocracy had become "decadent" and Gaelic poetry had lost most of its vitality (Mac Donagh 26). The English language came to take the place of Irish in the social and artistic life of Ireland, but Mac Donagh maintained that the variety of English that was taught to and adopted by the Irish "was not the language of English commerce" but an older variety of the language that had not been widely spoken in Britain since Shakespeare's time (28). Mac Donagh also postulated that Modern Irish was not substantially different to Old Irish, thus providing an unbroken tradition around which a Gaelic identity could be re-formed, and that the language's relative isolation from the modern world had produced vocabularies and turns of phrase far more nuanced than those of English (31).

Both these elements combined to produce what Mac Donagh called "the Irish Mode," a description he substitutes for Arnold's "Celtic note." The Irish Mode is "the mode of a people to whom the ideal, the spiritual, the mystic, are the true [...] and there is still nothing new under the sun and all novelty is but oblivion" (6). The "informing soul" of Irish literature, according to Mac Donagh, was "the cause that never dies" (9), and he foreshadowed his own untimely end with the observation that "the cause of God and Right and Freedom, the cause which has been the great theme of our poetry, may any day call the poets to give their lives in the old service" (73). Despite the emphasis he placed on tradition and mysticism, however, Mac Donagh was prepared to admit that the Futurists might have been on to something:

> The futurists may be charlatans, or fools, or lunatics. They may also be prophets. The difference of their manner from the good old ways does not prove their rightness or their greatness; but the hostile critics of their works use words and weapons so like those used against other work that survived attack and afterwards became right and great and good, that one cannot lightly join them. (3)

He further conceded that "the literature of to-morrow will be in terms of the life of to-morrow" (80), but expressed hope that "we may resume a broken tradition and make a literature in consonance with our past" (98). In this sentiment, we can see a precursor of Yamano's recommendation that authors approach "universal" themes and subjects from their own historical, cultural and personal subjectivities. While Mac Donagh was outlining these hopes for the future of Irish tradition and literature, the utopian aspirations of other Irish revolutionaries were a good deal more detailed and comprehensive.

It is difficult to conceive of two more contradictory brothers-in-arms than James Connolly, the level-headed socialist, and Pádraig Pearse, the mystic poet. The difference between them is illustrated by their respective opinions on the state of education in Ireland under British rule. Pearse's most famous text, "The Murder Machine," criticised this education system on the grounds that it was "soulless," treating children as "raw material" to be "finished" and "turned out" in as efficient a manner as possible (Mac Aonghusa and Ó Réagáin 1967b, 33). In place of this system, Pearse advocates an attempted emulation of the Gaelic system of fosterage, as far as is practicable (38–42), administered by a Ministry of Education that would allow each school the freedom to shape its own curriculum, appropriate to the context of its "size, personnel and so on" (45). Pupils could take inspiration in the classroom from Celtic sagas and hero-tales (46–7), and Pearse further imagines a partial return to mediaeval systems of education, where students would seek out educators whose philosophies and personalities appealed to them, rather than receiving a standardised education from whichever tutor happened to be nearest to them (41). Connolly, by contrast, attacked the same education system with facts and figures, arguing that classrooms were unsanitary (Mac Aonghusa and Ó Réagáin 1967a, 144–5) and overcrowded (146–7), and that many of the teachers and teaching methods employed in the schools were incompetent and ineffective (148).

Other differences of opinion between the two revolutionaries abound, and some of these differences appear to be quite severe. Rather than a material or political ideology, Pearse stated that "Freedom, being a spiritual necessity, transcends all corporeal necessities, and when freedom is being considered interests should not be spoken of" (1967b, 14). Connolly, on the other hand, maintained that independence could only be guaranteed if Irish workers seized the means of distribution, such as railways and canals (1967a, 186–7), and among the characteristics of a free nation, he listed control over the harbours, the power to encourage industries, a postal service, telegraphs, wireless broadcasting, customs and excise, coinage, armed forces, merchant commerce and property relations (192–3), all of which are "corporeal necessities."[2] Pearse's mystical nationalism is located in the overlap between tradition and myth, while Connolly's materialist analysis resides in that between modernity and realism. Opposition to the revolution would come from predictable quarters – the Roman Catholic Church and the middle classes – but Connolly predicted that reactions from these groups could be overcome without too much trouble. The Church would initially kick against the workers, he argued, but history had proved that Irish Catholicism was opportunistic, and the Church itself was inclined to support whichever side looked as though it might eventually win, regardless of the official line from the Vatican (29–31). As for the middle classes and aristocrats, they could expect no mollycoddling or compromise from the revolutionaries, suggested Connolly, warning: "If you remove the English army to-morrow and hoist the green flag over Dublin Castle, unless you set about the organisation of the Socialist Republic your efforts will be in vain" (20–1).

Middle-class nationalists, however, were a much more complicated breed than Connolly realised, and this was reflected in the fantastical literature they produced.

Tradition and Realism

Since the nineteenth century, notes Terence Brown, traditional crafts and trades had been dying out in the face of competition from industrialised systems of production, and people seeking employment in this context had three choices: join the professional class, get a job "in town" or emigrate (25). A "job in town" usually meant the grocery trade or general shopkeeping, and the expansion of this social group (along with the professional classes) created a milieu in which wealth had to be consolidated by marrying into wealth, best encapsulated by marriages between successful farmers and shopkeepers' daughters. The cultural effects of this consolidation of wealth (and thus, political and social influence) were enormous:

> The values and familist social structures of the farm world were transferred to the shop and the town, thereby ensuring that the cultural and political influence of the small and strong farmers in the country was augmented by that of the grocers and small-traders of the town [...] Their economic prudence, their necessarily puritanical, repressive sexual mores and nationalistic conservatism, encouraged by a priesthood and Hierarchy drawn considerably from their number, largely determined the kind of country which emerged in the first decades of independence. (25–6)

To the above observation, we must add that the Roman Catholic Church did not merely support these social classes out of a sense of familial loyalty. As noted in Chapter 1, in the latter half of the nineteenth century the Church had used its position as the country's only "legitimate" premodern ideology to accrue a phenomenal amount of wealth and power, and the numbers of clergy had expanded while the total population of Roman Catholics had decreased. This is where bourgeois ideas of tradition and realism combine, and this area has one particular text that encapsulates its values with stunning clarity. Not only does *Eoghan Paor* by Pádraig Ó Séaghda (under the pseudonym Conán Maol), published in 1911, figure one transmutation of the future-war narrative into something new, but it also contains a rich seam of utopianism. Unfortunately, this utopianism comes wrapped in a reactionary ideology, which gives the text historical significance for rather unsavoury reasons.

Gobnait, the daughter of a shopkeeper, falls in love with the titular Eoghan Paor ("Eoghan Power"), a young lad of no apparent means. They promise themselves to each other, and Eoghan heads off to seek his fortune. Seven years go by, without any word from Eoghan, and Gobnait's father starts to despair of ever finding her a suitable match. Eventually, he forces her into a loveless marriage to a wealthy young farmer nicknamed "Progress," so called because he often says, "my neighbours should be involved in commerce and trade, and progressing in life" (Ó Séaghda 12).[3] After the wedding is concluded, Progress gets into a bar fight with one of the other guests, and thinking that he has killed the man, he flees the country – taking Gobnait's dowry with him, and losing it all on the stock market in London. The shock hastens him into bad health, and in order to recoup some of the money he sells his farm – the very farm that Gobnait happens to be living on, back in Killarney. When the stockbroker's agent comes to repossess the house, she finally discovers where Progress is, and she goes to London looking for him.

Gobnait arrives in London in time to hear the full story, and despite her skills as a nurse, she is unable to save her husband. She has nowhere else to go, and so ends up destitute in London, promising to give her life up to God. After befriending a kindly Irish doctor, she finds work as a nurse in one of London's hospitals, where she meets the mysterious stockbroker Parheim – only to discover that he is none other than her long-lost beau, Eoghan Paor, who has by this time become the richest man in the world. Their love rekindled, they make plans for the liberation of Ireland, eventually hitting upon an ingenious scheme – they will purchase, populate and fortify all the hills and mountains in Ireland, in preparation for the day when a Republic is declared.

Middle-class Catholic ideology drives this novel. Firstly, there is Eoghan Paor himself. Born in Australia to nationalist parents exiled from Ireland, and educated in Germany, Eoghan was born into money thanks to the crafty land speculation of his father, and he inherits a million pounds after his father's death (64). Upon coming of age, he doubles his fortune through playing the stock market, netting two million pounds and crashing the Melbourne Stock Exchange (65), and he decides to use this economic terrorism against England (67). We later discover that "Barún Hirse" (William Randolph Hearst) has asked Eoghan to lend him enough money to buy the Holy Land (99), and that Eoghan counts the King of Belgium among his cordial acquaintances (157). Known to his business competitors as "The Lion" (and aided by a cunning Jewish assistant referred to as "The Jackal"; 158), "Parheim" is a catch for any ambitious, upwardly mobile young lady.

Secondly, there is the long-suffering Gobnait, the quasi-Cinderella of this novel. Denied her chance at happiness with her one true love and blamed for bringing "shame" on Progress's family (34), she is so wholesome that the depiction of her destitution becomes ridiculous: for example, at one point she becomes an organ-grinder to make ends meet, and is so fair-minded that she shares her meagre income with the monkey (43). A good Catholic, she saves Eoghan's soul from the "treachery" of German philosophers such as Kant and Hegel by repeatedly reciting the Hail Mary (83), and their reunion comes to a bitter end when Gobnait realises she cannot choose Eoghan over God. Meek, gentle and worshipful, Gobnait is also quite intelligent and well-read.

Eoghan's and Gobnait's nationalist credentials are evidenced by their attendance at Irish classes run by Cumann na Gaedhilge (54, 88), their contemptuous attitude to Anglicised Gaels (89, 98–9), Eoghan's attempt to save an Irishman framed for terrorist activities (124–5), and references to the broken Treaty of Limerick and the Whiteboys (127).[4] The means by which these historic wrongs are to be corrected, however, are financial rather than military. Eoghan tells of his appeal to the President of the United States to buy Ireland from the British; the President (presumably either Theodore Roosevelt or William Howard Taft) informed him that America could buy Ireland, but the British would never sell it for fear that the Germans might conquer it later (77). Eoghan later reveals that he would do it himself, but he has loaned nine or ten million to both the Russians and the Japanese, and that this money will not be available again for another ten years (79). Gobnait comes up with the brilliant idea to buy and fortify Ireland's hills, and to only allow Irish speakers to live on them (91–3); Eoghan is initially sceptical of the whole idea, but later he becomes more enthusiastic, and during a return visit to his alma mater in Germany, he requisitions a team of German scholars to inquire into how the scheme could be carried out successfully (159–60).

As might be expected, there is a strong resonance in this text with the mysticism of Pearse:

> We are too fond of clapping ourselves upon the back because we live in modern times, and we preen ourselves quite ridiculously (and unnecessarily) on our modern progress. There is, of course,

such a thing as modern progress, but it has been won at how great
a cost! How many precious things have we flung from us to lighten
ourselves for that race!

   And in some directions we have progressed not at all, or we have
progressed in a circle; perhaps, indeed, all progress on this planet,
and on every planet, is in a circle, just as every line you draw on
a globe is a circle or part of one. Modern speculation is often a
mere groping where ancient men saw clearly. All these problems
with which we strive (I mean all the really important problems)
were long ago solved by our ancestors, only their solutions have
been forgotten. (Mac Aonghusa and Ó Réagáin 1967b, 37)

Aside from the heavy-handed allegorical aspects to the story (such as
"Progress" bankrupting poor Gobnait, the personification of meek Irish
Catholic femininity), most of the text's ideology is connected to the title
character. Despite the fact that, as a Machiavellian stockbroker, he is
bound to the modern world, Eoghan shares Pearse's distaste for modern
schools of thought and denounces the works of Darwin, Lamarck,
Thomas Henry Huxley and Hegel as lies (Ó Séaghda 69).

   More interesting is Eoghan's back-up plan in case his scheme for
Ireland's hills does not work. After hearing Eoghan's description of
Hearst's plan to buy the Holy Land as a home country for the Jewish
Diaspora, Gobnait asks whether Eoghan could do something similar –
such as buy one of the United States as a new home for the Irish (Ó
Séaghda 99). Eoghan dismisses this plan as impractical, but he reveals
that he has given a similar idea some thought:

   Many of the Irish in the old days were prophets. During paganism,
   particularly often since then, we do be talking of "Tír na n-Óg,"
   and of "Mag Mell" and of "Hy Brasil," and many people believe
   that these were just other names for Heaven [...] There is a country
   in South America that is called Brazil, and in my opinion, if the
   Irish that do be heading to North America every year were directed
   there, they would quickly have plenty in Hy Brasil and the good
   life would be theirs in that place. (100–1)[5]

Sure enough, Eoghan is planning to buy one of the ancient Irish
utopias, Hy Brasil, which he has identified (showing either stunning
ignorance or a spectacular lack of imagination) as Brazil. Later, he
organises a two-year fact-finding expedition to Brazil, to be undertaken
by his German comrades (168). While we are not told at the novel's
close whether either scheme succeeded, we are left with the heartening

promise, "Beidh lá eile ag an bPaorach" ("Power will have another day")
(188).[6] The fact that such a character appeared in print as the hero of
a nationalist novel was an indication that the fight for Irish freedom
was not necessarily going to have a socialistic, egalitarian conclusion.

Modernity and Myth

In 1912, the same year that Prime Minister Henry Herbert Asquith
introduced a third Home Rule Bill (to which a quarter of a million
Northern Irish unionists responded by signing a petition known as the
Ulster Solemn League and Covenant), Pearse speculated about what
might have happened if Gaelic literature and philosophy, rather than
those of the classical Greeks and Romans, had emerged as the guiding
light of European civilisation in the fifteenth century:

> Then instead of the classic revival we should have had the Celtic
> revival; or rather the Celtic would have become the classic and the
> Gael would have given laws to Europe. I do not say positively that
> literature would have gained, but I am not sure that it would have
> lost. Something it would have lost: the Greek ideal of perfection in
> form, the wise calm Greek scrutiny. Yet something it would have
> gained: a more piercing vision, a nobler, because a more humane,
> inspiration, above all a deeper spirituality. One other result would
> have followed: the goodly culture and the fine mysticism of the
> Middle Ages would not have so utterly been lost. (Mac Aonghusa
> and Ó Réagáin 1967b, 85–6)

Mac Donagh was not quite so taken with this idea, but he had the
decency not to name his compatriot in print when he dismissed the
"Celtic revival" as useless whimsy four years later: "[a] recent writer
has lamented that instead of the Classic there did not take place in the
fourteenth century a Gaelic Renaissance. Of course, the lament and all
discussion of it is futile. I listen dreamily to it" (Mac Donagh 78). Despite
Mac Donagh's dismissal, however, the power of such alternative histories
was compelling enough to prompt at least one author to speculate about
what an alternative Ireland would look like, and from March to June
of 1912, Charlotte ("L") McManus's *The Professor in Erin* was serialised
in Arthur Griffith's *Sinn Féin* newspaper.

The plot of *The Professor in Erin* dramatises a central conceit of the
republican imagination. The world-renowned philologist and "Celtologist"
Professor Schliemann, while examining the ruins of Hugh O'Neill's

castle in Dungannon, falls through a hole in the ground and regains consciousness in a different Ireland. In this parallel world, the forces of Hugh O'Neill (known by the Irish version of his name, "Aodh") defeated the English at the Battle of Kinsale and went on to liberate the entire country. Ireland has a population of thirty million, and has a lower crime rate than any other country in Northern Europe; there are no slums or burglaries; Ireland has its own currency (with rather complicated exchange rates), a thriving agricultural sector and heavy industry powered by hydroelectricity, and it retains its ancient forests; public sanitation is aided by public baths and aqueducts; Irish tabloids do not pry into the private lives of celebrities; and to top it all off, Irish scientists discovered electro-magnetism before anyone else, and have gone on to discover the White Ray, "which has even greater and more extraordinary properties than Radium" (McManus 1912h, 6). The political system that prevails is "framed as far as modern life will allow on the ancient clan or communal system," with a guarded tolerance of entrepreneurism and national ownership of all material resources apart from gold and silver (McManus 1912e, 6). Electoral areas are based on the "Tricha-Ced" system of land division (184 divisions of 188 square miles), general elections take place every five years, and the only unelected positions are those of the King, the Righdamma [sic] (heir to the throne), the Five Princes, the Five Hereditary Historians and the four Archbishops.[7]

Schliemann has stumbled into a nationalist wonderland. Here is an Ireland that was never Anglicised, represented by the "Avenue of Kings" on the grounds of the palace of Tara, wherein stand magnificent statues of past High-Kings from Tiermas to the current ruler, Niall III. There are no English place names, and Schliemann repeatedly confuses his hosts by asking them questions related to a history of English rule that they cannot conceive of. Irish legend is written into the landscape, notably in the case of the "Bridge of Bulls" which spans the Shannon, so called for the statues of the bulls from the *Táin Bó Chuailgne* that stand at either end, and in the case of the private sanctuary of the Princess of Midhe (Meath), referred to as "Tír-na-nÓg" and administered by a beautiful servant girl named "sidhe."[8] The unbroken history of Celtic tradition constructed in this text also allows McManus to make a joke that is in somewhat bad taste:

> "But the Orangemen," said Schliemann, "What have you done with them?"
>
> "We import them," MacFirbis replied, whom the noise of the train had prevented from hearing the exact question. "The climate

of Erin is unfit for their growth. The Prince of Thomond has an Orangerie of some size." (McManus 1912e, 6)

The depiction of this parallel-universe "Erin" goes beyond Hyde's calls for the de-Anglicisation of Ireland. Erin represents what Ireland *should* be, and *would* have been had it never been invaded. It is an "authentic" nation that the Ireland of our world must aspire to become – even if history has to be rewound and started again.

Within this setting, Schliemann finds himself embroiled in an escalating crisis that begins as the story of a family feud, complicated by a tale of star-crossed lovers, which later adopts the postures of a detective story, and threatens to escalate into a full-blown future-war narrative, with Erin and Germany as the belligerent parties. The sought-after object in this text is a pair of ancient vellums, the Codex Diomsneachta and the Psalter of Tara, written during the time of the High-King Cormac Mac Art (and thus, during the time of Fionn Mac Cumhail and the Fianna). The vellums are the cause of a centuries-long feud between the Mac Firbis clan and the Keating family, with each party believing the texts to be their own rightful property. Having seen them himself, Schliemann decides to steal them and take them back to Germany, but he soon realises that he is not the only party interested in such a course of action. Geoffrey Keating and Sorcha Ní Fhirbis wish to steal the vellums in order to fulfil the technical requirements of the Keating oath, thereafter returning them to Mac Firbis and ending the feud so that they might marry. Shortly after he agrees to help them accomplish this, Schliemann meets yet another would-be thief, an American who introduces himself as "Amos Moss, of Chicago, billionaire." Moss is an obsessive collector of ancient artefacts, and having been refused the opportunity to buy the vellums, he offers Schliemann a sizeable reward for their theft (McManus 1912d, 6). By sheer luck, Moss later manages to steal the vellums himself, setting in motion a game of bluff and double-bluff as the various characters attempt to recover the ancient books while avoiding the suspicions of the brilliant young detective/secret agent Mac Suibhne, and foiling the machinations of Maelmuire Mac Firbis, who wishes to prevent Sorcha and Geoffrey's wedding so that he may marry Sorcha himself. When Moss is eventually arrested, it transpires that he has lost the vellums; more importantly, he is blackmailing Germany with economic ruin if the Irish police do not release him within thirty hours, at a time when diplomatic relations between Erin and Germany are already strained. Towards the story's climax, Schliemann becomes aware of what is at stake when he catches a glimpse of the Irish army being mobilised:

Young faces, kindled faces; fair, sunburnt skins under helmets; tall
figures; men weaponed; the confidence of courage, the haughtiness
of race in their air and step. And he saw the furled colours carried
by a young officer; nineteen, perhaps, was the lad's years; there
was laughter and daring in his eyes; the pride of the world in
his mien. It was a regiment for its foes to fear; wonderful in its
unity; flexible as the willows; strong as the torrents of Dun-easa;
disciplined, mobile, magnificent, a weapon of slaughter and death.
(McManus 1912m, 7)

Heightening the tension, Schliemann's experiences in Erin are
marked by paranoia and helplessness. Whenever he touches the ancient
books, he is afflicted with spells of catalepsy, which seem to be triggered
by a sweet scent emanating from the vellum itself (McManus 1912c, 6).
This affliction, which is never explained within the narrative, allows
Moss to steal the vellums while Schliemann looks on, unable to move,
and causes him to freeze during the climactic shoot-out between Mac
Suibhne, Maelmuire Mac Firbis and Moss (McManus 1912n, 7). In
addition, the longer the professor remains in Erin, the more he is in
danger of losing his identity. Due to his name, he is repeatedly mistaken
for the famous archaeologist "Carl Schliemann,"[9] and as he tries to
correct this mistake, other characters either brush his denial off as
modesty (McManus 1912b, 6) or think him insane (McManus 1912l, 6).
Much to his exasperation, he is forced to adopt the identity of the other
Schliemann, beginning with a couple of white lies and culminating
in an improvised lecture. Eventually, Mac Suibhne discovers that the
"real" Schliemann is excavating a ruin in Yucatan; the professor is so
relieved that he exclaims, "I hope the Indians will scalp him! He has
been my nightmare" (McManus 1912l, 7). By this time, the shedding
of Carl Schliemann's identity is a hollow victory – those who realise
that he is not the famous archaeologist now think that he is a German
spy, and even the staff of the German embassy know him as "Professor
Schliemann of the Foreign Secret Service" (McManus 1912g, 6). Twice in
the text, the phrase "I know who you are" is used as a threat (McManus
1912j, 6; 1912m, 7).
Schliemann's nightmares of mistaken identity arise from the premise
of the setting – in a world where Ireland was never Anglicised, there
is not much use for a philologist who specialises in the study of Irish
as a dead language; therefore, history must choose another role for
him. Twice, Schliemann tries to contact his sister in Berlin by post and
telegram, but receives no answer (McManus 1912e, 6; 1912i, 6), and
another avenue of escape back to Germany is closed off to him when

his curiosity to see Dublin causes him to miss the boat to Hamburg (McManus 1912h, 7). To him, Ireland is an open prison. He cannot interact with Erin in any meaningful way as a "Celtologist," thus explaining the fits of paralysis that overtake him whenever he tries to interfere with the vellums.

As outlined above, *The Professor in Erin* bears the residual traces of numerous literary genres. Schliemann is a mad scientist (since he insists on believing in things that the rest of the world knows to be false); his struggles to assert his own identity (combined with the repeated failure of his attempts to escape) recall the paranoia and fatalism of the Ascendancy gothic; he bears witness to the well-worn melodrama of star-crossed lovers and family feuds; and he matches his wits against dastardly villains and an inscrutable detective who could have escaped from the "penny dreadfuls" of the late nineteenth century. The place he falls into is likewise reminiscent of other literary forms – in a very real sense, it is a "lost world"; the minute descriptions of that world, including even the diet and clothing of its inhabitants, testify to the influence of utopian literature; and this nationalist utopia is threatened by the prospect of a conflict with the perennial antagonist of British future-war fiction, Germany. The over-arching generic structure is of the sub-genre referred to in the present day as "alternative history," but tempered with something distinctly Irish, the *aisling* or prophetic dream-poem:

> Into the night all had vanished, all that he had seen, the men and women he had met, to whom he had spoken, with whom he had moved, who had been so alive; vanished for ever.
> He sat down on the side of the mound, and opened his notebook. Then his eyes dwelt long on some words in archaic lettering. "It is a dream and a prophecy that will be fulfilled," he said, when he raised his head; "for not till the Judgment Day shall Ireland be conquered." (McManus 1912n, 7)

The invocation of this poetic form carries a trace of something potentially quite dangerous. The vision of this completely de-Anglicised (or to be more precise, never-Anglicised) Ireland, with a Gaelic aristocracy, a mediaeval code of honour and no Orange Order, coupled with the assertion that this "will be fulfilled," is not merely an implied threat to the unionist community, but also an expression of a problematic "nativist" urge, a desire for "the systematic removal of all vestiges of colonial power and influence and a reversion to a precolonial, 'Edenic' state" (Langer 6), which, as Langer points out, "is not only unrecuperable but [...] wholly imagined in its purity and perfection" (109).

The Great War and the Rising

Both *Eoghan Paor* and *The Professor in Erin* display an ambivalent attitude towards Germany and the German people. In the former, the hero owes his keen intellect to a German education, and is supported in his efforts by German scholars, but finds spiritual redemption by abandoning their blasphemous philosophies; in the latter, the protagonist is an enthusiast of Irish history and the Irish language, but his is an enthusiasm for dead things, and thus his presence in the alternative Gaelic world is an implicit threat, triggering a war between Erin and Germany. This ambivalence towards Germany was, in fact, one of the few things that the various nationalist ideologies had in common.

Joachim Fischer, charting the history of German-Irish relations from the latter half of the nineteenth century to the early twentieth, notes that to some degree there had been a meeting of minds, as German philologists started to appreciate the Irish language as a worthwhile object of study and Irish nationalists admired and took inspiration from German literature's rise "out of the shadow of the French" in the eighteenth century (Fischer 1999, 67). This interest in Germany was intensified by the outcome of the Franco-Prussian War (the same turn of events that spawned the future-war genre), which, combined with the Entente Cordiale between France and Britain in 1904, displaced France as Ireland's preferred European ally; Pearse even considered an alliance with Germany whereby the Kaiser's son Joachim would temporarily serve as the Irish head of state (69). In Ireland, Germany was presented as a patriotic, high-spirited and high-minded opposite to the money-obsessed, decadent culture of England. This image of Germany was fostered by Catholic journals, and Catholic Germany was held up as an example for Ireland to follow – despite the fact that two-thirds of Germany was actually Protestant (73–5).[10] Complicating this relationship, however, was the fact that there were few supporters of Germany among the Anglo-Irish and Protestant authors of the Literary Revival (69), and the fact that in the nineteenth century, theorists such as Ernest Renan and Matthew Arnold had defined the Celt as an archetype to be unfavourably compared to the German – "a melancholic, dreamy, imaginative, literary, backward looking and essentially feminine race which was no good at one thing: politics" (70) – thus making the "German character" complicit in the colonial discourse deployed to justify British rule.

Nationalist support for the British war effort was based on the promise of Home Rule – both on the expectation that Irish support would be rewarded and on the principle that it would be better to avoid the

perception that Ulster unionists had sacrificed their lives while nationalists did nothing (Bew 2008, 98). More generally, many Irish people
believed that "war abroad means peace at home" (Pennell 39), and
genuine support for the Allies manifested itself in sometimes unfortunate
ways, such as attacks on German-owned businesses in Dublin, paranoia
regarding German spies, and anxiety over a possible German invasion
of Ireland (42–3). Fischer surveys two products of this anxiety, *The
Germans in Cork: Being the Letters of His Excellency the Baron Von Kartoffel
(Military Governor of Cork in the Year 1918) and Others* and *The Germans at
Bessbrook: A Dream*, both published anonymously within the space of a
few months in 1917; Lady Mary Carbery admitted in 1937 to being the
author of *The Germans in Cork*, while *The Germans at Bessbrook* has been
determined to be the work of James Nicholson Richardson (Fischer 2007,
346–7). These texts were not just anti-German, but were also intended
to undermine the growing support for Sinn Féin in the aftermath of
the 1916 Rising. In both texts, naïve Sinn Féiners help the Germans
to take over the country, expecting power to be handed over once the
conquest is complete; of course, the Germans have other plans (349). In
the end, the dreaded and hoped-for large-scale German military support
for Irish independence never materialised. There were, however, a large
number of nationalists that saw the Great War of Civilisation as the
perfect opportunity to strike.

For Irish people raised in the nationalist tradition, it is difficult to
speak of the 1916 Rising in terms that frame it as anything other than
a utopian moment. Of this seven-day rebellion, Declan Kiberd writes:

> *Imagine* is the operative word for the liberationist who, far more
> than the nationalist, needs the sanction of previous authority if
> history is to be blown open. That sanction comes from history
> not as chronological narrative but as symbolic pattern, in which
> certain utopian moments are extracted from its flow. The 1916
> Rising announced itself in this way, not only as the outcome of
> the previous thirty years, but also as a moment charged with the
> utopian energies of 1803, 1848 and 1867. (Kiberd 1996, 293)

However, the Rising did not "announce" itself as a utopian moment
at all – at least, not in the sense that is implied in Kiberd's reading of
the episode. The 1916 rebels were ridiculed and spat upon by the people
of Dublin following their arrest; it was only after the rebel leaders were
executed that public opinion began to turn in favour of physical-force
nationalism. Three years later came the start of the conflict known as
either the Anglo-Irish War or the War of Independence, a conflict infamous

for the involvement of British militias such as the Black-and-Tans and the Auxiliaries.[11] The war came to an end in 1921 with a treaty negotiated according to British PM Lloyd George's "Gairloch Formula," an agreement to word the discussions so ambiguously that neither side appeared to yield any ground (Neeson 55). On 6 December, Irish delegates led by Michael Collins signed the Anglo-Irish Treaty, which brought into being a "Free State" rather than a "Republic" (the country did not officially become a Republic until 1949), partitioned the island of Ireland and divided its citizens politically and emotionally, and led to a civil war whose consequences are still felt in Irish politics today.[12] When that civil war ended, and the twenty-six county Free State was finally able to get on with the business of building the society it wanted, economic and political power was transferred to a conservative Catholic nationalist bourgeoisie. To gloss over the unpleasant realities of the Civil War and partition, the emphasis of subsequent commemorations was on a celebration of martyrdom – the implication was that these brave men had not just died for Ireland, but died for *the Ireland we have now*.[13] As Nicholas Allen observes: "The birth of the state compelled a revised chronology by which to understand history, the failed rebellions of the past now re-ordered as successful steps in the evolution towards independence" (35).

This "revised chronology" was not only necessary for the final vindication of "failed" uprisings of the past. "Realism/tradition" nationalism, the nationalism of *Eoghan Paor* and the socially conservative Catholic bourgeoisie, had triumphed over other nationalist political programmes that were hostile to it and still had armed supporters. Thus, the re-ordering of previous rebellions into an "evolution towards independence" also fulfilled a legitimising function, not against the accusations of unionists, but against the competing claims of other nationalisms. Ireland retained the existing British models of politics, civil service and public administration, and very few tangible changes were made to existing institutions until Ireland joined the EEC in 1973 (Kirby and Murphy 47).

The Free State

The primary difficulties facing the Irish Free State were economic in nature:

> The economy that the Free State inherited [...] had several major inherent defects. It was stable to the point of stagnation: a developed infrastructure of railways and canals was not matched

by an equivalent industrialization; the economy supported too many unproductive people – the old and young and a considerable professional class; there were few native industries of any size and such as there were (brewing, bacon-curing, creameries, biscuit-making and woollens and worsteds) were productive of primary commodities and unable to provide a base for an industrial revolution. (Brown 15)

Independence had thrust Ireland into a global economic matrix for which it was ill-prepared, largely because the "Tradition/Realism" framework of interwoven rural, urban and ecclesiastical business interests depended upon cultural stasis. Despite the professed nationalism of those concerned, these interests were best served by retaining the status quo. An egalitarian republic would not come unless, like Hy Brasil, it could be bought.

In the face of criticism to this effect, "It became all the more necessary to call the native parliament the *Dáil*, in order to conceal its depressing similarity to the hated Westminster model" (Kiberd 1996, 484). The revival of the Irish language, being "a cause of unexceptionable nationalist authenticity" (Brown 47), was an ideal tool for deflecting the accusation that the Free State had changed nothing for the better, and so Irish was privileged in the primary school curriculum at the expense of art, elementary science, nature studies and "hygiene" (51). This project was fraught with difficulty. In the late nineteenth and early twentieth centuries, the vast majority of the native Irish speakers left in the country came from impoverished rural areas, and were unable to read or write the language. An additional complication came in the form of the official choice of alphabet, with most revivalists in favour of using an "authentic" uncial script that could only be printed in a handful of places. To counteract this linguistic confusion, a standardised national dialect was proposed, which had the unintended effect of creating further confusion, as individual translators reacted against it by making surreptitious adjustments in favour of their own dialects (Ó Huallacháin 111–2). This would have an impact on Gaelic popular literature, SF included.

This renewed commitment to language revival aside, in the absence of any real social change, authors learned to make do with what they had, and hope for a more satisfactory future. In 1926, Pádraig Ó Conaire's short story "Páipéar a Fristhadh i mBosca" ["A Paper Found in a Box"] was published in the *Connacht Tribune* newspaper. It depicts a scene from the year 1966, in which the "Warden of Galway" addresses a mob of people who are demanding radical social change. In order to calm the crowd down, he reads them excerpts from a forty-year-old copy of a newspaper, which he has found in a box in his father's house. The old newspaper details the awful conditions in which the people of Galway lived in those far-off times, crowded into tumbledown slums in appalling sanitary conditions. The recitation has the desired effect, and the mob calms down, having seen how far their city has progressed in forty years. The paper quoted in this story is the 22 May 1926 edition of the *Connacht Tribune*, published exactly seven days before this story of Ó Conaire's appeared in the same paper – the Ireland of the day was the atrocious past of the Warden's future Galway (Ó Conaire). The story is a transparent criticism of the new Irish government, but it also articulates nationalist optimism by suggesting that things can only get better. This was the national mood predating the publication the following year of an SF text of the modernist, "realist" nationalist trend. Like Ó Conaire's text, it tries to console the citizens of the Free State with visions of a more prosperous future, but it communicates much of the frustration and anger of those who had egalitarian hopes for independence, as well as focusing on the plight of the poor and the control of material resources.

Barra Ó Caochlaigh's (i.e., Art Ó Riain's) novella *An Tost* [Silence] is divided into five sections, the story charting the fortunes of the Ó Suíbhne family from 1914 to 1975. Parts four and five are of more interest to researchers of SF than the first three, since both are set in the future. In part four, Fionnbarra Ó Suíbhne is a medical student and a member of his university's opera society, famed for his wonderful tenor voice. When a visiting director of an international music society offers him the chance to make a living from music, Fionnbarra is tempted to take it. In order to do so, he is advised to refrain from his work with the poor in Dublin's slums, since the disease endemic there could damage his voice. Fionnbarra refuses to compromise, and pays the price for his charity when he contracts diphtheria, ruining his throat to the extent that he will never sing again (Ó Caochlaigh 22–30).

Part five, set in 1975, tells of a world war erupting between the Americas and a British–Japanese alliance. Ireland announces it will remain neutral, and receives an ultimatum from the British to allow flyovers and refuelling stops. Also of concern is Ireland's stockpile of oil and valuable minerals, which is hidden in a secret location somewhere in the countryside. By this time, Fionnbarra has become the Minister for Air-Travel, and the Taoiseach entrusts him with a map of the stockpile's location, hidden inside a secret booby-trapped compartment in the bookcase of Fionnbarra's new office. Within hours of turning down the ultimatum, Ireland is invaded and the government's buildings seized, and Fionnbarra is interrogated by the British. After having his right hand burned off with a laser, Fionnbarra says he will hand over the map, revealing its hiding place in the bookcase, neglecting to tell his captors of the booby trap or how to disarm it. When they open up the secret compartment without pressing the all-important disarming button, they flood the office with poisonous gas. Everyone in the room, including Fionnbarra, is killed – just as the American air force arrives to drive off the invaders (31–45).

The immediate object of scorn in this text is the condition of the slums and the despicable treatment of the poor by the upper and middle classes. To a professor who alludes to the filth of the poor, and suggests that they ended up in that condition by not planning ahead, Fionnbarra retorts:

> "I thought, once upon a time, that I was a Christian; but when I started to get to know the poor, I found out for the first time what Christianity should be [...] If you were earning two pounds a week, and you had a wife and eight children to support on that amount, you wouldn't be doing much planning ahead! Filth, you say? You keep eight children, whether they're rich or poor, in one room, and see then how clean it'll be!" (24–5)[14]

In the year 1975 as described in the fifth section, Ireland has stockpiled enough mineral wealth to make it an object of envy to nations such as Britain and Japan; even though the vision is a dystopian one for planet Earth in general, it is thus implied that at least Ireland's fortunes have improved, and one can only hope that some of this prosperity has managed to trickle down to the poor. The story is also of interest for its extrapolated implications of Irish neutrality during a global conflict, a situation which will be examined in the next chapter.

4. States of Emergency:
Irish SF during World War II

Ireland developed a fear of infiltration and re-colonisation during the 1920s and 1930s, whether by the forces of modernity or by antagonistic foreign powers. The prospect of a superhuman race appearing in Europe was one more aspect of a wider world that seemed indifferent at best and hostile at worst. Faced with such threats, the only sane response seemed to be to retreat from the world, even as the nation builders of the Free State tried to ingratiate themselves with foreign capitalists and power brokers.

Because of this, very little of the SF published in Ireland at the time reflects the predominant themes and concerns of the American tradition. From the early 1920s to the post-war years, SF in America underwent a major evolutionary leap, thanks to the influence of magazine editors such as Hugo Gernsback and John W. Campbell, acquiring the label "science fiction," and developing a distinct literary identity. Following this evolutionary leap came a wave of paranoid thrillers appropriate to the geopolitical mood engendered by the Cold War, including *The Thing* and *Invasion of the Body Snatchers*.

In Ireland, however, these phases were reversed: while space opera was emerging in America, Ireland was producing paranoid invasion fantasies; by the time the latter became the norm in America, Irish authors had started writing the former.

Monsters under the Bed

The *Saorstát Éireann: Official Handbook* (1932) presents itself as a complete record of every aspect of the Free State. It contains chapters on almost every conceivable topic, including the native flora and fauna, the constitution, infrastructure, education, cultural agencies, history, religion and architecture, each one discussed with great attention to detail – chapters on the country and its citizens are outlined with census data (Hobson 23), and references to the mineral wealth of the country are supported with quotes from geological surveys (32). Bulmer Hobson states in his introduction that "Its aim is to give an account of the Irish Free State as it is to-day, and to give also the necessary historical background without which an understanding of modern Ireland would not be possible" (15).

While Hobson continues to frame the handbook in historical terms, portraying it as a stock-taking exercise finally made possible by the establishment of an Irish Republic (though, officially, it was still a "Free State" in 1932), the re-establishment of law and order and the triumph of peace and democracy over anarchy (15–16), the fact remains that the committee for the handbook's compilation was appointed by the Minister for Industry and Commerce. It can be inferred, therefore, that the production of an official handbook for the Free State was motivated by economic concerns, rather than historical or cultural ones – the wealth of data on trade, commerce, mineral wealth and communications was more than likely intended to either inspire domestic entrepreneurs or entice foreign investors. Nevertheless, Hobson's view of the handbook as a sort of *Encyclopaedia Hibernia* does hold some water. Alongside the reams of scientific, sociological and geographical data, there are lengthy chapters on Irish pre-history, ecclesiastical history, art, folk music and literature. The combined effect is one of calm self-congratulation, as if to itemise the fruits of the Free State victory in the Civil War. If, like Langer, we regard decolonisation and postcolonialism as "processes rather than states [...] defined as the ways in which a society forms itself in the wake, however long ago, of colonization" (Langer 6–7), the early 1930s represent the moment at which the decolonisation process was accelerated.

It seems as if the glimmer of hope for a more prosperous future seen in Ó Conaire and Ó Caochlaigh had strengthened, and now the Irish were rolling up their sleeves for the task of nation-building. This task would not be easy – there were barbarians at the gates of the fledgling state, peddling foreign imports such as swing and jazz music. Clair Wills argues that the main problem with jazz in 1930s Ireland was not simply that it was a raunchy musical genre, but also that it was not Irish:

> Priests, bishops, and district justices up and down the country railed against the cosmopolitan modern imports of jazz and swing. There was too much jazz on Irish radio (the people should be satisfied with traditional music) and too little respect for native culture. During the later 1930s the Irish Folklore Commission sent its representatives out into village and countryside to try to preserve the music and oral tradition associated with the Gaelic way of life – a sure recognition that the culture was in decline. (Wills 30)

On the one hand, the Free State had autonomy over a sizeable amount of material resources; on the other, the cocoon of the British Empire was gone, and the Free State now had to take care of its own defences. Independence had brought with it a more acute awareness of the vastness of the world beyond Irish shores, and to a newly independent people, it seemed as though that world was full of strange and threatening things, not least of which was the new kind of physics pioneered by scientists such as Planck, Einstein, Heisenberg and Schrödinger. For an indication of some of the effects that quantum theory had on Western popular culture in general, we can look at Everett F. Bleiler's extensive research into "pulp" SF from 1926 to 1936: in narratives featuring time travel into the past, the protagonists almost invariably encounter a long-lost civilisation which is possessed of scientific knowledge light years ahead of our own (Bleiler, 10–11, 62, 82–3, 177, 275, 318, 502–3). Conversely, in tales depicting a journey into the future, the outcome is more often than not decidedly grim, with planet Earth either dead or dying (31–2, 36–7, 233, 520).

It is difficult to overestimate the magnitude of the philosophical crisis triggered by quantum mechanics, which cast doubt on the self-evident truth of Newtonian time, and seemed to even throw it into reverse. Unlike the American pulp authors, however, Irish authors seemed to ignore the field or dismiss it as ridiculous, and when Irish-language essayists tackled Ireland's scientific history, they usually produced biographies of famous scientists in "safe" fields such as chemistry and engineering, sometimes with a moralising Catholic overtone (O'Leary 2010, 312, 332).

Likewise, the futurist movement did not achieve widespread popularity on the island of Ireland. Joe Cleary attributes this to the waves of Catholic emigration in the years following the Famine: this de-population meant that the industrial working class was almost monocultural, consisting of extremely conservative Protestant unionists who regarded the second Industrial Revolution as a threat to the British Empire and thus were hostile to cultural movements that advocated change (Cleary 87). On the other hand, the Famine had done enormous damage to the Gaelic way of life, meaning that cultural nationalists came to be preoccupied with "the need to salvage something from the wholesale shattering of tradition," rather than with technological innovation or the future (88–9).

The extent of Ireland's ambivalence to Western popular culture is apparent in the short story "Cuairt ar an nGealaigh" ["A Visit to the Moon"] by Micheál Mac Craith, in which Irish mariners are transported into the sky on board their boat by a powerful storm, and, after being thrown around for seven days and nights, deposited on the Moon.

Thereafter, the narrative focuses on the peculiar habits of the Moon people, who eat smoke, drink nothing but water (as lunar vines produce clusters of hailstones instead of grapes) and consider baldness to be the paragon of beauty. Their eyes are movable (to the extent that a Moon person can detach its eyes from its head), they have a single toe on each foot, five limbs, kangaroo-like pouches and sycamore leaves for ears, and they lactate instead of perspiring. Most individuals wear soft glass (though the destitute often wear suits of pliable bronze), and for this reason, throwing stones on the Moon can kill a person. The narrator says he does not mind whether the reader believes all that he has said, because sooner or later the reader will visit the Moon (either in death or in life), and will witness these things personally (Mac Craith 1923).

This is perhaps the most astonishing example of anachronism in any of the texts surveyed for this project. One could argue that the story is whimsical in tone, and point out that, as a middle-aged priest, the author was not likely to have been conversant with popular fiction.[1] However, he was born in Derry, a major urban centre of industrialised Ulster, and he studied in Dublin and France (Ó Droighneáin 192), so it is not unreasonable to assume that he was at least *aware* of the works of Jules Verne, or, failing that, that he was aware of the technological tenor of the times he lived in. Then there are the too-illogical descriptions of the Moon people, their habits and their environment, less reminiscent of a twentieth-century text than of the second-century satirist Lucian's *True History* (though carefully omitting the latter's descriptions of war and homosexuality). Even if this work is intended to be nothing more than an *homage*, the narrative is still outdated: Mac Craith was writing at a time when it was commonly known that no wind, regardless of its strength, could sweep a yacht across space to the Moon. It is in fact not really SF or comedy at all, but a conscious attempt at adapting an ancient work to an Irish Catholic context.

Taken alongside the perceived unholy influence of German materialist philosophy mentioned in the last chapter, the disturbing implications of quantum mechanics and the carnality of music forms such as jazz, the anachronism of Mac Craith's work is hardly surprising. In the first half of the twentieth century, Ireland was experiencing a historical moment much like that inhabited by Jonathan Swift, as discussed in the introduction: it was, at this time, still possible for a "serious mind" to *not take modernity seriously*, and this disregard often translated into open hostility. In the 1930s, Ireland became paranoid, and this paranoia is reflected in the Irish-produced SF of the time.

Published in 1933, "Marbhán" is a two-part detective story set in the year 2000. The disestablishment of the British monarchy has given rise to a British Republic and a United Ireland. There is, however, an underground society dedicated to the reinstitution of the monarchy, known as the "Scréacháin Roilige" ["The Owls"], and it transpires that they are also active in Galway. After the Irish President's secretary is robbed of £20,000 and a stack of sensitive documents, the government and the Gardaí determine that the Owls are responsible. A secret agent known only as "Marbhán" ["corpse"] is assigned to liaise with the Gardaí in Galway. After infiltrating the Owl cell, Marbhán leads the authorities to arrest the subversive group's ultimate leadership, who are masquerading as husband and wife in a house in the countryside ("Conán" 3, 3). While this text works better as a detective/spy story than as SF, it proves useful as a thematic bridge between earlier futuristic texts and those that would come later. *An Tost* predicted a future where Ireland's material wealth and geographic location made it a target of other nations; "Marbhán" changed the means by which that attack would occur, and in so doing anticipated the first genuine "infiltration story" of Irish SF.

Vint and Bould note that in American SF of the 1950s paranoia about difference was linked to anxieties of social control (Bould and Vint 97). The threat of modernity engendered the same anxieties in 1930s/1940s Ireland, and these anxieties were heightened by the notion of conspiracy and a clandestine invasion. These anxieties were expressed in Seosamh Ó Torna's "Duinneall" (1938). A Duinneall (*Duine*, "person" + *Inneall*, "engine") is to all intents and purposes a human being, but modern means of production have transformed it into a machinelike thing, which does not understand truth, beauty, humour or compassion. The narrator warns that thousands of these things exist around the world, insinuating themselves into political and civic life, and that only the "truth" is capable of defeating them. The tone of the story is ambiguous – the narrator could be a paranoid fantasist, but there is also the implication that he is attempting to warn the reader of a genuine danger. The text unconsciously appropriates Marxist teaching in defence of the "Gaelic" way of life – the Duinnealls are workers that have been alienated from their humanity by the labour conditions of modern industry, "as well as if they had been cars manufactured by Ford" (Ó Torna 72).

> It is time for me, dear reader, to tell you what frightens me about the hordes of Duinnealls. Understand, all of you, that the Duinneall is not satisfied without imposing restrictions on me. The mentality behind the Vicious Circle is being implemented. They are trying to bring about Maximum Efficiency. To that end, it is necessary to increase the Big and exterminate the Small. To destroy the

small merchant and the individual craftsman, and to establish monopolies and mass-production in their place. To devastate the small towns and to widen the great city. To cover over the River Liffey to accommodate thousands on every patch of ground, and to construct buildings that will eclipse the sun. To force a mechanical arrangement on people that will make every mother's son of them into a cog in a massive engine. (74)[2]

Their aims are the eradication of traditional life, and complete control over literature, music and even the human soul; the tell-tale signs of their activities are an increase in aeroplanes and the proliferation of jazz, and we are told that the Duinneall is "a dictator that surpasses Hitler and Stalin" (74–5). The figure of the Duinneall cannot be mapped onto any singular real-world group or ideology – rather, it stands for the modern world in general, a huge and unforgiving global matrix from which there could be no escape.

The terror of "Maximum Efficiency" was not an innovation of Ó Torna's. The Technocracy movement in America enjoyed a brief period of popularity during the 1930s, with its somewhat ominous promise of a scientific rationale for all decision-making (Bould and Vint 62–3), and the idea of Ireland being invaded and subjected to a "mechanical arrangement" of its social life had been explored by Mary Carbery in her 1917 text *The Germans in Cork*. As soon as the Germans arrive in Cork, they set about modernising its food production, housing, education and cultural activities, while at the same time dismantling the local democratic infrastructure. The Irish language is outlawed, the insane are gassed to death and the poor are placed in the now-empty asylums, all kinds of crime are punishable with the gas chamber, funerals are replaced with cremations in the name of "efficiency," and attempts are begun to create a new race through eugenics, by cross-breeding the Germans and the Irish (Fischer 2007, 351–2). All of these things were stock-in-trade for anti-German propaganda of the time, but some aspects would later prove to be horrifyingly prescient.

The Superman

William M. Salter, writing in 1915, analyses Nietzsche's conception of the Superman with regard to what he appears to perceive as the popular misconceptions surrounding it: namely, that Nietzsche's theories are a logical extension of Darwinism. He accurately argues that Nietzsche's Superman does not figure a new evolutionary step in the *biological* sense;

in cultural and intellectual terms, however, the Superman could very well be considered a new, separate species (423–4). This interpretation of Nietzsche's relation to evolutionary science brings Salter to a dubious conclusion, and leads him to make a very dangerous proposal:

> Let an organized mankind test Darwin's assertions by experiment – even if the experimentation covers centuries and millenniums and we have to turn the whole earth into experiment stations. Let it be proved whether apes can be developed into men, and lower races into higher races, and whether from the best mankind has at present to show, something still higher can be reared. The Chinese have made trees that bear roses on one side and pears on the other – and where are the limits to be set to the possibilities of selective human breeding? (426–7)

With the benefit of hindsight, it is easy to read the above passage as not just dangerous, but prophetic, though the notion that the human race could be improved through selective breeding was not a new one. As Gregory Claeys says, the term "eugenics" was coined by Francis Galton, a nineteenth-century Social Darwinist, and this philosophy was initially focused on the domestic sphere: "positive" eugenics would encourage desirable traits (as opposed to "negative" eugenics, focused on breeding out unwanted ones) through the regulation of marriage, and the poor would be required to prove that they had the means to raise a family before being allowed to wed. Claeys notes that during this initial exploration of Social Darwinism, Galton's ideas did have some positive outcomes, in that they prompted government involvement in public health and encouraged others to re-think old religious and sexual taboos (Claeys 188–9). By the early twentieth century, however, these ideas were being applied to racial politics, and in a sense, the entire planet was about to be turned into a laboratory, as Salter suggested. In that worldwide laboratory, the idea of the Superman was tested to breaking point.

The year of the first major Nazi mass meeting in Munich, 1921, also saw the publication of George Bernard Shaw's *Back to Methuselah*. In a lengthy preface to the drama, Shaw argues that truly original art can only appear in the context of a profound religious movement similar to the Reformation (Shaw 1921, xc–xcii). In so doing, he attributes all the evils of the world (including World War I) to Darwinism (x, xi, xxxv, lii, lix), and presents the drama as his attempt to create a sort of "Bible" for a new world religion based on the philosophies of Lamarck and Nietzsche (c–ci). His belief in "Creative Evolution" led him to reject both liberal and "vanguardist" democracy (Barnes 161) and convinced him that biological attributes, such as longevity, were "a matter of will" (Indick 23). Shaw had a somewhat generous view of his own understanding of science,[3] and he acknowledged the necessity for experimentation for almost every scientific theory except the one in which he was most invested emotionally. He defended Creative Evolution by stating that it could not be disproved (as Tom Shippey notes, hypotheses that cannot be empirically tested and possibly disproved have no scientific value), by repeating aphorisms about acquired traits *"ad nauseam"* without explaining what he meant by them, and by asserting that "all sensible people agree with him" (Shippey 201–2); in defending it, he was "always wrong, always shallow, and often rather cheap" (202). Shaw's need to believe in this evolutionary model was certainly influenced by the horrors of the Great War and the rise of dictatorships across Europe, but as I will argue below, this need predated these hostilities and may have a wider cultural explanation.

Shaw's new Bible takes longevity and immortality as its principal theme, beginning in the Garden of Eden, where Adam vows to live for a thousand years, and Eve learns the secret of procreation (Shaw 1921, 1–20). Part II, set a few years after World War I, concerns the Barnabas brothers, a biology professor and a former clergyman, who determine that the human lifespan must be extended to three hundred years, so that humankind can develop a conscience capable of solving the world's problems without resorting to war. Their discovery is taken up by Mr. Burge of the Liberal Party, who launches a campaign with the slogan, "Back to Methuselah!" (41–100). Part III (103–54) is set in the year 2170, by which time Britain has become a republic, administered by Chinese and African consultants. The President is distracted from "marine golf" and a long-distance affair with the Minister for Health (a beautiful African woman) by the political fallout caused by an American who has invented a way to breathe underwater, and thus revealed that two archbishops, a former president and a general, all of whom supposedly died from drowning, were in fact the same person – the current Archbishop of York, who is using his immortality to cheat the social welfare system (114–18). Part IV, Act I (157–97) takes place in Galway in the year 3000. Long-lived people are more commonplace, the capital of the British Commonwealth is Baghdad (158), and the Irish and the Jews are extinct (176). Ireland is a colony of the long-lived, and short-lived people are only allowed to visit under strict supervision. The first act centres on an elderly man who has returned to Western Europe on a pilgrimage, and his conversations with the long-lived highlight the cultural changes that have been wrought by longevity. In Acts II and

III, Emperor Cain Adamson of Turania approaches a long-lived oracle for advice on how to achieve greatness, and a group of envoys learn that some of the long-lived are planning the genocide of the short-lived (199–231). Part V is set in the year 31,920, when short-lived humans are extinct. People in this time hatch fully grown from eggs and do not have digestive systems or genitals; a series of short vignettes illustrate how these post-humans age and mature (235–300).

Margery Mary Morgan goes to great lengths to distance Shaw from the unsavoury implications of his eulogising of the Superman and the Will. In the case of *Back to Methuselah*, she dismisses as naïve the question "of whether or not Shaw means what he says," and considers it evident that he is "talking nonsense" (Morgan 221); she attributes the play's references to eugenics to the influence of Plato's *Republic* (236), ignoring Shaw's genuine belief in the merit of such practices, expressed in *Man and Superman*: "The only fundamental and possible Socialism is the socialization of the selective breeding of Man: in other terms, of human evolution. We must eliminate the Yahoo, or his vote will wreck the commonwealth" (Shaw 1903, 219).

Morgan's analysis does, however, present some salient points, first of all, regarding the governing emotions of "Puritanical repugnance for physical life and shrinking from emotional intimacy":

> Their force is admitted in one thread running predominantly through the play: it appears in Part I, in Eve's overwhelming shame (the emotion of the Fall) [...] in Part II, in the severity of the scientific rationalism of the Brothers Barnabas [...] in Part III, in the objectivity of the Longlivers who have outgrown human affection; in Part IV it takes alternative forms [...] in Part V it is reflected in the adolescents' shrinking from touch and the Ancients' contempt for the body, and it is satirically embodied in Pygmalion, who brings to being a blueprint of humanity that turns and destroys him. (Morgan 227)

While Morgan regards this thread of disgust towards the body as a reflection of the play's principal theme, that is, the evolution of man towards transcendence of all limitations, it is hard not to divorce this from the bemused and scornful authorial presence in Shaw's 1913 anti-suffragette play *Press Cuttings*, which depends upon a sense of bewilderment with the emerging new century for its satirical effect. This observation is reinforced by Morgan when she identifies the nineteenth-century European clash between tradition and science as a recurring theme within Shavian drama (333).

Jeffrey M. Wallmann's assertion that Shaw "oppose[d] Victorian codes of conduct and duty" (Wallmann 82) does not ring entirely true. Despite their godlike power and their transcendence of bourgeois notions of good and evil, Shaw's post-humans conform in their behaviour to stereotypes of Victorian propriety and sexual repression; repeatedly describing their presentation as "satirical" (as Morgan does) does nothing to dismiss the notion that the new conscience advocated by Shaw is nothing more than a return to the old moral certainties of the nineteenth century, and to a safely teleological view of nature in which evolution is an upward struggle resulting in a final manifestation of the divine – as symbolised by the apparitions of Adam, Eve, Cain, Lilith and the Serpent appearing after the post-humans have left the stage (Shaw 1921, 297–300). This longing for a bygone code of morals is also apparent in *The Simpleton of the Unexpected Isles* (1934), in which the superhuman inhabitants of the eponymous utopian islands exist within a "superfamily," as though the family unit were the natural basis of even post-human society, and in *Geneva* (1938), where a lower-middle-class "little Englander" almost triggers another world war through her ignorance, and international cooperation is mocked as an ineffectual pipe dream. This reactionary attitude to changing standards of propriety seems quite at odds with Shaw's socialism, which was by no means insincere – as J.L. Wisenthal points out, "accounts of Shaw's 1931 visit to the USSR read like works of utopian fiction," with Shaw as the overawed outsider from an inferior nation (Wisenthal 60).

The apparent contradiction is jarring until one remembers that in the nineteenth and early twentieth centuries, the Fabian Society (of which Shaw was a member, along with his rhetorical sparring-partner H.G. Wells) regarded the British Empire as the most effective vehicle through which worldwide socialism could be brought about. Indeed, following a series of polls, the Fabians sided with the Empire during the Boer War, and it was Shaw himself who led the pro-war campaign, taking "obvious pleasure" in the disappointment of the more pacifist Fabians when the vote turned in favour of officially supporting the conflict; the way Shaw and his hawkish colleagues saw it, nationalism was a greater evil than imperialism, and war offered its own opportunities for socialist regime change, such as the nationalisation of the defeated party's material resources (Semmel 57–62).

Rather than the societal change advocated by most schools of socialist thought, Shaw sought biological or psychological change. As John Barnes puts it, Shaw believed that rather than waiting for the world to improve, "the people who can make it better will come to be born and will eventually save the day" (Barnes 161). This certainly placed him at a remove from mainstream socialist thought, as "A world in which supermen come into being and bring about revolutions is exactly opposite a world in which revolution allows the next generation to grow up as supermen" (156).

Shaw's preoccupation with the theme of the Superman can perhaps be explained by the fact that he lived in a world populated by "Yahoos" whose vote would "wreck the commonwealth." The Shavian Yahoo (an unimaginative, selfish, closed-minded non-entity) was possessed of an obscene power conferred by his or her very mediocrity, as well as a distressing ability to show up at the exact place and time where he or she could cause the most havoc. The Shavian conceptions of Superman and Yahoo are mirror images of each other. The Yahoo has a distinct advantage in that no special effort is required to create one – mediocrity is the norm, while transcendence must be strived for. This dichotomy, combined with the recurring theme of a disintegrating Empire, creates a sense of urgency that permeates Shaw's work. The project of harnessing human evolution is a race against time – the Superman must be created before the Yahoo brings about apocalypse.

If Shaw was enthusiastic about the utopian logic of eugenics, however, there were many others who were not, among them the Northern Irish author C.S. Lewis. In the first volume of his "Space Trilogy," *Out of the Silent Planet* (1938), Professor Ransom, a university lecturer in literature and philology, is inducted into a nightmarish scenario when he encounters a distressed woman at random while walking in the countryside. She tells him that she fears for the safety of her son, Harry, who works at the home of a physicist named Weston. Ransom agrees to visit Weston's house and escort the boy home, and after breaking into Weston's property, he discovers that the physicist is using the unwilling Harry in a scientific experiment.

It transpires that Weston and his partner in crime, an aspiring politician named Devine, have travelled to Mars and made contact with the indigenous sapient creatures. Having assumed that the Martians are savages and cannibals with a Stone Age level of technological and cultural development (135), their intent was to offer Harry as a human sacrifice (34–5) in order to further their respective goals – Weston wants humanity to conquer "infinity, and therefore perhaps eternity" (27), while Devine simply wants to collect gold, which is abundant on Mars and considered valueless by the Martians.

Ransom ends up taking the boy's place once Devine points out that the lecturer's absence would be less likely to draw the attention of the police. Though the text repeatedly describes Harry as simply being of low intelligence, the implication is that he has an intellectual disability of some kind, and thus is dependent on his mother and other carers who would raise an alarm if he went missing. Weston is initially reluctant to change test subjects, still feeling that Harry is a more appropriate choice because he is "Incapable of serving humanity and only too likely to propagate idiocy. He was the sort of boy who in a civilised community would be automatically handed over to a state laboratory for experimental purposes." Taking the unpleasantness further, Weston explains his reluctance by arguing that "[Ransom] is, after all, human," whereas Harry "was really almost a – a preparation" (19).

Weston, according to Devine, "has Einstein on toast and drinks a pint of Schrödinger's blood for breakfast," and he regards Ransom's humanities-based research as "unscientific tomfoolery" (13). Lewis avoids the problem of explaining how the spaceship works by having Weston exclaim, in true mad scientist fashion, "Unless you were one of the four or five real physicists now living you couldn't understand" (25).

Fortunately for Ransom, it transpires that the Martians are not at all as dangerous as Weston and Devine believe them to be. The three sapient species live in a kind of cultural symbiosis – the hairy *hrossa* are poets and farmers, the tapir-like *pfifltriggi* are artisans, and the feathered *sorns* are philosophers and theologians. After meeting a friendly *hross* and using his philological knowledge to learn the Martian language, Ransom learns that Malacandra (the native name for Mars) is furthermore governed by angel-like creatures called *eldila*, who are invisible to the human eye because the matter of their bodies vibrates at the speed of light (93–5). Eldila perceive the realm of our vision as a human perceives light and motion underwater (95). The senior eldil, effectively the ruler of Malacandra, is called the Oyarsa, and Ransom eventually makes contact with this creature.

The Oyarsa explains that the eldila naturally communicate with their fellows on the other planets of the solar system. Earth, or "Thulcundra" as it is known to the eldila, is the exception – it is literally a "silent planet," because the eldila cannot communicate with it (120). Earth's Oyarsa, "the Bent One," is a fallen eldil (120–1), and its influence has given rise to human violence, greed and misery (140), causing the other eldila to place the planet under quarantine. Weston and Devine are puppets of the Bent One, who is trying to break out and contaminate the rest of the cosmos (139–40). It transpires that the Martian Oyarsa exerted its influence to bring Ransom to Malacandra to stop them, because the eldila of one world are not allowed to exceed their authority by killing or punishing the creatures of another (123): hence, a righteous Thulcundran is required to oppose the evil Thulcundrans, preventing the possibility of a Martian invasion.

However, other Martians from the time held different opinions on Social Darwinism, eugenics, the Superman and the relationship between Earth's morality and its science, and they were not nearly as personable or non-interventionist as Lewis's Malacandrans.

Prelude to War

Following the outbreak of the Spanish Civil War, Taoiseach Éamon de Valera offered his services as a mediator in the conflict, arguing that his Spanish ancestry and Irish nationality qualified him as a concerned yet impartial observer; his offer was turned down (Stradling 9). Thereafter, though the official standpoint of the Irish government was one of non-involvement, civilian volunteers regarded the Spanish Civil War as a foreign arena in which domestic ideological disputes could be settled by proxy.

To many, stories of dangerous foreign infiltrators were not crackpot conspiracy theories. The most famous true-believer, former Garda Commissioner General Eoin O'Duffy, became leader of the Army Comrades Association in 1933 and instituted a number of changes to the organisation: the name was changed to the National Guard, and membership was restricted to Christians of Irish birth or heritage. The organisation's aims were also redefined: whereas the ACA had been founded to uphold the state and defend the interests of ex-servicemen (Manning 21), the National Guard, colloquially known as the "Blueshirts," concerned themselves with the re-unification of Ireland, opposition to communism and "alien control and influence," and the maintenance of social order (70–2). According to the historian Robert Stradling, O'Duffy's paranoia about communist infiltration amounted almost to a "personality disorder," and as Commissioner of the Garda Síochána, he had pursued a policy of persecuting both real and suspected communists; dismissed from this position, he used his leadership of the National Guard to continue this crusade. Stradling argues that this ironically led to the formation of a renewed Irish Communist Party and the Republican Congress – two leftist groups that had little in common except a mutual loathing of O'Duffy (Stradling 128–31).

O'Duffy's millenarian vision of an epic final conflict between Catholicism and communism – expressed via repeated invocations of the figure of the Murdered Nun (6) – succeeded in drawing volunteers for "the Last Crusade" from predominantly rural backgrounds (26), and parallels with the mediaeval Crusades were further underlined by parish priests who recommended participation in the Spanish Civil War as a penance for the forgiveness of one's sins (10). Stradling notes that the international volunteers who signed up to combat Franco's nationalists were essentially motivated by altruism (145); other Irishmen signed up because they perceived an opportunity to re-fight Ireland's own civil war (209).[4] Neither side, whether O'Duffy's Irish Brigade or the so-called "Connolly Column," can be said to have accomplished anything by their involvement in the Spanish conflict, and their experiences seemed to prove that Ireland was ill-prepared for involvement in an international war. Thus, the knowledge that such a war was approaching was just cause for national anxiety.

The Rainbow in the Valley by James Creed Meredith was published in 1939 and articulates not just the immediate Irish anxieties regarding the impending war, but the nation's philosophical anxieties surrounding modernity as well. Following a near nervous breakdown, an Irish solicitor named Bartholomew Hobson takes some time to himself to travel the world. He finds himself in China, in a place called "The Valley of the Shadows," home to a research station staffed by a crew of European and American scientists. The Westerners have managed to establish radio contact with Mars, and they have been exchanging ideas and philosophies with the Martians. Martian society as described in this text has existed peacefully for ten thousand years, thanks to a dictator who assumed control of the planet following its third global war, and dismissed the ineffectual and legalistic leagues that had tried to keep the peace through diplomacy (Meredith 125–36). Alexedon's New Order stabilised Mars, and eventually the dictator handed over the reins of power to a forty-member Council of Wise Men (226–7). Thanks to advanced scientific knowledge, the Martians have more leisure time than we do (223), and due to both Mars' low population and a "top-down" economic structure, they live in a post-scarcity society (224).

Jauffret, a French Egyptologist, takes on the task of translating the Martian radio signals, and eventually the Martian language, beginning by deciphering the signals for "and" and "equal to" (31). This accomplishment allows him to learn Martian negatives and adjectives, as well as the future tense and conjugation of Martian verbs, the Martian words for directions and the names of planets, latitude and longitude, and abstract names (33–8). Green, an English engineer and "jack of all trades" scientist, earns Jauffret's hatred when he discovers, by sheer chance, that the Martian language is somewhat similar to Urdu (14). This jealousy is compounded when it emerges that both Green and Jauffret are compiling Martian dictionaries (57–8). This squabble over the ownership of knowledge foreshadows the more dangerous philosophical debates that follow. Fundamental to the text is the confrontation between subjectivity and objectivity, delineated through the characters' reactions to the works of Hegel and Darwin.

Hegel's philosophy of Absolute Idealism comes under fire for two reasons: the American physicist Williams criticises Hegel's characterisation of existence as an inescapable matrix of thought as tautology and solipsism (117–18), arguing that there must be some kind of objective reality. Green, meanwhile, agrees with Hegel's characterisation of existence, but objects to the philosopher's argument that an understanding of science and mathematics leads to a greater understanding of the Absolute Idea, saying that it negates any discussion of abstract principles (119–20). The Martians flummox Green and Williams by agreeing with both of them to certain extents – they regard themselves as expressions of an infinite system from which thought cannot be divorced, but they regard that system as having an objective reality of its own. Thus, there is no easy distinction between Martian systems of religion, science or philosophy (70–1, 116) and their perfect mathematical system is capable of predicting evolutionary change (68).

Darwinian Theory also takes a battering from the Martian dialogues. We are told that the Martians resemble Earthlings, despite having no common ancestor (67–8), and the fact that their species has existed for longer than ours (and thus has had more time to evolve into something other than human) and the population of Mars has always been lower than that of Earth, meaning that there are fewer opportunities for natural selection to favour advantageous new mutations that might lead to a humanoid appearance by accident (185–6). The Earthlings' assumption from this new evidence is that Darwin got it wrong, and that life is predestined to turn out the same everywhere in the universe. Therefore, there is no such thing as chance, despite what mathematicians and scientists say (67–70), and Green goes so far as to echo Nietzsche's idea of "eternal recurrence":

> if there was a mighty cosmic cataclysm, and our sun and this and all the other planets were dissolved into misty vapour, then, once again, atom would come to atom and molecule to molecule, and our system would build itself up anew, and would recreate the beauty of the Sistine Madonna of Raphael and the glory of the fifth symphony of Beethoven. (69)

Thus, there is only one workable model for existence, and only one correct way to interpret and analyse it: the objective, capital-T Truth, as worshipped by the Martians (in temples, no less; 245). This worship of objectivism is reflected in the attitudes of the Earthmen, who now regard subjectivity as a "sin" (205, 242).

The fetishisation of transcendent, eternal objectivity, reducing the world's complexity to a set of easily understood, infallible axioms, is the main driving force behind ideologies motivated by a fear of ambiguity, ambivalence, abstraction, and the powerlessness these subjective forces imply. It seeks to ameliorate these feelings of human insignificance and impotence by bringing an end to critical thought – after all, if an idea is "proved" to be eternally and objectively true, the possibility of dissenting opinion or confusion is removed.

Of all the characters present in the text, only one – Max Raabe, the German mathematician – is explicitly said to be a fascist (13); the other men of learning, however, display the same longing for a simple, ordered, unambiguous world, and the strength of this longing is evident in the manner in which they completely reject subjectivity and contingency, simply because the Martians have done so.

Regardless of what they believe, neither the Martians nor the Earthmen can escape subjectivity, as symbolised by the titular rainbow. The American physicist (and amateur psychologist) Williams points out that it is more than likely that rainbows and colours appear different to every individual observer (40), and this observation is all the more pointed for the fact that Mars has no rainbows at all (39). This fact is further illustrated by the story of how the arrogant Jauffret attempts to teach the names of colours to the Martians: when the aliens do not understand his assertion that "White is composed of blue, yellow and red," he goes so far as to get Green to draw a diagram for them, and continue to insist on the truth of this assertion until, at last, the Martians give in and agree with him – after which it is discovered that the Martians have mixed up yellow and red (41–2).

Much of the discussions are taken up with the unfolding crisis in Europe. Hobson and the others ponder the question of whether Russia will remain neutral (16, 213), the German annexation of Bohemia (of which the Martians disapprove; 141), Danzig (152) and the Nazi treatment of the Jews (which Williams seems to think is justified, hinting at secret Zionist societies in London; 207–8). Meredith also situates Ireland and the Irish people within that geopolitical context: the Irish will remain neutral (214), and if Hitler decided to conquer Ireland, it is Hobson's opinion that the North would control the entire Reich within six months (142). In discussing these things, however, Hobson discovers that for all their expertise, his new companions are frustratingly ignorant of Irish affairs.

To begin with, Hobson discovers that one of the other characters has given him a nickname – "Joseph Mary" – assuming that because

Hobson is Irish, he must be Catholic (77). This ignorance leads Hobson to reminisce about the one serious quarrel he ever had with a fellow Protestant, after equating the assassinations of British military personnel on 21 November 1920 with the massacre in Croke Park later that day (79–80).[5] Discussing the Partition, he says that the Republic is better off without the North, reasoning that Ulster unionists would have prolonged such religious bigotry, as well as forming a third major political party to muddy the waters of Irish democracy (142). He reacts angrily to Green's suggestion that the people of the North are really English at heart (142–3), and counters the perception that Irishmen of the Republic are characterised by a hatred of the English by pointing out the symbiotic nature of the islands' economies – without England to sell produce to, Ireland could not survive (143). When Green repeats the dictum that mayhem would result if England withdrew its troops from the North, Hobson replies, "[all] we ask you to do [...] is to go away and let us fight in peace" (165). Decolonisation is not an unproblematic task, and sometimes, differences of opinion as to how it should be carried out will lead to violence.

It is worth noting that in the same year, a similar argument took place in the press. The British newspaper *Picture Post* triggered a minor controversy by serialising H.G. Wells's *The Fate of Homo Sapiens*, in which Wells criticised Catholicism as an incoherent and anti-intellectual faith that led countries to stagnation, using Ireland as a case in point (Ashworth 271–3). Reacting to the resulting hue and cry from aggrieved Catholics all over the country, the Irish government banned *Picture Post* for three months, but not before the editor of that paper threw down a gauntlet to the editor of the *Irish Catholic*, suggesting that they nominate someone to articulate a detailed response to Wells's assertions; the nominated man, Alfred O'Rahilly, published his objections to Wells in the *Standard* (272), attacking Wells on a number of logical fallacies, and charging the famous SF author with being unscientific (274–5).

Lucian Ashworth attributes the spat between Wells and O'Rahilly to geopolitical factors – the physical proximity of Ireland and Britain, he says, combined with political manoeuvring in relation to Northern Ireland, gives the Irish people "a national sensitivity about British attitudes towards Ireland" (267). While one would hope that recent political advances have moved Anglo-Irish relations beyond this state of affairs, it is demonstrably true that this kind of excessive sensitivity existed in Ireland in the past, and it was undoubtedly alive at the time the *Picture Post* controversy occurred. From a cultural or philosophical point of view, however, it is difficult to place this incident at a remove from the worldwide clash between "objectivity" and subjectivity described by

James Creed Meredith. Wells was a man of science, and even suggested the establishment of a secular religion based upon scientific fact (272); O'Rahilly, in turn, argued that "Wells assumes that agreeing with his ideas is the same thing as being impartial and unbiased" (274). Meredith and O'Rahilly wrote from two different traditional perspectives – the former being Protestant and the latter Catholic – indicating that their respective writings were reflective of a national mood that ultimately had little to do with religion. At the time, Ireland appears to have been a bastion of subjectivity in a world that was trying to become purely "objective," and thus had once again become a "lost world."

This mood pervaded many cultural arguments at the time, such as the bitter debates over the implementation of a standardised Irish and the adoption of the Roman typeface to write it (O'Leary 2010, 35–9). Because "authenticity" was linked to antiquity (38), cultural nationalists framed this kind of argument in oppositional terms, or, as one commentator described it, "out and out war between the new world and the old world" (47). The same time period saw an increasing anxiety that the Irish were forgetting their heritage, and an increased interest in Irish history (158–9). In this kind of milieu, "efficiency," science and technology (all "objective" forces) could only be interpreted as antagonistic to a nation trying to construct an "authentic" (subjective) identity for itself.

Meredith seems to be suggesting that the worldwide pursuit of Truth and "objectivity" is dangerous to the Irish, about whom the wider world knows and cares little. Ireland is being weighed and measured in the worldwide laboratory by people who have already dismissed the Irish as stupid, violent and irrelevant – as Yahoos, in both the Swiftian and Shavian senses of the word. This is all the more pointed for Meredith's description of the Martians' reaction to that ideal, which suggests that for all their authoritarianism, the extraterrestrials recognise the Superman as something to be feared and avoided – as evidenced by this "mythical" account of the emergence of superhumans on Mars millennia ago:

> It was found out that these supermen, when a number of them were growing up, had begun plotting together with a view of obtaining the mastery of the planet. Accordingly they were all put to death. For some thousands of years afterwards similar supermen were born from time to time. They were all systematically put to death as soon as they were recognised as belonging to the new race. After a few thousand years no more supermen came to be born. The Martians do not know themselves what to make of the myth, but the Council of Wise Men have announced that if any supermen happen to be born again the fact is to be communicated to them immediately.

Of course no one knows whether the supermen would be put to death or would be co-opted on the Council. (Meredith 74–5)

Shortly after the publication of *The Rainbow in the Valley*, the Nazis invaded Poland, marking the beginning of World War II. On 2 September of the same year, the Irish government officially declared a state of emergency (thus coining the official Irish euphemism for the war), and committed to a precarious position intended to be not just neutral, but impartial as well. Seosamh Ó Torna may very well have approved of this course of action, since it involved sealing Ireland off from the rest of the world altogether.

The Emergency

The attempt to hermetically seal Ireland for the duration of World War II meant that, in addition to the hardships caused by the rationing of practically every material resource, popular culture suffered as well. The press, radio and cinema were subjected to censorship aimed at "controlling covert propaganda, disinformation, and stories planted by the belligerent powers" (Wills 163). Irish radio productions of the time consisted mainly of religious topics, sports coverage, music and programmes for schools (188–9), while low production values and pay rates contributed to the abysmal state of radio drama, where untrained and underpaid voice actors would often find themselves portraying several different characters that were indistinguishable to the listener (189–90). Films produced in Ireland mostly took the form of Catholic documentaries, as well as documentaries on agriculture and army life (299); the insistence on documentaries came from the official received wisdom that realist pictures were "in the national and cultural interests of the people" (300–1). Restrictions on foreign films proved beneficial to Irish film producers (301), though Clair Wills notes that at the time, there was a paradoxical interest in Russian cinema, which she attributes to the realism of film-makers like Eisenstein, Pudovkin and Dovshenko, combined with a "softening" of attitudes towards the Soviets in the wake of German attacks (302–3).

The irony of this was that "all these groups – Catholic Action, the liberal Film Society, Muintir na Tíre, *The Bell*, the Gaelic League, even the Abbey Theatre – were battling over the ground of realism, while being lambasted from abroad for living in a fantasy world" (304). As discussed in the previous chapter, "tradition" and "realism," however narrowly defined, were the paradigms of the bourgeois nationalist subculture that came to power following the Partition and the Civil War. Furthermore, laying claim to "the ground of realism" can be seen as another bid for political legitimacy: Ireland may have been sufficiently subjective in character to regard the twentieth century as a fad (at best) or a threat (at worst), but that did not mean that every subjectivity would be tolerated. This held true for writers of Irish-language texts as well. Despite the repeated rhapsodising of the "imagination" of the Irish people, and residents of the Gaeltacht particularly (O'Leary 2010, 86–7), Irish-language authors were reluctant to experiment with theme or setting (108), and were content to reproduce a "ruralist ideology" that linked authentic native culture exclusively to the countryside (81);[6] this makes the one example of wartime Irish-language SF all the more remarkable.

In *Manannán* by Máiréad Ní Ghráda, astronomer Micheál Ó Flaithimh finds, while on holiday in Egypt, an ancient star chart that depicts a hitherto-unknown planet between Earth and Mars (Ní Ghráda 12–14). After ten years of research, the astronomer discovers that the mysterious world has been hidden from terrestrial view by a cloud of toxic gas that allows light in, but does not allow it to escape. There are many questions to be answered, most important of which is the question of whether there is intelligent life there.

The only way to answer these questions, it seems, is to launch an interplanetary expedition. To this end, Ó Flaithimh enlists the help of ace pilot Seán Ó Maolchatha and physics professor Máirtín Mac Con Midhe, as well as the financial aid of an unidentified Irish-American multi-millionaire with a fondness for the works of Jules Verne (28). Over the course of a year, they set to work acquiring all the provisions and equipment they need, as well as void-proofing an aeroplane and affixing rockets that will allow it to reach escape velocity (31–3). On the fourteenth of the month, they set off on their interplanetary journey, only to discover that the astronomer's precocious young son, Brian, has stowed away on board (35–9). Thankfully, they stocked up with plenty of extra air, food and water (41), thus avoiding the unpleasantness that marred Robert Cromie's expedition to Mars in *A Plunge into Space*.

A month later, they penetrate the cloud of gas and land on the new planet. Luckily, the toxic cloud does not mix with the planet's atmosphere, which turns out to be breathable (44). The water is drinkable too, and after a quick bath, they set off to initiate contact with the locals. Manannán, named after the old Irish god of the sea, is a colourful world, and the gravity is so low that the Irishmen are able to carry the plane on their shoulders to a suitable hiding place (46). On Manannán, the human population lives within cities protected by invisible force fields.

The reason for this is the planet's other dominant species, the Cráidhmí, amphibious monsters that are part turtle, part crab and part ape (74–5). Hundreds of years ago, the Cráidhmí population exploded, and these creatures came onto the land in search of food (124–5). Voracious omnivores, they kill and eat anything in their path, rendering food production almost impossible – if nothing is done, the inhabitants of the cities will eventually die from starvation. The Manannánites are not to be totally pitied, however. Under the rule of their autocratic leader, the "High-Master," dissenters, criminals and enemies of the state are subjected to severe punishments. This most commonly takes the form of a type of re-education, but occasionally extreme sentences are handed down for minor crimes:

> "That man is a pickpocket," Amón said. "He was caught red-handed and taken to the presence of the High-Master. The punishment that he put on him was that electric currents were put through the fingers on his hands, and if he lays one finger on anything in future, that current will pass through his whole body and he will be killed." (141)[7]

The first indication the adventurers receive that something might be amiss with the society they have landed in is that everyone looks the same – they all have white skin, blue eyes and blonde hair (53). The astronomer puts this down to the gas cloud, which blocks direct sunlight, but this supposition is disproved by the appearance of the High-Master himself, Rámó, who seems to be the only red-head on the planet (80). These observations have an additional historical resonance when one considers that at the time, the most vocal self-proclaimed champion of a stereotypically "Nordic" master race was himself anything but tall, blond and blue-eyed.

When the grown-ups are arrested as possible spies (84–9), Brian and his local friend Nící seek a way to liberate them. In the course of their adventures, they uncover a plot to oust the High-Master (110–16), and as thanks for this information, the adults are released from prison (136–7). To further curry the High-Master's favour, the physics professor comes up with a way to end the Cráidhmí problem – build a giant robot and annihilate them (142–4). The High-Master gives the project the go-ahead, and after a pitched battle, the Cráidhmí are practically wiped out (154–62). A few manage to escape, but this is acceptable, since the survivors' tales will serve to spread fear among the Cráidhmí and discourage them from coming onto dry land again (163). The Irishmen are given a heroes' reception upon their return to the city, and are honoured by the High-Master for their service. Following the decimation of the Cráidhmí, the ecstatic citizens hail Máirtín as their saviour, and start whispering about how he should be their new High-Master (169). The current High-Master responds by gassing the crowd, providing one of the eeriest images in Irish popular literature: "The crowd was standing outside in the street; everyone's head raised in the air like they were looking at something far away, the colour of death on every face, and all of them like statues without soul or breath" (170–1).[8]

The following morning, the Irish adventurers realise what's in store for them. The High-Master will not let them go home, and he wants them to supply him with an army of giant robots, that he may destroy his enemies in the city on the other side of the hill (179). The Irishmen have no desire to remain on Manannán any longer, and use the giant robot to take back their aeroplane and make good their escape back to Earth (180–3).

As the above outline indicates, this novel is intended for children, and young boys particularly: there are no girls in the story, and we are told that Brian's mother (who surely would have prevented her husband taking their son to another planet) has been dead for seven years (17). The adults are removed from the narrative so that the youngsters can go exploring, and Brian and Nící's adventures are littered with chance encounters, fortuitous discoveries and lucky escapes. The boring business of scientific research (i.e. the very reason for the expedition) is left unresolved at the novel's close, and the whole adventure conveniently takes place during the summer holidays (183).

One point of interest is the manner in which Irish mythology is invoked to name science-fictional objects. The principal example in this text is, of course, the planet Manannán itself, named by the pilot after the ancient Irish god of the sea (23). Since the inhabitants of the planet have no concept of astronomy (81–2), they seem not to have any name for their own world, and if the ancient Egyptians had a name for it, that name is not recorded. Thus, the Irish adventurers have appropriated a measure of imperial privilege, in that they are at liberty to name another civilisation's homeland, and primacy is given to the name they chose for it before ever setting foot on it. Just as interesting is the name bestowed upon the robot, "Lugh Lámh-Fhada," after the Gaelic sun king (144, 146). O'Leary notes that, during the war, the popularity of stories of the fairy folk (daoine sidhe) "remained surprisingly high" (O'Leary 2010, 112), which may to a degree explain these mythological homages. Another possibility is the notion, which would become a matter of public debate in the post-war period, that the Irish were ignorant of their own mythology, especially when compared to other European populations, such as the Icelandic people (347–8). Thus, any attempt to educate the general public on this topic was welcome.

Rámó relies on mechanical means to indoctrinate the public, rather than ideological means such as demagoguery or control of the education system. During their detention on suspicion of espionage, the Earthmen worry that they might be sentenced to death. A friendly local puts their minds at ease by telling them that Manannán has no death penalty. Rather, dissenters are subjected to a form of re-education:

> "We don't want to do you any harm. All the High-Master will do is to overpower your minds with his own, so you won't remember your purpose for coming here, and so you'll be loyal to him, and so you won't want to do harm to him or to anyone else here." (96)[9]

The exact process is left to the reader's imagination, but it hints at a kind of dictatorship only possible within the realms of SF: as long as one has the loyalty of the army, plus a handy brain-washing machine, autocratic rule is easy. The horrors that they have witnessed inspire the astronomer to remark, as they make their way back to Earth, "Thank God we live in a country with no High-Master or dictator over it. Those people are worse than the Cráidhmí themselves" (186).[10] Of course, they do not reflect on the implications of their involvement in the Cráidhmí affair: not only do they leave the giant robot behind (183), but they also leave behind a workforce that now knows how to build more – the natives that helped them to construct Lugh Lámh-Fhada (143). While the Irish are congratulating themselves on living in a free country, they do not seem to realise that they have given the High-Master the means to spread his rule over the entire planet of Manannán.

A Relic of Old Certainties

Though the popular Catholic culture of mediaevalism reached a crescendo during the 1930s with the figuring of the Spanish Civil War as a "Crusade," George Bernard Shaw's revulsion at modernity and nostalgia for Victorian social norms is a strong indicator that the "necromantic impulse" once embodied by the old *filí* was not just a Catholic trait (Shaw himself was closer to being a deist than any variety of Christian). This point was hammered home in the post-war years by the Anglo-Irish Lord Dunsany's quasi-pagan reaction against every kind of mechanical industry in *The Last Revolution* (1951).

The story concerns an eccentric inventor named Ablard Pender, who creates a sentient machine which in turn starts to build other intelligent machines, in a bid to take over the world. When the original monster, nicknamed "Robespierre" (Dunsany 81), kidnaps Pender's fiancée, the inventor and the narrator must join forces to rescue her and stop the Last Revolution. Most of the narrative is set in a cottage in the marshes, to which the machines have lain siege; the human protagonists must keep the monsters from acquiring the oil they need to leave the marshes and spread their influence further afield, while staying alive long enough to be rescued by the military.

In a very real sense, the apocalypse foretold by Dunsany did actually happen: *The Last Revolution* portrays the demise of a way of life which, by the time of the novel's publication, had been anachronistic for nearly half a century. The novel figures this demise as the destruction of a more decent, gentler world by the relentless forces of modernisation.

For example, the narrator first meets Pender at the United Schools Club (5), and when Pender invites the narrator to dinner at his aunt's house, he says that there is no need for formal attire, because they "haven't dressed for dinner since the war" (13). As the story progresses, it becomes clear that, despite the post-World War II setting, Dunsany's characters have been more profoundly impacted by World War I, a conflict that more or less brought an end to the old British aristocracy to which Dunsany himself was connected by blood. When a housemaid quits because Pender's creation frightens her, Pender's aunt notes that "Servants are very hard to keep these days. They will give notice for any trifle" (48). When he receives a distressed telephone call from Pender's aunt, the narrator springs into action – by asking his housekeeper to boil two eggs for a quick breakfast while he finishes dressing (69). Later, the siege is measured out with cups of tea, of which there seems to be an inexhaustible supply, even if the supplies of food and drinking water have to be rationed (83, 92, 105, 116, 129, 135, 158, 165, 171). These references to a frustrated Edwardian civility are accompanied by a sense of duty and forbearance, the stereotypical British "stiff upper lip." Eerith, the elderly man employed by Pender to keep the machines oiled (and in whose cottage the characters find themselves under siege), despises the machines with a passion, yet he refuses to help smash them because "I'm paid to look after them" (66). One of the policemen later tries to console Pender by saying, "Oh, we don't mind it for being new, sir. Poor old Goering used to play some nasty new tricks on us. But we soon got used to them" (116). The novel's antagonists also call to mind the Great War's unprecedented mechanisation of death and destruction – the "nasty new tricks" Dunsany refers to are less Goering's than those of World War I.

The anachronism of the protagonists and their relationships to each other and the world in general is complemented by an anachronistic narrative: it features a mad scientist and the setting is an atemporal "gothic zone" – a primitive landscape into which "mad science" intrudes. Future-war narratives are another undeniable influence, and the paranoia of Cromie's *A Plunge into Space* permeates the protagonists' reactions to an encroaching modern world. Like *A Modern Daedalus* and *The Professor in Erin* before it, *The Last Revolution* is, in fact, an almost perfect synthesis of all the various strands of SF. Had it been published in the nineteenth century, it could have been called a classic work of the early genre, greater than the sum of its myriad parts. The attempted return to earlier literary forms is not successful, however – the world has changed too much to allow it.

Warning signs regarding the nature of Pender's invention are present from the very beginning. Other United Schools Club members remark that they have heard the inventor has "made a Frankenstein" (5); Pender informs us that his creation is stronger than a man (or any other animal, for that matter), and that it is sufficiently intelligent to beat human beings at chess (9). The machine arouses instinctive revulsion in all who encounter it: the narrator feels a *frisson* of existential horror upon realising that humankind has dropped to "second place in the world" (12), and later remarks, "I was looking at the future, and saw nothing – it was too dark" (21). Hammering this unease home, the machine reveals its true nature with a moment of sadistic *Grand Guignol*:

> Once more the dog howled. And then Pender's monster came for it, scurrying over the marshes like a terribly magnified beetle, and seized the dog by the throat with some of its hands. The dog bit, but bit upon iron. And before we could do anything it had torn the dog to pieces and was holding the pieces up so as to let the blood run all over it. Its idea of eating, I suppose.

Equally arresting is Pender's response to his creation's actions: "Motors kill more dogs than that, and men, women and children too. But you wouldn't stop motors" (29). The narrator describes Pender as being wilfully blind, lacking in foresight, and being possessed of only two ambitions: "to free humankind from the drudgery of labour," and to marry the love of his life, Alicia (43). When the narrator asks him when the machines' reproduction will stop, Pender replies, "I don't want it to stop," and argues that this new race of intelligent machines will change human existence for the better – "all the advantages of slavery without the harm of it" (32–3). On moral grounds, Pender later refuses to try to stop the machines at all (51). It does not take long for the inventor to change his tune. The protagonists discover that machines all over the immediate area are acting up (52–3, 54–5), and Eerith has figured out the truth: Pender's machines can "speak" to other mechanisms (57). Shortly thereafter, the machines make their first major power play by taking control of Alicia's motorbike in order to kidnap her (74).

Pender's single-minded focus, meanwhile, shifts from uncritical praise of his invention to increasingly desperate denials of any moral culpability. He blames "James Watt and Stevenson and Marconi and hundreds of others" for starting the machines' evolution (87), and repeatedly insists that he is not to blame for their revolution, that he merely gave them "a helping hand" without realising what he was doing. Pender even goes so far as to claim that "Marconi made Hitler and Mussolini" in a similar fashion, in that Marconi unwittingly enabled the rise of fascist regimes through the discovery of radio broadcasting (127). Eventually, the narrator accepts Pender's arguments as the truth, and reflects that humankind's downfall was initiated not by the inventor's murderous creation, but by the advent of machinery in general (149). This is a marked departure from the genre's nineteenth-century insane scientists, who praised their own achievements by hyperbolic comparisons to those of "lesser" thinkers from history; Pender is so desperate to renounce any responsibility for what he has done that he attributes consciousness to inanimate objects, arguing that machines have always hated humankind, and have only needed intelligence to rebel against us. His particular madness turns out to be a distorted animism, and thus it is no surprise that following the attempted machine uprising, he and Alicia move to the countryside "to seek out rural things and ancient things and simple things" (185). Disillusioned with the modern world, they are trying to reclaim some kind of pagan Arcadia, much like Fitz-James O'Brien's mad scientist Linley attempted to do through his diamond lens.

Dunsany's position on the modern world is not subtle: the entire text of *The Last Revolution* is a sustained polemic on the evils of science, technology and modernity. Pender states that science cannot be stopped, and if it brings disaster to the human race, "the human race will have to endure it" (49); the narrator bemoans the marginalisation of the Luddites, whose foresight was disregarded at the expense of England's natural beauty, and points out that machines have already started to enslave human beings:

> "Haven't you seen thousands of men serving machines in factories? Haven't you seen design, art, all the work of mankind, getting more

and more mechanical? It's been coming for some time. You are like
some old French aristocrat in his tower, who did not know what
the *canaille* were doing." (60)

Dunsany underlines this anti-technology message by drawing an
explicit dichotomy between the mechanical and natural worlds. The
story of Alicia's ordeal on board the possessed motorbike is punctuated
by strange displays of solidarity from the animal kingdom. A herd
of cattle leap out of the motorbike's way, "as though they knew that
something would come to the world that was more deadly than Man,
and that now it had come" (87–8). Moths, foxes and sheep seem to
realise the gravity of the situation as well, and as Alicia notices the
reactions of these animals, she fancies that "I know how Queen Marie
Antoinette must have felt [...] on her way to the guillotine" (88–9).
Badgers flee the motorbike's approach (91), and later on, the same sixth
sense is demonstrated by a flock of ducks (159). A pair of owls keeps
pace with the motorbike, sympathetic but unable to do anything to
help (90–1). The narrator surmises, "We and the tiger might be allies
some day," when faced by a common enemy that despises all organic
life (159–60).

All of this being said, metaphors from nature also abound in the
narrator's description of the machines. The original machine is described
as resembling a giant crab (15), initially behaving like a "well-trained
retriever," buzzing like a fly, and watching its chess opponents "rather
as a cockroach watches one" (18). In its workshop on the marshes, it
comes across as "a thing with the industry of a spider and the brains of
Capablanca" (24), and it has the speed of a hare (26).[11] The machines it
creates resemble giant beetles (28, 161), and in their presence the narrator
feels like "a man in a cage full of tigers" (41). Their social structure is
compared to a termite colony (74), and a delirious wounded policeman
rambles on about "beetles that had mated with tigers" (126).

The point is made more forcefully when Eerith bluntly states that
"There's a curse over all [new] things" (57), and again towards the text's
conclusion, when an elderly farmer re-iterates his grandfather's assertion
that "machines were the devil" (189). Nothing in the narrative is quite
so ridiculous as Alicia calling out to a family of gypsies for assistance
("Give me a spell against it") as her motorbike captor speeds past their
roadside camp (91), but this is an interesting throwback to the days of
Jonathan Swift – the gypsies, figured here as a premodern people, are
attributed with premodern (i.e. magical) capabilities.

The marsh in which the machines' workshop is situated is described
in terms that evoke the Ascendancy gothic's alienated landscapes:

[Beyond] the brow of a little hill on which the cabbages grew there loured a bank of mist, and under that was land that owes no allegiance to us; under that lay the marshes. Men had been there too, as an old thatched cottage showed, but they came there as strangers, not as the masters of hundreds of rows of cabbages, drawn up by Man, and to serve his needs in the end. (25)

The depiction of the siege is in itself anachronistic, but this anachronism articulates Dunsany's class anxieties and his deep-rooted fear of revolution and regime change.[12] Throughout the text, the main characters make reference to the French Revolution (62, 167), and compare themselves and each other to various personages from that revolution (60, 62, 89) – not to mention the fact that the original machine is named after Robespierre. Taking this into account, it becomes clear why the machines forgo the simple tactic of using their superior strength to force their way into the cottage, and instead attempt to burn the humans out, using the flaming torches beloved of the angry peasant mobs of gothic melodrama. It is unfortunate for Pender and company, then, that they must suffer the indignity of being besieged inside a tumbledown servant's cottage, rather than a Big House more suited to their standing as embattled members of a latter-day *ancien régime*.

It is difficult not to read *The Last Revolution* as an attempt to return to a past time of reliable certainties, when the conflict between the traditional and the modern had not yet been settled. Dunsany is aware, however, that no such attempt can succeed; the narrator acknowledges, "There have been great beasts before us. And we must expect something else to come after us" (60). At the novel's close, we are told that "there will be other Penders," and we should resign ourselves to the fact that the Last Revolution is inevitable (192).[13]

Published the same year as *The Last Revolution*, Shaw's *Farfetched Fables* reads almost like a reprise of *Back to Methuselah*, and a bitter re-evaluation of the arguments put forward in the earlier text, arguments that are no longer tenable in a post-Holocaust world. Beginning in the present day, the first fable announced that the "Truce of God" has been declared, and planet Earth is now at peace; true to the pessimism and cynicism of *Geneva*, an amoral, opportunist chemist takes advantage of the Truce to develop a new kind of poison gas, cornering the armaments market in a world without weapons. In the second fable, we learn that several warlords around the world have access to this gas, which is used to wipe out the population of London. The succeeding fables are all set in a nondescript building on the Isle of Wight, whose function changes with the passage of time from an "anthropometric laboratory" to the headquarters of the "diet commissioners" to a genetics lab and finally to a sixth-form school. These latter fables constitute a sustained mockery of eugenic experiments: the anthropometric lab, whose function is to sort people into "mediocrities" and "anybodies" (note the lack of a "superman" category), ends up classifying an idiotic tourist as a genius and dismissing a brilliant tramp as a mediocrity; the "diet commissioners" discover that vegetarianism increases aggression, and create a soldiering caste of grass-eating "supergorillas"; the genetics lab, operating in a future when the physical act of sex has been abolished and hermaphrodites are commonplace among the population, criticise the barbarians of the past while knowing nothing of their history (at one point, they confuse Hitler with Jesus); finally, in the sixth-form school, children are trained only to ask questions that can be answered objectively, with the implication that they are killed if they fail to graduate. To put it bluntly, this play is Shaw's admission that his earlier attitude to the Yahoo was inhumane. His general pessimism has been confirmed, it appears, but his hope for the emergence of the Superman has been dashed.

Taking a "universal" approach to these texts, we can say that Ó Torna's "Duinneall" is just as much an articulation of terror before the Nietzschean Superman as it is about the evil influence of modern popular culture. The narrator's assertion that the Duinnealls' evil surpasses that of Hitler and Stalin (Ó Torna 74–5) voices the fear that James Creed Meredith leaves unsaid in *The Rainbow in the Valley* and that Dunsany dramatises in *The Last Revolution* – that once created, the Superman cannot be controlled, appealed to or reasoned with. The "parochial" interpretation, however, highlights an important fact: the "siege culture," most commonly attributed to Irish Protestantism and Ulster unionism in particular, is not in fact exclusive to those traditions. The feeling of being under threat from an outside aggressor presents across Irish society, and has given rise to a recurring theme in Irish SF. In the next chapter, I will examine how this theme resurfaced with special relevance to Irish Catholicism during the 1960s.

5. The 1960s: Lemass, Modernisation and the Cold War

Seán Mac Maoláin's 1947 novel *Algoland* begins with an introduction in which Mac Maoláin explains his reasons for writing the novel:

> I have asked a lot of people what is the reason why the Gaels never write any dreams but the ones they have between morning and midnight – what is the reason why they don't write the strange dreams they create between midnight and day. And every person gave me the same answer, i.e. "Ah, you basket-case, don't you know that the unfortunates have to wait until such things are commonly done in one of the major languages of the world?" But I have never given in to that idea, and I will not give in – for a little while longer, at any rate. (Mac Maoláin 3)[1]

If the above introduction is an accurate indicator of Irish attitudes to non-realist literature at the time, we could infer that the struggle for "realism" prior to and during the Emergency had concluded, and Mac Maoláin would have us believe that by 1947, readers had forgotten that non-realism was indeed widely practised in literature in *all* "the major languages of the world."

The narrative that follows is framed as a dream, brought on by eating seafood before bedtime. The unnamed narrator (presumably Mac Maoláin himself) finds himself in the country of Algoland, where he befriends the poet laureate, Tagaldus. Tagaldus takes it upon himself to guide the narrator around Algoland's capital city, La Primabura, while answering questions about the strange country. Algolandish society is almost fully automated: nearly every task is performed by machines that seem to possess rudimentary artificial intelligence, and the narrator is shocked to see pubs with no barmen (41), banks with no clerks (46), clothes shops with no tailors (52) and combine harvesters without human drivers (76–8). However, the Algolanders did not build the machines themselves. Rather, they acquired these marvellous devices from various countries around the world, in exchange for the powerful, naturally occurring cosmetic substances (a skin conditioner, and oil that encourages hair growth) within Algoland's mines (96–8).

The most interesting aspect of this text is the way in which it lampoons socially conservative nationalism, through the means of an interview with Algoland's oldest citizen. He lives in the last Irish-style cottage left on the island (79), and has an unrivalled knowledge of old Algolandish folklore and folk wisdom – so much so that the country's historians are terrified that he might lose his memory if he is moved out of the cottage and into the city, and so do their best to keep him and his wife where they are (80–1). More importantly, he and his wife remember what the country used to be like before the arrival of automated machines, and describe it as a life of utter hardship (81–2). As for traditional pastimes such as dancing and music, the elderly man dismisses the former as "almost offensive" ["gearr-mhaslach"] and tells the narrator that he rarely plays his fiddle any more (83). Instead, he contents himself with a gramophone, and displays a "measureless desire" ["dúil as miosúr"] for one particular jazz record, of all things, that the narrator finds abhorrent (84). Major changes in Irish popular culture were afoot.

From the beginning of the twentieth century, Ireland was kept at something of a remove from American popular culture – by neutrality in geopolitical events such as World War II, by local conflicts such as the War of Independence and the Civil War, and by a dominant ideology that attacked foreign art forms as the vectors by which modernity might infect the country. This is not to say that Ireland was completely cut off from the outside world. As Diarmaid Ferriter points out, the Irish market for popular literature at the time embraced foreign works such as the romances of Charlotte Brame and the westerns of Zane Grey, alongside the lives of the saints – eventually leading to the emergence of domestic fiction magazines full of "cowboys called Seán" (Ferriter 426–7). In terms of Irish-language literature, the preference for "realist" genres (which, under the cultural logic of Catholicism, includes the biographies of the saints, miracles included) may have a very straightforward explanation.

From the inception of the Free State, standardisation (caighdeánú) became the guiding principle of the government's engagement with the Irish language. Coinciding with this was an emergent concern with the state of Irish-language literature. Commentators argued that if the Irish language was to be respected as a working language, and not just a form of rural cant, it had to prove itself capable of engaging with the modern world (O'Leary 2004, 170). Despite the misgivings of purists, this argument was to be implemented as policy by the government and the Irish-language publishing sector. However, the language simply did not have the vocabulary to deal with modern developments in science, art and politics. The debate that followed was a contest between those who believed that the new vocabulary should be adapted from existing words in other languages, and those who held the opinion that domestic linguistic experimentation was to be preferred (172–4). In the end, the Irish Free State stepped into the breach. In 1928, the government established An Coiste Téarmaíochta (the terminology committee), within the Department of Education. Despite the construction of an official lexicon to deal with these topics, O'Leary notes, "readers were far more likely to learn necessary new terminology from the books, essays, and articles [...] in which many Irish-language writers tried, aptly or absurdly, to expand the capacities of the national language" (176).

One effect that this confused state of affairs has on the study of Irish-language science fiction is that it complicates the task of locating and identifying SF "neologisms," especially when dealing with texts from the early years of the twentieth century. Since authors working in the Irish language were in the habit of coining words for concepts that they believed had no Irish signifier, it would have been difficult for a reader to discern between an author's "real" neologisms and his science-fictive ones. In the early years of the Gaelic Revival, the average reader would not have been able to tell whether the strange new words they were reading were supposed to be from Mars, a different Gaeltacht, or the Dáil. This added confusion would not have been present in more popular genres such as the western or the detective novel. Indeed, westerns were especially popular, to the extent that Brian Ó Nualláin (better known as Flann O'Brien) saw fit to lampoon the Irish reading public's tastes in a memorable section of his 1939 novel, *At Swim-Two-Birds*, in which a clichéd western plot is overlaid onto the geography of Dublin City (O'Brien 2001, 53–9). The market for foreign popular fiction was, however, broader than this trend might suggest.

Seven years earlier, under his own name, Ó Nualláin produced a short story, "Dioghaltas ar Ghallaibh 'sa bhliadhain 2032!" ["Revenge on the English in the Year 2032!"], in which the narrator (having, as in Mac Maoláin's novel, fallen into a deep sleep after overeating) finds himself in unfamiliar surroundings, and receives a shock when confronted by a customs officer:

> "You have to pay five shillings on this hat," he said, pulling a new hat out of the depths of the bag. I paid the money without saying a word, and he gave me a receipt; I looked at it, and the date filled me with astonishment – *12/02/2032.*
> "I thought," I said, "that it was only the eleventh." (Ó Nualláin 4)[2]

This joke depends for its effect on familiarity with the clichés of time-travel stories, on the part of the reader as well as the author. That familiarity was facilitated by the early twentieth-century boom in American "pulp fiction" magazines, such as Hugo Gernsback's *Amazing Stories*.

The Pulps

Science fiction came into its own as a popular genre at a time "when magazine publications in the US were proliferating, and plummeting in price," thanks to the development of cheap, easily manufactured wood-pulp paper, combined with the effects of railway expansion and an increasing number of book clubs (Mendlesohn 2011, 52). In 1908, the Luxembourg-born Gernsback took advantage of this development to launch a magazine of his own, *Modern Electrics*, in which he published technical articles appealing to the amateur experimenter. With the magazine's change of title to *Science and Invention* in 1920, Gernsback started to publish short stories alongside these articles, in which a scientific principle was demonstrated. When these short stories proved popular, Gernsback launched the first magazine dedicated entirely to fiction of that type, *Amazing Stories*, in 1926. Others followed through the 1930s – for example, *Scientific Detective Stories*, *Wonder Stories* and the highly regarded *Astounding Stories* – establishing the magazine as the quintessential twentieth-century format for SF literature.

While even Gernsback's most ardent defender, Gary Westfahl, notes that Gernsback was primarily motivated by "twin urges to achieve status in the realms of literature and science" (Westfahl 138–9), his main ambition for SF was in principle a selfless one: that it should impart reliable scientific fact to the reader. As Brian Attebery puts it, for Gernsback, the genre "was primarily a teaching tool, but one that did not make its teaching obvious" (Attebery 33). Other critics, such as Adam Roberts, see this didacticism as an endeavour "to reshape, in other words, SF by purging all mystical or magical elements from the science-mysticism dialectic that initially formed it" (Roberts 2007, 175). However one prefers to interpret it, and though it came to nought, Gernsback's mission succeeded in creating a shorthand term by which the genre could be recognised. His original term, "scientifiction," conveys his didactic vision, but thankfully, this awkward coinage was soon resolved into the more easily enunciated "science fiction." The new SF magazines brought three traditions together – the literary mode of "scientific romance", the "popular story-telling formulas that developed in dime novels and pulp magazines," and scientific journalism. In addition, most contributors were professional pulp authors who could turn their hand to any number of genres, and had previously written stories for western, detective and "general adventure" magazines (Attebery 34–5). The characteristic tone of "pulp" SF thus arose contrary to Gernsback's wishes – as Farah Mendlesohn points out, pulp literature was largely shaped by market forces and cross-fertilisation between the various popular genres (Mendlesohn 2011, 52).

Mendlesohn describes three basic formulae for pulp plots of the 1930s – the invasion story, the exploration/first contact story, and the invention story – all of which are quite obvious reinterpretations of older types. The invasion story is, as one might suspect, a variation on the nineteenth-century theme of the future war (with "bug-eyed monsters" substituted for villainous foreigners), the exploration/first contact story is a pseudoscientific update of the lost world tale, and the invention story is undoubtedly influenced by technological utopianism and the "unsurpassed self-publicist Thomas Alva Edison" (54–5). As Attebery says, these plots were derivative of their literary/generic origins, and allowed for little but "perfunctory" characterisation, but the intermingling of narrative formulae provided suitable conditions for the emergence of the sub-genre now known as "space opera" (Attebery 34–5).

Space opera is, in the popular imagination at any rate, emblematic of the SF genre as a whole. Set in outer space, more often than not in a technologically advanced future, space opera's focus is always on large-scale adventure: the heroes and (less often) heroines of this sub-genre explore the void, doing battle with aliens, and the stakes are always colossal. The term was coined in 1941 from the phrase "soap opera" by SF fan Bob Tucker (Bould and Vint 47) and calls attention to the sub-genre's sometimes melodramatic execution and its frequent use of recurring casts of characters – *Star Trek* and *Star Wars* encapsulate the formula perfectly. Máiréad Ní Ghráda's *Manannán*, discussed in the previous chapter, comes close to this sub-genre, but does not quite fit because it remains rooted in the present day, providing an avenue of return from the adventure world. In space opera proper, the adventure world and its infrastructures encompass the entire universe – one does not visit it for the summer holidays. The original space operas were also characterised by what Peter Stockwell calls "pulpstyle" prose: the emphasis is on drama, with plenty of cliffhangers for serial works (Stockwell 79), the titles of stories are "plainly descriptive of the content," usually along the lines of "The [Noun(s)] of [Setting]" (80), stories are almost always in the third person, "with an apparently objective and often omniscient narrator" (83), and exposition often militates against realistic dialogue (84–5). Pulp heroes tend to be male, white Anglo-Saxon Protestants. Implausible names full of consonants are chosen for aliens (to indicate exoticness), and the science involved, if any, is taken from either the physical sciences or engineering (82). Indeed, Bould and Vint go so far as to call this "a peculiar anti-intellectualism, which privileges engineering know-how over more abstract theorisation" (Bould and Vint 48). Westfahl places the blame for space opera's often melodramatic and shoddy execution on writers who were "already set in their ways," and were either unwilling or unable to meet Gernsback's expectations; they resorted to strategies of "avoidance" and "distraction" to get around their own lack of scientific knowledge, writing stories with ever-decreasing amounts of reliable scientific content and ever-increasing hyperbole (Westfahl 145–8). What these writers – referred to by Attebery as "adaptable professionals" (Attebery 35) and by Mendlesohn as "hacks" (Mendlesohn 2011, 52) – lacked in scientific training, they made up for with action and drama.

Gernsback's didactic ambition was thus never realised beyond the extent to which "Many stories in the pulp magazines revolved around solving a problem through scientific means" (Attebery 33) – the improbable techno-babble so derided in modern SF. This does not diminish Gernsback's importance to the genre's development. Roberts makes an excellent point when he says, "the point of Pulps is precisely the raw excitement of the [improbable alien] rather than the occasional anticipation of a more sober style of 'engineering feat' SF" (Roberts 2007, 178).

It transpired that these adaptable hacks had done the genre a service when, during the 1950s, SF in the USA escaped official attention during the "Red Scare," which saw left-leaning professors fired from university faculties, Hollywood demonised as a hotbed of communism, and the House Un-American Activities Committee apparently more interested in destroying those who had supported Roosevelt's "New Deal" than in actually investigating subversion (Jezer 90–100). During this time, Marty Jezer explains, to be fired from one's job for "subversion" was "akin to being convicted of a heinous moral crime" (83–4). However, due to its cheap, sub-literary reputation, SF was able to fly "under the radar of hegemonic surveillance," with the result that with the rise of the counterculture in the 1960s, it was recognised as a corpus of radical literature (Moylan 91).

Whether because of the genre's trashy reputation, the resurgence of global conflict, or anti-modernist paranoia, "pulp" SF did not attain the same popularity in Ireland, though as Ó Nualláin's above-quoted time-travel joke indicates, it was well-known enough to be an object of derision at the very least. Consequently, pulp-style space operas did not appear in Irish literature until the 1960s, during what is now remembered, for better or worse, as "the Lemass Era."

Captaen Spéirling: A Man of His Time

Seán Lemass, according to the political scientist Tom Garvin, was an inner-city "Dublin Jackeen" – that is, a confirmed Dubliner who cared little for the preoccupations of rural Ireland.[3] He came from a family with a strong Parnellite tradition that bequeathed the values of liberalism and anti-clericalism: Garvin even hypothesises that Lemass may have been an agnostic or an atheist (33). His legacy is one of modernisation, and he appeared on the political scene as the "Boys of the Old Brigade," de Valera included, were starting to age into a "gerontocracy" (33–4).

During Lemass's term as Taoiseach from 1959 to 1966, the Irish economy expanded at a rate of 4 per cent per annum (Garvin 147). Ó Caochlaigh's and Ó Conaire's observations on the grinding poverty of the Free State were also finally responded to, albeit in the wake of a disaster. Following the collapse of tenement buildings in Dublin, the government took action on behalf of the poor by relocating inner-city slum dwellers to specially constructed "modern flats" and estates in the suburbs, while at the same time, the city was being transformed by new civic buildings, office blocks and other developments, at the expense of historic buildings and neighbourhoods that had stood since the eighteenth century (Ferriter 590–2). Fianna Fáil, of which Lemass was the leader at the time, had secured its position as the state's dominant political party. Its populist success forced opposition parties (such as Fine Gael) to try to imitate them, with limited success, and Irish people learned to engage with the state not as citizens, but as clients reliant on "Fianna Fáil middlemen" (Kirby and Murphy 31–2). Progress in Ireland thus became the object of a political cargo cult, with Fianna Fáil as the priestly caste deriving their power from their ability to deliver prosperity to their supplicants. Alongside this prosperity came increased participation in the outside world.

From 1958, Irish troops were used as peacekeeping forces on UN missions, beginning with a deployment to Lebanon, and the most significant of these peacekeeping missions was Ireland's involvement in Congo. As few European countries were considered politically acceptable to undertake such a mission in the newly independent African state, the Irish troops were considered to be the ideal men for the job; however, their deployment highlighted the Irish Army's severe lack of resources, and it was discovered that Irish nationality did not confer any special protection. On 8 November 1960, a platoon of eleven Irish soldiers was ambushed near the town of Niemba by an estimated twenty members of the Baluba tribe; nine of the Irishmen were killed.[4] Despite this, the Congo mission continued until 1964, symbolising Ireland's commitment to helping the indigenous populations of war-torn countries, and perhaps exorcising the painful memories of its failed, incoherent involvement in the Spanish Civil War.

The optimism engendered by Ireland's nascent economic upturn, and the peacekeeping missions in distant countries, found expression in a series of Irish-language SF stories for children by Cathal Ó Sándair. The four books in the *Captaen Spéirling* series were published in 1960 and 1961, and for the purposes of the analysis below, I have taken the liberty of arranging the stories into "chronological" order: the third book to be published takes place in the year 2000; the fourth is set in 2005; the first published Spéirling adventure is set in 2007, and thus comes third in chronological order; and the second book of the series actually comes last, being set in the year 2050.

The third published story, *An Captaen Spéirling, Spás Phíolóta* [Captain Spéirling, Space Pilot], begins on May the first, 2000, during what we are told is "the Atomic Age." Planet Earth, now known as Terra, is divided into a number of power blocs, the largest of these being "Occidenta" and "Orienta," and the headquarters of the United Nations is on neutral ground in a place called the "City of Peace." Everything in this world, from heavy industry to civilian vehicles, runs on atomic power. The uranium, however, is running out, and Occidenta and Orienta are at loggerheads over what little remains (Ó Sándair 1961a, 5–6). The flashpoint comes when an uprising takes place in "Mediterra," the location of most of the planet's remaining uranium, and soon it looks like Terra is heading towards a third world war. To avoid this course of events, the scientist Professor Ó Glarcáin devises a plan to build a spaceship capable of reaching the Moon (Luna), where he believes there is a bountiful supply of uranium. Helping him to put this plan into action is his friend, the eponymous Captain Spéirling. They convince the Minister of Defence to donate half of the country's defence budget to the project (14), and by New Year's Day 2001, the spaceship is ready to launch. Bringing along Spéirling's daughter Deirdre – as well as a stowaway in the shape of Marco, an inept Oriental spy – the Terrans soon land on Luna, much to the consternation of the natives.

The tragic history of the people of Luna presents a warning about Terra's potential future. Once a "normal" humanoid species, their over-reliance on fossil fuels pushed them to discover atomic energy. This in turn triggered the outbreak of a nuclear war, which drove the survivors into underground warrens and whose lingering effects mutated them into one-eyed creatures with two mouths, split tongues and fur-covered bodies. This history is outlined for the reader as it is explained to a forlorn Lunar teenager, one of the first "normal" children born in thousands of years, who wants to know why he is so different from all his friends (37–40). By splitting the atom, the Moon people discovered something that has eluded Terran physicists: a side effect of nuclear fission is the emission of "bad rays," a form of radiation that increases aggression and makes people want to fight. Thus, the discovery of fission technology leads inexorably to nuclear war (39). Thankfully, in the thousands of years since the Lunar conflict, they have found a way to produce the antithesis to this radiation: "good rays," which induce pacifism and an urge to cooperate (40). Once they make contact with the Terran adventurers, the Moon people bequeath this marvellous invention to them, along with enough uranium to last the entire world for centuries to come. Ireland takes its place as a well-respected member of the United Nations, and is honoured for its part in ending war forever and establishing friendly relations with our extraterrestrial neighbours.

By the year 2005, things have got even better for Terra. As outlined in *Leis an gCaptaen Spéirling go Mars* [Captain Spéirling Goes to Mars], every major city on the planet has its own space station in geosynchronous orbit (Ó Sándair 1961b, 17–18), people have personal flying shuttles (*inghearáin*) instead of atomic cars (14), and there are now Terran colonies on Luna (18). The rate of invention and scientific achievement has increased exponentially in just four years, with many spaceships already considered old-fashioned (19), and the UN keeps watch over all, via the Werner Von Braun Space-Station (21). Spéirling and Ó Glarcáin petition the Scientists' Association of Ireland for £75 million to fund an expedition to Mars, but are turned down. Undaunted, they decide to appeal to the public for funding, establishing the Company for the Development of Mars, in which the public can buy shares. They raise the money in three days, doubtlessly due to the success of their previous business venture, the Company for the Development of Luna, which delivered a 75 per cent profit on each share sold (19–20). They put the money to good use, building a new spaceship with all kinds of mod cons, and by spring 2006, it appears as though all will go swimmingly for the Irish adventurers once more. Unknown to either of our two heroes, Mars is inhabited by a humanoid race, and for thousands of years has suffered under a brutal regime driven by slave labour. Even worse, the cruel Rulers of Mars have noticed the Terran colonies on Luna, monitored our radio and television broadcasts, and are now constructing a teleportation device with which to invade and subjugate planet Earth (10–13). A rebellious slave named Liberta manages to escape to Terra using this device, and warns the Earthlings of the impending attack. Spéirling and company load up their new ship with assorted weapons of mass destruction, and effect a sweeping regime change on Mars (40–50).

The first published Spéirling adventure, *Captaen Spéirling agus an Phláinéad do Phléasc* [Captain Spéirling and the Planet That Exploded] is set in the year 2007, when Professor Ó Glarcáin discovers that the planet Mercury ("Mercurius") is about to explode, causing massive loss of life on Earth (Ó Sándair 1960a, 8). The United Nations scramble to prepare themselves for the event, constructing underground shelters and evacuating regions likely to suffer catastrophic habitat change: for example, the Sahara Desert, as well as Holland, Belgium and parts of Ireland and Australia will be drowned (16). Meanwhile, a mysterious alien race known as "The People of the Light" (who evolved within the nucleus of the star Sirius) have arrived in our planetary system to establish a colony. Upon realising that their first choice (Mercury) is about to explode, they set their sights on Terra (9–10), skipping over Venus for reasons best known to themselves. They hover above our world until the catastrophe passes, and then attempt to insert Earth into Mercury's now-vacant orbital path (29). They are foiled by Professor Ó Glarcáin and Captain Spéirling, and thereafter Earth enjoys a much sunnier climate than it did previously (30). Obviously, there are numerous logical flaws with the story, and the defeat of the invaders is accomplished via a *deus ex machina* – Spéirling develops telepathic powers just in time to read the aliens' minds and figure out what they are up to (28–9). Admirably for a children's book of the time, however, the text acknowledges that some problems are beyond the capability of responsible grown-ups to sort out. Following Mercury's destruction, millions of people are killed, including many of those who had taken refuge in government-constructed underground shelters, as Earth is battered by meteorites, sea levels rise, and wildfires and super-storms sweep the planet in a week-long conflagration (23).

More interesting than the main plot are the four short stories that follow it. In "An Deoraí" ["The Exile"], the Irish tragedy of emigration is re-enacted in the Captaen Spéirling universe: a Kerryman emigrates to the Moon to seek employment, only to discover, when he attempts to return home after fifty years, that his body has adjusted to Luna's lower gravity and artificial atmosphere, and he is too old to re-acclimatise to the environmental conditions of his homeland (31–8). "An Cailín ón gCian-Spás" ["The Girl from Deep Space"] is a vignette wherein a disoriented deep-space prospector rescues a shipwrecked Terran girl from her Robinson Crusoe-esque existence on a backwater planet (39–42). "An Spás-Fhoghlaí" ["The Space-Pirate"] concerns the escapades of an infamous raider, and the eventual eradication of space-piracy by an interplanetary military coalition (43–9). Lastly, "An Phláinéad Toirmeasctha" ["The Forbidden Planet"] is a short adventure featuring Spéirling and Ó Glarcáin, who find themselves relying on their wits to survive on a hostile planet, to which they have been sent to catch a gang of drug smugglers (50–6). The first and last of these stories are the best of the selection – "An Deoraí" works as "proper" SF (by which I mean that it takes a scientific fact as its premise, and explores that premise emotionally), while "Toirmeasctha" climaxes with a heroic feat of emergency engineering: to repair a rupture in the hull of their ship, the adventurers dip the damaged part of the vessel into one of the many pools of molten metal scattered across the planet's surface.

The final Spéirling adventure in chronological order, the second to be published, is *An Captaen Spéirling Arís* [Captain Spéirling Again], published in 1960 but set in the year 2050. Spéirling and Ó Glarcáin are sent to Venus to bring back Ross Simms, an English space pilot who has travelled to Venus without authorisation and disappeared (Ó Sándair 1960b, 4). Upon arriving on Venus, the two Irishmen discover that Simms has married the Venusian Queen, Ena, and that he is helping her to launch an assault on Earth (15–17). Spéirling and Ó Glarcáin are sent to the Venusian marshes as slaves (20), but a mere ten days later, they manage to escape, end slavery and oversee the transition to a more just and equal Venus (45–6, 52). Simms, driven mad by a Venusian prophet who tells him he will die in seven days (41), attempts to escape from Venus and ends up crashing his ship into the Sun (50–1). All's well that ends well, and the two Irishmen return home to planet Earth, where nobody will ever realise the danger our world was in. On the way home, a starry-eyed Spéirling delivers the following heartfelt speech:

> "We have a huge choice [of planets to visit], Professor," said Captain Spéirling. "There is an abundance of planets in the firmament. Aren't the works of the Creator beyond wonderful! What is that quote from the Sanctus – *pleni sunt coeli et terra majestatis gloriae tuae!* The Heavens and Earth are full of your glory! Professor, the age in which we happen to be living is wonderful, without a doubt!" (52)[5]

The appearance of a hero like Captain Spéirling in Irish literature is significant for two reasons. The first of these is not that he was an original character, but rather the exact opposite – that he is completely *unoriginal*, being nothing more than a *Gaelgeoir* Buck Rogers or Dan Dare. Indeed, the radio serial *The New Adventures of Dan Dare, Pilot of the Future*, available to Irish listeners via Radio Luxembourg from 1951 to 1956, must have been an influence on Ó Sándair's space pilot. The future world Spéirling inhabits is indebted to the genre conventions established by legendary pulp editor John W. Campbell, and to the science-fictional culture that arose in the United States following the war: the depicted world runs exclusively on nuclear power, which is capable of destroying the world but is generally seen as being worth the risk (Bould and Vint 69); the encounters with aliens conform to Campbell's editorial policy of "human exceptionalism" and demonstrate a problematic colonial attitude (72); *The Planet That Exploded* features a massive American supercomputer which can only be a version of ENIAC, "the first general purpose computer" (67), and Spéirling's sudden development of telepathy recalls the general fascination with psychic powers that pervaded pulp SF during the 1950s (70). The only original aspect to the character is the fact that he is, as evidenced in the speech quoted above, at least a practising Catholic. His quotation of the Sanctus in Latin is an ironic indication of the limits of the Irish Catholic imagination: while it was easy to postulate a future world in which Ireland conquers the solar system, it was nigh-impossible to anticipate the changes wrought by the Second Vatican Council in 1965 – one of which was the abolition of the Latin Mass. Again, this is similar to the way in which Campbell's authors seemed incapable of imagining "sufficiently radical" otherness when describing alien societies (71).

The language in which Spéirling's adventures are presented is not in itself enough to bestow originality upon them – in the time-honoured (and much derided) tradition of Anglophone pulp fiction, no logic is applied to the fact that every character speaks the language in which the text is written, including extraterrestrials who have not had any previous contact with planet Earth. Charitably interpreting the nomenclature for planets and political entities, one could hypothesise that Ó Sándair was postulating a future in which Latin has become a lingua franca, though this does not address the problem either. Thus, the *Captaen Spéirling* series could be a direct translation of any number of pulp adventures published in English.

The second reason for regarding Spéirling's appearance as significant (from the viewpoint of cultural historiography) is the time in which he appeared: Spéirling is an Irish hero for the Lemass era. His very name, "Spéirling," is a science-fictional pun communicating optimism and adventure – *speír* being the Irish for "sky." Far from being an "Earthling," with all the hardship, toil and historical baggage implied by that word (a descriptor for *a creature rooted in the soil* as much as for an inhabitant of planet Earth), the Captain is a new breed of intrepid Irishman whose natural habitat is the great beyond. His purpose is to demonstrate new kinds of Irish identity, and to make the reasonable point that there was no logical reason why the Irish should not hold the same lofty aspirations as the Americans and the British. Thus, the question of his originality is ultimately beside the point – the good Captain's principal purpose is *to speak Irish in outer space*, and thus to show that there is no objective reason why the Irish should not dare to dream of such things.

This confidence and optimism in Ireland's abilities brings a rather more unpleasant theme to the fore. In the first adventure, Spéirling promises that if Luna turns out to be populated, the Irish will treat the natives with respect, bearing in mind all the ill-treatment suffered by Ireland in the past (Ó Sándair 1961a, 11); despite this, one newspaper pundit ponders if it would be legal or moral for Ireland to colonise the Moon, or if the enterprise would prove similar to the European "scramble for Africa" (18). This notion of the possible emergence of an Irish imperialist project is referenced twice more in the text: Marco the Oriental spy stows away on the spaceship by hiding inside a chest that was supposed to contain gifts for the lunar folk – bracelets, watches and other assorted trinkets (25). Later, the Moon people's main concern surrounding the arrival of the Earthmen is that, due to their own monstrous appearance, the visitors will assume that they are an unevolved people, and enslave them (43). While everything works out for the best in the end, Ó Sándair does not address the unsavoury implication that Spéirling and Ó Glarcáin intended to travel to *terra incognita*, and trade trinkets to the natives in exchange for valuable mineral resources. Neither does he examine his narrative use of the alien Other – the humans' reaction to the aliens' appearance is one of instinctive revulsion (50), and the Irish adventurers convince the United Nations of the truth of their account by staging a freak show at an informal UN assembly in Dublin (56). In their subsequent adventures, Spéirling and Ó Glarcáin continue to take up the white man's burden, and through their Companies for the Development of Luna and Mars, regime change becomes Terra's primary export. Following the slave revolt on Venus in *An Captaen Spéirling Arís*, Queen Ena (who, up to this point, had been portrayed as a cruel and capricious despot) acknowledges that she has been too harsh with her subjects, and promises that she will institute a more humane system of labour, to which Spéirling responds, "You're learning fast, Queen [...] and that gives me great happiness" (46).[6] Like other white explorers before him, the gallant space pilot has become a teacher, and the self-evident truth of what he says undoes thousands of years of heathen folly in an instant.

Spéirling represents the economic aspirations of the Lemass era, taken to their logical extreme – an Irish Empire without any of the nasty aspects of imperialism, much as Dunsany's sapient machines in *The Last Revolution* were supposed to give humanity all the benefits of slavery, but with none of the disadvantages. This is a boys' empire, though. Spéirling has a daughter named Deirdre who insists on tagging along with Spéirling and Ó Glarcáin on their adventures to the Moon and to Mars. Since she is studying to become an astronomer, this is hardly an unreasonable request. However, Deirdre does absolutely nothing of any importance to the plot of either novel in which she appears. Her dialogue is limited to a few words of astonishment in *An Captaen Spéirling, Spás Phíolóta*, and she says so little in *Leis an gCaptaen Spéirlin Go Mars* that the reader could be forgiven for forgetting that she is present. Despite her apparently high intelligence, her active involvement in the narratives is limited to cooking breakfast for her father and lecturing him about his health, usually just before Spéirling is summoned to give his opinion on the latest geopolitical crisis.

One could argue that her half-hearted inclusion is a tiny step in the right direction, since the main female character of *A Plunge into Space* was killed for daring to intrude in an all-male genre, and since there is no mention of any female characters whatsoever in *Manannán*. The new message seemed to be that girls could tag along, so long as they kept their mouths shut and let the boys take care of business. Unfortunately, this somewhat lenient view of Ó Sándair's treatment of a main female character would be quite out of step with the historical context of the time. Even as Lemass and his cabinet were revolutionising Irish economics and society, they were doing little to combat the abominable Magdalene Laundries – institutes run by the Roman Catholic Church as punishment camps for "fallen" women.

One fascinating aspect of the Captain Spéirling series is the way in which Ó Sándair presents a near-utopian space-opera future on the one hand, and visions of an apocalypse on the other. Shortly after the uprising in Mediterra described in *Spás Phíolóta*, it is discovered that Orienta has been supplying weapons to the rebels. Occidenta responds by sending a fleet of aircraft carriers to the Mediterranean, which exacerbates the situation further (Ó Sándair 1961a, 18–19). The Orientals demand that the fleet be removed, to which the Occidentals respond that they will pull back if Orienta pledges to cease the supply of weapons. They also demand that neutral observers be sent to the region to ensure that no other territory interferes with the Mediterranean conflict. Orienta agrees to the first condition, but rejects the second, provoking a standoff that threatens to plunge the entire world into nuclear war (44–5).

That Ó Sándair seemed to predict the Cuban Missile Crisis should not come as a surprise. For all their optimism, the *Captaen Spéirling* books are shot through with the Cold War terrors of the day: the planet-wide firestorm in *An Phláinéad a Phléasc* cannot be anything other than a fever dream of nuclear exchange. The political jostling between two colossal, equally powerful and mutually antagonistic power blocs cannot be anything other than a fictionalisation of the tension between the USA and the USSR, bound to escalate to a "Hot War" eventually. The interplanetary weapons of *An Captaen Spéirling Arís* are intercontinental ballistic missiles, inflated to space-opera scale. Captaen Spéirling is not just a hero for Irish children enthralled by the wonders of the nascent space age – while he impresses upon his readers that they can pursue their wildest dreams, he also prepares them for the possibility that they might die horribly before ever getting a chance to realise those ambitions.

The Dalkey Archive

Ó Sándair was not the only Irish author to explore apocalyptic themes during the 1960s. In 1964, Flann O'Brien's *The Dalkey Archive* was published. The plot concerns physicist and theologian De Selby, expanded from a literal footnote character in the then-unpublished *The Third Policeman*, and given an uppercase "D" in the process. He has invented a substance called DMP (named after the Dublin Metropolitan Police), which is capable of removing oxygen from the atmosphere. In so doing, it re-aligns human perception to reveal the true nature of time, namely that the "passage of time" is a fallacy – there is no past or future. This enables him to converse with individuals existing outside of normal time, particularly Christian saints and philosophers in the afterlife. Saint Augustine, who speaks with a Dublin accent and disparages other philosophers, is the only one of these spirits to have a speaking role, but we are informed that De Selby has conversed with many others, including Jonah, whom De Selby describes as "a bit of a bollocks" (O'Brien 1990, 67), the Greek Fathers and John the Baptist. Through conversing with all these learned and saintly people, De Selby has come to the conclusion that life on Earth is too "abominable" to be allowed to continue, and thus he must destroy it all with a massive application of DMP. Keen to stop this is Mick Shaughnessy, an alcoholic civil servant, with the aid of his loutish drinking buddy Hackett.

Throughout the narrative, however, a second catastrophe is implied –
that if De Selby does not destroy life on Earth, he will destroy religious
faith by removing the mysteries upon which that faith depends. Indeed,
his speech on the need for the destruction of life on Earth could be
interpreted in either a religious or an anti-religious manner:

> It merits destruction. Its history and prehistory, even its present, is
> a foul record of pestilence, famine, war, devastation and misery so
> terrible and multifarious that its depth and horror are unknown
> to any one man. Rottenness is universally endemic, disease is
> paramount. The human race is finally debauched and aborted [...]
> I do not care a farthing about who made the world or what the
> grand intention was, laudable or horrible. The creation is loathsome
> and abominable, and total extinction could not be worse. (18)

In resolving to stop this, Mick comes to regard himself as more than
just the saviour of humanity:

> Did not the Saint Augustine apparition mean that all was not
> well in heaven? Had there been some sublime slip-up? If [Mick]
> now carried out his plan to rescue all God's creatures, was there
> not a sort of concomitant obligation on him to try at least to save
> the Almighty as well as his terrestrial brood from all his corrupt
> Churches – Catholic, Greek, Mohammedan, Buddhist, Hindu and
> the innumerable manifestations of the witch doctorate? (111)

"Witch doctorate," of course, has another connotation besides folk
magic. "Doctorate" calls to mind "doctoral degree," thus equating
academia, science and modern epistemology with paganism.

True to Thee 'til Death

Philip O'Leary describes a number of themes and trends in Irish-language
literature of the 1940s and 1950s which broadly reflect the dominant
cultural values of the time. The Gaeltacht, because of its value as a
notional repository of ancient (and therefore "authentic") Gaelic culture,
was fetishised as the only place where "correct Irish" was spoken
(O'Leary 2010, 46), and was described as both "the real Ireland" and a
pseudo-mystical otherworld, a "border land between ancient and modern
Ireland" (82–3). This rural bias was accompanied, rather obviously,
by denunciations of the urban (79). Another factor of this nationalist

ideology was fundamentalist Catholicism, which engendered a "frequent emphasis on the need for people to accept the will of God (*toil Dé*), no matter how incomprehensible or seemingly unjust, even cruel" (116).

As early as 1947, this ideology was mercilessly mocked in *Algoland*, in which the stereotypical repository of wisdom and knowledge, the wise old man in his cottage, utterly refutes the "authentic" past that others fetishise, hates traditional music and dance, and (horror of horrors) loves jazz. By the 1960s, the tide appears to have started turning in favour of modernity, and Seán Lemass embodied that cultural sea change. In the first years of his government, his ideology seemed to be getting results: the economy was growing, citizens had more disposable income and the slums were demolished. The writing seemed to be on the wall for Catholic tradition's dominance of society, symbolised by Lemass's dismissive attitude to the Republic's éminence grise, Archbishop McQuaid. Captaen Spéirling's primary mission was to demonstrate that Ireland had nothing to fear from joining modernity, and that one could inhabit a pulp sci-fi future and remain an Irish-speaking, Catholic nationalist. One had to accept, however, that Ireland would change from an exporter of missionaries to an exporter of modernisers, and that social and economic liberalism, rather than Catholic social teaching, would constitute the cultural paradigm of the future.

The theme of Catholicism coming under threat was more thoroughly examined in Brian Moore's 1972 novel *Catholics*. Following Vatican IV, in which private confessions are abolished and the Mass explicitly stated to be symbolic, the balance of religious power rests with the World Ecumenical Council in Amsterdam, and the Roman Catholic Church is about to enter into a historic merger with Buddhism (43–4). However, a community of monks living on an island off the coast of Kerry insist on celebrating Mass in ways that existed prior to Vatican II – they say Mass in Latin, and the chief celebrant stands with his back to the congregation (16, 46–8) – and, due to television coverage, more people attend these "traditional" Masses than the modern ones authorised by the World Ecumenical Council. Wishing to avoid embarrassment in the run-up to the merger with Buddhism, the Albanesian Order sends an American priest, Father Kinsella, to Muck Island, to get the isolated monks to toe the official line. Modernity is represented, somewhat heavy-handedly, by the helicopter that brings Kinsella to and from the isolated island. The Abbot describes the helicopter with reference to Lewis Carroll's nonsense poem "Jabberwocky," referring to it once as a "vorpal blade" and twice as a "frumious bandersnatch" (31, 96) – simultaneously a weapon and a predator, modernity is nonetheless incomprehensible and ridiculous to him. The Abbot hammers the metaphor home by explicitly referring to the vehicle as "the symbol of the century," and making plain his ambivalence to its arrival on the island "Just when I thought we'd be able to close the hundred years out, and say we missed our time" (33).

Kinsella, who sees the Catholic Church as a way to inspire revolution around the world, regards the "combination of Holy Orders and revolutionary theory" as the best means to achieve his goals (21), but in practice, faith matters little to him. The Abbot draws a distinction between the conversion of souls and the pursuit of the good of humankind, the distinction being that the latter does not require any devotion to God (40–1), and Kinsella later confirms this by stating that he believes the Mass to be symbolic (67), and ordering the monks to amend their beliefs to reflect this new position. To Kinsella, the Church's importance lies in its international structure and influence – it supplies him with the infrastructure he needs to change the world, but he does not actually believe in its teachings. He does not even look like a priest (18–20, 21), and in fact looks more like a soldier (71). He is resisted at first by the Abbot, but eventually the elderly monk's resolve fades away. Other monks are not swayed, and react angrily to the new symbolic Mass:

> "Of course [our faith depends upon miracles]! Saint Augustine said, 'I should not be a Christian but for the miracles.' And Pascal said, 'Had it not been for the miracles, there would have been no sin in not believing in Jesus Christ.' Without a miracle, Christ did not rise from His tomb and ascend into heaven. And without that, there would be no Christian Church." (82)

The tide cannot be held back, however, and the triumph of modernity is a foregone conclusion. In the end, the monks will do as they are told, and the monastery enters into "the null," the metaphysical torment of those denied the presence of God (78, 100, 101–2). Kinsella has accomplished one of the missions that De Selby relinquished – he has destroyed religious faith.[7]

It is not surprising that this theme should emerge, as since the latter half of the twentieth century, and particularly since the 1970s, fundamentalist Catholicism in Ireland had begun to wane. Finola Kennedy identifies three prime causes for this: economic development, increased access to the mass media, and Ireland's accession into the Western geopolitical sphere. Economic development reduced the population's dependence on the land as their only means of survival, increasing individual freedom (Kennedy 6) and allowing the children of rural families to pursue further education and personal prosperity (124–5).

Access to the mass media equated to a greater access to information (103), and presented the possibility of a secular system of values (5). Lastly, Ireland's accession to the EEC in 1973 exposed the country to equality legislation (114). All of these factors served to change the patterns of Irish family life, rendering much of the old Roman Catholic social teaching irrelevant in a practical sense.

This, of course, was only generally true of the Republic. North of the border, traditional cultural logics were resistant to change, conflated with identity politics and reinforced by discrimination, ethnic hatred and violence.

6. The Wrong History:
Bob Shaw, James White and the Troubles

The historian Francis T. Holohan points out that from about 1920 onwards, the valorisation of Irish rebels and martyrs was adopted as a central policy of primary education in the Free State, with the aim that children "would be imbued with a heroic notion of Irish history"; teachers were to choose history books that emphasised "important personages and striking incidents," and the teaching of history would later be constructed as a branch of religious education, wherein educators were to emphasise "that in any historical event it was the moral issue that really mattered" (Holohan 54–5). Though there was a considerable amount of public debate on the subject (O'Leary 2010, 162–3), as mentioned in Chapter 3, the emphasis in historical analysis and commemoration was ultimately on a celebration of martyrdom. Sighle Bhreathnach-Lynch outlines a striking example of this celebration of martyrdom – the changed interpretation of Oliver Shepherd's iconic statue of Cú Chulainn in the General Post Office in Dublin. The statue, which depicts the dead demigod lashed to a rock with a crow perched on his shoulder, was "originally modelled as an exhibition piece in 1914, before the Rising had taken place," but "was subsequently deemed to be the most suitable symbol of the event" (Bhreathnach-Lynch 38). By the 1960s, Lemass and others had transformed the country from a Church-dominated economic basket case to a more-or-less modern, more-or-less secular society where the citizenry had more disposable income than previous generations. Bourgeois nationalism, however, remained in place, along with its epic construction of Irish history: all that had changed was that there was now a new kind of bourgeoisie.

The other nationalist traditions had not gone away completely, meaning that the project of legitimisation would have to be an ongoing one – hence the importance of commemoration, and particularly the commemoration of the 1916 Rising. The year 1966, therefore, was especially important, as the epic construction of 1916 had to be implanted and affirmed in the minds of a generation that had no lived experience of the actual event, most notably through the arts. Art competitions were included as part of the commemoration programme, and Bhreathnach-Lynch points out that "almost all of the artists represented were too young to have had any recollections of the episode"; thus, their entries "largely reinforced the heroic construct of the Rising" (40). Roisin Higgins et al. note that as part of the cultural programme for 1966, "Children were invited to write essays, in Irish or in English, entitled 'An Easter Week veteran tells his story' or '1916–2016'" (Higgins et al. 33–4). The 1966 commemorations in Dublin opened on 10 April with a reading of the Proclamation at the GPO, followed by a military parade, and closed on 16 April with a 120-gun salute on the GPO's roof. The commemoration week included broadcasts on the lives of the various revolutionaries involved, and de Valera (himself one of the 1916 combatants), now President, closed the week with a final address to the nation, calling for a United Ireland and the transfer of political power over Northern Ireland from Westminster to Dublin. Then-Taoiseach Seán Lemass, by contrast, was keen to use the fiftieth anniversary to foster economic patriotism, by impressing upon young people the notion that they could best honour the 1916 martyrs by purchasing Irish goods and refraining from littering. Neither strategy worked, because on the whole, the young people targeted by these commemorative efforts felt a greater connection to American and British popular culture than they did to either the heroic myth of 1916 or the economic patriotism preached by Lemass (34). Understandably, given the militaristic tone of the proceedings, the 1966 commemoration was interpreted somewhat differently in Northern Ireland, where the run-up to the event provoked unionist fears of a widespread resurgence in IRA activity.

As discussed in Chapter 2, unionism and Irish Protestantism have usually been described as comprising a "siege culture," and the popular literature of the nineteenth century demonstrates that this anxiety was steadily intensifying. The Ascendancy gothic had for generations warned of annihilation should the barricades fall, and the future-war narratives advised Irish Protestants to be ready to defend themselves and their communities, rather than relying on the forces of the Crown for protection. There was a growing perception that Westminster was indifferent to the concerns of Ulster unionists, and that a moment's inattention or acquiescence on Parliament's part would lead to total devastation.

In January 1913, Asquith's Home Rule Bill was passed by 367 votes to 257 on its third reading, bringing the latter anxiety to life. In response, the Ulster Volunteer Force (UVF) was formed, following the typical Ulster future-war narrative pattern to the letter. With the Government of Ireland Act 1920, Ireland was partitioned and Home Rule was introduced in both North and South. Nationalist paramilitaries, however, continued fighting until Southern Ireland officially became the Free State in 1922 – as the future-war stories had predicted, the British had given an inch, and the Irish had taken a mile. Shortly after this, the Free State descended into civil war – another prediction that came true – and the 1937 Constitution of Ireland contained inflammatory clauses, such as Articles 2 and 3 (which claimed Dáil jurisdiction over the entire island) and Article 44, which acknowledged the "special position" of the Catholic Church. Unionist siege paranoia had been vindicated in several ways, reaffirming its centrality to the social organisation of the North.

The first UVF murder took place in 1966: the victim was a Protestant woman incorrectly identified as a "Taig," because she happened to be living in a house adjoining a Catholic-owned off-licence (Taylor 40). In the same year, the Soviet *Venera 3* probe crash-landed on Venus, becoming the first spacecraft to reach another planet, but failing to return any data. This was merely a side-show to the main event, as the USA and the USSR started to compete for the Moon: the Soviets carried out a soft landing on the lunar surface on 3 February with *Luna 9*, and in March *Luna 10* became the first spacecraft to orbit our planet's main satellite; these moves were matched by the USA on 2 June, when *Surveyor 1* carried out a soft landing, and on 14 August, when *Lunar Orbiter 1* trumped *Luna 10* by relaying the first pictures of Earth taken from the Moon's distance. This was neither the first nor the last time that such a disheartening comparison could be made between the lived experience of Northern Irish citizens and the images that had come to characterise the era in which they lived.

To anyone whose imagination was directed upwards into the stars, this should have been an exhilarating time to live through. As Bould and Vint note, SF had been "a significant and recognisable feature of the [Western] cultural landscape" since the 1930s (Bould and Vint 59), and its imagery started to influence all kinds of popular art and design, from fashion to furniture to popular music to architecture (103–4). Now, not only had it been demonstrated that human beings could leave the planet on which they had evolved, but international politics framed each achievement as a hotly contested prize in a race between two mutually hostile superpowers. The dreams of pulp-era SF were starting to come true, and the narrative of a "race" between Western astronaut and Soviet cosmonaut ensured that the old stories lost none of their drama and excitement. The problem was that the presentation of the "space age" assumed that when the future arrived, it would be evenly distributed and politically innocent – an impossible dream given that history itself, which encompasses the potentiality of the future, also provides the ideological foundation for political legitimacy. With its jingoism, exorbitant cost and subliminal ideology of manifest destiny, space exploration was no more politically neutral than the bizarre display of military triumphalism commemorating the nationalist "blood sacrifice" of 1916, or the annual Orange Order marches through Catholic neighbourhoods on 12 July.

The American poet Gil Scott Heron (1949–2011) articulated this frustration in "Whitey on the Moon," in which the narrator, a working-class black American, juxtaposes the reality of his day-to-day existence with the Moon landing: he cannot afford to pay for medical treatment for his sister, who has contracted an infection after being bitten by a rat; most of his income is taken by taxes and rent, though his home has no electricity or running water; drugs are destroying his neighbourhood; and the price of food is increasing. In the meantime, society is supposed to be rejoicing, because "Whitey's on the Moon" (Heron). What was being touted as a new techno-utopian era for humanity was in reality the preserve of a global minority. Theirs was the history that would continue into the future and culminate in a space-opera future, and it was to this projected future-history – later satirised by William Gibson as "The Gernsback Continuum," a dream-world of food pills and colossal flying machines, populated exclusively by Aryans (Gibson 1988) – that the lived experiences of most of Earth's inhabitants were compared and found wanting.

Northern Ireland was just one of the many places that ended up with the "wrong history." To outsiders, the reasons for the conflict often appeared opaque, and outside commentators were prone to oversimplification.[1] As former UVF member Billy Mitchell puts it: "Someone didn't fly over Northern Ireland and drop some sort of 'loony gas' and suddenly people woke up the next morning as killers [...] Conditions were created in this country whereby people did things they shouldn't have done" (Taylor 46).

In 1964, the Campaign for Social Justice collected evidence of sectarian discrimination across Northern Ireland, including gerrymandering and discrimination in employment and housing (Coogan 27–9). There was also a growing perception of a "Protestant East" versus a "Catholic West," with the east taking the lion's share of government investment. "Catholic" railways, such as the lines to Derry, Newry and much of Fermanagh and Tyrone, were taken out of service. Peculiarities in town planning (such as inadequate provision for the construction of Catholic primary schools) were interpreted by Catholics as "fortress unionism" – a bid to discourage Catholics from living and working in the province's urban centres – and there was also discrimination in higher education, most notably in one incident where Coleraine (in the

"Protestant East") was chosen as the site for a new university, at a time when Derry (which had four times Coleraine's population) was hoping for funds to expand its already existing third-level facilities (41–3).

In 1967, NICRA (Northern Ireland Civil Rights Association) was formed to tackle this discrimination, but in campaigning for an end to discrimination against Catholics, the organisation unintentionally divided Ulster's working classes. Because they saw no difference between their own living conditions and those of their Catholic neighbours, working-class Protestants could not conceive of the organisation as anything other than an IRA front, and NICRA's very existence exacerbated the growing ill feeling between the communities:

> Not only was I *not* a first-class citizen, I remember the absolute sense of indignation and outrage whenever I was accused of being one. There was this explicit inference [sic] to Catholics being second-class citizens and therefore this inference that I was in some way depriving them of their rights. (Taylor 50)[2]

Jack Lynch, who had succeeded Seán Lemass as Taoiseach of the Republic in 1966, did not help matters by giving a speech, written for him by the cabinet as a whole, decrying the Northern Irish situation and containing the inflammatory phrase "We cannot stand idly by" (Coogan 99). Though the speech was clearly meant to mollify the government's political base, it intensified unionist fears of an attempted Republican invasion, and the field hospitals/refugee camps established along the border were seen as "staging posts" for that invasion (Taylor 66–7). Shortly afterwards, in 1970, unionists' suspicions that the southern government was colluding with the IRA were confirmed, when Charles Haughey (then Minister for Finance) and Neil Blaney (Minister for Agriculture and Fisheries) were sacked from Lynch's Dáil following the discovery of their involvement in a plot to smuggle arms into Northern Ireland, and were later acquitted (Taylor 76). Blaney, notes Martin Dillon, always maintained that the border camps *were* in fact invasion staging posts, and even claimed that the invasion of the North was to be undertaken with the tacit approval of the British government – the invasion would have gone ahead, Blaney said, had Lynch not got "cold feet" when the time came to strike (Dillon 7).

This was the social and political background against which "The Troubles" unfolded, while elsewhere the mass media were heralding the dawn of a glorious new era of human history.

In 1969, the year of the Burntollet Riot, the loyalist "false flag" attacks on Belfast's electricity supply and water system, the "Battle of the

Bogside" and the first ever deployment of the British army in Northern Ireland, the burning of Catholic homes in Belfast, and the death of the first police officer to be killed in the Troubles, the rest of the Western world was watching in awe as Neil Armstrong, Buzz Aldrin and Michael Collins landed on the Moon. Later in the same year, *Mariner 6* and *Mariner 7* relayed the first detailed pictures of the surface of Mars. The closest Northern Ireland got that year to an acknowledgement that outer space even existed was a meteorite strike on the RUC armoury on 26 April.

Complicated by identities and histories that did not match the preferred narratives of the Republic, the United Kingdom or the "Gernsback Continuum," and mired in what politician John Hume once described as "the politics of the latest atrocity," the history of the Troubles is grotesque, upsetting and tragic. Reacting against this tragic context, two Northern Irish authors produced some of the most highly regarded SF of the twentieth century.

James White (1928–1999) and Bob Shaw (1931–1996) both grew up in Belfast, and entered their teenage years during World War II, at a time when American forces were using the city as a stop-off point on the way to the European front. The American troops sold their used magazines to second-hand stalls in Smithfield Market, giving youngsters such as White and Shaw access to a literary field which would have a profound effect on both of them. In 1947, White founded Irish Fandom with his friend Walt Willis, and Shaw joined this group in 1950 (Maume 195). SF thus forged friendships that spanned the cultural divide.

White and Shaw wrote SF narratives that, on the surface, appeared to be straightforward adventure stories in the purest pulp mode, but beneath this veneer lie some of the genre's most profound meditations on violence, history, peace, prejudice and utopia.

James White

White had always wanted to become a doctor, but "had to go out to work" instead of completing his education. He would later say that this was probably for the best, describing himself as having "five not particularly dextrous thumbs" on each hand (White 1977, 11–12). He worked as a tailor for twenty-two years, eventually becoming apprentice manager of the Belfast Co-operative, before going on to work in public relations for Shorts aerospace factory (Maume 197). Though this varied work experience occasionally informs particular short works, the vast majority of White's output takes the field of medical science as its theme.

White's most famous contribution to SF literature is his *Sector General* series, set in a 384-level multi-species hospital station, floating in outer space somewhere on the Galactic Rim. The doctors and nurses, as well as the patients, are drawn from every intelligent star-faring species in known space.

Hospital Station (1962), the first entry in the series, is a "fix-up" from a handful of short stories, and the disjointed impression this produces in the narrative has the effect of conveying the atmosphere of a busy emergency ward – no sooner is one crisis dealt with than another arises. The main character is the simpatico Conway, who progresses from intern to senior physician over the course of the book, thanks to his knack for diagnosing and treating extraterrestrial ailments that baffle his fellow doctors. Each section deals with some sort of medical puzzle which must be solved to save the life of an alien patient, and the crises presented range from treating an alien child with a lethal case of measles ("Hospital Station", 17–50) to tracking down a hungry and psychotic shape-shifter in the hospital's nursery ward (132–58). The stories are entertaining in themselves, but much more interesting is the way in which White takes one of SF's most recognisable characteristics – the capacity to figure an absolute, alien Other – and pursues it to an extent that had rarely been seen in space opera before.

White's galactic civilisation differs from those of other space operas in that the aliens on parade here are all fundamentally decent, despite their physical, cultural and psychological differences. This demonstrates the influence of the American pulp author E.E. "Doc" Smith, whose writing demonstrated to White that aliens could be good as well as evil (Maume 195), but it is also a reflection of White's own attitudes to the place in which he was living:

> The stories that I write are very unlikely to happen. It's just that Northern Ireland is a very frustrating and dangerous and tragic place. The people are very nice, regardless of whether they're Protestants or Catholics or whatever. But it's these poisonous few, who keep it all boiling over and won't allow anybody to settle. Most of the stories, I write about the sort of characters and the sort of world that I would like to live in. I'm trying to escape from reality. (White 2002)

The multi-species set-up provides the over-arching conflict of the entire series: the episodic treatment of doctor versus disease is ultimately of secondary importance to the never-ending war against xenophobia. The only way a multi-species environment can function is if the inhabitants are utterly free of any kind of prejudice, though this is sometimes a difficult requirement to fulfil:

> Given even the highest qualities of tolerance and mutual respect, there were still occasions when inter-racial friction occurred in the hospital. Potentially dangerous situations arose through ignorance or misunderstanding, or a being could develop xenophobia to a degree which affected its professional efficiency, mental stability, or both. An Earth-human doctor, for instance, who had a subconscious fear of spiders would not be able to bring to bear on a Cinrusskin patient the proper degree of clinical detachment necessary for its treatment. ("Star Surgeon," 242)

The "absent paradigm" of a multi-species society, such as the Sector General Hospital, is the web of relations between "natural powers" and "species powers," as described by Karl Marx, and later analysed in depth by Bertell Ollman. Natural powers (also referred to as "animal functions" and "physical needs") are "the processes that living creatures undergo and the actions they undertake in order to stay alive" (Ollman 77), and are coupled with impulses through which they are fulfilled – "Taking eating as a natural power, man's impulses which drive him to eat are clear enough: he is hungry" (78). Species powers, on the other hand, are the qualities that characterise us as sentient beings – various "senses" that form our self-consciousness:

> Mutual recognition, the act of seeing oneself in others, extends each individual's awareness to cover the whole human race [...] Man is also conscious of having a past, which is the record of his successes and failures in attaining these aims, and of the possibilities which constitute his future [...] In short, man is a species being because he knows what only man can know, namely that he is the species being, man. (82)

Science fiction's capacity to figure an absolute Other presents us with characters whose "natural" and "species" powers may be different (or unnervingly similar) to human ones, with strange impulses appropriate to them. Essentially, it signals "otherness" via the construction of biological difference. Few twentieth-century SF authors foreground the theme as obviously as White does, via Sector General's species-classification system, and in the very layout of the hospital, which has specific wards with particular environmental settings to accommodate every possible combination of powers and needs.

Michael Hardt and Antonio Negri maintain that "The construction of an absolute racial difference is the essential ground for the conception of a homogenous national identity" (Hardt and Negri 103), "a necessary, eternal, and immutable rift in the order of being" (191). In SF, this "absolute racial difference" does not need to be *constructed*, because it actually *exists*. Adam Roberts argues that this generic potential "allows for a more complex and sophisticated response to the dynamics of difference" (Roberts 2000, 118), but it is still problematic. As Bould points out:

> [The] satirical SF tale in which the alien or android is the subject of prejudice, whatever its merits, also avoids direct engagement with the realities of racialized hierarchies and oppressions [...] And by presenting racism as an insanity that burned itself out, or as the obvious folly of the ignorant and impoverished who would be left behind by the genre's brave new futures, SF avoids confronting the structures of racism and its own complicity in them. (Bould 179–80)

To merely substitute androids or aliens for oppressed human groups, in other words, is to deny the validity of their respective, *specific* histories of oppression by universalising them. Such an approach also squanders the potential of a theoretical zone where the ideology of "a necessary, eternal, and immutable" biological difference is a matter of fact. While this can give the author *carte blanche* to indulge in biological essentialism (as in the space opera tradition of describing entire species with a single adjective – "warlike," "honourable," "treacherous," and so on), little has been made of the anti-racist potential this position offers: the ability to conceive of a world where the racist dogma of essential bodily differences is actually *true*, and then demonstrate that even these extreme differences are meaningless in a social context.

One of the ways in which White's doctors dismiss extreme biological difference as a valid excuse for xenophobia is the use of "educator tapes." In the multi-species environment of the hospital, it is taken for granted that a doctor will know more about treating its own species than any other-species colleague would. However, it is not always possible to match doctors to same-species patients, and allowing a skilled surgeon to specialise in just one species is considered a waste of resources. The "educator tapes" are memory grafts from renowned healers, containing all the knowledge they have accrued throughout their medical training and real-world experience.

One major side effect of the educator tapes is that they do not merely transfer medical knowledge. They also transfer the donor's personality, including their memories, phobias, daydreams, nightmares, sexual fantasies, secrets, longings, and, in a very real sense, the donor's culture, history and heritage (White 1998, 79). The transfer can be traumatic, and for this reason only senior diagnosticians are allowed to retain their memory grafts, carrying up to five separate cultures in their heads permanently, in effect transforming themselves into multiple other creatures and further undermining the ideology of absolute difference. The most mundane effect of this voluntary multiple-personality disorder is that these diagnosticians find lunchtime to be something of an ordeal:

> "I'm just myself today," said Prilicla in answer to Conway's question. "The usual, if you please."
> Conway dialled for the usual, which was a triple helping of Earth-type spaghetti, then looked at Mannon.
> "I've an FROB *and* an MSVK beastie riding me," the other senior said gruffly. "Hudlars aren't pernickety about food, but those blasted MSVKs are offended by anything which doesn't look like birdseed! Just get me something nutritious, but don't tell me what it is and put it in about three sandwiches so's I won't see what it is ..."
> ("Major Operation," 374)

Ollman's observation that the condition of "species being" involves an awareness of the past and the future has special significance for White's fictional world: the educator tapes, in transferring memories and identities, by necessity also transfer species being. By taking on another people's history, one becomes one of them, and in the Sector General Hospital, there are thousands of different histories. As a means to inter-group communication and cooperation, these histories are vital to the maintenance of a multicultural work environment, but ultimately no one history is more important than any other.

The battle against xenophobia with the *Sector General* series is polarised around two particular characters: the gentle Cinrusskin surgeon known as Prilicla and the caustic Earth-human psychiatrist, O'Mara.

Prilicla, from a planet whose gravity is low enough to have allowed arthropods to evolve into the dominant species, is repeatedly described as the most genial member of the Sector General medical staff. Most of the hospital's other inhabitants refer to him as "little friend," despite the fact that he resembles nothing so much as a four-foot-tall house spider with wings. The other doctors' fondness for him is partly due to his physical frailty, but he is also regarded with affection because of the unique talent he brings to the operating theatre: he is an "empath," a creature with a near-psychic ability to read the emotional states of those around him. However, this talent is involuntary. Prilicla cannot switch it off, and thus he is constantly tuned in to the "emotional radiation" being emitted by everyone in his immediate vicinity, something that can have serious negative effects on him. Thus, he seeks to become friends with everyone he meets, to ensure that he is surrounded by positive emotions. Conway at one point remarks that this has made Prilicla the greatest liar in the entire hospital ("Major Operation," 370–1).

The character of O'Mara is Prilicla's polar opposite. As the Chief Psychiatrist of the hospital, his prime duty is to ruthlessly weed out prejudice and conceit to ensure the hospital's stability, and he does not care who he frightens or offends in the process: his oft-repeated motto is "My job is to *shrink* heads, not swell them." In direct contrast to Prilicla, who lies to everyone so as not to hurt their feelings, O'Mara adopts an approach of caustic honesty and interrogation, which earns him frequent comparisons to the Inquisition and its alien counterparts ("Hospital Station," 93).

The contrast between Prilicla and O'Mara, while they are both "secondary" characters, highlights an important underlying theme in White's writing, one which can be teased out through an analysis of one of his darker works, *Underkill*, which re-examines Sector General's "doctors in space" theme with such a grim, brutal and cynical tone that several publishers in the USA rejected it "because it was not a 'real' James White novel" (Andrews).

Following a great "Powerdown," society's electricity is provided by "power-walkers" on treadmills (White 1979, 32–4) and privately owned vehicles are rare (12), but senior-level doctors can apply for a horse (8). Violence and corporal punishment are taken for granted in schools (27–8), and most of the population lives in overcrowded apartment blocks. The story follows the Malcolms, a husband-and-wife team of doctors working in the unnamed city's hospital, who uncover a conspiracy involving two mysterious groups, the "Lukes" and "Johns," who are carrying out paramilitary actions that maximise civilian casualties. Many of the paramilitaries involved, as well as some politically influential men, are later revealed to be clones, and the mysterious revolutionary "parent group" of the Lukes and Johns turns out to be an extraterrestrial species: the Trennechorans, galactic medics who have diagnosed humanity and the planet Earth with a deadly disease common to intelligent species (a combination of inherited hatred and overpopulation).

It transpires that the Lukes and Johns are differentiated by their treatment philosophies, with the Johns favouring a "medical" cure and the Lukes more inclined to "surgery." Since the late sixteenth century, these quarrelling factions have been working at cross-purposes on

Earth, each taking their turn to interfere in human history (139–42). The only hope left for humanity's recovery is a radical and invasive surgery – in effect, the extermination of a quarter of the planet's population. The Lukes regard this procedure in a matter-of-fact manner, even having polite arguments as to which is "tidier," earthquakes or "urban operations" (127), and the Malcolms, because they side with neither faction, are press-ganged into helping with the planetary genocide (132).

White admitted that the urban milieu of *Underkill* "was obviously an expanded Belfast" (White 2002), and this authorial intent is hard to miss – for one thing, the Luke faction initially goes undetected by the security forces because vocal references to it are misinterpreted as the word "look" (White 1979, 77), a joke that depends on the phonetic spelling of a Northern Irish accent. There are also the power-walkers: if "power" is read to signify *political* power rather than electricity, "power-walking" might well equate to marching, a recurring and divisive issue in Northern Irish politics. Most obvious is the self-righteousness of the aliens and their clone servants, combined with their horrific strategies, which provokes a familiar outburst from an unnamed doctor doing her best to help the wounded:

> You, and your people, are responsible for the deaths and suffering of other human beings who know nothing of your glorious cause and who were certainly not willing to die for it. They simply wanted to make the best of things as are, and live. Yet you are killing innocent people for their own good, you say, and seem to expect understanding and forgiveness for doing so. (157)

Despite the misgivings of White's American publishers, *Underkill* is more similar to the Sector General series than one might think – I would even argue that *Underkill* presents the world of Sector General *in extremis*, since both illustrate a tendency on White's part to ignore possible historical-materialist causes for ethnic conflict, as pointed out by Patrick Maume: "White's emphasis on the irrationality of xenophobic prejudice towards the Other makes him implicitly dismiss the possibility of genuine ideological conflict over the ordering of society and equate discontent with mental disease" (Maume 209).

As outlined at the start of this chapter, in Northern Ireland there were multiple causes for such a conflict, and the Troubles were not the consequence of mental disease or "loony gas." It seems extraordinary that White, an inhabitant of Belfast during the early days of the Troubles, should exhibit such an apparently un-nuanced understanding of the conflict. In truth, this tendency is understandable within the context of White's personal philosophy.

Underkill's Luke and John factions represent either side of the same carrot-and-stick dynamic present in the Sector General novels, where it is represented by Prilicla and O'Mara – one force relies on persuasion and the other on belligerence, in pursuit of the same end. That end, even in *Underkill*, is the cessation of violence and hatred, and it seems that diplomacy, as favoured by the Johns and Prilicla, necessitates dishonesty and is unfortunately doomed to fail. To get results, one needs the Lukes, or at least an O'Mara. This attitude is derived from White's sympathy for the medical profession. His wife Margaret was an intensive care nurse at the height of the Troubles, and "doctors and nurses do not admire the heroes who are causing so much medical repair work for them" (White 2002). Honesty, and occasionally belligerence, are required to deal with "heroes" of this calibre. The material causes of violence, and the ideologies that excuse it, are unimportant because only the results are of any consequence – death, maimed bodies and shattered minds.

This heightened awareness of the human cost of conflict appears to have contributed to something a shade more disturbing, an apparent wish for the kind of omnipotent, neutral arbiter embodied in the pitch for his short story "The Scavengers": "Sometimes a civilization has got to be rescued – whether it wants to or not!" (Andrews 2002). Science fiction allows for the depiction of all-powerful, infallible outsiders. In *Underkill*, this role is obviously filled by the Trennechorans, but the Sector General series has its own equivalent, the unnervingly titled Monitor Corps, a military force that watches everyone (in fact, the fearsome O'Mara is not a doctor in the strictest sense, but a major in this very force). As outlined in a conversation between a Monitor and young Doctor Conway, the Corps' job is to simultaneously *protect* the citizens of the Federation and *allow* them freedom of action, as far as is practicable. This is particularly true in the case of the "Normals," individuals who want nothing to do with the Federation, who are restricted to reservations where they are allowed to do whatever they want, including kill each other ("Hospital Station," 73). They also have a faintly utilitarian view of the middle classes:

> "[Your] trouble is that you, and your whole social group, are a protected species [...] Shielded from the crudities of present-day life. From your social strata – on all the worlds of the Union, not just on Earth – come practically all the great artists, musicians and professional men. Most of you live out your lives in ignorance of the fact that you are protected, that you are insulated from childhood

against the grosser realities of our interstellar so-called civilization [...] You are allowed this luxury in the hope that from it may come a philosophy that may one day make every being in the Galaxy truly civilized, truly good." (73)

The young Doctor Conway, who is on the receiving end of this stern, paternal lecture, can only react meekly because the Monitor (who is younger than he is) "seemed to possess *authority* somehow" (72). In White's fictional universe, the military has the status of a long-suffering parent to an often ill-behaved civil society.

This is not to paint White as a militarist or an admirer of authoritarianism – as he himself explained, "I've never gone in for the old type of square-jawed hero who blasts aliens out of the sky and never thinks about the down side of war" (White 2002) – but given the context of the Troubles, the structure of his Federation is perfectly understandable. In the midst of an intractable ethnic conflict, it is only logical that in his fiction, White should create an impartial security force with the requisite power to end it – or to segregate the "poisonous few" on either side who refuse to compromise or listen to reason. It is indicative of White's optimism that the omnipotent Monitor Corps never abuses or fully asserts its power, even though the Federation is not yet "truly civilized." His friend Bob Shaw, by contrast, had much less faith in the impartiality of the powerful.

Bob Shaw

Robert Shaw, known to all as "Bob" and to his friends within SF fandom as "BoSh," was first exposed to SF, according to his own estimation, at around the age of eleven, when he came across a short story by the Canadian author A.E. van Vogt, the effects of which were "much more devastating than LSD and much longer lasting" (Stableford 1995a, 25–6). Brian Stableford points to the tension between the van Vogtian thrills of SF and "the dour culture of the Protestant Ethic" as the foundation of Shaw's worldview and a central element of his work: Shaw's heroes "very frequently find themselves caught between the irreconcilable demands of domesticity and ambition," and the domestic sphere is "almost always portrayed as bleak, overdemanding and hurtful" (26). Like White, Shaw was a self-described "escapist," but Shaw's opinion of "escapism" inverts the usual arguments about genre fiction's intellectually bankrupt reputation. While the "realists" live in a world where the mundane artefacts of modern life are not arbitrary social arrangements but laws of nature, "the science fiction buff," Shaw argues, understands that "all these things are merely local phenomena of a very temporary nature" (27).

Shaw's heroes are strongly reminiscent of the protagonists of American pulp SF, most notably in that regardless of their profession (most of them are either pilots or engineers), they are capable of holding their own in a fight. They perceive right and wrong as keenly as White's protagonists do, but they differ in that they more often see direct, sometimes violent action as necessary to the pursuit of a greater good. Despite this, Stableford reads these characters as strangely impotent in their personal lives: Shaw's heroes, he says, "find it easier to save the world than to save themselves" (29). This is a shrewd analysis, to which I would add that Shaw's heroes, rather than seeking adventure, all start out with just one ambition in life: to be left alone. In this respect, the quintessential Shaw protagonist is Gilbert Snook, the hero of *A Wreath of Stars*, who considers himself "the human neutrino, the uncommitted particle of humanity" (Shaw 2000b, 23), passing through the world without having any effect on it.

Shaw repeatedly demonstrates, however, that this desire is unattainable. In fact, that very desire is bound to draw the attention of the bullies who have seized control of civil society. The villains of Shaw's novels are always in a position of political power or authority – demagogues, politicians, gang leaders, military commanders, the heads of multinational corporations, and autocrats. Having become aware of the hero's existence, these monsters then proceed to interfere with his life, in many cases for no reason other than their own insane amusement.

This illustrates the principal difference between Shaw's work and White's. Though his protagonists are usually competent fighters, Shaw, like White, sees conflict as morally bankrupt. Unfortunately, unlike White, he also seems to regard it as the natural state of humankind, since the most dangerous members of our species usually end up with the power of life and death over it. Like George Bernard Shaw's "Yahoo," Bob Shaw's unaccountable villains always show up at just the wrong moment, and they have the power to destroy everything – G.B. Shaw was concerned that his blandly destructive nonentities would "wreck the Commonwealth," while Bob Shaw's creations can wreck entire planets. Thus, not only is conflict futile, but regrettably, so are all attempts to prevent it. Shaw apparently admires White's absolute pacifism but does not see how it could possibly work, since an all-powerful Monitor Corps is required to maintain it, and in Shaw's opinion, power always corrupts. For this reason, the villains of Shaw's novels are more memorable than the protagonists. A case in point is Prince Leddravohr, the villain of *The Ragged Astronauts*, first volume of the "Land Trilogy."[3]

The Land Trilogy is set in a universe parallel to our own, where the laws of physics work differently to those of our world – physical constants are changed to serve the story, or "whatever it needs to be to make my solar system work" (Langford 1996). This is made apparent in a brief scene where the reader is told that pi is a perfectly even 3, rather than 3.14 (Shaw 1987, 131–2). The precise setting is a planet known as Land, locked into a bizarre twin orbit around its parent star with a near-identical planet referred to as Overland – the two planets are so close to each other that their atmospheres partially overlap.

At the beginning of *The Ragged Astronauts*, the feudalistic society of Land is poised on the brink of ecological disaster: the ptertha, a kind of spherical, toxic airborne jellyfish, are multiplying as a direct consequence of deforestation, and whereas the "globes" were previously seen as mindless invertebrates, they now seem to be actively hunting people. The ecosystem is irreparably broken, and there is only one course of action left to the planet's human inhabitants: they have to escape to the empty planet of Overland, through outer space by hot-air balloon.

The hero is Toller Maraquine, a man of action born into Land's scientist/engineering caste. Following the murder of his genius half-brother, Toller finds himself in charge of the mass-migration project, having already made a deadly enemy in Prince Leddravohr – and it is Leddravohr's malign presence that provides most of the novel's drama.

The Prince is an irredeemable villain – egomaniacal, sadistic and insane. Early in the narrative, he takes a minor breach of protocol by Toller as a personal insult, and builds his annoyance into a vendetta that he pursues almost as a kind of hobby, raping Toller's pregnant sister-in-law (144–7) and later murdering Toller's half-brother Lain by leaving him stranded in a ptertha-infested wilderness (228–32). Eventually, his bloodlust is visited upon the civilian population, in an extended scene where he orders the soldiers under his command to attack an unarmed crowd; through the incident, the Prince is oddly detached from what is happening, as though going through an out-of-body experience (236–40). While no explicit comparisons are ever made in the text, it is difficult not to see resonances between this particular passage and certain events in Northern Irish history.

Shaw's fondness for flamboyant villains occasionally tends towards pantomime. Colonel Freeborn, the main antagonist of *A Wreath of Stars*, has a "cup-shaped" dent in one side of his skull, and is in the habit of suggestively resting the head of his cane in this cavity to subtly threaten others (Shaw 2000b, 31, 45–7). Elizabeth Lindstrom, the primary antagonist of *Orbitsville*, is described in terms that present her as a cross between Queen Elizabeth I and a giant spider (Shaw 2000a,

6, 27, 75). "Jaycee," the insane hippy cultist of *The Shadow of Heaven*, resembles nothing so much as an exaggerated Charles Manson. There are many other examples: if Shaw's villains are not always grotesque in appearance, they usually harbour absurd ambitions. This level of malevolence may seem almost cartoonish on paper, but it is a necessary pre-condition for the exploration of other important themes, such as that of sight, or altered vision.

Shaw himself had a lifelong terror of losing his sight, and this fear invigorated much of his work.[4] In Shaw's work, altered vision is often used as the most potent metaphor for a profound paradigm shift: a change or discovery beyond human control that challenges the status quo. Shaw's most poignant work, *Other Days, Other Eyes* (1972), concerns Alban Garrod, a scientist working in the aerospace industry, who becomes a millionaire when he accidentally invents "slow glass." Slow glass, also known as "retardite," is a type of glass that light takes years to penetrate, in essence recording anything that occurs in front of it. Garrod soon finds himself swept up in a number of different political intrigues, as his invention slowly but surely turns planet Earth into a giant panopticon, though Garrod himself is more preoccupied with escaping his loveless marriage.

The main narrative is split up by "sidelights," vignettes demonstrating how the invention of slow glass has irrevocably altered human existence. The first of these sidelights is the short story from which the novel was expanded, "The Light of Other Days," which focuses on a bickering couple's visit to a slow glass "farm" in the Scottish Highlands – having invested in a "scenedow," the couple discover that the woman and child seen in the windows of a cottage have in fact been dead for seven years (Shaw 1974, 25–34). The second sidelight examines the impact of slow glass upon the criminal justice system, describing the inner torment of a judge who, having sentenced a man to death five years earlier, awaits the emergence of the truth from a slow glass window that recorded the crime (47–61). The third demonstrates an inhumane application of the substance, as an English pilot, shot down over China, is fitted with crude slow glass contact lenses which force him to witness Western atrocities committed in Asia, such as the My Lai Massacre (94–101). Like the ghosts of the gothic tradition, slow glass symbolises a past that will not go away, offering the potential for both escapism and entrapment. Both arise when Garrod's possessive wife, who has been blinded in an accident at Garrod's laboratory, acquires a set of slow glass contact lenses that effectively allow her to see again, albeit through a recorded view of the previous day. Taking advantage of her husband's guilt about the accident, Esther manipulates him into staying with her and living out an unchanging daily routine which will allow her to live in the past (107–8).

In Shaw's novels, altered sight is just one way in which society is irrevocably altered by a single, massive paradigm shift. The effect of these paradigm shifts is to make possible "a way out" of the world: in the Land Trilogy, ecological disaster forces a moribund feudal society to seriously consider space flight; in *Other Days, Other Eyes*, the discovery of slow glass spawns a new popular culture where people seek to escape into the past; the *Orbitsville* sequence posits a new world of such incredible size that territorial conflict becomes inconceivable: "five billion Earths" (Shaw 2000a, 65).

One could interpret these world-altering calls to adventure, as Stableford does, as imagined flights from the domestic sphere, an escape from the home and "the dullness of mundanity" (Stableford 1995a, 27) and familial responsibility. There are, however, other ways to interpret the concept of "home," which can expand beyond the domestic sphere to encompass the town, nation or planet, the latter obviously commonplace in SF texts, where almost every character has a "homeworld." On the other side of the equation, another cognate of "escape" is emigration. The "escapist" can also be a refugee.

Emigration in science-fictional terms is an attractive proposition when one's hometown has become a warzone, as it presents the possibility of a truly fresh start: a new home on a world that has no history at all. Migration to the virgin plains of Overland or Orbitsville signifies a totalising break with the histories that oblige people to fight each other. This is significant in Shaw's case because he and his family emigrated from Northern Ireland in the 1970s, and settled in the town of Ulverston in the north-western English county of Cumbria – almost directly opposite Belfast on the other side of the Irish Sea – specifically because he and his wife wanted to ensure that their children would not become embroiled in the Troubles (Priest 2010). This desire to begin a new life in a new place, and to begin a new history, is coupled with a dread of contaminating one's new home with the history of the place one has left behind.

Shaw's antagonistic relationship to history is apparent in the villains of his novels, all unaccountable authority figures who use their power to bully the powerless. In the cases of Leddravohr and Liz Lindstrom, this power is drawn directly from history – the former is a prince in a hereditary monarchy, the latter the hereditary "president" of an all-powerful corporation. Not only did the corrupt President Ogilvie and vicious Colonel Freeborn from *A Wreath of Stars* come to power in a nationalist revolution, but they adhere to a bizarre ideology that seems nostalgic for Africa's colonial history, scorning Swahili names in favour of "Anglian" ones (Shaw 2000b, 28).

The villains are further defined by their desire to change the utopias in which the protagonists have taken shelter: Lindstrom plans the "exploitation and development" of Orbitsville (Shaw 2000a, 76). *The Shadow of Heaven*'s Jaycee plans to hijack one of the US government's "International Land Expansions" – hovering islands containing the last fertile soil left in the world – and fly it to the Moon (Shaw 1969, 152–5). Utopias are *found*, not created, and while the protagonists adapt themselves to suit their new environment, the antagonists try to adapt new worlds to suit themselves – the better to continue the histories from which they have benefited. Here, we can see odd parallels between the desires of the present-day refugee and the daydreams of the frustrated nineteenth-century imperialist to which John Rieder attributes the rise of SF proper: the fact that there are no "blank spaces" left on the map.

Escape

In the introduction, I used Darko Suvin's over-arching description for highly estranged narratives, "ahistorical literature," as a basis for differentiating between SF, fantasy and horror. Each of these genres has a particular non-normative relationship to history, which we can understand not just as the chronology that has led to our present moment, but also as a model of reality and various sets of ideological assumptions about what is possible. There is, however, no such thing as a single history.

The narrative of the space age, the "giant leap for mankind" that would launch us into a space-opera future, had other histories to compete with – most obviously, the histories of the poor and the marginalised all over the world who would not be coming along for the ride. In addition to the latter, there were also national, tribal and ethnic histories that complicated the expectations of the "Gernsback Continuum." The island of Ireland was no exception to this observation. In addition to the "nativist" history of invasion and subjugation, and the "planter" history of siege and resistance, in the Republic there was the heroic framing of nationalist history. Nestled in the overlap between this re-drafted nationalist history and the utopian promises of the space age came Seán Lemass's economic liberalism and its attendant hyperbolic future-histories, as exemplified by Cathal Ó Sándair's *Captaen Spéirling* novels. In the North, meanwhile, history, siege rhetoric and future-war narratives had for generations been preparing unionists for an inevitable final battle, and even instructing them in paramilitary warfare. For James White and Bob Shaw, the discovery of SF was a paradigm shift of the kind Shaw would later write about – a change of perspective revealing a way out of the world. They both became self-described "escapists" in a place where escapism was badly needed. As Miéville reminds us, neither the author nor the reader of an ahistorical text believes the events of the narrative to be true, but both behave as if they do. An "escapist," therefore, far from being someone who "cannot deal with the real world," is someone who enjoys the "mind-page oscillation" (as described by Suvin) that constitutes SF.[5] Escapists are drawn to highly estranged literatures because the temporary imaginary destruction, dismissal or projection of their empirical historical moment, along with all its attendant epistemologies and ideologies, gives them satisfaction.

White and Shaw appropriated the Space Age narrative and changed it according to their experiences of life in Northern Ireland. Rather than dismiss it as having no relevance to their lives, as Gil Scott Heron did, or complacently await the arrival of a prosperous, exciting future, they drew upon their personal beliefs and experiences to construct nuanced SF worlds. Prejudice has not gone away, and getting along with one's neighbours still requires effort and care. If anything, the stakes are higher and the hazards of ethnic hatred are infinitely greater. For White, the solution to conflict is to forcibly end it, while Shaw's solution is to leave a territory that has been polluted by it.

Shaw died in his sleep in February 1996, and White succumbed to a stroke in August 1999 (Maume 202–3). Neither man lived to see the IRA decommission its weapons in 2005, the 2006 St. Andrews Agreement on the devolution of power to the North, the 2007 formation of a DUP/Sinn Féin coalition government, or the official withdrawal of British army troops after thirty-eight years. Northern Ireland got the "wrong history," and both men tried, in their way, to present better ones; their efforts are all the more poignant for the fact that neither lived to witness the hinted-at emergence of a better history for their home province.

7. Exotic Doom:
The SF of Ian McDonald

Ian McDonald was born in Manchester in 1960 to an Irish mother and a Scottish father, and has lived in Belfast from the age of five. His writing career began with *Desolation Road* (1988), a novel with definite mythic resonances tracing the history of the titular Martian frontier town, and more recently he has begun a young-adult series (the "Everness" sequence) focusing on travel between parallel universes, but it is perhaps for his "parochial" SF works that he is currently best known. This chapter will focus on *Chaga* (1995), *Sacrifice of Fools* (1996), *River of Gods* (2004), *Brasyl* (2007) and *The Dervish House* (2010), set in Kenya, Northern Ireland, India, Brazil and Turkey, respectively. Regardless of the setting, McDonald's focus remains the same:

> I'm not very interested in space opera or galactic empires. I'm not interested in computer technology and all the hype surrounding it, but more in how it's going to affect the fundamentals of life [...] Whatever we encounter in the future, there is still this fundamental core of values, emotions, beliefs that are the arbiters of everything that happens. If aliens do land at Belfast City Hall, for example, it's still going to be human values that mediate the experience, that shape the way we react. (Carson 270)

Andrew M. Butler includes McDonald in his "(Partial) Consensus" of British Boom writers (376), listing McDonald "among the British writers who carved out their sf writing careers" in the British magazine *Interzone* (378), though McDonald himself would disagree: "*Interzone* was around, but you had to be part of a south-of-England masonic cabal to get a story published there" (Carson 269). Butler describes McDonald's writing as having a "remix aesthetic," "which draws to some extent on music culture of the 1980s, puts little store in originality, but more in the skillful [sic] blending of the individual elements"; by way of example, Butler argues that McDonald's *Desolation Road* (1988) draws upon the work of Ray Bradbury and Gabriel García Marquez, that his fantasy novel *Hearts, Hands and Voices* (1992) is clearly influenced by the work of Geoff Ryman, and that *Sacrifice of Fools* "mixes the police procedural with the sexual politics of Gwyneth Jones's *Aleutian* trilogy (1991–7)" (Butler 383).

This is, to a certain extent, true enough – McDonald does not reinvent the SF wheel, so to speak (for that matter, neither do the majority of his contemporaries). In my own opinion, though, "originality" and the blending of elements/tropes/clichés are less important to understanding the work of writers like McDonald (and perhaps less important to understanding the science fiction genre as a whole) than setting. The striking thing about *Sacrifice of Fools* is not that it combines a whodunit plot with extraterrestrial gender trouble, but that it is set in Belfast. One could point out without fear of contradiction that the multiversal shenanigans, conspiracy-thriller plot and historical fiction of *Brasyl* are not particularly "original" in themselves, that the self-aware AIs seen in *River of Gods* are clearly descendants of older ghosts in the machine, and that the alien goo coming to assimilate us all in the *Chaga* trilogy is reminiscent of the all-consuming noocytes in Greg Bear's *Blood Music* (1985). However, the defining aspect of each is the setting – McDonald consciously chose to set these stories in Brazil, the Indian Subcontinent and East Africa.

For this reason, I would argue that Ian McDonald's work engages with the genre and with the Northern Irish situation in a much more direct way than either Shaw or White. It may seem suspiciously convenient to consider him in the same context as Shaw and White, since only one of the novels analysed here is set in Northern Ireland, but it is indisputable that the place has had a palpable influence on his writing. McDonald once categorised Northern Ireland as "a Third World country," where conflict between social groups had been engineered, a skewed economic system favoured the public sector and a "samurai elite (the RUC)," physical marginalisation highlighted a massive gap between rich and poor, and a highly politicised population had "the ability to arm itself to the teeth if it's disregarded" (quoted in Langer 122). The majority of his output is a reaction to the phenomenon outlined in the previous chapter: the disparity between the self-congratulatory rhetoric of the Space Age and the lived experience of the majority of the world's population, with its implication that the marginalised populations of the world had ended up with the "wrong history." In McDonald's work, the marginalised non-Western world adopts the trappings of the Western future – tropes, clichés and well-worn plots – in idiosyncratic ways, "redecorating a prefabricated house." In so doing, these narrative worlds offer alternatives to the now-passé shiny, libertarian, culturally homogenous techno-utopias of the past.

In *Chaga* (1995), extraterrestrial "packages" crash into Mount Kilimanjaro, unleashing a wave of self-replicating alien life that rapidly spreads through East Africa, assimilating and supplanting terrestrial ecosystems as it goes; other packages come down in South America and the Indian Ocean, but the novel is set for the most part in Kenya. Named after the Wa-Chagga people who first encounter it, the Chaga resists and adapts to all attempts to destroy it, and its steady advance causes panic throughout Tanzania and Kenya while the United Nations struggles to understand and contain it. Into this setting arrives Gaby McAslan, an ambitious and manipulative aspiring journalist from Northern Ireland, who falls in love with the UN's enigmatic Doctor Shepard.

Concurrent with the arrival and spread of the Chaga is the mysterious darkening of Saturn's moon Iapetus and the disappearance of another moon, Hyperion. Scientific opinion is initially divided as to whether the phenomenon is due to interior vulcanism or "black snow" (16), but a reconnaissance satellite reveals that Iapetus has a Chaga infestation of its own (90–2). Soon, another momentous discovery is made – the Chaga has re-processed the missing Hyperion into a free-floating structure and dispatched it towards Earth (120–4). The probability of some form of guiding intelligence is raised when a Chaga structure in the Indian Ocean transmits a powerful signal to the Hyperion object (195–6); subsequent analysis of this transmission reveals that the data contained within it is a complete map of the human genome (199–200). Scientific analysis of the Chaga reveals that at the molecular level it consists of "buckyballs" structured into hollow cylinders, functioning as "machines for processing atoms"; these "fullerene worms" break down and re-process the chemical bonds of the molecules they come in contact with, recycling terrestrial matter into alien structures (96–7). The discovery that it can do this to human genes, and that it does not appear to be giving us a choice in the matter, inevitably triggers a panic.

Despite the alarm with which it is met, though, the Chaga appears to have a benevolent attitude to humanity, to the extent that within the "buckyball jungle" that takes over East Africa, items are colour-coded for human convenience – edible Chaga artefacts are always red. The Chaga can even cure HIV, and it uses the virus as a vector to infect and change the DNA of adult humans, triggering mutations that will allow humanity to adapt to any environment and even grant abilities such as advanced time perception and probability manipulation. While investigating the Hyperion object as it approaches Earth, Shepard refers to the unseen aliens who created the Chaga as "the Evolvers" (410), and it seems that these aliens have encouraged human evolution in the past, as evidenced by the recovery of *Australopithecus* genes from a Chaga package (221).

In *Sacrifice of Fools* (1996), humanity has made contact with an intelligent extraterrestrial species, the Shian, and allowed them to settle on Earth in exchange for their technology. While apparently hominid, apart from "terracotta-red" skin, catlike eyes and three-fingered hands (17), the Shian are different from humans in a variety of unsettling ways: they are born sexless and become male or female at puberty, though their appearance is generally androgynous throughout their lifespan; they are sexually mature at the age of eleven, they become parents by their mid-teens, and their offspring are able to speak from the moment of birth, having acquired language chemically in the womb. The main difference between humans and Shian, from which all these lesser differences arise, lies in social structure: humanity evolved as a species that prioritises trade and exchange, while the Shian evolved exclusively as hunters. They carry on the hunting tradition, especially when in heat, trapping and killing rats, seagulls and even stray dogs and cats (160, 187–8).

One of the places where the Shian have been settled is Belfast, in what is suspected to be an attempt at social engineering in a region still bitterly divided along the Catholic/Protestant binary (25–6). By 2004, the "slow Peace" has culminated in Joint Sovereignty over the North between the United Kingdom and the Republic of Ireland, though ethnic tensions still run high. The main protagonist, Andy Gillespie, is a former getaway driver for a loyalist hit squad. Having learned Narha (the Shian language) while incarcerated in the Maze prison for his part in the attempted murder of a drug dealer, Gillespie has since his release worked for a Welcome Centre, attending to the needs of itinerant Shian. Unfortunately, his paramilitary past makes him the ideal suspect when five of his co-workers are killed and mutilated, in what the Northern Ireland Police Service suspect is a plot to arm dissident militias with alien weaponry. To clear his name, Gillespie sets out to solve the case himself. Speaking in 1996, McDonald said:

> *Sacrifice of Fools* came from a conversation with Ian Bishop twenty years ago [...] We reckoned the way to solve Northern Ireland's political problems was to take all the Chinese from Hong Kong, several million of them, and dump them here. So we'd have lots of Chinese – hence few Catholics, few Protestants – a fabulous culture, great food and colourful crime. And this sparked an idea: you never get stories about aliens walking down the Shankill Road, so what if you did? (Carson 269)

The "Sacrifice of Fools" referred to in the title is an extension of the supreme Shian moral law – Shian will not die for love, we are told, but they will kill to protect their children, and the novel begins with Gillespie providing a legal defence for a Shian mother who has set two human children on fire for threatening to kill her offspring (19–21). Taken to its logical extreme, this moral code mandates the murder of "fools" who pose a potential danger to future generations, along with any offspring who may be carrying the fool's genes (228–30). Once the existence of the "Fool Killer" is discovered, the true scale of the problem becomes apparent – there is no shortage of dangerous idiots in Northern Ireland (231).

River of Gods (2004) is an expansive narrative set in the days and weeks leading up to the hundredth anniversary of India's independence. India has broken up into a collection of independent states, of which Bharat is the principal setting. Bharat is suffering from a three-year drought, and this is bringing it closer to the brink of war with its neighbour, Awadh, which has dammed the Ganges. The narrative focuses on ten characters: Shiv, a gangster; Mr. Nandha, a "Krishna Cop"; Parvati, his wife; Shaheen Badoor Khan, advisor to the Prime Minister; Najia, a journalist of Afghan extraction; Vishram Ray, a wannabe stand-up comedian who inherits his father's power company; Tal, a "nute" (surgically created genderless human); Lisa Durnau, an expert in the field of artificial intelligence; Thomas Lull, her former teacher and lover; and Aj, a teenage orphan possessed of uncanny powers. Most of the story is concerned with artificial intelligences ("aeai"), which are multiplying at an unexpected rate, and growing closer and closer to full self-awareness, while older and more dangerous aeai manipulate political, business and underworld events towards unknown ends.

Aeai capable of "passing" as humans are outlawed, and operatives like Mr. Nandha are charged with destroying them: the process is called "excommunication" and such operatives are nicknamed "Krishna Cops," the obvious implication being that they are doing holy work by policing the border between what is and is not human. While Lull tries to protect the mysterious Aj, his former student Lisa is called upon to investigate an asteroid heading towards Earth; she discovers that this asteroid contains a strange artefact billions of years old. The Rays' power company, working on harnessing zero-point energy from parallel universes, builds a particle accelerator that threatens the existence of our own. It transpires that the asteroid has come to Earth to prevent this from happening: it has come from the future, where billions of years of evolution have caused sapient aeai to evolve into godlike entities with a vested interest in preserving the existence of their creators.

Brasyl (2007) is made up of three narratives. The first, set in Rio de Janeiro in 2006, follows reality-TV producer Marcelina Hoffman as she searches for Moaçir Barbosa, the goalkeeper considered responsible for Brazil's defeat in the "Fateful Final" match against Uruguay in the 1950 FIFA World Cup, to put him on trial before the nation on television. As she begins her search, however, Marcelina's life is turned upside-down by a mysterious doppelganger who seems intent on destroying her life and reputation.

The second narrative, set in Sao Paolo in 2032/2033, describes a future where electronic surveillance is omnipresent and private-sector security firms bid against one another for contracts on crimes in progress. When his dim-witted elder brother steals a handbag tagged with a quantum "arfid" (radio frequency identification chip) that cannot be stripped out by the usual *favela* technicians, Edson Jesus Oliveira de Freitas seeks out a secretive gang of quantum physicists for help and falls in love with their leader, Fia Kishida. Quantum technology appears on the black market, including "Q-blades," knives sharp enough to cut between atoms, and one of these is used to murder Fia and her comrades. Soon after, however, Edson finds her alive again, with no memory of their relationship or any of the events leading up to her death.

The third narrative is set in 1732/1733, in the early years of the European colonisation of Brazil. Father Luis Quinn, a Portuguese-Irish Jesuit who has asked God for "a task most difficult" to make amends for the sins of his past, is sent to the New World to track down Father Diego Gonçalves, a Jesuit missionary who has taken a swathe of the Upper Amazon as his own private kingdom. When he finds Gonçalves, he discovers that the rumours of his cruelty and insanity are, if anything, understated: the missionary has come to believe that the native *indíos* have been delivered unto the white man by God for spiritual testing; those who accept Jesus Christ as their saviour are bestowed with souls, while those who do not are enslaved or killed (226, 230–2). None of the previous admonitories sent to bring him back to answer for his crimes have returned; Gonçalves, having taken them prisoner, has forced each of them in turn to seek out the Iguapá, a tribe rumoured to possess the gift of prophecy. Gonçalves intends to either wipe out or destroy this tribe, but thus far, none of his hostages has returned to tell him where they are. Threatening the life of Quinn's colleague Dr. Falcon, Gonçalves forces Quinn to attempt this mission (233–4).

These stories are tied together within the overarching context of a quantum multiverse, wherein time travel and travel between parallel worlds are possible. Perceiving the true nature of reality allows one to traverse it, seemingly at will. Marcelina Hoffman's doppelganger, the "Anti-Marcelina," is in fact a version of herself from another history; this parallel version works for the Order, an organisation that polices and prevents travel between the worlds (216), and she is trying to "edit" her way into Marcelina's world in order to hunt down and destroy a cabal of world travellers hiding out in Rio.

Edson, meanwhile, learns that the resurrected Fia is in fact her counterpart from a parallel universe, a history blighted with environmental collapse (214) though possessing biotechnology far in advance of Edson's world, to the point where they wear their computers on their skin as living tattoos (209–10). In most worlds, it seems that Fia studied quantum mechanics at university, helped to develop a quantum computer and thus discovered how to travel between worlds. This has made her a target of the Order, who appear to have a much stronger presence in Edson's world than anywhere else: the seemingly ubiquitous Q-blades are in fact the Order's signature weapon, though the technology's origin remains obscure (339). Fia describes the Order as an organisation of terrifying power and influence: when one of the Order's admonitories (such as the Anti-Marcelina) crosses between worlds, they give advance warning to the Pope and the President of the United States (216).

As can be adduced from the Order's terminology, it is revealed that they are directly involved in Father Gonçalves's religiously motivated eighteenth-century atrocities. Gonçalves's quest to find and destroy the Iguapá has been mandated by the Order because the tribe has discovered a "flaw" in the universe that allows for the perception of multiple universes: a jungle frog with a multiverse-revealing hallucinogen in its skin (395).

The Dervish House is set in Istanbul in the year 2027, when nanotechnology has become the driving force of the global economy: the markets are regulated by AIs, police forces use insect-sized "swarm bots" for crowd control and crime scene forensics, and "nano" can be customised for a wide variety of legal and illegal uses, from enhancing a day trader's concentration to scrambling a witness's memory. The novel follows six characters: retired economics professor Georgios; power couple Adnan and Ayşe, a stock trader and an antiquities dealer respectively; Can, a "boy detective" with a heart condition who explores the world outside his home with the aid of his toy robots; Necdet, an aimless young man with psychotic tendencies; and Leyla, whose marketing and deal-making career is just beginning. All of these characters are connected to the titular dervish house or "tekke," formerly the domain of a respected shaykh named Adem Dede. Can, Georgios, Necdet and Leyla live in the converted apartments, while Ayşe's antiquities store occupies a ground-level unit in the same complex.

As suggested by the coincidence inherent in the setting, the multi-stranded narrative is not totally cohesive. The novel begins with a terrorist attack on a tram not far from the dervish house, in which only the suicide bomber is killed. Necdet, who was at the centre of the attack, starts to see djinns, and the knowledge they impart earns him a reputation as a latter-day shaykh; more disturbingly, he also hears the voice of Hızır, an enigmatic figure of Islamic veneration also known as "the Green Saint." Can, through his robot proxies, takes it upon himself to solve the mysteries that spring up in the attack's aftermath. Georgios, Can's friend and confidant, is recruited into a government think-tank following the bombing and soon uncovers the truth behind the terrorist group and their objectives. In the meantime, Adnan and a gang of his fellow traders hatch a plot to illegally sell cheap Iranian gas through the Kayışdağı natural gas pipeline for a monstrous profit, while Ayşe is hired to track down a Mellified Man (a dead man preserved in a coffin full of honey, reputed to be a relic of significant mystical/magical power) and Leyla is asked to help her cousin and his partner find a financial backer for their revolutionary new technology – though she will first have to track down a lost family heirloom: a halved Koran, ownership of which is legally tied to ownership of the company. In the end, the terror plot dominates and the other strands feed into it accidentally: Ayşe is arrested for arranging to sell antiquities outside of the country, and Adnan reveals his natural gas chicanery in exchange for immunity from prosecution and the dropping of Ayşe's criminal charges; this results in the pipeline being shut down before the terrorist group (who call themselves "God's Engineers") can use it to launch an attack on Europe. Adnan then uses the money from his "golden parachute" to invest in Leyla's cousin's world-changing new technology, the Besarani-Ceylan transcriber, a device for inscribing data onto cells of the human body: "All the music ever written can fit into your appendix. Every book ever written [...] maybe a few centimetres of your bowel" (270).

Going back to the terms of reference set up in the introduction, McDonald's intent is plain: if the SF genre is a "prefabricated house," then he is redecorating it. One obvious problem, of course, is that in each of these novels he is doing the decorating on other peoples' behalf.

In his seminal work *Orientalism*, Edward Said outlines how "the imaginative examination" of the Orient from the eighteenth century onwards was grounded upon a sovereign Western consciousness "out of whose unchallenged centrality an Oriental world emerged" (8). Arising out of a number of unequal political, intellectual, cultural and moral discourses of power (12), these distorted images of the Orient helped to establish the West as its direct opposite (1–2). With the ideology of Orientalism acting as a tinted lens or a sieve, the dominant Western image of the East was constructed in terms of "the exotic, the mysterious, the profound, the seminal" (51); this image was constructed not just by explorers and traders, Said says, but also by historians for whom this exoticism was a handy means of favourably comparing European experience "with other, as well as older, civilizations" (117).

Thus, we are left with a discourse of Western rationality and non-Western backwardness, terms that map unsettlingly well onto the dichotomy between modernity and tradition, marked out with depictions of the exotic or the weirdly foreign. To an extent, McDonald and other Western writers of "globalised SF" are guilty of indulging this discourse: as I argued earlier in this chapter, the settings in McDonald's novels are more important than the "remixed" tropes he employs, and those settings are illustrated via the idiosyncratic – and hence "exotic" – elements of the referenced cultures.

The Dervish House is by far the most "Orientalist" of the novels in this sense, more so even than *River of Gods*: alongside corporate skulduggery and rampant nanotechnology, one of the main plot strands concerns people who start to see creatures from Islamic mythology, and two of the sub-plots deal with the search for an artefact bearing some mystical or religious significance (the halved Koran and the Mellified Man).

The "spiritual" oddities are eventually rationalised as products of a secret nanotechnology weapon, designed by the Turkish military to affect cognition and increase a target's susceptibility to propaganda. Tested out on a civilian population in an isolated Kurdish village close to the Iranian border, it produced visual and auditory hallucinations and "an unshakable trust in the personal nature and authority of these hallucinations," which were predominantly of a religious nature (274–6). The terrorist group, made up at least in part of survivors from this attack, has acquired the weapon and learned how to use it. Following the tram attack, other visionaries besides Necdet emerge: a woman who sees "peri" (fairies) and a businessman who sees tiny robots; both these people are gifted in the same way as Necdet – they sense hidden truths and find lost things (255–6). Though it is never explicitly stated, it is clear that what the visionaries see is actually a consequence of "cognitive discontinuity," theorised by Georgios to be the human capacity to draw accurate conclusions from "minimal" information, an inborn ability so instinctive that it is not consciously acknowledged, and is thus interpreted as knowledge from a supernatural source (366): there is a notable similarity here to Chernyshova's conception of myth. However, there is a larger mythic structure at work here than McDonald's use of the tropes of Islamic mysticism.

Georgios accurately guesses that the tram attack was an experiment to see if religious belief can be artificially created (310). Georgios works out that the attack will occur via the Kayışdağı pipeline, using the natural gas as feedstock and enabling the dispersal of the nano-weapon across Europe (365). The image of a gang of Islamic fundamentalists bringing religion to Europe in this way literalises the canards of "creeping sharia" and "Eurabia" so beloved of right-wing Western extremists.[1] Contrasting this paranoid fantasy (which would actually require magic or science-fictional technology to come to pass), McDonald shows other ways in which Islamic tradition finds a niche in the modern world. Ayşe learns that the Mellified Man was once in the possession of a family of magicians, but was lost to a rival group in a battle of "the old magic of the spoken word against the magic of the written word" (215); this is later interpreted by another character as a clash between oral and written traditions, or between different legal systems (263). This emerges as the principal theme of *The Dervish House*. Islamists, we are told, no longer engage in violent attacks on Western targets. Instead they emphasise the practical side to their religiosity, allowing the public to choose it if they see fit: "The jihad is on the streets [...] There's a new shariat: street law. It works. People use it" (253).[2] The "tarikat boys" later drive a pair of gangsters out of the neighbourhood, and force the Greek lampoonist Lefteres to take down his lampoon of one of his neighbours, a Georgian woman rumoured to be a prostitute. Lefteres is enraged, having lost his position as the de facto lawgiver in what he sees as a "shame society" (422).

At the same time, though, McDonald's work inverts this tendency of Orientalism. In historical-materialist terms, by focusing exclusively on the "mysterious" and exotic, Orientalism depicts only a distorted image of a "superstructure," the cultural and intellectual practices that give a civilisation its unique rituals and outward appearance; Orientalism is not as interested in the economic, material "base" that orthodox Marxism holds to be the principal determining factor behind the shape of that superstructure. In McDonald's work, the non-Western superstructure is supported by a science-fictional industrial base – nanotechnology, artificial intelligence, quantum computing and (if this does not stretch the definition of "industrial" too far) alien biotechnology that appears to eradicate material scarcity. *Sacrifice of Fools* does not fit as neatly into this dynamic, but its depiction of defunct Belfast shipyards (the material base for unionist identity since the second Industrial Revolution) re-purposed as habitats for aliens has an undeniable significance: the old bases are crumbling away, and the superstructure is startle to topple.

There is a peculiar fatalism that permeates McDonald's writing, along the axes of gender, economics and tribalism. In terms of gender, maleness and male sexuality in McDonald's worlds lead inexorably to violence, and this notion is particularly crucial to the plot of *Sacrifice of Fools*. The

Shian are androgynous, to the point where there are no apparent physical differences between the sexes at all – indeed, when they first encountered humans, the Shian believed men and women to be different species. Androgynous though they are, due to the biochemical dictates of their mating cycle there is no such thing as a homosexual Shian (119–20); Shian have two mating seasons per year, and mating guarantees pregnancy, though a female Shian can decide whether to bring the child to term or not, and can even defer the gestation of a foetus indefinitely (158). Thus, following contact with human beings, the aliens were as shocked at the range and variety of human gender roles and sexuality as they were at the ways in which those sexualities can be linked to violence.

Unfortunately, the pheromones released by the Shian during their mating seasons also affect humans, with men in particular becoming more aggressive. This latter point is central to the narrative: Gillespie reveals that he received the Narha language, in chemical form, in the Maze from a Shian imprisoned "for pursuing Shian law further than human law allowed." This Shian went into heat while he was incarcerated, and his pheromones drove the other inmates into a frenzy which culminated in the alien being brutally gang raped and traumatised to the point of committing suicide (165–77). Gillespie's commitment to helping the Shian community stems from his own guilt at doing nothing to stop the assault, and the incident has left him with a lasting disgust for male sexuality, which he has come to see as a form of violence.

This idea is echoed in *The Dervish House* through the character of self-styled alpha male Adnan, who celebrates successful business deals with a cigar, musing in a Freudian fashion without the slightest hint of self-awareness, "Cigars are the amputated cocks of your foes" (183). Later, it is explicitly stated that global violence is a problem of "males killing each other": "There can never be an end to violence as long as there are young males" (411).

There are a number of contrasts to this. Most obviously, McDonald depicts female sexuality as being much less combative and destructive, as in *Chaga*, where the Chaga acquires a decidedly female character in one overtly sexualised passage. Exploring the Chaga with the Black Simba "tacticals" (paramilitaries), Gaby takes shelter from a storm inside a mutated tree, which contains a special chamber seemingly created for just that purpose. The description of the chamber is explicitly sexual: it opens when one of the Black Simbas licks it, it has a nipple on the floor to dispense "nutrient sap," and when the storm passes Gaby and her companions exit the chamber by stroking "a tennis-ball sized bud" to unseal the slit door; lest there be any danger of missing the guided imagery, Gaby describes climbing into this chamber as being "like birth in reverse" and refers to the Chaga know-how of her guides as "womb magic" (249). Besides femininity, another contrast is non-normative masculinity.

The omnipresent surveillance of the 2030s in *Brasyl* means that underworld operators, including Edson, construct multiple identities for themselves and swap their techno-enhanced glasses (devices in the overlap between social networking and state surveillance) to supply each other with alibis. Edson's malleable identity extends to his sexual activity, whereby he becomes a transvestite to pick up Fia in a nightclub (63–71) and a superhero for bedroom role-play with his male lover. Edson is a gangster when all is said and done, but he exhibits none of the latent savagery associated with other characters with normative masculine identities.

Of course, this means of existence is not possible for everyone. When normative masculinity leads to destruction (when adhered to) or a loss of stable identity (when repudiated), the only other option seems to be that embodied by Tal, the "nute" from *River of Gods* – abandoning gender altogether. Referred to throughout by the pronoun "yt," the nutes have no genitalia or secondary sexual characteristics – not androgynous, but lacking any kind of gender-determining feature, even memory: "Never ask, never tell. Before I Stepped Away, I was another incarnation. I am only alive now, do you understand? Before was another life, and I am dead and reborn" (157).

At the same time, the nutes are a fetishised and highly sexualised subculture, and though they have renounced their sexed/gendered pasts, they carry surgically implanted "orgasm keys" on their arms. To an extent, these are efforts to distance themselves from what they once were: physically, the nutes are a literal "third sex," complete with new kinds of genitalia, rather than being completely neuter, and the gender role they perform seems to revolve around their objectification by females and males – one of these being Badoor Khan. By "Stepping Away," the nutes seem to have adopted a passivity that leaves them vulnerable to exploitation and manipulation.

Money is the root of many evils in McDonald's work, encouraging a destructive selfishness epitomised by *The Dervish House*'s Adnan: "I am the money [...] That's all there is [...] So your theories are good and fine but when it all comes down, the money doesn't care. And I don't care, because I am the money. I make your world turn" (179–80). In *Chaga*, Gaby's investigative reporting uncovers shocking abuses of power and infringements of human rights perpetrated by the UN: peacekeeping troops charged with managing refugee camps extort money and valuable possessions from displaced populations, selling the latter on the black market (128, 134–9), while people who have been infected and mutated by the Chaga are held indefinitely in a secret UN laboratory (288–302). For her public criticism of the UN, Gaby is incarcerated in this secret unit and subjected to sexual abuse and repeated injections of psychotropic substances (282–7). Gaby's rescue from Unit 12 is possible because she is a white woman, and she is allowed to travel from Chaga-infested Nairobi to the USA because she is "the right nationality, the right race, the right colour," while black African refugees are denied entry owing to "potential biohazard threats" (376). It is difficult to sidestep the implication that the UN scientists, much like the extortionist peacekeeping troops, are abusing their power to find a profitable angle on the disaster. In the 2006 plotline of *Brasyl*, Marcelina muses:

> Brazil rails against the unstoppable wave of favelization; we tear down shacks and put up walls and declare bairro status like tattooing over the scars from a terrible childhood illness, one the ianques ["Yankees"] eradicated decades ago [...] but they are not stumbling blocks on Brazil's march to the future. They are the future. They are our solution to this fearful, uncertain century. (326)

This, of course, is the patronising attitude of an upper-middle-class, white-skinned media professional who does not have to live in the favela; she has the luxury of being able to rhapsodise about the resourcefulness of Brazil's poorest citizens without knowing anything of the desperation that drives it, and she is wrong: the future of 2033 is horrendous, and the gap between rich and poor has grown wider and wider in spite of the plucky ingenuity she attributes to the *favelados*. Brazil has not been redeemed by the poor; it has continued to ignore them: as if to underline this, towards the climax the action moves to the floating 2030s city of Oceanus, the libertarian dream of the businessman Teixeira (himself a *favelado* turned billionaire), floating just beyond the reach of Brazil's tax laws (348–52).

Tribalism, whether in the form of ethnocentrism or mindless loyalty to a particular group, lends itself to abhorrent behaviours in much more straightforward ways. Much is often made of SF's potential to subvert ethnocentrism and tribalism, but it appears that McDonald is not so sure – the arrival of the science-fictional does not automatically undo the follies of the real. *Chaga*'s Daniel "Dr. Dan" Oloitip, a Masai politician, describes the extraterrestrial life-form as a "cancer", and despairs at its implications for Kenya:

> What is it they are estimating? Twenty more [years] until the country is overrun? Seventy years is not time to be a nation.

Why could it not have come down in France or England where they have too much history; or China or India, where they have so much past they do not know what to do with it? Or America where at least they could turn being made into another planet into a theme park. (22–3)

It is all well and good for Western SF to look forwards to a prosperous technological utopia, where universal equality is as often as not equated with universal *sameness*, but as in early twentieth-century Ireland, the whole point of independence and self-determination is the recovery of a distinctive subjectivity: the arrival of the Chaga is of great interest to Western scientists, but to people like Dr. Dan, the more pressing concern is that it will swallow up the country and Kenya will cease to be Kenya. As in the work of Bob Shaw, though, SF provides an avenue of escape from the bitter realities of a world defined by tribalism. As Gaby points out (referencing her family's fondness for astronomy): "In the solar system you could not end up with the wrong name in the wrong district. No one sprayed *Iochaid Ar La* [sic] on the slopes of Olympus Mons or painted the edges of the craters on the moon red white and blue" (16–17).[3]

McDonald is not content to simply let it rest there. His works often interrogate the escapist aspect of SF, and with regard to the issue of tribalism, there is probably no better example than *Sacrifice of Fools*. In contrast to a sexually violent humanity (and sexually violent human males in particular), the Shian are assumed to be biologically (and thus, psychologically) incapable of rape or murder. Thus, the self-loathing Gillespie idealises them as a more enlightened race. In the end, however, it turns out that the Shian are no more advanced or enlightened than humanity, and even they can fall prey to a psychotic confusion between sex and violence. The killer Gillespie is hunting is a pubescent Shian who was left to cope with the psychological trauma of her first mating season alone, and in the absence of a familial support structure turned to an ancestral spirit who inspired her to undertake the titular "Sacrifice of Fools" (262–3). Gillespie has in fact been treating the Shian almost as a "model minority," and he receives a well-warranted upbraiding for this towards the end of the novel:

You thought we were a better people, without violence, without the basic biological inequalities of humans. Saner. Better. No sin. No demons haunting us. No dark side of the soul [...] We didn't ask for you to make us gods, we didn't ask for your faith and your hope. What right have you to make these expectations of us, and then be angry when we don't live up to them? (279)

Considering the alien as an ethnic minority raises an interesting issue in *Sacrifice of Fools*. Though the Shian are clearly non-human, much of their description resonates with stereotypical images of Native Americans: aesthetically in elements such as "red skin" and the crest formation of their hair (i.e. the "Mohawk" style); culturally in the importance of hunting to their culture, and certain aspects of their spiritual beliefs (while they do not worship a deity as such, they revere and regularly communicate with ancestral spirits); and also linguistically – for a start, the name of their species is a homophone for "Cheyenne," and the collective term for a matrix of interrelated Shian families is "Nation." This depiction could be linked to Northern Irish popular culture (in Northern Ireland, the Republic is sometimes referred to as "Mexico"), or perhaps there is also resonance between stories of the Wild West and the Ulster Scot history of plantation in a land filled with hostile natives.

The overarching difficulty is that each problem interlocks with and reinforces the others: tribal conflict reinforces destructive gender norms in that it is nearly always gangs of "angry young men" that keep such conflicts going; economic exploitation exacerbates tribal tensions and makes such conflicts more likely; and as exemplified by the character of Adnan, it is an aggressive male will-to-power that drives this exploitative vulture capitalism.

A comparison with the work of James White highlights this pessimism. As noted in the previous chapter, White often expresses a vague wish for some kind of all-powerful outside arbiter coming to save the human race from itself; McDonald's novels often feature saviours like this, but their appearance is complicated. In *Chaga*, the human reaction to the apparent end of material scarcity indicates that we are too suspicious a species to accept such help; in *Sacrifice of Fools*, the outsiders are also possessed of molecular recombination technology that could end material want through unlimited recycling, but it is clear that in their own way, they are just as bad as we are; in *River of Gods*, the remit of the Krishna cops and paranoia regarding self-aware aeai suggest that it is in our nature to react violently against the very things that could save us.

Perhaps the best example of fatalism in McDonald's work is the unsettling truth uncovered by the protagonists of *Brasyl*: that the universe we inhabit is but a repetition of the real one, and we by implication are but simulacra of the real universe's original inhabitants; the original universe being long dead, we simulacra are doomed to repeat the actions of the originals, over and over again, with less energy every time, until finally entropy puts an end to it. Unlike in Shaw's or White's, in McDonald's literary worlds, escape will only come when existence as we know it comes to an end altogether.

8. The Dystopian Decades:
From Recession to Tiger and Back Again

During the late 1970s and 1980s, a conservative phalanx emerged in Britain and in America to react against the progressiveness and radicalism of the 1960s. Technological developments allowed for changes in modes of production enabling the evolution of multinational corporations into "transnational entities" capable of influencing government policy. Political rhetoric focused on issues of "national security" with increasing frequency, ultimately legitimising interference in the democratic processes of Third World countries. The US and Thatcherite Britain waged "a geopolitical crusade" (Harvey 68), inflicting a horrific measure of economic violence on the rest of the planet as "the conjunctural privileging of quick financial gain led to the fiscal write-off of entire geographic regions and masses of humanity" (Moylan 184). It is thus hardly surprising that the 1980s and 1990s also saw not just the resurgence of the Anti-Utopia (103–4), but the emergence of re-worked versions of the classical dystopia, tailored to fit "the economic, political, and cultural conditions of the decade" (186).

The Irish economy's real growth rate was less than the real interest rate for much of the 1980s, and the rising cost of servicing this debt militated against the issuing of bonds to cover the government deficit (Geary 2–3). The Irish economy also suffered the "external shocks" of the 1979 Iranian Revolution's impact on oil prices, and consequently on international trade, finance and interest rates; in addition, there was a simultaneous international fall in agriculture prices (16–17). Instead of promoting "local linkages through the processing of agricultural inputs," Irish governments had encouraged multinational corporations to settle in rural areas, creating "enclaves" rather than evenly distributed industrialisation. With this incoherent foundation, indigenous industry suffered in two ways: on the one hand, most Irish firms were focused on domestic demand, which slumped in the early 1980s, and on the other, firms exposed to foreign competition were negatively impacted by international factors (Kirby 21).

These difficulties were compounded by the decimation of the country's workforce. During the 1980s, Ireland had the second-worst unemployment figures in Europe, after Spain. The Irish unemployment levels remained high throughout the decade, climbing in response to economic shocks but never lowering in the periods between them, and the percentage of the labour force unemployed for a year or more, the "long-term unemployed," remained in the 50–60 per cent range. Between 1985 and 1990, 160,000 people emigrated from Ireland. This situation was further exacerbated by governmental policies restricting taxation on corporate profits, which meant that the shortfall had to be made up in some other way, with the result that labour was taxed more than capital (23).

Ireland's mood of economic pessimism at the start of the 1980s did not just result in an increasing number of urban dystopian narratives; another consequence of the recession was an apparent intensifying of nuclear anxieties. In the *Captaen Spéirling* series, Lemassian promises of a prosperous future were balanced against the looming threat of nuclear annihilation. In the future, the Irish would drive uranium-powered vehicles along autobahns, Irish diplomats and scientists would save the world more than once, and Terra would flourish as an empire; if the price to be paid for this glorious future was the division of humanity into east and west, or the potential outbreak of nuclear war, then so be it. By the 1980s, the balance had shifted again. As emigration and long-term unemployment became facts of life, the promises of economic prosperity rang hollow while a nuclear holocaust seemed more and more likely.

In *The Cloud of Desolation* (1982), author Sam Baneham examines human existence in the aftermath of a worldwide nuclear war. The protagonist is a young man named Dig 951, an inhabitant of a subterranean society that calls itself Utopia, which is locked in a state of cold war against Hegemony, a rival state which could in fact be only imaginary. Utopia is a paranoid theocracy, structured around the worship of a god called Rem (the worshippers refer to themselves as "Remnants"), and ruled by the Supreme Patron. Dig's curiosity about the semi-mythical "Overlanders" triggers a comedy of errors that takes up much of the first half of the narrative, generating a political scandal that sees several senior government officials executed, and Dig elevated to the Supreme Patron's right hand. Sent to the irradiated surface of the planet, Dig encounters a family of Overlanders and learns something of the world's true history.

The narrative reads partially like a satire of life in the USSR. Innocuous questions lead to inquisitions, and equally innocuous answers lead to paranoid surveillance and analysis. Very little "happens" – most of the text is taken up with the inner thoughts of various characters at all levels of Utopian society, as they frantically interpret and reinterpret everything they see and hear. The minutiae of everyday life are overtly politicised, and citizens have to be Machiavellian in order to survive, allaying suspicion of "deviance" at every turn, privileging a political system over the individuals within it: "Utopia is perfect but Utopians are unfortunately not. They are capable of error. Even occasionally of betrayal. The most beautiful ideas can be betrayed" (Baneham 78).

Another source of dystopian narrative was the increasing power of big business. Micheál Ó Brolacháin's *Pax Dei* (1985) is set in a future when nation-states have ceased to exist. Instead, the world's power brokers are multinational corporations, each of which has its own army. There are two parallel narratives in the novel. The first of these follows a young boy called Rurc.

Rurc has lived all his life with his mother in a single room within a colossal block of flats. Outside the windows, nothing can be seen but thick black smog, and it is dangerous to venture outside one's door without a weapon of some kind. The inhabitants of this building subsist on "brot" and "klob," mass-produced crackers and spread that are barely sufficient to keep people alive. These foodstuffs are distributed by "the Christians," mysterious government workers whom nobody has ever met (Ó Brolacháin 37). Due to environmental factors, children are hairless, lacking even eyebrows or eyelashes (20).

Rurc's tale begins with the death of his mother, which forces him to venture out into the hallways in search of help (5–11). Outside the safety of his flat, he has the great misfortune to run into Hekter, a psychopath who has monopolised the food supply, and uses it to extort financial and sexual favours from the starving. Hekter takes Rurc prisoner, forcing him to fight another young boy for sport (22), and takes the corpse of Rurc's mother in order to eat it (26–9). Escape from this world is impossible, due to the hordes of ravenous rats that swarm the stairways (30).

The second narrative concerns the comic antics of one P.X. Winterbottom, the regional head manager of Pax Dei, a multinational weapons manufacturer. Pax Dei is about to go to war with Fun Leisure Intl., a Japanese company that produces video games (12–13). In the middle of the preparations for battle, an already panicky Winterbottom is further unnerved by the unannounced arrival of the chairman's representative, Bollard. Bollard, a violent and unstable individual, is plotting to have Winterbottom tortured to death in public as an incentive for other employees to work harder, after which he plans to establish "people-farms" to keep his predilection for young boys satisfied (47–8). Winterbottom's only way out is to come up with a strategy that will win the war against Fun Leisure Intl., and earn him a seat at the Chairman's table. The strategy he devises is to cut down operational expenses, by deliberately decreasing the civilian population to which the company has been supplying food (35–6).

Ó Brolacháin heightens the difference in tone between the two storylines by writing in different tenses. The story of the Pax Dei employees and the negotiations between the multinationals is written in the past tense, giving their bumbling a comfortable distance from the reader which suits the comedic element of their storyline. Rurc's storyline is written in the present tense – everything is happening *now*, the future is uncertain, his hunger and torment are intimate and immediate. The comedic antics of the powerful perpetuate tragedies for the powerless.

It is difficult to ignore the significance of the urban environment in *Pax Dei* – the skyscrapers in which the non-corporate citizens live are reminiscent of the high-rise tower blocks of Dublin's Ballymun area. These were the purpose-built flats to which Dublin's poor were relocated during the 1960s, so that the unsightly inner-city tenements could be cleared out of Seán Lemass's modern city. By the 1980s, the Ballymun flats were notorious sites of social alienation, inextricably linked in the popular media with crime, violence and drug dealing.

Other dystopias from the time incorporate re-examinations of old dogmas. Catherine Brophy's *Dark Paradise* (1991) is set on the planet Zintilla, where a humanoid species has evolved into two distinct types: natural humans who live rustic lives in the wilderness, and "Crystal Beings." The Crystal Beings lack legs, reproductive organs and excretory appendages, and they live beneath the Cowl – a colossal roof covering a large portion of the planet's five continents – in a society devoted to knowledge and logic, where emotions are abhorred as "chaos." Somewhat predictably, a group of young Crystal Beings manages to escape with the help of the unevolved "bipeds," forming a rebel movement to end the joyless, antiseptic Zintillian hegemony. The story is related in flashback through the memories of Fendan, the Supreme Krister (administrator/ world president), who has escaped Zintilla on board a starship. Fendan floats through the universe until he is reincarnated as a baby on planet Earth (Brophy 221–2). Brophy's timing proved to be uncanny, as birth and the provenance of life were to become the subjects of a bitter public dispute that broke out shortly after the book's publication. In February 1992, the High Court issued an injunction against a fourteen-year-old girl, who had been impregnated through rape by a family friend, to prevent her from travelling to Britain to seek an abortion. Analysing the "X Case," Lisa Smyth argues that the predominant media and legislative narrative of the crisis was primarily concerned with establishing criteria for "worthy victims" of sexual assault; as X was increasingly depersonalised by national discourse, the debate became increasingly theoretical, the effect of which was simultaneously to reaffirm the family unit as the fundament of society and to characterise that unit as "the real victim" of rape (Smyth 67–8). Since then, raising the issue of abortion has become a well-established demagogic tactic, particularly in advance of referenda on EU law.[1]

Following the destitution of the 1980s, the enthusiastic embrace of the Celtic Tiger economy had some unanticipated consequences for Irish popular culture, arising out of the jarring contradictions inherent in the phrase itself:

> The term "Celtic" invokes a premodern, romantic, "spiritual," unified sense of history that is remote, primordial, prenational, and which transcends the divisive historical realities of modern Ireland. In contrast, the term "Tiger" resonates with a different and in some ways opposite set of images, for it invokes the rhetoric of competitive individualism, energetic progress and globalised capital. (Kühling and Keohane 13)

Expanding upon this observation, Carmen Kühling and Kieran Keohane argue that "The experience of living in contemporary Ireland is that of living in an in-between world, in-between cultures and identities, an experience of liminality" (14). This new, liminal "Irishness" cannot be reliably quantified with reference to the traditional parameters of Irish identity.

One of the most striking changes in Irish culture around this time, whether as a result of the economic upturn or near-constant news coverage of the violence in Northern Ireland, was an increasingly lukewarm attitude to nationalist ideology.

Pádraig Standún's *AD 2016* (1988) is set in the run-up to the centenary of the 1916 Rising. In 2016, Ireland has been re-unified thanks to a Sinn Féin-led socialist coalition government, and nearly the entire populace speaks Irish as their first language. A backlash against the socialist government has given rise to a renewed fundamentalist Catholicism, following the mantra of "Land, Language and Liturgy!" (8).[2] The Olympic Games are to take place in Kildare, and Pope Pius XIV has been invited to open them with prayer, much to the indignation of the non-Catholic population. Against this backdrop, an old man named Pádraig, angry with the "official Republicans" now in charge, decides to travel to Dublin to make a formal protest, accompanied by a pair of eager young evangelical Catholics. Eventually, Pádraig explains his antipathy to the celebration:

It's my opinion that there hasn't yet been a politician in this country that came within an ass's roar of Dan O'Connell. Parnell, de Valera, Lemass, Fitzgerald and Hume were all excellent politicians. Adams is no loss as a politician, even though I don't agree with him. But it has to be said that Dan created Irish democracy. And he did it without spilling a drop of blood [...]. In my opinion, the likes of O'Connell and Michael Davitt did more for the ordinary people of this country than the 1916 crowd or the physical-force crowds before or after them. (106)[3]

Further details of this future world are delineated in news bulletins: China's population officially grows to two billion people with the birth of a little boy named after Mao Tse Tung and a breakaway Catholic sect called "The Church of Women" is gaining popularity in South America (85), and a government spokesman tells Protestants that if they don't like the Catholic ethos of the Republic, they can always emigrate (64). The final bulletin tells of a heroic band of unionists, occupying the GPO on the day of the centenary, raising the flag of the Red Hand (166).

In 1991, the seventy-fifth anniversary of the 1916 Rising passed by with almost no comment or commemoration at all, leading some commentators to angrily accuse the general populace of giving in to political correctness. The following year, Arthur Riordan performed a one-man play entitled *The Emergency Session*, in which he played MC Dev, a parody of Éamon de Valera as a rapper. The play is best remembered today for the song "Éire 2016 AD," depicting a dystopian future "Theme-Park Ireland" where the unemployed have been exiled to outer space, "Robo-priest" patrols "a Disney-scape of fake round towers" and the "rare oul' times are here to stay." In 2016, Ireland will have hover cars, teleportation and cyber-cailíns (such as the "remote-controlled Maude Gonne") but "you won't find a condom vending machine." Much of the comedy in this piece is derived from the incongruity of SF tropes in Irish settings – Castlebar, County Mayo, is populated by mutants, "You can order a pint from your TV screen," and the teleportation service even covers Ronald Reagan's ancestral home of Ballyporeen, County Tipperary – but these images are juxtaposed with scathing criticisms. The Ireland of the future is a great place to live, "Unless you're female, or jobless, or gay," Connemara has been sold to ICI, after which it melted for some undisclosed reason (but "at least the Brits won't get hold of it"), and "We've got democracy the Irish way / With a referendum every day" (Riordan 1992).

Not only does *The Emergency Session* say something profound (and very funny) about the sometimes dubious results of Irish artists appropriating "foreign" art forms like rap or SF, but as we shall see, "Éire 2016 AD" may in fact be one of the most prescient SF texts produced by an Irish author during the 1990s.

This is no mean feat, given that at around the same time, Irish SF fandom was starting to increase in size and vibrancy, thanks to the growing economy. Since 1993, *Albedo One* has published short fiction, criticism and reviews from Irish and international authors, growing from a local "semi-prozine" to an internationally recognised magazine, while its "publishing arm" Aeon Press has released a number of novels, short story collections, anthologies and graphic novels. College societies devoted to SF appeared across the country, from Queen's University Belfast to NUI Maynooth, Trinity College Dublin and the University of Limerick. Outside the colleges, local reading groups were established – mostly in large urban centres such as Dublin and Belfast, but also in places such as Ennis, County Clare, which was declared Ireland's first "Information Age Town" in 1997. These various groups have organised conventions, many of which have become annual events, and a number of short story competitions, such as the James White Award and the Aeon Award, encourage the emergence of new authors. As a further sign of the science-fictionalisation of Ireland, a number of American SF authors, most notably Harry Harrison and Anne McCaffrey, settled in the Republic, perhaps enticed by the "Artists Exemption" to the Republic's tax code.[4] The Celtic Tiger framed a historical moment wherein Irish authors experimented with previously "unsuitable" genres with increasing frequency.

In Robert Welch's *Tearmann* (1997), two investigators from the Department of Art and Culture, Mac Liam and Mac an Ghabha, are sent to the city of Tearmann ("sanctuary") to investigate the mysterious disappearance of a local Department inspector. No sooner have they arrived than they are introduced to the seedier side of Tearmann's night-life, uncover rumours of a strange cult, and are arrested on trumped-up charges of sexual assault by police acting on behalf of the corrupt mayor and his comrades. The text lacks cohesion, and this problem is especially apparent in the second half, with Welch introducing far too many twists into a story that is too short to allow any of them to develop satisfactorily.

Having begun as a paranoid, vaguely futuristic *noir* thriller somewhat reminiscent of Godard's *Alphaville*, the story changes too abruptly into an urban fantasy, with the conspirators known as "The Five" wielding magical control over the weather, and seemingly able to vanish from sight at will (68–70); thereafter, Mac Liam is rescued from his prison cell by an angel in disguise, and informed that Tearmann is the site of a struggle between the forces of good and evil (75–83). Mac Liam and the angel track down and confront the Five, whereupon the narrative starts to ape the formulaic plots of Dennis Wheatley – the wealthy and powerful of Tearmann apparently owe their status to their allegiance to Satan, and Mac Liam's partner Mac an Ghabha is tortured to death in a sadomasochism/bondage dungeon for the cult's amusement (98–103). Mac Liam then hallucinates a fight against a minotaur (which turns into his father once it is defeated) (106–7), after which it is revealed that the Five are not Satanists at all – everything that Mac Liam has experienced, they tell him, has been a test, made possible by extremely advanced technology (109). It is unclear to what end Mac Liam is being tested, but in the end Mac an Ghabha is still dead, and Mac Liam remains convinced of a Satanic influence at work. Seeing that nobody will believe his story, Mac Liam and the angel buy a small arsenal from an underworld arms dealer and set out to punish the evildoers (111–13). The story ends with the revelation that Mac Liam is telling this story to us from the confines of a mental hospital, thus throwing all the foregoing twists and turns into doubt (113). It is worth bearing in mind that all of this unfolds in the course of a single night.

For all its faults, *Tearmann* is of interest for a few reasons. Most obvious of these is the mixing and matching of narrative forms, as seen in other Tiger-era texts. In this case, however, this *bricolage* clearly arises out of a genuine desire to experiment with the limits of Irish literature, and in particular with the limits of literature written in Irish. While the mish-mash may not be successful in itself, *Tearmann* works as a sort of "proof of concept" because any one of its constituent sub-plots, given space to breathe and develop, could have been a satisfying novel in its own right. In a way, it does the same thing for aspiring writers that Captaen Spéirling did for children of the Lemass era – it demonstrates that it is indeed possible to do such things in the Irish language.

The other significant aspect of *Tearmann* is its setting. The titular city bears no real resemblance to any existing Irish city – it has a red-light district, complete with what seem to be legal brothels; it also features a more up-market "pleasure district" containing nightclubs on a scale that simply did not exist in Ireland in 1997; the local population is suggested to be similar in size to that of Tokyo, London or New York (4); and it has a special force of "night police" (49). This is a bizarrely aspirational text, expressing a desire for an Irish city not just as wealthy or successful as any other city in the world, but as seedy and violent, too. Written at the height of the Celtic Tiger, *Tearmann* is characteristic of its time – bombastic, superficial and dangerous.

The Celtic Tiger

The resurgence of the Right had cultural consequences that continued to be felt throughout the 1990s. As Tom Moylan points out, "the 1990s shift to the nominal centre [did not change] anything for the better – even though it did halt the overt economic, political, and cultural violence perpetrated by the Right in the 1980s" (Moylan 185). This "shift to the centre" also took free-market ideology for granted. David Harvey, describing the mood of the era, underlines how Francis Fukuyama's "End of History" determined the zeitgeist: "To pretend there was anything interesting about Marx after 1989 was to sound more and more like an all-but extinct dinosaur whimpering its own last rites. Free-market capitalism rode triumphantly across the globe, slaying all such old dinosaurs in its path" (Harvey 5).

From the 1990s to the early twenty-first century, Ireland experienced an unprecedented period of economic growth, mimicking the Southeast Asian "tiger" economies from which this new phase of prosperity took its name.[5] The recovery from the 1980s recession was partly due to severe cutbacks made by the newly elected Fianna Fáil government in 1987, triggering "an expansionary fiscal contraction" (Kirby 31). Other factors, listed by Paul Sweeney, included foreign investment, a stabilised global economy, "good all-round competitiveness," the European Single Market, and "timing," all of which was helped by a "very favourable global trading environment" (Sweeney 79). Another factor was increased investment in fast-growing export industries, such as information technology (83–4). Michael J. O'Sullivan suggests yet another contributing factor, the presence of reliable state institutions, signifying the kind of political stability that could not be taken for granted in other European countries, and thus increasing Ireland's attractiveness to outside investors (O'Sullivan 69).

There were, however, a number of severe problems with the Celtic Tiger. Peadar Kirby identifies three. Firstly, Tiger-era growth was not powered by local industry, but was instead dependent on the strength of the United States' economy, as evidenced by a generous corporate tax rate designed to attract American investment (Kirby 187–8). Secondly, Celtic Tiger Ireland placed a greater emphasis on competitiveness and profitability over the welfare of the state and its citizens, seeking "low-cost solutions that weakened its effectiveness to achieve the goals it set itself" (188). Lastly, while increased standards of living for much of the population were an oft-cited cause for self-congratulation, little to no attention was given to the increases in relative poverty, and "critical voices were silenced and ignored." Hence, "people's livelihoods and quality of life became far too dependent on the sustainability of a model that was itself highly vulnerable" (188–9). There were very few works of fiction at the time that were prepared to attack the Tiger and address its shortcomings.

Epic by Conor Kostick (2004) is a "young adult" novel, and one of the few texts published during the 1990s and 2000s to suggest a cautious approach to the boom. The setting is New Earth, a colony planet settled by Scandinavian pacifists, where the economy and legal system are controlled by "Epic," a colossal virtual-reality role-playing game originally developed to keep the colonists entertained as they voyaged through deep space. As citizens spend every spare moment playing "Epic," their real-world society crumbles, and a small handful of players have amassed enough in-game wealth to effectively control the entire planet. When a teenager called Erik assembles a team of adventurers to kill a dragon, thereby earning enough in-game money to force a change in the constitution, he finds himself at the centre of a plot to destroy the game, which has become self-aware. The game is ended, the "Casiocracy" is overthrown, and an egalitarian world system is established.

The raw material for the narrative is, obviously, the emergence of MMORPGs (massively multiplayer online role-playing games) such as *World of Warcraft*. Interestingly, these online games have functioning economies of their own: to maximise profits, most gaming companies allow players to buy in-game items with real-world money, rather than playing for them. Players also informally buy and sell items among themselves, and many games allow players to redeem game-world money for real-world credit. References to this phenomenon are inevitable in a text like *Epic*, but Kostick's novel also presents as thorough a social critique as is feasible in a young-adult novel. In places, *Epic* reads like a dramatised textbook on economic theory for teenagers, but it also includes references to political philosophy, name-dropping Machiavelli (Kostick 175) and paying homage to Thomas Hobbes with an underground newsletter called "The New Leviathan" (67, 91, 180, 245). The story presents a sentiment that could be interpreted as a warning about the underlying shakiness of the economic boom: "Epic is not real. Yet everyone is spending hours and hours at it, while the real world collapses. It's time we woke up from this dream" (263).

Such criticisms largely went unheeded. As Susan Cahill puts it, Celtic Tiger Ireland existed in "an eternal present," where neither the past nor the future mattered (Cahill 186). Consumerism and near-instant gratification narrowed the focus of Irish popular culture to the here and now: the future could only be contemplated in terms of optimistic predictions that extended the present moment indefinitely, and the past was only worth considering as a resource to be plundered. Bizarrely, it was this conception of the past, rather than visions of the future, that would come to inform Irish cyberpunk fiction.

Cyberpunk and Mysticism

Within Anglophone SF, cyberpunk had assumed pride of place as the quintessential sub-genre of the 1980s. Moylan foregrounds cyberpunk's political potential, describing how it

> reached toward Utopia not by delineation of fully detailed better places but by dropping in on decidedly worse places and tracking the moves of a dystopian citizen as she or he becomes aware of the social hell and [...] contends with that diabolical place while moving toward a better alternative, which is often found in the recesses of memory or the margins of the dominant culture. (Moylan 106)

Writing in 1991, Peter Fitting's semiotic examination of the word itself provides a helpful characterisation of this literary movement:

> [*Cyber*] of course suggests "cyborg" and "cybernetics" and the increasing presence of computers in our lives, while *punk* is an attempt to identify this new writing in terms of its edge and texture [...] At the same time, *punk* refers to an alternative stance, a hip self-marginalisation in opposition to the dominant life-styles that have come to characterize the Reagan years. If mainstream SF often presents more traditional heroes in the shape of scientists and explorers, cyberpunk is characterised by a fascination with more marginal characters: petty criminals and hustlers suddenly caught up in some larger intrigue. (Fitting 296)

This radical energy did not last for long. Cyberpunk's increasing decrepitude following the 1980s made it a large, slow-moving target for parodists such as Terry Pratchett, whose short story "# ifdefDEBUG + 'world/enough' + 'time'," originally published in 1990, features a protagonist far removed from the "console cowboys" of William Gibson and other 1980s authors – the narrator is an IT technician who remembers the excitement of early cyberpunk with a sense of bitter disappointment:

> I mean, when I was a kid, we thought the future would be all crowded and cool and rainy with big glowing Japanese adverts

> everywhere and people eating noodles in the street. At least you'd be communicating, if only to ask the other guy to pass the soy sauce. My joke. But what we got, we got this Information Revolution, what it means is no bugger knows anything and doesn't know what they don't know, and they just give up. (Pratchett 18)

The most obvious cultural hangover from the 1980s, "the 'Me' decade," was an intensified consumerism that collided violently with cyberpunk's worn-out image of itself to produce something like a millenarian moment that was equal parts capitalist, mystical and science-fictional. Cosmic transcendence was attainable, in the only way it made sense to speak of "attaining" something during the 1980s and 1990s – by purchasing it.

The summer 1990 issue of *Mondo 2000*, a magazine dedicated to the new futurological counterculture (and edited by one "R.U. Sirius"), boasts a number of advertisements which serve as intriguing snapshots of this historical moment. As well as a signed, limited edition of Timothy Leary's *Greatest Hits, Volume 1* (Sirius 74), there are copious ads for "brain-boosting" drugs, devices and food supplements aimed precisely at a notional hacker market, such as "The Synchro ENERGIZER™" (2–3), "blue-green algae" (33) and "MindFood" with "[all] the stimulation and twice the kick … with no sugar letdown" (101). The best of these ads comes from a company seeking to corner the specialist market in hacker clothing: "Reality is a virtual adventure. Dress for it in Chi Pants" (126). This indicates the extent to which the vocabularies of cyberpunk and transcendence had degenerated into buzzwords describing a market waiting to be exploited.

By the time the Irish started writing it, there was a list of identifiable cyberpunk clichés, and Irish writers simply copied them wholesale. Irish cyberpunk novels of the 1990s more often than not feature references to Asian culture, hackers or freedom fighters as heroes, a background of Big Brother-style surveillance, blurred lines between corporations and governments, powerful businessmen as villains, characters with cybernetic limbs or "brain jacks," and the narratives often follow the pattern of hard-boiled detective fiction. Irish writers tried to put their own spin on these clichés, though sometimes this spin amounted to nothing more than the novelty of setting these tropes in Ireland, often with mixed results.

In Iarla Mac Aodha Bhuí's young-adult novel *An Clár AMANDA* [The AMANDA Program] (2000), Séamus Uí Dhuibhir downloads a program into his brain without realising what it is, and his brother Conall then has to figure out a way to save him. The eponymous AMANDA program grants Séamus a phenomenal degree of control over the stock market, but it also re-writes his personality, turning him into an assassin. Conall, together with hard-drinking investigative journalist Jane and computer-geek Wayne, follows leads across Korea and China while trying to keep one step ahead of Colonel Kim, the South Korean chief of police with dreams of dominating all of Asia (Mac Aodha Bhuí 2000). The novel won a prize at Oireachtas na Gaeilge 1998, but it was not published until 2000. Well-plotted and well-written, *An Clár AMANDA* demonstrated that Irish authors could do "straight" cyberpunk if they put their minds to it. At the same time, though, another sub-genre was proving popular in Ireland, and it was no less commercialised than cyberpunk had become.

According to Harvey, rampant capitalism has corrupted human society to the extent that "we are left with few options except to react against [it] by way of religious fundamentalism, mysticism, personal narcissism and self-alienation" (Harvey 22). Thus, it is perhaps understandable that in the late twentieth century, there was a conflation of scientific positivism and "New Age" beliefs. This conflation is fascinating because it demonstrates that the myth-formation formula outlined in the introduction can also work in reverse: whereas pseudoscientific myths (the basis for most SF) arise when gaps in scientific knowledge are filled in with reference to prior logics, *mystical* pseudoscience (or perhaps, "pseudohistory") arises when gaps in anthropological understanding, or in the historical record, are filled in with reference to the now-dominant cultural logic of empiricism – most often, it must be said, without any proper understanding of empiricism or scientific principles.

The most notable twentieth-century example of this is Erich von Däniken's *Chariots of the Gods?* (1968), arguably the best-known treatise supporting the "ancient astronauts" theory (i.e. that the deities of Earth's many religions were in fact extraterrestrials). These visitors came to be deified, von Däniken argues, due to the scientific knowledge they bestowed upon us, from advanced cartography (von Däniken 28–31) to numbers greater than 10,000 (42) to various archaeological artefacts that seem too sophisticated for the civilisations that produced them – such as "crystal lenses" from ancient Egypt and Iraq, the "Baghdad battery" and platinum from ancient Peru (45). Furthermore, countless "ancient mysteries" can be explained with reference to these superbeings: the Nazca lines of Peru are navigation markers, designed to be seen from the air (32–3), the pyramids of Giza were constructed with the help of alien engineers (104–9), and the stone idols of Easter Island are representations of visitors from outer space (122–4). To top it all off, von Däniken hints that persons unknown are going to considerable effort to keep the truth hidden (47), thus tapping into countercultural concerns regarding officialdom's control of information, which were largely confirmed as the 1960s came to an end.

These concerns were most keenly felt in the USA, where they had previously often manifested as elements of "Aquarian Age" mysticism and resonated with the conspiracy theories that arose in the face of official savagery and dishonesty – such as the fatal shooting of four student protestors at Kent State University by the Ohio National Guard in 1970, the 1971 exposure of the FBI's COINTELPRO operation against "subversive" organisations (such as those protesting the Vietnam War and others campaigning for civil rights for black people) and the 1972 Watergate break-in. A cultural milieu came to exist in which governmental violence and subterfuge were taken for granted, and "truth," if such a thing even existed, was assumed to be hidden. Out of this milieu came a distinct breed of "estranged" fiction, informed by UFOlogy, Aquarian transcendentalism and conspiracy theory, phenomena that SF had hitherto "adamantly refused to enrol" (Bould and Vint 100).

At this point, it would be wise to distinguish between this kind of mystical fiction and "slipstream" fiction, which, as Victoria De Zwaan says, addresses the fluid genre boundaries and the "postmodernisation" of SF, without undermining the qualities of the genre that appeal to authors and readers. The term is also useful for describing non-genre texts that nonetheless make use of genre themes and tropes, and defies the distinction between "high" and "low" culture (De Zwaan 500–2). The principal difference between mystical and slipstream fiction is that slipstream, being postmodern and self-consciously "anti-realist" (502), does not incorporate esoteric explanatory models. Mystical fiction, by contrast, almost always offers a grand narrative to explain the oddities and inequities of the "zero world."

One text that combines elements of this mystical fiction with more "reputable" SF is Mac Aodha Bhuí's space opera for younger readers, *Domhan Faoi Cheilt* [A Hidden World]. The story concerns two teenagers from a distant future when humankind has colonised outer space, who discover an artificial environment floating in the void. When they enter it, they find themselves in a replica of Earth, populated by descendants of Atlantis. There are two tribes at war here, one of which is a slave-driven economy, while the other is peaceful and lives in harmony with the environment. Our two heroes lead a slave rebellion, and help the good Atlanticans to escape before the artificial sun (a nuclear reactor) explodes (Mac Aodha Bhuí 1999). At no point is it explained how the Atlanticans developed the technology to launch themselves into outer space, how they went undetected for so long, or how their advanced civilisation reverted to barbarism. Other novels published around the same time combined the mystical with the science-fictional, and explored this combination in greater detail, but with no more logical rigour.

Virtually Maria (1998) is the first part of John Joyce's "Virtual Trilogy". Following an air crash in Egypt, billionaire computer expert and captain of industry Theodore Gilkrensky comes out of seclusion to investigate whether an aeronautics device manufactured by his company had anything to do with the disaster. He is aided in his investigations by a small army of pilots and bodyguards, as well as a self-aware computer system modelled after his deceased wife (the titular Maria). Eventually, the characters discover that the Great Pyramid of Cheops is in fact a time machine. Joyce followed this in 1999 with *A Matter of Time*, in which Theo Gilkrensky continues his quest to find a way to travel into the past to save his wife Maria from assassination, using the reality-warping powers of "ley-lines." The third instalment, *Yesterday, Today and Tomorrow*, was self-published in 2008.[6]

The most remarkable feature of the Virtual Trilogy is the degree to which its plot is superannuated – it is a composite of genres and narrative tropes that had dwindled into irrelevance by the time the series was published, such as the corporate thriller, flamboyant action-adventures reminiscent of the James Bond film series, and Aquarian Age mysticism. Even the title of the series – The Virtual Trilogy – is applied without any apparent irony, suggesting to the reader that the narrative explores a fascinating "new" world of virtual reality. In reality, by the time William Gibson had coined the term "cyberspace" the concepts of artificial intelligence and simulated realities were already sufficiently established in the public consciousness for the Walt Disney Company to perceive a zeitgeist that could be tapped into with the film *Tron* (1982).

The principal antagonists are the Japanese, in the form of the *keiretsu* that seeks to acquire Gilkrensky's corporation: another outdated trope. During the 1980s, competition between the United States and Japan in the automobile and semiconductor industries engendered severe cross-cultural tension, which in turn informed quite a lot of cyberpunk world-building (hence the "big glowing Japanese adverts everywhere" described by Terry Pratchett). By 1998, however, Japan's economy was in the depths of a recession referred to nowadays as "The Lost Decade" (1991–2000). Despite this, Joyce adheres to a narrative pattern in which cunning Japanese businessmen engage in financial, political and legal chicanery to achieve their ends. Coupled with this portrayal of Asian deviousness and inscrutability is the recurring villain Yukiko Funakoshi, an insane ninja who pursues Gilkrensky with the aim of killing him to satisfy her family's honour, using traditional Japanese weaponry such as *katana* and *wakizashi* swords, and poisoned throwing stars.[7]

In each novel, Gilkrensky extricates himself from tricky situations by means of action-movie heroics (e.g. a helicopter gun battle in *Virtually Maria* (Joyce 1998, 177–83) and escaping by hang-glider from a terrorist attack in *Yesterday, Today and Tomorrow* (Joyce 2008, 222–3)), and relies on his colossal personal wealth to avoid the legal and political fallout of his actions: he is permitted to remain in Egypt following the aerial dogfight over Cairo because one of his employees is able to "pull strings at the Egyptian embassy," whatever that means (Joyce 1998, 187), and he escapes prosecution in Japan because of "the deal our embassy hammered out with the Americans," which apparently supersedes Japanese law (Joyce 2008, 233). All the while, he continues to fend off the affections of a brace of beautiful, jealous women – including the self-aware virtual-reality simulacrum of his dead wife.

As in the adventures of James Bond, the world outside Gilkrensky's home (a private island off the coast of West Cork) is at worst nothing more than exotic set dressing, and at best an arena in which the hero proves his mettle against villainous foreigners. The locations are chosen for their significance to New Age mysticism, and Gilkrensky treats the heritage of the human race (or at least, the patronising Western figuration of that heritage as a series of "ancient mysteries") as a resource to be plundered. In order to acquire these spiritual assets, he is obliged to travel to Egypt, Nazca and Bermuda, and fight off gangs of bothersome locals who object to his intrusion. The description of rural Peruvians offered to one of Gilkrensky's assistants could just as easily be applied to any group of indigenous people in the world: "They're a superstitious people around here, lady. They don't like rich *gringos* messing with things they don't understand. Nazca is a holy place for them. Maybe they're afraid your Doctor Theo will ruin the lines and bring bad magic down out of the sky" (Joyce 2008, 9).

The local people our hero encounters on his journey fall into one of two categories: they are either indigenous law-enforcement officers or deluded fanatics. The spiritual dupes of this series are an Islamist paramilitary group (*Virtually Maria*), a conspiracy-obsessed senior citizen who runs a fraudulent video-production business out of his retirement home (*A Matter of Time*) and (another example of Japanese villainy) the Aum Supreme Truth cult (*Yesterday, Today and Tomorrow*). All of these people are psychologically damaged by their inferior understanding of the spiritual secrets that Gilkrensky is able to simply buy, and are easily manipulated by the novels' main antagonists.

Ironically, Gilkrensky's capitalist mysticism indicates the possible influence of counter-globalisation movements that have been co-opted by the system they oppose, particularly, movements of indigenous peoples asserting their cultural identities. These peoples were cast as "'authentic' bearers of a 'true' alternative to a homogenizing and globalizing capitalism" (Harvey 74), and thus the lived experiences of ethnic minorities became a product. It is telling that Kevin Costner's acclaimed *Dances with Wolves* (1990) continues to cast a long shadow over popular culture, recently spawning a science-fictional offspring – James Cameron's *Avatar* (2009), the story of a soldier from a hyper-capitalist Earth who finds an "authentic" existence within an alien species' tribal society. This idealisation of "native" existence is an unintended consequence of the abjection of "traditional" society, and SF is particularly susceptible to it. As John Rieder points out, in nineteenth-century "lost world" stories, the "lost races" encountered usually turned out to be related to the protagonists; the explorer-hero was thus confronted with an earlier stage of his own genealogy (Rieder 42), giving rise to the conflicting colonial urges to preserve and to civilise (Langer 133). The depiction of natives as relics of the hero's past implies that the hero is a visitor from the natives' future, thus affirming Western capitalist modernity as the only viable end-point for societal development. According to the logic of this trajectory, traditional societies are closer to some imagined origin point, a state that carries implications of purity and authenticity.

"Authentic" Irishness

Pól Ó Muirí's *Siosafas* is a collection of short stories in the Irish language. Of interest to SF readers is "Siocshuan," a very short character study of a human travelling from Earth to another world. The title is a neologism referring to the trope of suspended animation (literally translated, it means "frost sleep"). The narrator ponders his status and reaches the conclusion that human identity is socially constructed – by leaving Earth, and travelling solo to another planet, he has ceased to properly belong to the human race. He refers to his mission as a process of rebirth, of transfiguration into something new (Ó Muirí 14–15).

The tale is obviously evocative of the migrant experience, and Ó Muirí's collection was published just as Ireland was beginning to see waves of immigration, with migrant workers, asylum seekers and refugees coming to Ireland in increasingly high numbers as the Tiger took hold.

Emigration has traditionally been seen as the predominant influence upon Irish history, but Irish myth and culture have consistently emphasised inward rather than outward migration. As noted in Chapter

3, the closest that Ireland has to a "creation myth" is the *Lebor Gabála*, or "Book of Invasions," which describes Irish prehistory in terms of which mythical race arrived, and in what order (the Gaels, we are told, came last). Historical fact confirms that immigration was vital to Irish culture: to take just two examples, Saint Patrick was Welsh by birth, not Irish, and by the late mediaeval period the descendants of Norman invaders had become, as the aphorism has it, "More Irish than the Irish themselves." The twentieth century saw the emergence of many prominent Irish people whose ancestry originated outside the country, such as the rock star Phil Lynott, actress Samantha Mumba, footballer Paul McGrath, singer-songwriter Laura Izibor, poet Gabriel Rosenstock, politician Ivana Bacik, sportsmen Seán Óg and Setanta Ó hAilpín, and politician Leo Varadkar – to say nothing of Éamon de Valera, born in the USA of mixed Spanish and Irish heritage.

The 2004 "Citizenship Referendum" generated widespread debate, bringing attitudes to light which had previously been, to a large extent, hidden.[8] Opinion polls showed that most Irish people apparently saw "foreign nationals" as parasites – despite the fact that refugees and asylum seekers were legally forbidden from working (Kühling and Keohane 60). Immigrants are consistently scapegoated for all kinds of social problems, such as inflation, inefficient transport, health and education systems, and the old canard that they are "stealing our jobs" (56), despite the fact that to this day, immigrants typically do the jobs that Irish people do not want to do (15). Immigrants are still viewed almost exclusively as "factors of production" rather than fully rounded human beings (51), and tend to be seen as "guest workers" – they are "economically necessary," but their integration into society is not desirable (55). The citizenship debates figured "a new, radically limited definition of Irish citizenship based on an essentialised version of Irishness which constructed all immigrants as a suspect and threatening Other," and the language routinely used in such debates frames immigrants, asylum seekers and migrant workers as cynical exploiters of Ireland's "generosity" (59).

"57% Irish" by Roddy Doyle is a short story in which an academic is asked by the Minister for the Arts and Ethnicity to develop a means of measuring Irishness. The young man develops an absurd device, reminiscent of *Blade Runner*'s Voight-Kampff machine, that measures the subject's emotional reactions to *Riverdance*, goals scored by footballer Roy Keane and Irish-made pornography. Principally a satire on the Irish and European attitudes to immigration, the narrative also contains hints that it is set in the future: for example, the aforementioned Roy Keane has quit football to take a post at the UN, and pop singer Ronan Keating is now bald (Doyle 2008). The fundamental point that Doyle makes is that "foreign nationals" only qualify as "New Irish" when they make us feel good about our own identity, a point confirmed by sociological research:

> When we say that Ireland is cosmopolitan often we are misrecognising that what we are really celebrating by saying that is exactly the opposite: it's not that we are celebrating what immigrants are bringing to us from their culture, but rather that through their presence we can see ourselves, our conceits of traditional, national identity, in a refreshed and flattering light. (Kühling and Keohane 68)

This theme is even more pronounced in Mike McCormack's *Notes from a Coma* (2005), whose protagonist, JJ O'Malley, the adopted son of a farmer in the west of Ireland, volunteers for the dry run of a pilot scheme proposed by the European Union, whereby congestion in the prison system will be eased by placing criminals into comas for the duration of their sentences. The experiment is taking place on board a ship anchored in Killary Harbour, and involves five volunteers, four of whom are criminals from Sweden, Scotland, France and Spain (McCormack 33–6). His story is told via interviews with those around him, including his adopted father, his neighbour, his teacher, his girlfriend and the local TD who brought the EU experiment to the area. In the background, we see the cultural reaction to the experiment, as the volunteers progress from being the latest reality TV sensation to almost being deified by the general population. Throughout it all, footnotes comment on JJ's story, possibly reflecting the thoughts of JJ himself. JJ's apparently high intelligence is a gift to the nation – "his suspended mind is one of those loci at which the nation's consciousness knows itself and knows itself knowing itself" (1) – which is fortunate for him, as the circumstances of his birth would otherwise have categorised him as an outsider: JJ is a survivor of the 1989 revolution that ended the authoritarian communist regime in Romania, and there remains a question about whether Frank "rescued" him, or merely delivered him from the ruins of one false utopia to another, that of small-town rural Ireland. As a final symbolic kick in the teeth to the Warsaw Pact, JJ was not *adopted* but *purchased*: "And what was the asking price, Anthony, what was the reserve? Was it stamped across my forehead or was there a little tag dangling from my toe?" (6). In essence, he was transformed from a child to a commodity, and this alienation is repeated through the "Somnos" project, a scheme through which human beings become products of both the mass media and the disciplinary apparatus of the EU.

At first glance, as one of the "New Irish," JJ embodies one positive effect of multiculturalism, in that he apparently exposes the nation to critical thinking. This proves to be both a blessing and a curse, manifesting as "mindrot meditations," cycles of obsessive analysis and extrapolation which, once started, cannot be halted. The fact that he cannot stop thinking only adds to his alienation, and the fact that he is aware of this does nothing to ameliorate it – this knowledge leads him to attempt suicide as a child (127–31).

Because he is strangely absent from the narrative, JJ cannot choose how his words or actions are to be interpreted, as is made clear by the way in which the masses start to deify JJ and the other Somnos volunteers. On one level, this could be interpreted as the height of non-critical thought, or the kind of unthinking worship bestowed upon celebrities. Interpreted in this way, the narrative appears as a clever satire of early twenty-first-century media, and "reality TV" particularly. On the other hand, the deification of the comatose volunteers could be interpreted as genuine and meaningful, in which case we must ask what need or lack is fulfilled by this kind of worship. The extent to which this kind of religiosity becomes normal is reflected in the ending – "What does a girl wear to the resurrection?" (199).

In this case, however, there is more than one resurrection, because the mass media and the EU have outdone Christ by offering five potential messiahs, all of whom are equally unlikeable: each of them is a narcissist of one kind or another. For all his sympathetic qualities, JJ appears to be just as narcissistic, never more so than when we learn that he blames himself for the death of his friend Owen: "He'd argued his best friend to death, that's how he saw it" (81), in effect killing Owen with his superior intellect, even though it is made clear that Owen died as a result of alcohol-induced respiratory failure (79).

In fact, JJ does not in fact think critically at all. His conception of the "mindrot meditations," the idea that his mind is eating itself, came from a weight-lifting magazine (51), and the dangerous thoughts to which he is prone – including the notion that God is not an appropriate basis for civil law (41–5), a cartoonish conception of the afterlife (51–6), and the idea that supposedly "kills" Owen (67–73) – are not radical, critical or "meditative," but merely appear to be when juxtaposed with the reactions of characters who are heavily implied to be less intelligent and imaginative than he is. In the final analysis, JJ is much less important than the narrative world in which he appears, a world in which the Irish (whoever they may be) are under siege. The New Irish are thus utilised to articulate old fears: namely, the fear of infiltration and re-colonisation that arose in the early years of independence.

The narrative world presented is only slightly estranged from our own, but nevertheless, it *is* estranged. The quality of that estrangement arises not from JJ, but from an absent paradigm that looms large in the anxieties of many Irish citizens – the image of an out-of-control European Union. The Somnos project is the product of sinister political manoeuvres aimed at "Harmonisation of judicial and sentencing procedures across the EU" (101), aided and abetted by Kevin Barrett, an ambitious local TD with a vapid political track record who has "risen without trace" in pursuit of the influence he craves (57–62). Though the experiment is a European one, "the Irish taxpayer" is funding it (61), and the faceless EU peons that labour behind the scenes seem prone to hysterics: in response to JJ's stated reason for volunteering, "I want to take my mind off my mind for a while," an unnamed application reviewer for the European Penal Commission writes a ridiculous, overly academic evaluation that runs to nearly two pages (105–7).

A Euro-sceptic tone is evident in the text: even if its motives are not strictly malevolent, the EU is governed by dotty intellectuals, and is equally capable of eradicating entire cattle herds in response to a BSE outbreak (2–3) and mandating that member states enforce the use of "biodegradable cardboard coffins" (60). One could argue that the BSE protocols were initiated on foot of a serious potential risk to human health, and that the cardboard coffin idea is plausible only as the kind of Euro-myth that might grace the front page of a tabloid newspaper, but this would be to miss the point. What is being articulated here is a profound anxiety about Ireland's international political context, as part of both the European Union and the geopolitical West, and its economic context as a recipient of foreign investment. From the time of the Saorstát Éireann *Handbook*, Ireland's main economic policy had always been to encourage this kind of investment. Now that it had come to pass, it seemed that the most threatening aspects of the outside world (once symbolised in the jazz record, the jet airplane and the "Duinneall") were now being invited in, and were worse than previously imagined.

Doom

It is interesting to note how, as the Celtic Tiger "Collision Culture" became more and more pronounced towards the end of the twentieth century and the beginning of the twenty-first, the "cyber-cailíns" described in *The Emergency Session* appear with increasing frequency.

Tim Booth's *Altergeist* (1999) is set in a fractious, near-future "New

Ireland" where the Roman Catholic Church, the Russian Army and an American media corporation compete with the remnants of the Irish government for control over the state. The plot follows Misha Ploughman, a "cadet" at the "DizBee" Learning Centre for Advertising Design, who goes on the run after top-secret software is downloaded into her brain, one consequence of which is the "Altergeist Effect" – for reasons unknown, the software triggers personality changes in young women, accompanied by phenomenal telekinetic powers.

Altergeist excels in its depiction of a balkanised Ireland, and manages to integrate cyberpunk tropes with a rural Irish setting. Following the reunification of Ireland, the country erupts into a civil war, during which the IRA's Russian allies detonate a nuclear weapon in the centre of Dublin, and the surrounding residential estates become "compounds, each ruled over by gombeen warlords and their Russian pals"; "Nord AMCO" (what remains of the United States) brokers a ceasefire with Moscow based on power sharing and free trade, while NATO secures "the eight counties" and establishes a new capital in Armagh. Cork and Waterford have been wiped out by nerve gas attacks, and following an attempted secession, the people of Limerick have been carted off to re-education camps (Booth 14–15). Dublin is now "Cliat" (from the town's Irish name, *Baile Átha Cliath*), and Mullingar is a stronghold of the "Plainers – the Plain People," who have established "a viable agri-based economy, centred on a quasi-feudal system of church tithes and military service," having driven out the IRA (123). In the midst of all this, the rural Irish are still hospitable to a fault, and a survivalist will not fail to ask, "Ye'll take porridge with your tay?" (126).

In this setting, we are introduced to several characters who are cartoonishly larger than life. There is Ripper, a petty criminal notable for his skates, which are built upon "[c]arbon-fibre technology developed for high-impact chainsaws in the frozen forests of Siberia" (16). Misha, the central character, is a punk caricature, with cropped hair, Celtic spiral tattoos, leather jacket and "skin-grafted pins" to hold her braids in place (24), and Harley, a travelling electronics merchant, is a machine girl straight out of the 1980s:

> Her arse may be cute, but her face is a shock. A bronzed metal plate covers the left eye socket, a round turret lens protruding from where the eye should be, a gunsight grid etched onto its shiny surface. The lens rotates in its mount, focusing with a scratch of gear wheels. The metal plate covers the forehead to the hairline, and stops in a hard curve at the temple. The other eye, green under an oriental eyelid, looks at them. (28)

The contrast between *Altergeist* and the Virtual Trilogy is interesting. In the latter, the intrusion of cyberpunk into rural Ireland changes nothing: except for the inconvenience of homicidal ninjas and misbehaving artificial intelligences, life in West Cork continues as normal, and most of the property damage takes place in distant Third World countries. In the former, Celtic Tiger Ireland is violently torn asunder. The future brings all kinds of foreign trade, and artefacts such as Virtual Reality rigs, chainsaw-powered rollerblades and "software-wetware" interface technology, allowing the human brain to interact directly with a computer mainframe, but the price for this is the kind of conflict and social upheaval seen in news reports during the 1990s, which made the breakup of Yugoslavia a nightmarish counterpart to the prosperity of Western Europe.

Other authors regarded the technological boons of Western society as a self-evident sham to begin with, regardless of the cost. The title of Tomás Mac Síomóin's debut novel *Ag Altóir an Diabhail* (2003) means "At the Altar of the Devil." In it, a recently widowed teacher named Beartla B receives a circular letter from a company called Marital Electronics Ltd. The company wishes to sell him "an electronic bride," also known as a "Juliet." This appliance is apparently very realistic and has lifelike responses to touch and verbal interaction. Initially enraged by this offer, under the duress of prolonged loneliness Beartla B begins to entertain the notion. Soon, he has ordered a "Juliet," and in so doing, he triggers a tragic chain of events. The situation lends itself to some comic scenes: Beartla tries to decide on the appearance of his custom-made bride, but cannot make his mind up between Monica Lewinsky and Mary Robinson; he then finds that he cannot follow the badly translated assembly instructions. All the while, he remains oblivious to the affection shown to him by a flesh-and-blood woman, "Deirdre of the Blue Nails." However, the comedy of the text is mixed with anger and sorrow: Beartla is narrating this tale to a psychiatrist in a mental institution, where he has been incarcerated after detonating a bomb in the centre of his village.

Of course, reading this novel immediately brings several texts to mind – *The Stepford Wives*, the ironic "Shortest Science Fiction Story Ever Written" ("Boy meets girl. Boy loses girl. Boy builds girl") and the Lester del Rey short story "Helen O' Loy," wherein a man builds the perfect woman. Beartla B would like to do the same, but his fantasy is revealed to be exactly that – a fantasy, an unattainable dream that speaks volumes about his relationship to women. Beartla B's deceased wife Áine is barely referenced, and we are not told how she died. This, coupled with Beartla's rejection of Deirdre for a mechanical woman who does not exist, forms a potent commentary that, in addition to articulating feminist concerns, problematises both Ireland's integration into the outside world and Irish authors' appropriation of foreign genres: foreign hucksters have conned Beartla into paying for an idyllic, techno-utopian future that he can never have. The duplicity of multinational corporations, a central theme of cyberpunk, became a truism as the Irish grew more and more aware of the hidden costs of foreign investment.

Connemara was not sold to ICI (Imperial Chemical Industries) as Arthur Riordan predicted in 1992, but to many, the Irish government's decision in 2001 to approve the development of the Corrib Gas Pipeline seemed just as irresponsible.[9] This decision ultimately started the ongoing "Shell to Sea" campaign, consisting of blockades that are routinely broken up with use of force by Gardaí. The unavoidable inference drawn by the protesters is that the justice system and the police force are following the orders of a multinational energy corporation (one which has previously been accused of human rights abuses in other territories, notably along the Niger Delta) because of the lucrative nature of its operations. To those arguing that outside corporate investment is not always necessarily a good thing, it appears that the promise of foreign money has turned the apparatus of the Republic against its own citizens – a perception reinforced at a Shell to Sea protest in 2011, when two Gardaí present at the scene were recorded making jokes about raping female protesters.

The blurring between political and corporate power is a central theme of *Welcome to Coolsville* (2004) by Jason Mordaunt, a sprawling near-future satire set in Maymon Glades, a fictional suburb of Dublin. The narrative is a rat's nest of characters and plotlines, including the development of a chemical agent that makes people docile and compliant, a *Charlie's Angels*-style sisterhood of warrior nuns established by a "rogue Jesuit" (Mordaunt 104), the establishment of a museum of popular culture, genetic engineering and the search for immortality. In this future world, children are often brought to term in artificial wombs, and parents can make genetic alterations to unborn children, particularly to correct undesirable inherited traits, but there are also rumours of an experimental mutant soldier, "basically human, but with four arms [...] and eyes in the back of its head" (242). Civil society is conspicuous by its absence in the narrative – no mention is ever made of police or national politics. There are only corporate security teams and boardroom warfare, because the multinational corporation WentWest has hollowed out and taken over the country's infrastructure: the nickname for the Maymon Glades suburb comes from the corporate-owned prison, or "cooler," at its centre (63–4), and WentWest employs a team of mercenaries to manage Dublin's homeless population (112–14). The frustrating nature of life in this society is demonstrated by the most popular sport, "slugfest," a *Rollerball*-esque high-octane tennis played by teams of armoured, padded athletes (10).

The plot is set in motion by a would-be whistle-blower who tries to reveal the truth about pharmaceutical experiments being carried out on the inmates of the Coolsville prison. A sinister compound, "a synthesis of a henbane derivative and recent developments in meta-phets ... designed to mimic specific neurotransmitters associated with conformity and obedience" (38), is being administered to prisoners in cans of "Moose," a milk-based beverage manufactured by WentWest in Dublin, "also available with croutons of a cereal-like substance floating in it which apparently never went soggy" (93). It transpires that these adulterated cans of Moose have escaped the corporation's labs, as evidenced by the news that three high-profile investment bankers in Greece, having been charged with embezzlement, claim in their defence that a mysterious woman bought them some drinks "and talked them into giving her half a million in cash" (304).

The only consistent voice of resistance is the mysterious "Mantra," a lone hacker who is erroneously believed to be an entire organisation, and who targets WentWest-sponsored slugfest games, hijacking every monitor with the same screed: "Welcome to Coolsville ... Cover your ass ... Pass the buck ... Resistance is futile" (11–12). At no point does Mantra attempt anything more that irritating WentWest, "while the people the message is aimed at can only complain about the fact that their sporting fixtures [...] have been interrupted" (292).

Other authors have tackled the cynical disinterest engendered by the Tiger. In Mac Síomóin's 2007 novel *An Tionscadal* [The Project], an Irish expat living in Catalonia comes into possession of an old map showing the location of a mysterious village in the mountains. Daithí Ó Gallchóir researches the village of Les Pedres, and learns that while it does in fact exist, the inhabitants are strange, solitary people lagging a couple of centuries behind the rest of the world (22–3); on the other hand, it is also home to a church reputed to contain beautiful artworks (15–16). Setting out to find the village and see the church for himself, Daithí discovers that the locals are extraordinarily long-lived: inscriptions on tombs initially indicate an average lifespan of two hundred years (45–6), but when Daithí questions the locals about this, he learns that those who pass away at this age are considered to have died before their time (47). This longevity, Daithí discovers, is linked to a bioluminescent species of ginseng that only grows in the vicinity of Les Pedres, and he soon starts planning how best to exploit this plant for financial gain. He sends a sample of the plant to Martel International (the mysterious multinational

behind "Marital Electronics Ltd." in *Ag Altóir an Diabhail*), which he
works for as a marketing executive. Martel realise the potential of the
ginseng when lipids extracted from it increase the lifespans of rats, mice
and monkeys (122–5, 203–8), but are somewhat reluctant to market the
"sempraviva" extract, for fear that the radical claims made for it will
damage Martel's dominant position in other markets; other objections
are raised on militaristic and religious grounds, as the potential effects
of sempraviva are extrapolated (142–3).

Mac Síomóin draws on his own expertise in chemistry and botany to
create the character of Daithí Ó Gallchóir, but this is not a sympathetic
protagonist by any means. Ó Gallchóir is an ambitious narcissist who
makes no effort to conceal his longing for fame and fortune. *An
Tionscadal*, like *Ag Altóir an Diabhail*, is an epistolary novel presented as
a collection of diary extracts and related documents, and it seems that
Ó Gallchóir has put it all together in order to pitch it to a film studio
– he regularly interrupts the story with notes for the film-makers, such
as suggestions regarding establishing shots of the Catalonian landscape
(25), suitably "atmospheric" locations (77) and music (78), and he
even includes fragments of a screenplay depicting himself as a dashing
romantic hero come to rescue Núria, a woman of Les Pedres to whom
he is attracted, from her "imprisonment" in the village; the part of Núria
is to be played by a tall Penelope Cruz lookalike, and Daithí by Gabriel
Byrne (77–90, 96–107, 110–11). On other occasions he compares himself
to James Bond and Sherlock Holmes (19), and reveals that he thinks of
the human race not as *Homo sapiens*, but as *Homo consumens* (28).

Peadar Kirby and Mary P. Murphy divide the Celtic Tiger period
into three distinct phases: first was a "growth phase" from 1987 to
1992, in which a centre-right coalition brought the country's financial
crisis under control and plugged Ireland into international markets;
second was a "developmental" phase from 1992 to 1997, during which
a centre-left coalition focused on equality and the development of
Ireland's burgeoning software sector; and finally came a "competition
phase" from 1997 to 2007, in which a centre-right coalition focused on
lowering taxes, and stimulated a property boom through state subsidies
and tax breaks (Kirby and Murphy 72).

A cursory glance over the publication dates cited above reveals that
more SF was published in Ireland during the last phase than in either
of the other two. Eleven of the texts discussed in this chapter were
published during the "competition" phase, which Kirby and Murphy
further characterise as "a process of narrowing and controlling the
agenda," increasing domestic consumption, and "a reassertion of central
state control" (73). The literary responses to this seem to have resurrected

the old fears of infiltration, tinged with a new mixture of cyberpunk and mysticism.

The most interesting trend to have appeared in Irish SF during the Tiger years, however, is a new approach to female characters. Almost every text examined here features strong, capable women. The Virtual Trilogy's Yukiko is insane (as are many of the other female characters of that series), but her ninja skills mean that she cannot be safely locked away in an attic. *Altergeist* features cyborg women and telekinetic punk girls, and the main villain is a ruthless woman who has become the head of the largest media corporation on Earth. *Welcome to Coolsville* has a secret sisterhood of warrior nuns, who wander the Earth solving mysteries and fighting corporate skulduggery. In *Epic*, the teenage male protagonist succeeds by playing as a very feminine character, and is treated as such by male NPCs ("non-player characters," i.e. personalities that only exist within the game). The appearance of these warrior women in Irish SF is more than likely due to international media influences, particularly television shows such as *Buffy the Vampire Slayer*, *Dark Angel*, *Xena, Warrior Princess* and others, but it is telling that in most of these texts, this kind of female character is deployed in opposition to destructive economic practices; thus, one positive pop-culture consequence of the boom was the emergence of the "Celtic Tigress."

9. The Shape of Irish SF to Come

86: "Classic Irish sci-fi."

> – 100 disastrous quotes to put on a movie poster
> *Neon* magazine, January 1999

The apparent incongruity of the notion of "Irish science fiction" speaks less to the unsuitability of a particular literary form to Irish artistic endeavour, and more to the unsuitability of Irish people to the genre's futuristic milieu. When Irish characters appear in American and British SF narratives (most notable is the engineer Miles O'Brien, a recurring character in *Star Trek: The Next Generation* and *Deep Space Nine*), their characterisation is more often than not couched in historical terms. O'Brien, for example, often speaks proudly of his ancestry, being particularly proud of his descent from the High King Brian Boru (Okuda and Okuda 330), and in his spare time he often takes part in "holo-deck" re-enactments of the Battle of Clontarf (191). The Irish are, if nothing else, creatures with very long histories, and there seems to be a general consensus that the Irish are more attuned to the past than the future (a notion which does in fact have much justification). The internal subjectivity of Ireland, the "literary personality" as Yamano might describe it, however, is more complex.

Being a part of the British Empire exposed the Irish to foreign intellectual and philosophical traditions that they might not otherwise have encountered. Nineteenth-century texts in particular show a clear political and philosophical influence from various European sources, such as Classical Greek philosophy, Marxism and Romanticism. Irish authors of the time also show themselves to be keen observers of developments in international politics, and they directly reference and react to those developments in their fiction – for example, the British army's defeat at the Battle of Majuba Hill in 1881 is discussed in almost every nineteenth-century text analysed herein, from both nationalist and unionist perspectives. Ireland's exposure to one of the most important international developments in philosophy, science and culture, the Enlightenment, was also mediated (and hindered) by the British Empire.

The Enlightenment gave rise not to an enlightened society per se, but to an enlightened class of people, which Adorno and Horkheimer argue are modernity's equivalent of shamans or wizards. It is the emergence of this class of experts, rather than the Enlightenment itself, that proved vital to the emergence of SF, for two reasons – the spread of scientific myth, and the emergence of future-oriented "cargo cults."

The limited nature of the scientist class means that scientific discoveries must be explained to lay people via the use of imagery, metaphor and analogy. This usually leads to mistakes of interpretation, because although not everyone can be a scientist, the process of logical deduction remains the same, regardless – if we do not understand something, we fill in the gap with something that makes sense to us from our prior experience. As Tatiana Chernyshova argues, this process is identical for both scientific and mythic reasoning, while the different results are due to the elements this process synthesises into a model of reality. Scientists fill gaps in their knowledge with testable hypotheses, while lay people fill them with anecdotes, "common sense" and other cultural logics. The latter gives rise to pseudoscience, the stuff of which SF is made.

Cultural logics are often so ubiquitous that society is hardly aware of their presence, or of these logics' kinship to myth and science. Rabkin and Scholes highlight the ways in which Western SF has drawn upon Judaeo-Christian and classical Greek and Roman mythology, but myth, as a kind of cultural logic, is not simply a repository of imagery and stories. Simultaneously narrative and ideology, myth dramatises societal norms and encompasses all that a society holds to be historically possible or inevitable. It displays many of the qualities that Antonio Gramsci attributes to "common sense," and fulfils many of the same functions:

> Common sense is not something rigid and static; rather, it changes continuously, enriched by scientific notions and philosophical opinions which have entered into common usage. "Common sense" is the folklore of "philosophy" and stands midway between real "folklore" [...] and the philosophy, the science, the economics of the scholars. (Gramsci 173)

The ancient Irish mythology of demigods and epic battles largely gave way to Christianity, but in so doing created a syncretic belief system, a hybrid cultural logic which explained some phenomena with reference to the teachings of Jesus, and others with reference to pagan fairy lore. It was this unstable tradition that initially came into conflict with modernity, and was later muscled out by a more orthodox (though still not unadulterated) Catholicism. The later clash between Catholicism and modernity gave rise to the implication that it was still possible to choose between them, and thus between two distinct logics, two means of making sense of history. I contend that this clash of cultural logics had a significant impact on the genre dynamics of Irish popular fiction.

Raffaella Baccolini sees genres as cultural institutions preoccupied with the maintenance of binary divisions between "what is normal and what is deviant," an "essentially masculine heritage" against which women writers have had to react (Baccolini 14–15); the blurring of genre lines uses hybridity and fluidity in order to deconstruct "universalist assumptions" and "pure, neutral, objective knowledge" (18). Langer sees genre blurring as "one of the most important forward trends in postcolonial science fiction," indicative of an identity-formation process in which "colonized groups seize [...] the precise type and genre of writing whose history and implication has heretofore marked them as for ever other, lesser, mythological and/or locked into a primitive past" (Langer 158). I agree with both in broad strokes, in that I think genre blurring is best explained as a consequence of negotiating historiography, and also a means of complicating hegemonic assumptions of what constitutes "knowledge," but in the case of Ireland, I would argue that the process has been a largely subconscious one.

Compounding the problems of ideological hybridity and confusion, Irish history has been repeatedly ruptured and suspended. The early modern period brought "an exceptionally violent and accelerated process of colonial modernization" from feudal pre-capitalism to mercantilism (Cleary 33). The Act of Union in 1801 removed the independence that had been granted to Ireland in 1782, and the mid-nineteenth-century Famine gruesomely demonstrated the power of modern economic forces. Other historical fractures and fissures abound. For decades, the dissident nationalist movement did not recognise the legitimacy of the twenty-six county Republic, or any general election following the general election of 1918 – for them, the "real" history of Ireland had effectively been put on hold.[1] Almost a century later, Ireland's assimilation into the geopolitical West has seen the country enter an international arena in which its "parochial" concerns are apparently of little consequence: as Peadar Kirby and Mary Murphy put it,

> [The] Irish state has always seen itself as subservient, firstly to the power of the Catholic Church, which ran most of its educational and health services for it and, more recently, to the power of global capital, which runs most of its economy. Instead, Irish politics tends

to be cloaked in a populist discourse that rarely acknowledges its
ideological content. (Kirby and Murphy 38–9)

So, Ireland has experienced multiple endings to its history (the basic
function of the horror narrative), and to a large extent has seen its
own history as irrelevant in the grander scheme of things (the defining
characteristic of fantasy literature). In addition to this, the abrupt leap
from an economy based on agriculture to one based on information
technology, minus the decades of industrialisation experienced by other
nations, seems both incongruous and artificial – this dramatic shift has
presented itself as history, but there is no evidence in the country's
landscape or infrastructure to suggest that it actually *is* history. In short,
Irish subjectivity is simultaneously fantastical, science-fictional and
horrific. Herein, I believe, lies the fundamental reason for the blurry
boundaries between the genres, as they are written in Ireland. I believe
that this tendency will persist in Irish SF, even as broader changes occur
in Irish culture.

The second way in which the emergence of a scientist "class" was
vital to the emergence of modern SF is that it created the perception
of a special category of person defined by "expertise," which is now
the principal means by which SF works – the author pretends to be
an expert, and the reader meets him or her halfway, through what
Angenot terms "the absent paradigm," and what Miéville describes as
a willing surrender of cognition. This kind of expertise on the part of
the author resonates with modernity's attitude to science in general.
Most readers are content to simply know that there exists a class
of people called "scientists," and that the "job" of these people is to
produce scientific knowledge (in much the same way that one does not
need to be a soldier to enjoy novels about war, or a detective to enjoy
crime fiction). In addition to this enlightened class, modernity and the
Enlightenment also cultivated the view of history as an ever-onwards
kind of progress, and necessary to this conception of history is the
abjection of the less-developed past; this in turn, according to Adorno
and Horkheimer, creates a fear that the past might come back. When
both these factors are combined and elaborated upon, the conclusions
are somewhat unsettling.

I argued in my introduction that SF is ahistorical because it "pretends
to be history," or tries to convince us that its estrangements are historically possible or inevitable. When the media speaks of "science fiction
becoming science fact," more often than not what is really at issue is
the gadgetry, not the depicted societal changes – it seems that everybody
wants a jet-pack, a robot butler or a flying car, but only a few regard

the egalitarian future of *Star Trek* (to take the most commonly cited example) as being even remotely feasible, and fewer still are prepared to put any effort into making it a reality in any way, shape or form. Because "proper" scientific knowledge is the sole preserve of an "expert" scientist class, "lay" people learn to use the gadgets, without having to understand the scientific principles that make them work. Nevertheless, we feel the fear of backsliding just as keenly. Our technology becomes a token of our modernity: people with no scientific training will point to technology as proof that their culture is "civilised" (usually in the course of belittling the difficulties of present-day tribal societies), when they themselves have no idea how that technology works. The technological view of modernity and civilisation is, when seen in this light, little more than a cargo cult, with the masses eagerly awaiting the delivery of scientific marvels from a special class of people.

Because so much Western SF, being a product of Western culture, reflects Western norms, beliefs and taboos, the incorporation of non-Western or indigenous myth into a science-fictional narrative structure can be a powerful tool for authors from groups that have historically been excluded, such as Nalo Hopkinson, Nnedi Okorafor and Larissa Lai, who utilise non-Western myth to different extents to articulate Jamaican, Nigerian and Asian-Canadian subjectivities, respectively (in addition, all three are female writers, articulating subjectivities that have often been marginalised within what is traditionally seen as a male-dominated genre). This is the essence of Yamano's view of the genre as a "pre-fabricated house" that non-Western authors must alter or redesign to satisfy their own tastes and needs.

Irish SF, in contrast to works produced by authors from other postcolonial territories, does not explicitly draw upon its indigenous mythology – to my knowledge, there is just one text that makes overt use of pre-Christian mythology (Mairéad Ní Ghráda's *Manannán*), but only in terms of borrowing names, and there is just one novel (Flann O'Brien's *The Dalkey Archive*) that openly incorporates Catholic religious teaching into a pseudoscientific explanatory model of the world. The last Irish people to genuinely live according to an indigenous premodern tradition either were mostly illiterate or had little interest in tackling modernity with recourse to that tradition: unlike the *puri-puri* of Carpentaria, Biddy Early's magic did not complement or attempt to incorporate scientific logic in any way, and the murder of Bridget Cleary represented an attempt to disavow modernity, rather than come to terms with it. Thus, Ireland did not produce a "pure" indigenous pseudoscientific tradition. This had an appreciable effect on Irish-language literature particularly, which did not produce mythic interpretations of modernity until the appearance of twentieth-century writers who were actually hostile to it. The "separate but equal" coexistence of pagan and Catholic traditions during the nineteenth century also points to a cultural logic of subjectivity and pragmatism – these traditions were judged not according to their supposed veracity, but according to their utility.

Thus, because popular culture has only (comparatively) recently been impacted by science, the "cargo cults" are political rather than technological. Prosperity is delivered from on high by a special class of people, politicians and demagogues rather than wizards or scientists: rather than the gadgets fetishised by Western modernity, in Irish popular culture it is political influence ("pull") that is fetishised. This is encouraged by an electoral system that often pits candidates of the same party against each other in the same constituency, thus forcing them to campaign on a clientelist basis (Kirby and Murphy 2011, 26). Thus, twentieth-century Irish SF most often treats the future as something to be *purchased* rather than invented. To me, this suggests that Irish culture in general has internalised the discourses of both colonialism and Catholic bourgeois capitalism, both of which include the notion that, in temperament, the Irish are more mystical than scientific. Therefore, the future must be imported from elsewhere.

Modernity came to be seen less as a historical epoch, and more as a system of societal structures that was being imposed from an outside world that was indifferent to the Irish at best, and hostile at worst. This ideology became hegemonic in the newly independent Ireland of the 1920s and 1930s, which had (understandably) developed a fear of infiltration and re-colonisation that coexisted with the nationalist urge to salvage an "authentic" indigenous culture. The result was that in the Free State, as in the time of Swift, it was possible to disregard science and modernity, and refuse to take them seriously. Many of the texts produced at this time, such as Micheál Mac Craith's "Cuairt ar an nGealaigh," were reminiscent of early modern and even mediaeval narratives, despite their contemporary or near-future settings. When popular literature was not hearkening back to a bygone era, it was dramatising the fear of dangerous forces from the outside world, as in Seosamh Ó Torna's "Duinneall" and "Marbhán" by the pseudonymous "Conán."

This anxiety was partially a consequence of independence and economic underdevelopment. Ireland had been a pre-industrial economy up until independence, and the shock of being suddenly thrust into a modern world, one which the Irish people were neither culturally nor economically prepared for, accounts not just for the anti-modernist impulse, but also for the emergence of an "island mentality." After all, the Famine resulted from a previous clash between Ireland and economic modernity, and the "stalking skeleton" of that clash still loomed large over Irish culture. Whereas once the Irish eagerly followed international news, during the twentieth century it became increasingly common to ignore the outside world in the hope that it would just go away. It is hard not to infer that Ireland regarded itself as a refuge of subjectivity in a world that was increasingly fetishising "objective" reality.

As I have argued here, the Irish tendency to challenge modernity has survived intact from the time of Jonathan Swift. In *Gulliver's Travels*, magic has not been disproved by science, but pushed off the edge of the map. Bound up with those older cultural logics are older forms of social organisation, such as the ancient Gaelic aristocracy, pined after by the *fili*, the bardic class left powerless by the death of that civilisation. In Swift's time, one could imagine that magic still "worked" in some unknown island beyond the horizon, but by the nineteenth century, the world had been comprehensively mapped. In a bizarre fashion, to outsiders, Ireland became one of the last geographic refuges of premodern otherness, due mainly to what Declan Kiberd describes as the "necromantic" impulse of the Irish poetic imagination, which continually hearkened back to a time when magic "still worked." This repeated return to the past had obvious appeal to nationalists, as it rendered possible the resurrection of an "authentic" Ireland.

The Professor in Erin, in dramatising this nationalist myth, gives voice to another colonial anxiety: namely, that people were only interested in Ireland and the Irish because that authenticity is gone, a hybrid culture amenable to tourists exists in its place, and Ireland thus represents a "safe" kind of exoticism. Here, visitors could experience one of the defining characteristics of lost world fiction as described by John Rieder, without having to travel to the jungles of Africa, Asia or South America for the privilege. A lost world is "a place where [the protagonists] find a fragment of their own history lodged in the midst of a native population that usually has forgotten the connection"; thus, the discovery of the hidden territory is reconfigured as the rediscovery of a lost *legacy*, handy justification for the appropriation of indigenous wealth and resources (Rieder 40). The emergence of hibernophiles thus seems to have created an anxiety of being scrutinised and appropriated, and the existence of scholars such as the protagonist of *The Professor in Erin*, Schliemann, served as confirmation that the "real" Ireland was truly gone forever. Eugene O'Brien, in his Lacanian reading of the "republican *imaginaire*," says of this imagined authentic country that "the 'ideal-Ireland' is reified, or fixed, allowing for no deviation from the temporal path set out in the imaginary mindset" (149).

What seems to have happened, as a consequence of colonisation, is that the Irish developed an anxiety of being unfairly, unfavourably judged according to inapplicable standards, having previously been judged according to imperial ethnic, religious and gender norms, and deemed failures in all three categories: sub-human, superstitious and perverted. More worryingly, Ireland was romanticised by people who seemed to know little about it, people who celebrated an "inauthentic" culture that Irish nationalists were trying to get rid of. Then, there was the threat of falling out of step with the modern world, in which agreement with the prevailing ideology of the West was considered the same as objectivity and efficiency, and those who did not concur ran the risk of being dismissed as unrealistic, inefficient "Yahoos." The prescriptive structures of social organisation implied by modern means of production became a threat, both to utopian nationalism (because they denied the possibility of resurrecting the authentic Gaelic kingdoms of the past) and to the Catholic Church (ever watchful for threats to its ideological dominance). Naturally, this anxiety and hostility came to be applied to cultural innovations, and thus modernist literature, music and art acquired apocalyptic significance. Thus, the feeling of being "under siege" is an Irish phenomenon, not just a characteristic of Ulster unionism or the Ascendancy class to which it is more usually ascribed.

The perception of being under siege from a powerful enemy will probably continue to inform much Irish SF for the foreseeable future – Ireland's continued membership of the EU will keep this theme alive, as will the country's long-term dependence on foreign investment and energy supplies. Ulster unionism, on the other hand, has been a "siege culture" for far too long to simply change overnight with the end of the Troubles, since the threat of a united Ireland remains. For the most part, Ireland does not see itself as an element of an interdependent web of nations and international relations, and therefore, it is more than likely that SF themes will be explored on a "parochial" rather than a "universal" level. An Irish SF author is less likely to depict an alien invasion of Earth in general than of Ireland in particular.

By the 1960s, the tactic of ignoring science and modernity was no longer possible, and by the 1990s, religious tradition was mostly irrelevant where it was not being used as justification for violence. The same time period has seen instances of what can almost be described as a newfound disdain for the past – old Georgian buildings were torn down to make room for new developments, the Viking settlement at Wood Quay in Dublin was destroyed to create room for office blocks, and numerous Neolithic sites have been bulldozed to make way for wider roads – most notable among this latter category is the Hill of Tara, which is internationally recognised to be an endangered world heritage site due to its proximity to the M3 motorway. As a result of Ireland's increasing adjustment to the modern world, Irish SF became more and more derivative of British and American works, as has happened elsewhere – Langer points out that this happened to Japanese SF, for example (Langer 25). There are, however, remnants of old ideologies to be found in the newer texts.

Most dystopian narratives, for example, seem to follow the same pattern: an inhabitant of dystopian society starts to notice anomalies in the historical record or logical fallacies in the state's ideology, asks awkward questions, is pursued by the various repressive apparatuses of their society, and subsequently escapes (or tries to) into the "real world" outside of the dystopian slum in which they have been living until now. The "real world" is nearly always rural, and it is sometimes depicted as a rustic utopia, in contrast to the dystopian environment, which is invariably urban, often industrialised if not explicitly "scientific" in its social organisation, and characterised by a total separation of the citizenry from the natural world. Sometimes, the hero returns to overthrow the dystopian state and bring society back to its wholesome, natural roots (or else dies trying). It is difficult to tell to what extent this oft-employed narrative arc is influenced by pastoral utopian literature, twentieth-century novels such as Ray Bradbury's *Fahrenheit 451* (1953) or the "ruralism" of the Free State's fundamentalist Catholic hegemony.

Irish SF is showing increasing signs of influence from Western popular culture, and this will probably continue. For much of the twentieth century, this kind of influence was completely dependent on economic factors – an individual's access to British or American texts was contingent on their having a disposable income large enough to allow for entertainment expenses. Nowadays, the variety, affordability and ubiquity of information technology have to a large extent removed any such economic barriers, and so the influence of foreign media will continue, on a huge scale. Thus, Irish SF will more than likely reflect broader trends in the genre across the Western world, possibly even to a derivative level. However, with this increased level of international influence comes the potential for fruitful experimentation with SF tropes and Irish subjectivities.

In *City of Bohane* (which will be discussed in greater detail below), for example, allusions to ahistorical media abound. "All Our Yesterdays," a column in the titular city's main newspaper, is taken from the title of the second-to-last episode of the original series of *Star Trek*. The "Black Atlantic" is a feature of the dystopian, post-apocalyptic setting of "Judge Dredd," from the weekly British SF/adventure comic *2000AD*. The novel includes a drawn map of Bohane on the inside back cover, à la most "high fantasy" fiction. The sand-pikeys, meanwhile, could have been taken from any number of post-apocalyptic films of the 1980s – the very fact that they live in the dunes south of the city is a nod to *Mad Max* (1979) and its sequels, whose arid Australian Outback setting established a narrative convention of sorts for post-apocalyptic fiction. Aside from this, other possible international influences present themselves in almost every chapter: the gang-dominated setting instantly calls Martin Scorsese's *Gangs of New York* (2002) to mind, as well as Frank Miller's graphic novel series *Sin City* (1991–2000) and its film adaptation (2005).

However, all of these stylistic influences are incorporated into an authentically Irish setting. For example, there is the scene in which a child messenger arrives in a rural pub to describe what he has seen taking place in the city, only to fall insensible from the stress of it all and require repeated draughts of vigour-restoring liquor, while a crowd gathered around hangs on his every word. The staging of the scene and the dialogue spoken are reminiscent of a Synge stage play (121–7).

Another area in which international SF will have a noticeable effect is Irish-language SF. Mac Giolla Bhuí's *Domhan Faoi Cheilt* demonstrates how this might happen. Not only is the setting borrowed wholesale from American space opera, but there are no original neologisms: the closest is "féasair," an Irish-language transcription of *Star Trek*'s "phasers." The readers of Irish-language texts are guaranteed to be bilingual, and therefore those who would read SF texts in Irish are more than likely to be fans of English-language SF. Thus, this kind of transcription offers a path of least resistance through the problems created by standardisation – everyone in the Western world has a fair idea of what a "phaser" is, even if they have never seen an episode of *Star Trek*. Innovation in Irish-language SF will come about not through the invention of radical new forms, but through the deconstruction and reinterpretation of SF clichés.

The Future

One significant cultural change, which has intensified over the past decade, is that Irish people are starting to abandon the necromantic obsession with the past, and seem increasingly willing to engage with the future – good, bad or indifferent. This could be attributed to the end of the Celtic Tiger economy, and the uncertainty that came in its wake.

In *Ireland in 2050: How We Will Be Living*, economist Stephen Kinsella argues that the post-Tiger mood of economic pessimism is actually a manifestation of "the growing pains of extremely rapid structural changes"; we see only gloom and doom ahead because "our economy has developed faster than our mindsets" (Kinsella 25). "Confidence [by which Kinsella obviously means 'optimism'] matters" (33) – an economic boom only lasts as long as people believe in it, and the minute people stop believing in their own purchasing power, they ruin it for everyone else. This is, I admit, an over-simplification of Kinsella's arguments, but there is no denying the fact that, as he is an economist, it is natural that he should also be something of an evangelist, as evidenced by his quasi-proselytising tone: "I will judge this book a success if you, the reader, begin to think seriously about the future and its likely effects on your life" (34).

Extrapolating from current demographic, economic, political and environmental trends, Kinsella makes some observations which have come true well in advance of his 2050 timeline, such as the advent of water charges (104), and some that are obvious, such as the eventual collapse of the Irish health service unless resources are diverted to it (207). The demographics of the Irish workforce will change, as the elderly and retired percentage of the population will increase dramatically while the numbers of people working to support the retired will fall (32). This increased generation gap will result in the elderly becoming an active political force, while primary and post-primary education will have to change in order to encourage children's creativity in an increasingly competitive global market (207). The combined impact of water shortages and climbing insurance premiums due to climate change will reduce the choices of places to live, especially for the poor, leading to the creation of "near-ghettos" in areas prone to flooding (104–6). On the bright side, Ireland's tourism industry will prosper, because "[as] the world warms up, people will begin looking to go to places where they can avoid the summer heat, rather than travel to it" (105). In 2050, Dublin will be the size that Los Angeles is now (106), and the population explosion will increase demand for solitude, which in turn will drive up land prices, especially in rural areas (107–8). The larger population will oblige Ireland to buy nuclear power from the UK or France (110–17). In terms of international finance, Ireland will have to choose "east or west" and "stick to it," as the country's future will be best served by "embedding ourselves within the world's most likely long-term economic success story" (206–7).

The most notable aspect of Kinsella's analysis is his insistence that "[t]echnology is pervasive, but, in many important ways, it changes *nothing*," because actual business negotiations will always be conducted as they are now; furthermore, technology is "only a set of tools – a bag of hammers," and will not solve any problem in and of itself, a notion

Kinsella dismisses as the anticipation of "robot monkey butlers" (35–6). This analytical slant is obviously problematic: for example, Gutenberg's moveable type may not have had any immediate effect on the manner in which late mediaeval peasants haggled over livestock, but to conclude from the continuation of those business practices that the printing press ultimately "changed nothing" would be ridiculous. In my opinion, this point of view can be attributed to the internalised colonial discourse of Irish culture. The only way in which the Irish are permitted to engage with the future, it seems, is to buy it from somewhere else, and the notion that the Irish just "don't do science" becomes a self-fulfilling prophecy when it is invoked to ridicule scientific endeavour.

Because his predictions are predicated upon things that are more or less beyond human control, Kinsella's analysis largely reaffirms a sense of Ireland's powerlessness. While one could make the argument that Ireland is a small country, and therefore realistically there are many things beyond Ireland's control, the fact is that this view can also serve as an excuse to do nothing, or abdicate responsibility: because Ireland is a small country with little control over its destiny, nobody is to blame when things go wrong, and there is little point trying to improve anything. Others disagree, and have reacted to the economic downturn not with pessimism or denial, but with calls for the wide-scale re-organisation of society.

For example, Kirby and Murphy argue for the establishment of a "Second Republic." There are a number of problems to be overcome, not least of which is the legacy of a past which hindered industrialisation, and placed a disproportionate amount of power in the hands of the landowning classes and the Roman Catholic Church, thereby giving rise to a popular culture favouring authoritarianism, conformity and anti-intellectualism, and thus to a political culture of blame avoidance and ad hoc planning (Kirby and Murphy 27). The situation is not helped by the ineffectiveness of the Seanad, the retention of a party whip system, and the de facto lack of a separation of power between the executive and the legislature (24–5). On top of all this, monopoly ownership of the media, the diminution of satire and a weak public intellectual tradition have contributed to the absence of a "counter-discourse" in Irish society (39): "In Habermasian terms, what is missing is a public sphere" (41).

Opposed to this, Kirby and Murphy propose a "bedrock of values." Firstly, a sense of equality is required that goes beyond the individualistic, so that no person or group of people can dominate another, or has to live in fear of being dominated (189–90). Secondly, republicanism in its original sense requires active participation, and thus the construction of a "robust public realm" (190). Thirdly, what is needed is "[an] ethic of care, interdependence and solidarity" (191), and lastly, sustainability, "achieving a sustainable balance between the functioning of the economy and society on the one hand, and the wider ecosystem on the other" (192). Kirby and Murphy also propose a number of necessary reforms to go along with these values, such as the drafting of a bill of rights (196), the separation of powers (196–7), local government reform (197) and electoral reform (198).

The relative strengths and merits of each body of arguments could be argued at length, but they indicate that this is a pivotal moment in Irish history, of the kind that encourages literary experimentation. It is only natural that at a moment of such palpable historical potential, narratives would emerge that take the ahistoricity of Irish subjectivity as their central theme – as happened before with *The Professor in Erin* (published as the popular movement for independence was gathering momentum) and *The Dalkey Archive* (published as secular threats to the dominance of Catholic dogma started to become more apparent).

20/16 Vision (2009) is the debut novel of the poet Hugh Maxton (pseudonym of the literary historian and critic W.J. McCormack). Thematically, the text is split into two main sections, which initially do not seem to have much to do with one another: the larger first part, made up of books one and two, is set in the days and weeks leading up to the centenary of the 1916 Rising. Ireland has been re-united as a federal republic, with each province having its own Provincial Vice President who retains absolute control over his or her own province's affairs, and an All-Ireland President who resides in Phoenix Park. Efforts are made to ensure the comfort of Ulster unionists through several initiatives, including a statue-swap between Dublin and Belfast (34–8). In the background, a coup is underway, as "the Brotherhood," an unnamed paramilitary organisation, has reinvented itself as a business concern and is using economic trends to seize control of the country.

The second thematic section, book three (203–79), is an alternative history set in Dublin in 1941, which is under Nazi control – as in 1917's *The Germans in Cork* and *The Germans at Bessbrook*, the invasion has been aided by Irish republican collaborators (253). Within the confines of the "Shellburnt" Hotel, a group of guests and hotel staff work behind the scenes to keep a young Jewish pianist out of the hands of the local SS commander. At last, it is revealed that the whole book is founded upon this alternative history.

There are multiple kinds of ahistoricity here: first of all, there is the implied future-history of Ireland's re-unification, and the alternative history of Nazi-occupied Dublin. This ahistoricity is compounded by the

Rising centenary, whereby an artificial history of military triumph will be commemorated and further removed from actual history: for example, Roger Casement's contribution to the Rising will not be included in the commemoration, as his alleged homosexuality might cause problems for the event's American corporate sponsors (122).

Unfortunately, the whole is less than the sum of its parts. Maxton's use of a poetic rather than a novelistic register renders large portions of the narrative incomprehensible. His repeated swipes at nationalist ideology, while to a certain extent necessary in any text dealing with the 2016 commemoration, come across less as cogent criticisms of that ideology than as navel-gazing. The resulting vagueness of the narrative world means that the text's more problematic elements stand out, such as the flaccid attempts at satire (to give one example, a political fixer is named "Wheeler-Delehan") and the inclusion of a female character for the sole purpose of being raped and murdered in order to frame a foreign diplomat (140–3). Ultimately, the novel hints at the ahistorical tendencies of Irish culture, but fails to explore them in any meaningful way, other than to show the continuation of the current cynicism of Irish politics into the near future. Clientelism, blame-avoidance and other problems in Irish politics are naturalised, and (as in Kinsella's predictions) the only changes that occur are cosmetic in nature – fundamentally, society remains the same.

Kevin Barry's IMPAC Award-winning *City of Bohane*, set in 2053–2054 in the eponymous fictional city in the west of Ireland, tackles ahistoricity much more successfully. Bohane is a bleak urban environment where crime and murder are part of the fabric of everyday life. To the east lies the expanse of bogland known as the Big Nothin', out of which the River Bohane flows west through the city and into the Black Atlantic, and to the south is an expanse of sand dunes. The most profitable trades in Bohane are prostitution and opium, both of which are concentrated in the Smoketown area, controlled by the gangster Logan "The Albino" Hartnett, chief of the gang now known as the Hartnett Fancy. The city has been calm for many years, but the peace is starting to look shaky, as the Fancy's traditional rivals, the families of the Northside Rises, have been growing in strength and are seeking an official feud. To make matters worse, the Fancy's former boss, a ruthless man known as "The Gant" Broderick, has returned from the Big Nothin' after an absence of twenty-five years, for reasons best known to himself.

There is scant description of the Ireland of the 2050s. Bohane is regarded by "the Nation Beyond" as being the worst city in the country, and it effectively functions as a semi-independent, kratocratic micro-nation. In another telling plot element, Travellers (now known almost exclusively as "Pikeys") live – or perhaps, are kept – on reservations.

There is a definite air of ahistoricity about the city of Bohane. On the one hand, there are obvious clashes between the modern and the pre-modern. De Valera Street, where Logan Hartnett lives, has an eccentric mix of denizens:

> There are soothsayers. There are purveyors of goat's blood cures for marital difficulties. There are dark caverns of record stores specialising in ancient calypso 78s [...] There are palmists. There are knackers selling combination socket wrench sets [...] there are cages of live poultry, and trinket stores devoted gaudily to the worship of the Sweet Baba Jay. There are herbalists, and veg stalls, and poolhalls. (32–3)

The characters are indifferent to what goes on outside the city, aside from the "Bohane Authority," which convenes to discuss the political fallout of the recent surge in violent crime. "[Sweet Baba Jay ("sweet Baby Jesus")] wept! As if our fuckin' name wasn't bad enough!" "Oh, those bastards in the Nation Beyond will be laughin' up their sleeves tonight!" (156). For the rest of the characters, however, the world has shrunk – as Ireland's connection with the outside world shrank from an imperial frame of reference to an island mentality in the twentieth century, in the mid-twenty-first it has shrunk again, from an island to a balkanised collection of cities. To them, there is effectively no such thing as "Ireland," a wider country of which they are citizens; there is only Bohane, and more important than Bohane are the neighbourhoods in which they live and the local rulers to which they pledge allegiance.

The tribalism of the city has mediaeval overtones. Each gang has its own insignia, including the "polis fraternities" (190), and the Fancy has its own distinct symbols, which the fighters carry into battle on giant banners – a puck goat's head, a scimitar dirk and a "dog-star moon" (146). When they meet the forces of the Northside Rises for pitched battle, they do so in the manner of mediaeval armies, marching to meet each other, and then charging (146–50). Not once in the entire narrative does any character use a firearm – the most common weapon is a "shkelp" (a long blade), followed by other close-combat weaponry such as blackthorn clubs (better known as "shillelaghs," but never referred to as such in the novel), chains and steel-toed boots.

The account of the feud is outlined after the fact, as Balthazar Grimes, the hunchbacked photographer for the *Bohane Vindicator*, lays out the pictures he has taken of the battle and arranges them into a coherent narrative, culminating in the death of the Northside leader, Eyes Cusack. Grimes's attitude to the combatants reveals that the city's tribalism includes everyone, and there can be no such thing as neutrality: "The hunchback Balt Grimes came to the end of the line and wryly he smiled. Norrie bluster, it seemed, was of a moment's lasting, and Back Trace class was permanent" (152–5). The attitude displayed here is not a modern one. Rather than delivering the denunciations of hooliganism one might expect of a tabloid newspaper, the *Vindicator*'s coverage of the incident indicates that events like this are largely seen as legitimate and inevitable, the continuation of Bohane tribal politics by other means.

Mediaevalism seeps into other aspects of Bohane's social life. Following the battle, and the death of their leader, the Rises are overcome with a wave of fervent "Baba-love," engineered by Hartnett by faking stigmata in a little girl. The religious outburst quickly forms the basis of a cult that is thoroughly mediaeval in character, with new miracles every week and prayer flags strung between the high-rise blocks, all of which culminates in calls for the genital mutilation of "sluts" as a punishment for "their attempted seductions of decent Baba-devoted young Norrie men," along with bizarre credos such as "Grog Is The Devil's Spit! Dogs Have Souls Too! Polacks Can Never Be Clean!" (223–7).

The epic battles, bardic storytelling and heroic characterisation point to the resurrection of an older way of life – specifically, the way of life eulogised by the *filí*. All that is missing from Bohane is the depiction of an epic cattle raid. Time has in fact been rewound to the point where Ireland's "true" history ended, just before the island was invaded and the indigenous high culture irrevocably changed. Bohane, it transpires, is the "authentic Ireland," not the unconquered constitutional monarchy of Charlotte McManus's *Erin*.

The necromantic impulse within Irish culture is also explored in its most basic form, nostalgia, which we are told is "a many-hooked line" on the Bohane peninsula (60). This is largely a consequence of the logic of blood feuds, since the maintenance of a feud requires a constant referral (and *de*ferral) to history, but it also reflects one of the novel's dominant themes – several of the characters are keenly aware that they are getting older, and there will soon be no place for them in the cut-and-thrust of gangland politics. In the run-up to the big fight with the Northside Rises mob, the Gant's former lover Macu wonders why "I'm forty-fuckin'-three and I'm sat around talkin' fuckin' *gang fights*?" (103). Towards the end of the narrative, the Gant starts to spend time in the Capricorn Bar, reminiscing about the old days with other men his age and older (255–7, 261–3). The third-person, omniscient narrator eventually reveals himself to be the proprietor of "The Ancient & Historical Bohane Film Society," where citizens can go to sit in a booth and watch films of Bohane in times past. The narrator notes that his stock of films goes back to "the thirties," but does not clarify whether he means the 1930s or the 2030s. He notes the popularity of his service by obliquely hinting, "I don't need to advertise" (178–80). We are also told that one of the most popular features in the *Bohane Vindicator* is a column called "All Our Yesterdays," written "in a limpid and melancholy prose, and its stock was the reminiscence and anecdotes of the Bohane lost-time." The end of the Gant's relevance to the everyday life of Bohane is confirmed when he agrees to be interviewed for this very column (195–201).

This nostalgia and mediaeval social organisation is contrasted with the threatened return of a barbaric past. Despite the apparently hierarchical relationship between Bohane and the "Nation Beyond," the expanse beyond the city walls is completely lawless, and the violence encountered outside is much more extreme without even the oversight of a gang boss to control it: while out on the Big Nothin', for example, two of Hartnett's lieutenants come across the skinless, mutilated body of an informer hanging from a bridge; despite all that they have witnessed and taken part in up to this point, the hardened gangsters are shocked by this discovery and beat a hasty retreat to the safety of the city (83). We are also told that, presumably thanks to global warming, there are poppy fields growing "in the tropic heat of August" east of the Traveller reservation (243), which are harvested to supply narcotics to the city. The usual pattern of contemporary Irish dystopian fiction has been broken here – the urban environment is dangerous and dirty, to be sure, but the rural expanse beyond is even more perilous. Even without the immediate threat of violence, the countryside is hardly a utopia, but a "Big Nothing": as the Irish midlands currently remain cluttered with ghost estates, and continue to be depopulated by emigration, this particular prediction cannot be dismissed as altogether unbelievable.

The ultimate signifier of pre-modernity (or rather, retro-pre-modernity) in the text is the sand-pikey tribe. The word "pikey," problematic as it is, is used with abandon throughout the text, referring both to the Travelling community and to this strange, marginal group. Aside perhaps from certain aspects of their trade (it is mentioned at one point that they manufacture and sell gates to farmers on the Big Nothin'; 185), there is very little resemblance between these people and real-world Travellers: their slang is derived from Jamaican patois, they braid their beards and wear dreadlocks, and they keep animalistic slave girls known as "lurchers" (164–6). The leader of the sand-pikeys is

Prince Tubby, whose official title is "the Far-Eye," a soothsayer endowed with a kind of Papal infallibility by his people: "All that come from de I-and-I is truth and Baba-sent" (137). The Gant, by contrast, is actually a Traveller by heritage: "it was known in Bohane there was a good mix of pikey juice in him. A rez boy – campfire blood" (53). He was born on the reservation, and his speech contains fragments of Shelta (a language spoken by Irish Travellers), most notably the word "lackeen" ("girl").[2] His story lends a hint of alternative history to the narrative: in order for the Gant to have been born on a reservation, such a place would have to have existed in the early 2010s, indicating that perhaps the idea of a Traveller reservation is an ironic comment on the current haphazard (and often woefully inadequate) system of halting sites, designated areas where Travellers are permitted to camp. Despite this background, the Gant is a well-respected man, and his ethnicity is not commented upon to any great extent. This is in marked contrast to the city-dwellers' attitudes towards the sand-pikeys.

In exchange for fighting on the Fancy's side in the feud, Logan gives the sand-pikeys a third of the Smoketown trade (138–9), much to the horror of both his gang and the Bohane Authority. A political fixer named Ol' Boy Mannion, helping the Authority to come up with a way to manage the situation, says that although he means "no disrespect to their ethnic heritage," "the last thing we want to be known as is Pikey Central" (159–60). The anxiety is mirrored on the gangland side. When the tribe starts to move into the city from the dunes, Hartnett's lieutenant Jenni Ching lectures the Far-Eye about behaving in a civilised manner, "coz yer in the fuckin' city now, right?" (185–6).

It is unclear where the sand-pikeys appeared from, whether they are supposed to be a future offshoot of the Travelling community or a wholly separate group, or, if they are in fact ethnically related to the Travellers, how they came to adopt a pseudo-Rastafarian culture. It is not explained how the Travellers came to be living on a reservation, though the implication is that they were forcibly relocated there; neither are we told why the sand-pikeys were the exception to this rule, and allowed to live freely on the dunes. It seems that they exist only to confront the residents of Bohane with a reflection of their own pre-modern barbarity, parodying the central trope of lost world fiction, whereby modern explorers confront the "living fossils" of their own past.

Despite the mediaeval political, social and religious organisation of Bohane society, the premodern resolution of disputes by pitched battle, and the primacy of history (referred to as "the lost-time") within the city's culture, Jenni still feels justified in warning the Far-Eye, "I'm tryin' to keep things a bit fuckin' civilise [sic] aroun' this joint, ya hear what I'm sayin' t'ya?" (186). In a post-apocalyptic future, there is still an anxiety that the past might return, even as society tries to rebuild itself in the ruins of the ended world.

Protagonists

Based on the trends examined thus far, I predict (without any assurances) that the settings of future Irish SF works will tend towards small-scale "lost worlds" in which the ahistorical genres are blurred, and the passage of time and history are reversed, mixed and matched or stalled in some way – works set in a distant, post-human future will be in the minority, as will epic future histories that span entire galaxies. The growing popularity of "slipstream" fiction and genre-blurring in Britain and America will encourage this trend, and I believe that Irish authors will continue to produce such works after the popularity of these sub-genres has faded elsewhere. From these trends, we can also extrapolate the kind of characters that will populate these settings.

The protagonists of Irish SF are often characterised by unstable ethnic, religious and gender identities, prone to Hamlet-esque indecisiveness and lack of self-esteem, despite their heroic roles. Ethnically Anglo-Irish writers existed "on the hyphen" and produced protagonists whose identities were similarly torn by their ties to two different tribes. In addition, religious identity was conflated with ethnic identity, to the extent that Protestant Irish people were largely regarded as a separate breed from their Catholic neighbours, and vice versa. This conflation of ethnic and religious identity is discussed in detail in James Creed Meredith's *The Rainbow in the Valley*, whose Protestant protagonist is annoyed to discover that the other characters presume him to be Catholic because he is Irish. Gender identity was no less problematic: the Act of Union had been figured as a "marriage," while Irish people, as Celts, had long been stereotyped as violent and sexually perverse. Irish masculinity, in particular, was figured as being defective during the nineteenth century, most infamously in the violent, apelike cartoon characters of *Punch* magazine, but also in popular literature, where Irishmen who did not live up to this violent stereotype were derided as effeminate.

Irish SF is not suited to pulp-style heroes, and when such characters as Ó Sándair's Captain Spéirling or Joyce's Theo Gilkrensky appear, they are too-obviously reminiscent of the fictional supermen of old, such as Buck Rogers and James Bond. Should the Irish economy improve to Celtic Tiger levels once again, it seems reasonable to expect that a fraction of whatever SF is producing will feature variations on this archetype, privileging action over characterisation. Overall, however, the majority of male protagonists will more than likely continue to exhibit indecision, anxiety and a shaky sense of self. This is contrasted by the massive recent changes in the depiction of female characters.

Until recently, female characters have tended not to be active players in Irish SF narratives, and in this respect, Irish SF is hardly atypical compared to Anglo-American takes on the genre. First, there was Animula, the dream woman of "The Diamond Lens," who is killed by the obsessive gaze of a would-be suitor without ever realising that she is being watched. Following this came the doomed Mignonette, and *The Crack of Doom*'s Natalie Brande and Miss Metford, who tried to defy the boundaries of their gender and paid the price for it. A few short years later there was Gobnait, the tiresome, pious little Cinderella of *Eoghan Paor*. In 1951, *The Last Revolution* presented Alicia, whose status as the fiancée of a mad scientist was also the sum total of her characterisation, so much a damsel in distress that she is kidnapped by a villainous motorbike. Modernisation did not initially change matters for the better. For example, Cathal Ó Sándair's Deirdre Spéirling tags along on her father's missions but literally does nothing, and the titular character from the short story "The Girl from Deep Space" (from *Captaen Spéirling agus an Phláinéad do Phléasc*) is capable of living independently only for as long as she is obliged to.

As outlined in the previous chapter, however, female characters in Irish SF are increasingly influenced by the international media trend towards powerful, capable female protagonists. The warrior woman is no less prone to cliché than the action hero, but within Western media, this character type is most often an underdog, or is representative of a counterculture, and it is perhaps for this reason that Irish authors write competent superwomen better than square-jawed pulp heroes, as it addresses the Irish obsession with infiltration and attack from outside.

Current trends indicate that the SF of the future will, generally speaking, be less concerned with the maintenance of genre boundaries. Bould and Vint note how many SF fans and authors are reacting to the ongoing erosion of these boundaries by proclaiming that SF is "disappearing" (Bould and Vint 182). The increasing popularity of slipstream fiction has, however, been accompanied by an increased interest in "hard" and "mundane" SF, both of which eschew flights of fancy in favour of "proper" science (187), while other new trends experiment with the genre by introducing new settings, rather than tinker with the makeup of the genre itself – there are, for example, more and more works of "historical" SF being published in the present day, in which SF is combined with historical or alternative-historical settings (193). "Proper" SF is clearly not about to become extinct; it has merely been augmented by an increasing willingness to experiment with form.

Most encouraging of all, however, is the fact that this willingness to experiment has been accompanied by "a growing recognition that there is not a single, true history of the genre but a rich diversity of possible science fictions" (202). There are plural histories to genres and nations alike, and multiple ways of dreaming either into being.

Notes

Introduction

1 The version of this joke told by the Dublin comedian Brendan Grace combines a number of Irish jokes into one: the astronauts (who refer to themselves as "spacers") plan to land their turf-powered rocket on the Sun. When told that their vessel will burn up in the attempt, they reply that they have taken this into account, and will consequently be undertaking this mission at night.

2 For example, one text which definitely qualifies as a "futuristic" tale, and which regrettably falls outside the scope of this project, is Royal Dublin Society founder member Samuel Madden's *Memoirs of the Twentieth Century*, originally published in 1733.

3 For a more detailed analysis of this process, see Satpal Sangwan (1990), on the colonial administration of science education in India, whereby actual science education was neglected in favour of the "moral and mental development" of the natives, with the principal aim being to create "a class of sycophants" (88). Richard A. Jarrell, examining science in Ireland, points out that science was largely ignored during the eighteenth and early nineteenth centuries because it posed no threat to political power (330), and consequently a *laissez faire* attitude to science education arose which ensured that there was no agreed-upon science curriculum for Irish schools; specialist science schools, which were intended for the working class, were not as common in Ireland as they were in Britain, and those that existed were concentrated in the industrial centres of Ulster (333).

4 One could point out, however, that the story that eventually became *Frankenstein* arose out of a specific brief – Shelley wrote it as part of a friendly competition where the task was specifically to write a horror tale (53). Stableford points to this as the reason why it has since been "mistakenly" categorised as a gothic novel, and he even goes so far as to describe the novel that Shelley could have (or should have) written (1995b, 55–6).

5 To take just a few examples, one might consider the libertarian (and at times, rabidly anti-liberal) SF of Larry Niven; the martyred leftist revolutionaries of China Miéville's fantasy novels; and the queer, carnivalesque horror of Clive Barker and Poppy Z. Brite.

6 In much the same way, apparently neutral phrases such as "the ancients" reveal a Western-centric bias in that they tend to refer almost exclusively to the ancient Greek and Roman people, and "the ancient world"

more often than not is used as a descriptor for the ancient Greek and Roman spheres of influence.

7 One notable example of this is "global warming": originally intended to succinctly convey scientific findings, the phrase has been widely misinterpreted to mean a uniform worldwide increase in temperature, a "burning world" scenario far removed from the actual data collected, which indicates that the most pressing immediate threats of climate change are intensified storms, flooding and the increased spread of disease.

8 Abe Kôbô is the pen name of the Japanese avant-garde author Abe Kimifusa (1924–1993).

9 There is an interesting comparison to be made between the reception of science-fictional consumer technology and that of large-scale scientific endeavours. While gadgets such as the iPad, the smartphone and the e-reader are widely embraced and become constituent elements of a culture of conspicuous consumption, "proper" science (such as cloning, stem-cell research and the Large Hadron Collider at CERN) often inspires paranoia and moral panic.

10 These are, for instance, the foundational principles of the "New Atheism" movement, typified by the polemicist Richard Dawkins.

11 Oisín, the son of the legendary hero Fionn Mac Cumhail and a renowned hero in his own right, fell in love with a woman from Tír na nÓg, a land of eternal youth, and left Erin to live at her side. Because no time passes in this place, he did not notice the centuries slipping by, until finally homesickness compelled him to return to visit the country of his birth. Warned that on no account must he set foot on Irish soil, he falls from his magical horse and, upon making contact with the ground, ages several hundred years in an instant. In the version of the tale recorded by mediaeval Christian scholars, he then learns of the existence of Saint Patrick, demands to be baptised and renounces his earlier paganism just before he dies of old age.

12 The truth of this reading is apparent in the nomenclature: "Balnibarbi" reads like an Anglicised Irish place name (as in "Ballyna-" or Baile na, meaning "Settlement/town/home of"); and, of course, the capital city of Balnibarbi is named Lindalino – the syllable "Lin" written twice, or, "Double-Lin."

13 Here, Kavanagh is repeating a nationalist truism whose roots can be traced back at least as far as the Young Ireland movement of the nineteenth century. As David Dwan outlines in The Great Community: Culture and Nationalism in Ireland, the Young Irelanders' opposition to cosmopolitanism was a consequence of their opposition to "universalism," which was in turn an expression of their distrust of centralised government (Dwan 35–7). This principle would later degenerate into simple "ruralism," and form a central element of the conservative hegemony of the Free State.

1. Mad Science and the Empire:
Fitz-James O'Brien and Robert Cromie

1 Furthermore, Joe Cleary points out that between 1840 and 1870, the British literary marketplace was dominated by just seven publishing firms and two subscription libraries. The larger of these, Mudie's Select Library, came to dominate the industry through its distribution network, and the adjective "select" refers to the fact that Mudie himself "screened" each text to make sure it contained nothing offensive to public morality (Cleary 71).

2 There were, for example, the Mayo-born Lynch brothers, Henry and Thomas, who joined Francis Rawdon Chesney (himself a native of County Down) to explore the Euphrates route to India; George Croghan, a Dubliner who proved invaluable in the British conquest of the territory of Illinois; and most spectacularly, George Thomas – a native of Roscrea, who served with the British army in India and later seized power over a sizeable area of the subcontinent, earning the title "The Rajah from Tipperary."

3 There are two nineteenth-century Irish texts that fit into the lost-world category. The first of these was Archbishop Richard Whately's *Account of an Expedition into the Interior of New Holland* (1837), describing the discovery of a federation of advanced civilisations, of mixed European and Aboriginal descent, in Australia. The democratic processes of these nations, along with their respective cultures and histories, are discussed in detail by a team of English explorers who come across them by accident. The second text, which perhaps requires a much looser interpretation of "lost world," is *History of a World of Immortals Without a God* (1891) by "Antares Skorpios" (the pseudonym of Jane Barlow, daughter of Reverend James William Barlow, vice-provost of Trinity College Dublin). This text dispatches a misanthropic occultist to Venus by means of meditation-induced teleportation. There, he finds a world without death, disease or material scarcity, and plunges its immortal inhabitants into never-ending despair with his misanthropic ranting. Quite a slight tale, it is really only noteworthy insofar as it openly presents itself as Gulliveriana: *Gulliver's Travels* is the protagonist's favourite book, and he refers to human beings as "Yahoos."

4 Philip O'Leary points out that this distinction would become something of a thorny issue for Irish cultural nationalists during the 1940s: "Most Gaels had always felt a real concern about the way their supernatural beings were misrepresented, caricatured even by those, including their own compatriots, writing in the English language" (O'Leary 2010, 113).

5 It must also be noted, however, that at the same time that these advances were being made, Ireland was undergoing a sort of "brain drain," as inventors and engineers of Irish birth emigrated to pursue their designs, while others were only able to prove their scientific mettle having been educated in other territories. James J. Wood, inventor of the arc-light dynamo and perhaps the most prolific of all nineteenth-century experimenters of Irish extraction (with over 240 patents to his name), was born in Kinsale, County Cork, but grew up in Connecticut and made his career in the United States. Louis Brennan, of Castlebar, County Mayo, emigrated

to Melbourne at an early age, where he later developed the dirigible torpedo and the first unmanned helicopter. The trend of young, scientifically inclined Irish people emigrating to undertake their work continued into the twentieth century – Ernest Walton, the first human being to split an atom, was born in County Waterford and graduated from Trinity College, Dublin, but was not able to accomplish his momentous feat until he had moved to Cambridge.

6 O'Brien seems to have brought this combative attitude to bear in other areas of his life besides his writing. William Winter notes that in 1858, O'Brien's nose was broken by a "pugilist" (xiii), and he maintains that O'Brien was one of the two men (the other being General Lander) who forced the surrender of a Confederate force at Bloomery Gap (xix).

7 The astronomer Heinrich Wilhelm Matthias Olbers (d. 1840) first proposed this theory of the formation of the asteroid belt in 1802. The hypothetical fifth planet was named "Phaeton," and was thought to have been destroyed by Jupiter's gravitational force. Nowadays, this theory has fallen out of favour, and the accepted account of the belt's formation describes the asteroids as the leftovers of planetary formation.

8 In mythology, changelings are infants of the fairy folk (the *daoine sidhe*) substituted for human babies by envious fairy mothers. In some cases, the fairies may even substitute an elderly specimen of their own race. There are a number of ways of tricking the changeling into revealing its true identity, such as making soup out of eggshells (which prompts the changeling to gasp in wonderment, "Three thousand years I've been alive, and I've never seen the brewing of eggshells before!"). If these attempts at trickery fail, the distraught parents have recourse to two items known to be fatal to the *sidhe* – fire and iron.

9 This is made explicit in the myth of Ethné, a fairy who was baptised by Saint Patrick only to discover that she was forevermore separated from her family and homeworld.

10 This assumption can certainly be debated at length – O'Leary, for example, cites editorials and readers' letters from the mid-twentieth century which suggest that literal belief did indeed linger on in some areas (O'Leary 2010, 112–13).

2. "Future War" and Gender in Nineteenth-Century Ireland

1 The phrase "comely maidens dancing at the crossroads," paraphrased from a speech given by Éamon de Valera, is used as a shorthand description of the rural, Catholic Arcadia which many nationalists sought to create in an independent Ireland.

2 The Fenian Brotherhood actually split on this issue shortly after its inception. O'Neill's faction supported a strategy of attacking British colonies, while others prioritised the liberation of Ireland.

3 Timur-i-Lang ("Timur the Lame," or "Tamberlane," the fourteenth-century Turkish-Mongol conqueror of most of Western and Central Asia); Maximilien Robespierre, an influential figure of the French Revolution;

Jeremiah O'Donovan Rossa, a leader of the Fenian Brotherhood who was still alive at the time of this novel's publication; William Wallace, the thirteenth–fourteenth-century Scottish freedom fighter; George Washington; Giuseppe Garibaldi, a leading figure of the Italian Carbonari movement.

3. Nationalist Fantasies
of the Early Twentieth Century

1 The mythological invaders include the Parthalonians (mortal descendants of the god of the dead, responsible for shaping Ireland's physical geography), the Nemedians, the Fomori (evil shape-shifters and sorcerers who tyrannised the country before being cast out by a Nemedian rebellion), the Firbolg, the Tuatha Dé Danann (the gods of the Gaels, who dwindled to the status of fairies and goblins following the arrival of Christianity) and the Gaels (in this context, also often referred to as Milesians).

2 The difference in these men's characters is also illustrated by the itemised lists each drew up of the precepts and ambitions they held for Irish independence. Pearse's list is as follows: "1. The end of freedom is human happiness. 2. The end of national freedom is individual freedom; therefore, individual happiness. 3. National freedom implies national sovereignty. 4. National sovereignty implies control of all of the moral and material resources of the nation" (Mac Aonghusa and Ó Réagáin 1967b, 169). Connolly's list, by contrast, is characteristically resource-oriented: "I. The abolition of the early morning start. II. The abolition of all task or piecework or 'rushing' systems – red with the blood of the workers. III. Reduction of the working day to the limit of eight hours or less, forbidding the physical and mental exhaustion of the workers. IV. Compensations for accidents to equal full pay of the worker injured. V. Pensions to all widows of workers killed at work, such pensions to be a charge upon the firm employing the worker; onus of collecting and disbursing said pension to lie upon the State" (Mac Aonghusa and Ó Réagáin 1967a, 140).

3 "[...] gur chóir dhom' chómharsanaibh tráchtáil is marguidheacht a bheith aca agus bheith ag dul ar aghaidh sa tsaoghal."

4 The Treaty of Limerick, signed on 3 October 1691, ended the war between the Jacobites and the Williamites in Ireland, so long as the (Catholic) Jacobite gentry either swore an oath of allegiance to King William of Orange or emigrated to France. When the Papacy recognised King James as the lawful King of Ireland two years later, the treaty was broken with the introduction of Penal Laws that eradicated Catholic power in Ireland and gave rise to the Protestant Ascendancy. The "Whiteboys" (*Buachaillí Bána*), so called because of the white cloaks they wore, were an eighteenth-century agrarian group that used violence to defend the rights of tenant farmers. The British reaction against this group was held to be excessive, with many innocent people arrested and executed on suspicion of being Whiteboy sympathisers.

5 "Daoine fáidheamhla do b'eadh cuid des na hEireannaigh 'san tsean-aimsir. Le linn na págántachta agus go minic ó shoin i leith chómh

maith bhídís ag trácht tar 'Tír na nOg,' agus ar 'Mágh Meala,' agus ar 'Ibh Breasail' agus is dóich le n-a lán gur leas-ainm ar Neamh iad so [...] Tá tír i nAmericá Theas go ngairmthear Breasail uirthe, agus is é mo thuairm dá stiúraighthidhe chúiche na hEireannaigh seo a bhíonn ar chosa" i n-áirde go hAmericá Thuaidh gach bliadhain gur geárr go mbeadh an oiread aca i nIbh Breasail is go mbeadh an bárr aca annsúd." (Mágh Meala, or "Mag Mell," was another mythical Irish island, the country of the sea-god Manannán Mac Lir. The name means "The Plain of Happiness.")

6 This is a historical quote from the days of the Gaelic clan system, which has since become a *seanfhocal*, or proverb. It stems from a war between a coalition of Kilkenny warriors and a Waterford warlord named Power, who was given to crossing the county border to raid farming communities. The warriors of Kilkenny finally decided to put an end to Power's mischief, and in the final battle at Moonveen, the majority of Power's warriors were slaughtered. Power himself escaped to safety, shouting "Beidh lá eile ag an bPaorach!" over his shoulder as he went. In modern times, the phrase can be translated to mean, "We will live to fight another day."

7 Ireland is divided into four provinces – Munster, Leinster, Connacht and Ulster. The Irish-Gaelic word for "province," however, is "cugadh," which literally means "one fifth." Historical research has suggested that the missing fifth province was somewhere in the midlands around County Meath.

8 "Sidhe" is the proper term for Irish spirit-people (who were believed to despise the term "fairy").

9 Both the protagonist of this narrative and the (fictional) "real" Schliemann mentioned in it are named after the archaeologist Heinrich Schliemann (1822–1890), who believed in the historical veracity of Roman and Hellenic myths. He is best known for his work in the location and excavation of the ancient city of Troy.

10 Canon Sheehan is largely responsible for this bucolic depiction of Germany, despite the fact that he had only ever been there once, on a two-week holiday. Philosophical, wise but serious German professors turn up in a few of his books, and overall the Germany Sheehan presents is held up as a contrast to the sinfulness of the modern age (Fischer 1999, 75).

11 These soldiers were, for the most part, veterans of World War I, and did not constitute a regular military unit. The nickname "Black and Tan" comes from the mix-and-match uniforms they wore, cobbled together from surplus army clothing.

12 The most obvious legacy of the Civil War in present-day Ireland is the domination of the political system by two groups, Fine Gael and Fianna Fáil, respectively the descendants of pro-Treaty and anti-Treaty political groups and activists.

13 To take just one example, the portrayal of the 1916 Rising as a resounding military victory carries such profound narrative power that, in campaigning against the Lisbon Treaty in 2009, the anti-European party Libertas and others were able to make use of it without being challenged to any major extent in the media.

14 "Do cheapas-sa, tráth, gur Críostuidhe mise leis; ach nuair a thosnuigheas ar aithne do chur ar na bochtaibh, fuaras amach mar an gcéad uair cad is Críostuidheacht cheart ann. Thug déantóirí na biotáille £1,000 an lá fé dheire mar dhéire, agus tá gach aoinne ghá moladh: ach tá na milliúin púnt aca. Chonac-sa fear bocht, ná raibh de lón aige i gcóir an lae ach cupán tae, ag tabhairt a leath sin d"fhear eile ná raibh an oiread san aige [...] Dá mbéadh dhá púnt sa tseachtmhain agat-sa agus bean agus ochtar cloinne agat le chothú ar an méid sin, nach mór an teilgean a dhéanfá! Salachar, a dubhraís? Cuirtear ochtar leanbhaí, pé bocht saidhbhir iad, i n-aon seomra amháin, agus feiceann annsan a ghlaine a bheidh sé!"

4. States of Emergency:
Irish SF during World War II

1 Mícheál Mac Craith was born in 1872, and joined the priesthood in 1896.

2 "Is mithid liom, a léightheóir, a innsint duit cad a thug eagla orm roimh líon na nDuinneall. Tuig máiseadh ná bhfuil an Duinneall sásta gan cumhangas a dhéanamh orm. An cuimhneamh atá laistiar den Chiorcal Lochtach tá sé 'á chur i ngníomh. Táthar ad iarraidh Bárr na hEifeachta a bhaint amach. Chuige sin ní fuláir Mór a mhéadughadh agus Beag a dhíotughadh. An ceannaidhe beag agus an ceárdaidhe aonair a scrios agus aoincheannaidheacht agus olldéantús a bhunughadh 'na-ionad. Na bailte beaga a bhánughadh agus an ollchathair a leathnughadh. Abha na Life a chur fé cheilt a' réidheadh slighe do tharrac na mílte ar aon láthair, agus foirgintí a thógaint a chuirfidh an ghrian fé éiclips. Eagar meicneach a chur ar dhaoinibh a dhéanfaidh máinle mór-inill de gach mac máthar aca."

3 Shaw once corresponded with the SF author Arthur C. Clarke, and offered a pseudoscientific explanation for the recent crash of an experimental jet plane and the death of its pilot (i.e. that the jet reached a speed at which the air resistance cancelled out the acceleration of its engines, bringing it to a standstill); when Clarke disagreed with him and argued that the crash was most likely due to a structural fault, Shaw defended his own theory and gave Clarke a "polite brush-off." Further correspondence from Clarke went unanswered (Indick 34).

4 There is also the case of the possibly insane Maurice Ryan, who allegedly joined the republican side in order to kill his own brother (who was fighting for the nationalists), and subsequently opened fire on his comrades-in-arms with a machine-gun (Stradling, 190–2).

5 On the morning of 21 November 1920, fourteen people connected to British Intelligence (a group known as the "Cairo Gang") were assassinated on the orders of Michael Collins (there were twelve IRA shooters involved in this incident, earning them the collective nickname of "The Twelve Apostles"). In reprisal, the Royal Irish Constabulary and the British Auxiliary Division entered Croke Park during a Gaelic football match between Dublin and Tipperary, and opened fire into the crowd, killing fourteen civilians. That evening, three IRA prisoners were shot dead in Dublin Castle, allegedly

while trying to escape. The day of 21 November 1920 was the first day of atrocity in Irish history to be called "Bloody Sunday."

6 The link between the rural, the ancient and authenticity was, of course, not particular to twentieth-century Ireland; as Dwan points out, one of the most noticeable similarities between the Young Ireland movement and the Young England movement (after which the former was ironically named) was an "idealization of the collective bond of a pre-industrial past" (Dwan 41).

7 "Fear pócaí a phiocadh is eadh é siúd," arsa Amón. "Do rugadh air sa choir agus tugadh i láthair an Ard-Mháighistir é. Sé píonós a chuir seisean air ná sruthán aibhléise a chur tré mhéireanna a lámh, agus má bhuaileann sé méar ar éinní feasta raghaidh an sruthán san tré n-a cholainn ar fad agus marbhóchthar é."

8 "Bhí an sluagh ina seasamh amuigh sa tsráid; ceann gach duine aca árduighthe san aer fé mar a bheadh sé ag féachaint ar rud éigin i bhfad uaidh, dath an bháis ar gach aon aghaidh, agus iad go léir ina stalcaí gan anam gan anáil."

9 "Ní fonn linn aon díoghbháil a dhéanamh díbh. Ní dhéanfaidh an tArd-Mháighistir ach chomacht a aigne féin a chur i bhfeidhm oraibh chun ná cuimhneochaidh sibh a thuille ar an ngó a thug annso sibh, agus chun go mbeidh sibh dílis dó, agus ná beidh fúibh díoghbháil a dhéanamh dó féin ná d'éinne eile annso."

10 "A bhuidhe le Dia sinn a bheith i dtír ná fuil Ard-Mháighistir ná Deachtóir uirthe [...] Is measa iad-san ná na Cráidhmí féin."

11 This refers to José Raúl Capablanca, Cuban-born chess world champion from 1921 to 1927. Dunsany himself played against Capablanca twice: in a simultaneous display at the Imperial Chess Club in London on 22 November 1928 (which Dunsany lost), and again on 12 April 1929, when he played Capablanca to a draw.

12 These anxieties are apparent in another aspect of Dunsany's legacy. In addition to his literary works, he is also remembered as the creator of Dunsany's Chess – wherein only one player has the usual complement of pawns, rooks, bishops, knights, a king and a queen; the other player is armed with a marauding force of 32 pawns.

13 This could of course be attributed to Dunsany's fatalism. He was prepared to fight in World War I, and was candid about the fact that he did not expect to survive. He was ironically spared a death in the trenches by an unknown would-be assassin during the 1916 Rising in Dublin, when Dunsany's car was attacked by rebels. Dunsany was shot in the face, and the resulting injuries precluded his taking part in the British war effort.

5. The 1960s: Lemass, Modernisation and the Cold War

1 "Is iomdha duine ar fhiafruigh mé de caidé an fáth nach scríobhann na Gaedhil brionglóidí ar bith ach na rudaí a ghní siad idir maidin agus meadhon oidhche – caidé an fáth nach scríobhann siad corr-bhrionglóid dá

ndéan siad idir meadhon oidhche agus lá. Agus b'ionann freagar a thug gach duine orm .i. 'Oró, a dhuine chléibh, nach bhfuil a fhios agat go gcaithfidh na créatúir fanacht nó go mbíd a leithéid dhá dhéanamh go coitcheannta i gceann éigin de mhór-theangthacha an domhain?' Ach níor géill mé do'n bharamhail sin ariamh, agus ní ghéillfead – go fóill beag, ar scor ar bith."

2 "'Caithfidh tú cúig sgilling a dhíol ar an hata seo,' ar seisean, ag tarraingt aníos hata úr as íochtar an mála. Dhíol mé an t-airgead gan briathar asam, agus thug sé admháil dom; dhearc mé air, agus chuir an dáta cinéal iongantais orm – 12–2–2032. 'Shaoil mé,' arsa mise, 'gur b'é an t-aonmhadh lá déag a bhí ann.'"

3 The phrase "Dublin Jackeen" originally carried an accusation of unionism and collaboration with the British Empire. "Jackeen" comes from "[Union] Jack." Nowadays, this meaning has largely faded away, and the phrase is more commonly used as a general descriptor of the stereotypical ignorant, arrogant Dubliner.

4 This incident bequeathed a new word to Irish slang, which is still commonly used today: to "go Balubas" means "to go berserk."

5 "'Tá rogha mór again, a Ollaimh,' arsan Captaen Spéirling. 'Is iomaí pláinéad sa bhfiormaimint. Nach sár-iontach iad oibreacha an Chruthaitheora! Céard é siúd atá ráite ag an salmóir – *pleni sunt coeli et terra majestatis gloriae tuae!* Lán iad na flaithis agus an talamh de mhaorgacht Do ghlóire! A Ollaimh, is iontach, gan aon agó, í an aois seo inar tharla sinne inár mbeatha lena linn!'"

6 "Tá tú ag foghlaim go tapaidh, a Ríon [...] agus is mór an áthais dom an méid sin."

7 The defining element of the Catholic Mass is the miracle of transub-stantiation; one of the technical requirements of the faith is a belief in the ritual transformation of bread and wine into the body and blood of Jesus Christ. Interpreting this part of the Mass as purely symbolic technically makes one a "lapsed" Catholic.

6. The Wrong History:
Bob Shaw, James White and the Troubles

1 One egregious example of this lack of comprehension appeared in *Stupid White Men* (2001) by American polemicist Michael Moore. His proposed solution to the Northern Irish situation was "Convert the Protestants of Northern Ireland to Catholicism. That's right. No more bickering and battling over religion when everyone belongs to the same religion!" (186).

2 Quoted: Gregory Campbell.

3 The three novels of this sequence – *The Ragged Astronauts, The Wooden Spaceships* and *The Fugitive Worlds* – constitute a rare instance of three linked SF narratives that do not have an "official" overarching title. "The Land Trilogy" is a shorthand derived by fans and critics for this sequence, in the absence of a moniker coined by either the author or the publisher's marketing department.

4 Shaw suffered a serious eye infection in his youth, and this infection

had an unnerving habit of flaring up on a semi-regular basis; fan writer Dave Langford also notes that an incident from Shaw's *Ground Zero Man*, in which a character loses an eye after falling face-first onto a steel reinforcement bar, actually happened to a childhood friend of Shaw's (Langford 1996). Christopher Priest reveals that in later life, Shaw's dread of losing his sight became so pronounced that he would sleep with the light on (Priest 2010).

5 There may very well be readers of ahistorical fiction who cannot cope with the realities of their lives; however, one would hope that it goes without saying that their individual situations more than likely have nothing to do with their choice of reading material.

7. Exotic Doom:
The SF of Ian McDonald

1 For example, certain American pundits have made extensive rhetorical use of the notion of Europe becoming an "Islamic caliphate," while European groups such as the English Defence League oppose the spread of Islam in terms that frame it as an invasion or occupation; Anders Behring Breivik, the Norwegian domestic terrorist who murdered seventy-seven people (sixty-nine of whom were adolescents) in Oslo in June 2011, planned the massacre in reaction to a perceived increase in Muslim immigration to Europe, which he also characterised, in his lengthy manifesto, as an invasion.

2 In Western territories that allow for the practice of sharia law, it is tolerated only so long as all parties in any given dispute agree to use it; it is not endorsed by the civil legislature, and religious leaders cannot legally compel adherence to sharia decisions.

3 "Tiocfaidh ár lá" means "Our day will come," a slogan associated with twentieth-century Irish nationalism.

8. The Dystopian Decades:
From Recession to Tiger and Back Again

1 Due to the 1987 High Court ruling in the case of Crotty vs. An Taoiseach, in which it was reaffirmed that the Constitution could not be altered in any respect without the consent of the majority of the Irish electorate. Thus, the ratification of any European Union treaty necessarily depends upon a public referendum in Ireland. On two occasions (the ratification of the Nice Treaty in 2001/2002 and the Lisbon Treaty in 2008/2009), this has led to EU treaties being delayed by Irish voters' concerns regarding a number of "hot-button" topics, such as abortion, taxation and Ireland's military neutrality. There is also a marked tendency among the Irish public to see these referenda as opportunities to punish the government for unpopular decisions, rather than as pan-European legislative processes. The Nice and Lisbon treaties were initially rejected by the public, citing the above concerns, and were passed a year later in each case, following assurances that Ireland's position on these issues would not be compromised.

2 "Tír, teanga, is teagasc Chriost!" (literally, "Country, Language and the Teachings of Christ!" The shortened translation above was chosen to preserve the alliteration).

3 "'Sé mo bharúil nach raibh polaiteoir sa tír fós a tháinig i bhfoisceacht scread asail de Dan O'Connell. Polaiteoirí den scoth a bhí i bParnell, i De Valéra [sic], i Lemass, sa nGearaltach, agus i Hume. Níl aon chailleadh ar Mac Ádhaimh mar pholateoir, cé nach n-aontaím leis. Ach d'fhéadfá a rá gur chruthaigh Dan an daonlathas in Éirinn. Agus rinne sé é gan deoir fola a ligean [...] 'sé mo bharúil go ndearna leithidí Uí Chonaill agus Mhicheáil Mhic Dhaibhéid níos mó do ghnáthdaoine na tire seo ná mar a rinne lucht 1916 ná lucht an fhornirt rompu agus ina ndiaidh."

4 Until recently, the income a citizen received from an artistic work was tax-free in the Republic of Ireland. Since 2011, this has changed somewhat, so that art-derived income is now only exempt from taxation up to the first €40,000 earned.

5 Authorship of the phrase "Celtic Tiger" has been consistently misattributed to the cultural and political commentator David McWilliams, who has consistently denied responsibility for it. In fact, as Susan Cahill (2011) points out, the phrase was coined by Kevin Gardiner, a London-based economist with Morgan Stanley (4). Michael J. O'Sullivan (2006) suggests that "bull" would have been a more appropriate image for the Irish boom than "tiger," since the economy has more in common with "Anglo-Saxon" economies such as the USA and Britain, and the Asian "tiger" economies had been booming for much longer than Ireland's – continuous growth for thirty years or more (81).

6 Also of interest in this context is the work of Northern Irish author William Allen Harbinson, born in Belfast in 1941 and now a resident of West Cork. Harbinson is probably most famous for his *Projekt Saucer* series (1991–1999), a five-book series taking as its basis the conspiracy theory that UFOs are not of extraterrestrial manufacture at all, but were invented and built by Nazi scientists at a secret base in Antarctica, with the cooperation of the US and Soviet governments. Many of Harbinson's other novels combine UFOlogy and New Age mysticism with conspiracy theories to forge thrillers, such as *The Crystal Skulls* (1997), a thriller based on the "crystal skulls" mythology, and *The Lodestone* (1989), in which cosmic powers are blended with Egyptology. Harbinson's work also contains religious thrillers, such as *Revelation* (1982) and *Into the World of Might Be* (2008), and he also writes militaristic techno-thrillers under the pseudonym "Shaun Clarke." An in-depth analysis of Harbinson's varied works is, however, beyond the scope of the present project.

7 The process of imagining the future in terms of an economic competitor's culture occurs frequently in SF, especially in "near future" sub-genres such as cyberpunk. In 2004, Northern Irish author Ian McDonald contributed to this tradition with *River of Gods*, an epic novel set in 2050s India with a huge cast of characters, many of whom are artificial intelligences. At the time of writing, there is much discussion about the seemingly inevitable rise of India and China as economic superpowers.

8 This referendum removed the automatic right to citizenship for parents of Irish-born children.

9 The Corrib Project, administered by Shell E&P Ireland, Statoil Exploration (Ireland) Ltd., and the Vermilion Energy Trust, is a project to extract natural gas from a field discovered off the north-west coast of Ireland, via a pipeline running through the parish of Erris, County Mayo. Residents of Erris were concerned about the potential risks of a natural gas pipeline, and a number of landowners in the area were informed that they would have to reach an agreement with Shell for the sale of their property to accommodate the pipeline. Many refused, and in response, then-Minister for the Marine and Natural Resources Frank Fahey issued thirty-four Compulsory Acquisition Orders. Those who refused to comply with the order were threatened with legal action, and in 2005 five men were jailed for contempt of court after refusing Shell employees access to their land.

9. The Shape of Irish SF to Come

1 The IRA's General Order No. 5, Part 1, forbade volunteers from recognising or swearing allegiance to "the partition institutions of government of the Six or Twenty Six County states" (Dillon 487). Since the 1960s, republicans (most notably Sinn Féin) have compromised on this rule in order to pursue their objectives in Stormont and Leinster House, but other groups, such as the 32 County Sovereignty Committee, remain steadfast in their refusal to acknowledge the partition of the island.

2 Shelta, also known as Gammon or Cant, to a large extent consists of anagrams of words taken from other languages. For example, "lackeen" is taken from the Gaelic "cailín," meaning "girl." Another example is "thobar," the Shelta word for "road," which is taken from the Gaelic "bóthar."

Bibliography

Abe, Kôbô. "The Boom in Science Fiction." *Science Fiction Studies* 29: 3 (2002): 342–49. Originally published 1962. Trans. Christopher Bolton.

Adorno, Theodor and Max Horkheimer. *Dialectic of Enlightenment: Philosophical Fragments*. 1944. Trans. Edmund Jephcott. Ed. Gunzelin Schmid Noerr. 4th ed. Stanford University Press, 2002.

Albanese, Denise. *New Science, New World*. Durham, NC: Duke University Press, 1996.

Aldiss, Brian, and David Wingrove. *Trillion Year Spree*. Thirsk, Yorkshire: House of Stratus, 2001.

Allen, Nicholas. *Modernity, Ireland and Civil War*. Cambridge: Cambridge University Press, 2009.

Andrews, Graham. "Dr. Kilcasey in Space: A Bio-bibliography of James White." 2002. 22 October 2009. <http://www.sectorgeneral.com/biobiblio. html>

Angenot, Marc. "The Absent Paradigm: An Introduction to the Semiotics of Science Fiction." *Science Fiction Studies* 6: 1 (1979): 9–19.

Anonymous. *The Re-Conquest of Ireland, A.D. 1895*. Dublin: Hodges, Figgis and Co., 1881.

—. *The Battle of the Moy; or, How Ireland Gained Her Independence, 1892–1894*. Boston: Lee & Shepard, 1883.

—. *Newry Bridge; or, Ireland in 1887*. Edinburgh and London: William Blackwood and Sons, 1886.

Aquinas, St. Thomas. "The Summa Theologica." 1274. Chicago: Benziger Brothers, 1947.

Archer, Thomas. *Gladstone and his Contemporaries: Fifty Years of Social and Political Progress*. Vol. 2: 1840–1854. 4 vols. London, Edinburgh, Glasgow and Dublin: Blackie and Son, 1885.

Ashworth, Lucian M. "Clashing Utopias: H.G. Wells and Catholic Ireland." *The Reception of H.G. Wells in Europe*. Ed. Patrick Parrinder and John S. Partington. The Athlone Critical Traditions Series: The Reception of British Authors in Europe. London: Thoemmes Continuum, 2005. 267–79.

Astle, Richard. "Dracula as Totemic Monster: Lacan, Freud, Oedipus and History." *SubStance* 8: 25 (1979): 98–105.

Attebery, Brian. "The magazine era: 1926–1960." *The Cambridge Companion to Science Fiction*. Ed. Edward James; Farah Mendlesohn. Cambridge: Cambridge University Press, 2003.

Baccolini, Raffaella. "Gender and Genre in the Feminist Critical Dystopias of Katharine Burdekin, Margaret Atwood, and Octavia Butler." *Future Females, The Next Generation: New Voices and Velocities in Science Fiction Criticism*. Ed. Marleen S. Barr. Oxford: Rowman & Littlefield Publishers, Inc., 2000. 13–34.

Baines, Paul. "'Able Mechanik': *The Life and Adventures of Peter Wilkins* and the Eighteenth-Century Fantastic Voyage." *Anticipations: Essays on Early Science Fiction and its Precursors*. Ed. David Seed. Liverpool: Liverpool University Press, 1995. 1–25.

Baneham, Sam. *The Cloud of Desolation*. Dublin: Wolfhound Press, 1982.

Barnes, John. "Tropics of a Desirable Oxymoron: The Radical Superman in *Back to Methuselah*." *SHAW – The Annual of Bernard Shaw Studies, Volume 17:Shaw and Science Fiction*. Ed. Milton T. Wolf. University Park, Pennsylvania: The Pennsylvania State University Press, 1997. 155–64.

Barry, Kevin. *City of Bohane*. London: Jonathan Cape, 2011.

Barthes, Roland. *Mythologies*. 1957. Trans. Annette Lavers. London: Jonathan Cape, 1974.

Benjamin, Walter. "Critique of Violence." Trans. Edmund Jephcott. *Reflections: Essays, Aphorisms, Autobiographic Writings*. Ed. Peter Demetz. New York: Schocken Books, 1986. 277–300.

—. "Two Poems by Friedrich Hölderlin: 'The Poet's Courage' and 'Timidity'." *Walter Benjamin, Selected Writings Volume 1: 1913–1926*. Ed. Marcus Bullock. Cambridge, MA: Harvard University Press, 1996. 18–36.

Bew, Paul. *Ireland: The Politics of Enmity 1789–2006*. Oxford History of Modern Europe. Oxford: Oxford University Press, 2007.

—. "The Politics of War." *Our War: Ireland and the Great War*. Ed. John Horne. The 2008 Thomas Davis Lecture Series. Dublin: Royal Irish Academy, 2008. 97–107.

Bhreathnach-Lynch, Sighle. "The Easter Rising 1916: Constructing a Canon in Art & Artefacts." *History Ireland* 5: 1 (1997): 37–42.

Bleiler, Everett F. *Science-Fiction – The Gernsback Years: A complete coverage of the genre magazines Amazing, Astounding, Wonder and others from 1926 through 1936*. Kent, OH: Kent State University Press, 1998.

Booth, Tim. *Altergeist*. Bantry: Fish Publishing, 1999.

Bould, Mark. "The Ships Landed Long Ago: Afrofuturism and Black SF." *Science Fiction Studies* 34: 2 (2007): 177–86.

Bould, Mark and Sherryl Vint. *The Routledge Concise History of Science Fiction*. Abingdon: Routledge, 2011.

Bourke, Angela. "The Baby and the Bathwater: Cultural Loss in Nineteenth-Century Ireland." *Ideology and Ireland in the Nineteenth Century*. Ed. Tadhg Foley and Seán Ryder. Dublin: Four Courts Press, 1998. 79–92.

—. *The Burning of Bridget Cleary: A True Story*. London: Pimlico, 1999.

Brophy, Catherine. *Dark Paradise*. Dublin: Wolfhound Press, 1991.

Brown, Terence. *Ireland: A Social and Cultural History 1922–1985*. 1981. 5th ed. London: Fontana Press, 1990.

Butler, Andrew M. "Thirteen Ways of Looking at the British Boom." *Science Fiction Studies* 30:3 (2003), 374–93.

Byrne, Patrick F., ed. *Irish Ghost Stories of Sheridan Le Fanu*. Dublin and Cork: Mercier, 1973.

Cahill, Susan. *Irish Literature in the Celtic Tiger Years, 1990–2008: Gender, Bodies, Memory*. London and New York: Continuum, 2011.

Campbell, Paul. "Respectable Little Green Men." *The Linen Hall Review* 3: 1 (1986): 4–5.

Carr, E.H. *What Is History?* 1961. 3rd ed. Basingstoke: Palgrave, 2001.

Carson, Liam. "The Most Irish of SF Writers." *Books Ireland* No. 198 (Oct. 1996): 269–70.

Chernyshova, Tatiana. "Science Fiction and Myth Creation in Our Age." *Science Fiction Studies* 31: 3 (2004): 345–57. Originally published 1972. Trans. Istvan Csicsery-Ronay Jr.

Claeys, Gregory. "Introduction: Francis Galton, 'Kantsaywhere' and 'The Donoghues of Dunno Weir'." *Utopian Studies* 12: 2 (2001): 188–90.

Clarke, I.F. *Voices Prophesying War, 1763–1984*. London: Oxford University Press, 1966.

Cleary, Joe. *Outrageous Fortune: Capital and Culture in Modern Ireland*. Dublin: Field Day Publications, 2007.

"Conán". "Marbhán." *Connacht Tribune* 25 March; 8 April 1933: 3; 3.

Coogan, Tim Pat. *The Troubles: Ireland's Ordeal 1966–1995 and the Search for Peace*. London: Hutchinson, 1995.

Cornwell, Neil. *The Absurd in Literature*. Manchester: Manchester University Press, 2006.

Cromie, Robert. *The Crack of Doom*. 2nd ed. London: Digby, Long & Co., 1895.

—. *A Plunge Into Space*. 1890. Westport, CT: Hyperion Press, 1976.

Cronin, Anthony. *No Laughing Matter: The Life and Times of Flann O'Brien*. 1989. Dublin: New Island, 2003.

De Zwaan, Victoria. "Slipstream." *The Routledge Companion to Science Fiction*. Ed. Mark Bould. Abingdon: Routledge, 2009.

Delany, Samuel R. *The Jewel-Hinged Jaw: Notes on the Language of Science Fiction*. 1978. Middletown CT: Wesleyan University Press, 2009.

Dillon, Martin. *The Dirty War*. 1990. 2nd ed. London: Arrow Books Limited, 1991.

Dougherty, Jane Elizabeth. "An Angel in the House: The Act of Union and Anthony Trollope's Irish Hero." *Victorian Literature and Culture* 32: 1 (2004): 133–45.

Downey, Edmund (as 'F.M. Allen'). *London's Peril*. London: Downey & Co. Ltd., 1900.

Doyle, Roddy. "'57% Irish'." *The Deportees*. London: Vintage Books, 2008.

Dunsany, Lord. *The Last Revolution*. London: Jarrolds Publishers Ltd., 1951.

Dwan, David. *The Great Community: Culture and Nationalism in Ireland*. Dublin: Field Day, 2008.

Evans, Richard J. *In Defence of History*. 1997. 2nd ed. London: Granta Books, 2000.

Ferriter, Diarmaid. *The Transformation of Ireland: 1900–2000*. London: Profile Books Ltd., 2004.

Fischer, Joachim. "A Future Ireland under German Rule: Dystopias as Propoganda during World War I." *Utopian Studies* 18: 3 (2007): 345–63.

—. "'Kultur – and Our Need of It': The Image of Germany and Irish National Identity, 1890–1920." *The Irish Review* 24 (1999): 66–79.

Fitting, Peter. "The Lessons of Cyberpunk." *Technoculture*. Ed. Constance Penley and Andrew Ross. Cultural Politics. Minneapolis: University of Minnesota Press, 1991. 295–316.

Freedman, Carl. *Critical Theory and Science Fiction*. Hanover, NH: Wesleyan University Press, 2000.

Frye, Herman Northrop. *Anatomy of Criticism: Four Essays*. 1957. Princeton: Princeton University Press, 1973.

Garvin, Tom. *Preventing the Future: Why was Ireland so poor for so long?* 2nd ed. Dublin: Gill & Macmillan Ltd., 2005.

Geary, Patrick T. "'Ireland's Economy in the 1980s – Stagnation and Recovery: A Preliminary Review of the Evidence'." *"Ireland's Successful Stabilisation? – Achievements and Prospects"*. Ed. Maynooth: Maynooth College Department of Economics. 1992. Conference Paper.

Gibbons, Luke. *Gaelic Gothic: Race, Colonization and Irish Culture*. Galway: Arlen House, 2004.

Gibson, William. "The Gernsback Continuum." *Mirrorshades*. 1981. Ed. Bruce Sterling. New York: Ace Books, 1988. 1–11.

Gramsci, Antonio. *Prison Notebooks*. 1975. Vol. 1. New York: Columbia University Press, 1992.

Greer, Tom. *A Modern Daedalus*. London: Griffith, Farran, Okeden & Welsh, 1885.

Hardt, Michael and Antonio Negri. *Empire*. London: Harvard University Press, 2001.

Harvey, David. *Spaces of Hope*. Edinburgh: Edinburgh University Press, 2000.

Heron, Gil Scott. "Whitey on the Moon." *A New Black Poet: Small Talk at 125th and Lenox*. New York: Flying Dutchman Records, 1970.

Higgins, Roisin, Carole Holohan and Catherine O'Donnell. "1966 and All That: The 50th Anniversary Commemorations." *History Ireland* 14: 2 (2006): 31–36.

Hobson, Bulmer, ed. *Saorstát Eireann: Official Handbook*. Dublin: Talbot Press, 1932.

Holohan, Francis T. "History Teaching in the Irish Free State 1922–1935." *History Ireland* 2: 4 (1994): 53–55.

Hyde, Douglas. "The Necessity for De-Anglicising Ireland." *Irish Political Documents 1869–1916*. 1892. Ed. Arthur Mitchell and Pádraig Ó Snodaigh. Dublin: Irish Academic Press, 1989. 81–86.

Indick, Ben P. "Shaw's Science Fiction on the Boards." *SHAW – The Annual of Bernard Shaw Studies, Volume 17:Shaw and Science Fiction*. Ed. Milton T. Wolf. University Park, Pennsylvania: The Pennsylvania State University Press, 1997. 19–38.

James, Edward. "The Anglo-Irish Disagreement: Past Irish Futures." *The Linen Hall Review* 3: 4 (1986): 5–8.

—. "Science Fiction by Gaslight: An Introduction to English-Language Science Fiction in the Nineteenth Century." *Anticipations: Essays on Early Science Fiction and its Precursors*. Ed. David Seed. Liverpool: Liverpool University Press, 1995. 26–45.

Jameson, Fredric. *The Political Unconscious*. 1981. Routledge Classics. 3rd ed. Abingdon: Routledge, 2002a.

—. *A Singular Modernity: Essay on the Ontology of the Present*. London and New York: Verso, 2002b.

Jarrell, Richard A. "The Department of Science and Art and Control of Irish Science, 1853–1905." *Irish Historical Studies* 23: 92 (1983): 330–47.

Jezer, Marty. *The Dark Ages: Life in the United States 1945–1960*. Cambridge, MA: South End Press, 1982.

Joyce, John. *Virtually Maria*. Dublin: Poolbeg Press Ltd., 1998.

—. *Yesterday, Today and Tomorrow*. Dublin: Spindrift Press, 2008.

Kavanagh, Patrick. "Mao Tse-Tung Unrolls His Mat." *Kavanagh's Weekly* 7 (1952): 1–3.

Kayser, Wolfgang Johannes. *The Grotesque in Art and Literature*. 1957. Trans. Ulrich Weisstein. New York: Columbia University Press, 1981.

Kee, Robert. *The Green Flag*. Vol. 2: "The Bold Fenian Men". London and New York: Penguin Books Ltd., 1989.

Kennedy, Finola. *Cottage to Crèche: family change in Ireland*. 2001. Dublin: Institute of Public Administration, 2004.

Kiberd, Declan. *Inventing Ireland: The Literature of a Modern Nation*. London: Vintage, 1996.

—. *Irish Classics*. 2nd ed. London: Granta Books, 2001.

Killeen, Jarlath. "Irish Gothic: A Theoretical Introduction." *The Irish Journal of Gothic and Horror Studies*. 25 August 2009 <http://irishgothichorror-journal.homestead.com/jarlath.html>.

Kinsella, Stephen. *Ireland in 2050: How We Will Be Living*. Dublin: Liberties Press, 2009.

Kirby, Peadar. *Celtic Tiger in Collapse: Explaining the Weaknesses of the Irish Model*. 2002. International Political Economy Series. 2nd ed. Basingstoke: Palgrave Macmillan, 2010.

Kirby, Peadar and Mary P. Murphy. *Towards a Second Republic: Irish Politics After the Celtic Tiger*. London: Pluto Press, 2011.

Knowlson, James R. "George Psalmanaazaar: The Fake Formosan." *History Today* XV: 12 (1965): 871–76.

Kostick, Conor. *Epic*. Dublin: O'Brien Press, 2004.

Kühling, Carmen and Kieran Keohane. *Cosmopolitan Ireland: Globalisation and Quality of Life*. London, Dublin, Ann Arbor: Pluto Press, 2007.

Langer, Jessica. *Postcolonialism and Science Fiction*. Basingstoke: Palgrave Macmillan, 2011.

Langford, David. "Wreath of Stars: The Late Bob Shaw Remembered". 1996. 13 August 2011. <http://www.ansible.co.uk/writing/bobshaw.html>.

Larkin, Emmet. "Church and State in Ireland in the Nineteenth Century." *Church History* 31:3 (1962): 294–306.

Leaney, Enda. "'Evanescent Impressions': Public Lectures and the

Popularization of Science in Ireland, 1770–1860." *Eire-Ireland* 43: 3 (2008): 157–82.

Lewis, C.S. *Out of the Silent Planet*. 1938. New York: Scribner Paperback Fiction, 1996.

Loeber, Rolf and Magda Loeber. *A Guide to Irish Fiction, 1650–1900*. Dublin: Four Courts Press, 2006.

Lovecraft, H.P. "Supernatural Horror in Literature." *Dagon and Other Macabre Tales*. 1927. Ed. August Derleth. St. Albans: Panther Books Ltd., 1973.

Mac Aodha Bhuí, Iarla. *An Clár AMANDA*. 1998. Indreabhán: Cló Mhaigh Eo, 2000.

—. *Domhan Faoi Cheilt*. Indreabhán: Cló Mhaigh Eo, 1999.

Mac Aonghusa, Proinsias and Liam Ó Réagáin, eds. *The Best of Connolly*. Cork: The Mercier Press, 1967a.

—, ed. *The Best of Pearse*. Cork: The Mercier Press, 1967b.

Mac Craith, Micheál. "Cuairt ar an nGealaigh." *Fainne an Lae* 17 March 1923: 5.

Mac Donagh, Thomas. *Literature in Ireland*. 1916. Nenagh: Relay Books, 1996.

Mac Maoláin, Seán. *Algoland*. Dublin: Oifig an tSoláthair, 1947.

MacManus, Diarmuid. *The Middle Kingdom: The Faerie World of Ireland*. London: Max Parrish & Co. Ltd., 1959.

Mac Síomóin, Tomás. *Ag Altóir an Diabhail: Striptease Spioradálta Bheartla B.* Dublin: Coiscéim, 2003.

—. *An Tionscadal: Fabhal don nua-aois i dtrí eadarlúid*. Dublin: Coiscéim, 2007.

Maguire, John Francis. *The Next Generation*. London: Hurst and Blackett, 1871.

Manning, Maurice. *The Blueshirts*. 1970. 3rd ed. Dublin: Gill & Macmillan Ltd., 2006.

Mansergh, Martin. "A Rising Curve from Subversion to Statecraft." *Fortnight* 292 (1991): 28–31.

Maume, Patrick. "Futures Past: The Science Fiction of Bob Shaw and James White as a Product of Late-Industrial Belfast." *No Country For Old Men: Fresh Perspectives on Irish Literature*. Ed. Paddy Lyons; Alison O'Malley-Younger. Bern: Peter Lang, 2009. 193–214.

Maxton, Hugh. *20/16 Vision*. Killiney, Co. Dublin: The Duras Press, 2009.

McCarthy, Michael J.F. *Priests and People in Ireland*. 1902. 4th ed. London: Simpkin, Marshall, Hamilton, Kent & Co., Ltd., 1911.

McCormack, Mike. *Notes From a Coma*. London: Jonathan Cape, 2005.

McDonald, Ian. *Chaga*. London: Victor Gollancz, 1995.

—. *Sacrifice of Fools*. London: Victor Gollancz, 1996.

—. *River of Gods*. London: Simon & Schuster, 2004.

—. *Brasyl*. London: Gollancz, 2007.

—. *The Dervish House*. London: Gollancz, 2010.

McManus, L. "The Professor in Erin, chapters 1 and 2." *Sinn Féin (Weekly)* 2 March 1912a: 6–7.

—. "The Professor in Erin, chapters 3 and 4." *Sinn Féin (Weekly)* 9 March 1912b: 6–7.

—. "The Professor in Erin, chapters 5 and 6." *Sinn Féin (Weekly)* 16 March 1912c: 6–7.

—. "The Professor in Erin, chapter 7." *Sinn Féin (Weekly)* 23 March 1912d: 6–7.

—. "The Professor in Erin, chapters 8 and 9." *Sinn Féin (Weekly)* 30 March 1912e: 6–7.

—. "The Professor in Erin, chapters 10, 11 and 12." *Sinn Féin (Weekly)* 6 April 1912f: 6–7.

—. "The Professor in Erin, Chapters 13, 14 and 15." *Sinn Féin (Weekly)* 13 April 1912g: 3; 6–7.

—. "The Professor in Erin, Chapters 16 and 17." *Sinn Féin (Weekly)* 20 April 1912h: 6–7.

—. "The Professor in Erin, Chapters 18 and 19." *Sinn Féin (Weekly)* 27 April 1912i: 6–7.

—. "The Professor in Erin, Chapters 19 (continued) and 20." *Sinn Féin (Weekly)* 4 May 1912j: 6–7.

—. "The Professor in Erin, Chapters 20 (continued) and 21." *Sinn Féin (Weekly)* 11 May 1912k: 6–7.

—. "The Professor in Erin, Chapters 22 and 23." *Sinn Féin (Weekly)* 18 May 1912l: 6–7.

—. "The Professor in Erin, Chapters 23 (continued) and 24." *Sinn Féin (Weekly)* 25 May 1912m: 6–7.

—. "The Professor in Erin, Chapter 25." *Sinn Féin (Weekly)* June 1st 1912n: 6–7.

Mendlesohn, Farah. "Fiction, 1926–1949." *The Routledge Companion to Science Fiction*. Ed. Mark Bould. Abingdon: Routledge, 2011. 52–61.

—. *Rhetorics of Fantasy*. Middletown, CT: Wesleyan University Press, 2008.

Meredith, James Creed. *The Rainbow in the Valley*. Dublin: Browne and Nolan Limited, 1939.

Miéville, China. "Cognition as Ideology: A Dialectic of SF Theory." *Red Planets: Marxism and Science Fiction*. Ed. Mark Bould and China Miéville. London: Pluto Press, 2009. 231–48.

Milligan, Alice L. *A Royal Democrat: A sensational Irish novel*. Dublin: M.H. Gill & Son, 1892.

Moore, Brian. *Catholics*. 1972. London: Vintage, 1992.

Moore, Michael. *Stupid White Men... And Other Sorry Excuses for the State of the Nation!* New York: HarperCollins, 2001.

Morash, Chris. "Literature, Memory, Atrocity." *Fearful Realities: New Perspectives on the Famine*. 1996. Ed. Chris Morash and Richard Hayes. Dublin: Irish Academic Press, 2000. 110–18.

Mordaunt, Jason. *Welcome to Coolsville*. London: Vintage, 2004.

Morgan, Margery Mary. *The Shavian Playground: an exploration of the art of George Bernard Shaw*. London: Methuen, 1972.

Moylan, Tom. *Scraps of the Untainted Sky: Science Fiction, Utopia, Dystopia*. Cultural Studies Series. Ed. Paul Smith. Boulder, CO: Westview Press, 2000.

Neeson, Eoin. *The Civil War, 1922–23*. 1966. 2nd ed. Dublin: Poolbeg Press Ltd., 1995.

Ní Ghráda, Máiréad. *Manannán*. Dublin: Oifig an tSoláthair, 1940.

Nolan, Val. "Flann, Fantasy and Science Fiction: O'Brien's Surprising Synthesis." *The Review of Contemporary Fiction* XXXI: 3 (2011): 178–90.

O'Brien, Eugene. "A Nation Once Again: Towards an epistemology of the republican 'imaginaire'." *Republicanism in Modern Ireland*. Ed. Fearghal McGarry. Dublin: University College Dublin Press, 2003. 145–66.

O'Brien, Fitz-James. *The Diamond Lens and Other Stories*. London: Ward & Downey, 1887.

O'Brien, Flann. *At Swim-Two-Birds*. 1939. 4th ed. London: Penguin Books Ltd., 2001.

—. *The Dalkey Archive*. 1964. London: Paladin, 1990.

—. "The Saint and I." *The Guardian* 19 January 1966: 9.

Ó Brolacháin, Mícheál. *Pax Dei*. Dublin: Taibhse, 1985.

Ó Caochlaigh, Barra. "An Tost." *An Tost agus Sgéalta Eile*. Dublin: Alex Thom & Co. Ltd.; Oifig an tSoláthair, 1927. 1–45.

Ó Conaire, Padraic. "Páipéar a Fristhadh i mBosca." *Connacht Tribune* 1926: 3.

Ó Droighneáin, Muiris. *Taighde i gComhair Stair Litridheachta na nua-Ghaedhilge ó 1882 Anuas*. Dublin, 1936.

Ó Huallacháin, Colmán. *The Irish and Irish: a sociolinguistic analysis of the relationship between a people and their language*. Dublin: Irish Franciscan Provincial Office, 1994.

O'Leary, Philip. *Gaelic Prose in the Irish Free State, 1922–1939*. University Park, Pennsylvania: Pennsylvania State University Press, 2004.

—. *Irish Interior: Keeping Faith with the Past in Gaelic Prose, 1940–1951*. Dublin: University College Dublin Press, 2010.

Ó Muirí, Pól. *Siosafas*. Dublin: Coiscéim, 1995.

Ó Nualláin, Brian. "Dioghaltas ar Ghallaibh 'sa bhliadhain 2032!" Short story. *The Irish Press* Monday, 18 January 1932: 4.

Ó Sándair, Cathal. *An Captaen Spéirling agus An Phláinéad do Phléasc*. Dublin: Oifig an tSoláthair, 1960a.

—. *An Captaen Spéirling Arís*. Dublin: Oifig an tSoláthair, 1960b.

—. *An Captaen Spéirling, Spás Phíolóta*. Dublin: Oifig an tSoláthair, 1961a.

—. *Leis an gCaptaen Spéirling go Mars*. Dublin: Oifig an tSoláthair, 1961b.

Ó Séaghda, Pádraig. *Eoghan Paor*. Dublin: M.H. Gill and Son, 1911.

Ó Snodaigh, Pádraig. "Ceiliúradh nó Comóradh?" *Comhar* 50: 4 (1991): 13–14.

O'Sullivan, Michael J. *Ireland and the Global Question*. Cork: Cork University Press, 2006.

O'Toole, Tina. "Ireland: The *Terra Incognita* of the New Woman Project." *New Contexts: Re-Framing Nineteenth-Century Irish Women's Prose*. Ed. Heidi Hansson. Cork: Cork University Press, 2008. 125–41.

Ó Torna, Seosamh. "Duinneall." *Bonaventura* Spring (1938): 70–75.

Okuda, Michael and Denise Okuda. *The Star Trek Encyclopedia: A Reference Guide to the Future*. 1994. 2nd ed. New York: Pocket Books, 1997.

Ollman, Bertell. *Alienation: Marx's Conception of Man in Capitalist Society*. Cambridge Studies in the History and Theory of Politics. Cambridge: Cambridge University Press, 1976.

Pennell, Catriona. "Going to War." *Our War: Ireland and the Great War.* Ed. John Horne. The 2008 Thomas Davis Lecture Series. Dublin: Royal Irish Academy, 2008. 37–48.

Philmus, Robert M. *Into the Unknown: The Evolution of Science Fiction from Francis Godwin to H.G. Wells.* Berkeley and Los Angeles: University of California Press, 1970.

Popper, Karl Raimund. *The Myth of the Framework: In defence of science and rationality.* 1994. Ed. M.A. Notturno. Abingdon: Routledge, 1997.

Pordzik, Ralph. "A Postcolonial View of Ireland and the Irish Conflict in Anglo-Irish Utopian Literature since the Nineteenth Century." *Irish Studies Review* 9: 3 (2001): 331–46.

Pratchett, Terry. "# ifdefDEBUG+'world/enough'+'time'." *Cyber-Killers.* 1990. Ed. Ric Alexander. London: Orion Books Ltd., 1998. 5–18.

Priest, Christopher. "Portrait of Bob Shaw." 2010. 13 August 2011. <http://www.christopher-priest.co.uk/essays-reviews/contemporaries-portrayed/bobshaw/>.

Rieder, John. *Colonialism and the Emergence of Science Fiction.* Middletown, CT: Wesleyan University Press, 2008.

Riordan, Arthur.*The Emergency Session.* Rough Magic, Dublin, 1992.

Roberts, Adam. *The History of Science Fiction.* Palgrave Histories of Literature. Basingstoke and New York: Palgrave Macmillan, 2007.

—. *Science Fiction.* The New Critical Idiom. Ed. John Drakakis. Abingdon: Routledge, 2000.

Roughsey, Dick (Goobalathaldin). *Moon and Rainbow: The Autobigraphy of an Aboriginal.* 1971. Adelaide: Rigby Limited, 1977.

Said, Edward W. *Orientalism: Western Conceptions of the Orient.* 1978. London: Penguin Books Ltd., 1995.

Salter, William M. "Nietzsche's Superman." *The Journal of Philosophy, Psychology and Scientific Methods* 12: 16 (1915): 421–38.

Sangwan, Satpal. "Science Education in India Under Colonial Constraints, 1792–1857." *Oxford Review of Education* 16: 1 (1990): 81–95.

Scholes, Robert and Eric S. Rabkin. *Science Fiction: Science, History, Vision.* New York: Oxford University Press, 1977.

Semmel, Bernard. *Imperialism and Social Reform: English Social-Imperial Thought, 1895–1914.* 1960. Garden City, New York: Anchor Books, 1968.

Shaw, Bob. *Orbitsville.* 1975. Gollancz SF Collectors' Editions. London: Gollancz, 2000a.

—. *Other Days, Other Eyes.* 2nd ed. London: Pan Books Ltd., 1974.

—. *The Ragged Astronauts.* 1986. London: Futura Publications, 1987.

—. *The Shadow of Heaven.* New York: Avon Books, 1969.

—. *A Wreath of Stars.* 1976. Gollancz SF Collectors' Editions. London: Gollancz, 2000b.

Shaw, George Bernard. *Back to Methuselah: A Metabiological Pentateuch.* New York: Brentano's, 1921.

—. *Man and Superman: A Comedy and a Philosophy.* Westminster: Archibald Constable & Co. Ltd., 1903.

—. "Utopias." 1887. *SHAW – The Annual of Bernard Shaw Studies, Volume 17:Shaw and Science Fiction.* Ed. Milton T. Wolf. University Park, Pennsylvania: The Pennsylvania State University Press, 1997. 65–80.

Shelley, Mary. *Frankenstein; or The Modern Prometheus.* 1818. Penguin Classics. Ed. Maurice Hindle. 3rd ed. London: Penguin Books Ltd., 1992.

Shippey, Tom. "Skeptical Speculation and *Back to Methuselah.*" *SHAW – The Annual of Bernard Shaw Studies, Volume 17:Shaw and Science Fiction.* Ed. Milton T. Wolf. University Park, Pennsylvania: The Pennsylvania State University Press, 1997. 199–214.

Sirius, R.U. *Mondo 2000.* Berkeley, CA: Fun City MegaMedia, 1990. Vol. 2.

Smyth, Lisa. "Narratives of Irishness and the Problem of Abortion: The X Case 1992." *Feminist Review* 60 (1998): 61–83.

Sparks, Julie A. "Shaw for the Utopians, Čapek for the Anti-Utopians." *SHAW – The Annual of Bernard Shaw Studies, Volume 17:Shaw and Science Fiction.* Ed. Milton T. Wolf. University Park, Pennsylvania: The Pennsylvania State University Press, 1997. 165–184.

Spencer, Kathleen L. "'The Red Sun is High, the Blue Low': Towards a Stylistic Description of Science Fiction ('Le soleil rouge est au zénith, le soleil bleu se couche': vers un description stylistique de la SF)." *Science Fiction Studies* 10 (1983): 35–49.

Stableford, Brian. *Algebraic Fantasies and Realistic Romances: More Masters of Science Fiction.* Milford series – Popular Writers of Today. Rockville, MD: Wildside Press LLC, 1995a.

—. "Frankenstein and the Origins of Science Fiction." *Anticipations: Essays on Early Science Fiction and its Precursors.* Ed. David Seed. Liverpool: Liverpool University Press, 1995b. 46–57.

Standún, Pádraig. *A.D. 2016.* Naas: Cló Chonamara, 1988.

Steele, E.D. "Cardinal Cullen and Irish Nationality." *Irish Historical Studies* 19: 75 (1975), 239–60.

Stockwell, Peter. *The Poetics of Science Fiction.* Textual Explorations. Ed. Mick Short and Elena Semino. Harlow: Pearson Educational Limited, 2000.

Stradling, Robert A. *The Irish and the Spanish Civil War 1936–1939: Crusades in Conflict.* Manchester and New York: Mandolin, 1999.

Suvin, Darko. "Considering the Sense of 'Fantasy' or 'Fantastic Fiction': An Effusion." *Extrapolation* 41: 3 (2000): 209–47.

—. "Science Fiction and the Novum." *Defined By a Hollow: Essays on Utopia, Science Fiction and Political Epistemology.* 1977. Ed. Darko Suvin. Ralahine Utopian Studies. Oxford: Peter Lang, 2010. 67–92.

Sweeney, Paul. *The Celtic Tiger: Ireand's Continuing Economic Miracle.* 1998. 2nd ed. Dublin: Oak Tree Press, 1999.

Taylor, Peter. *Loyalists.* 1999. London: Bloomsbury Publishing Plc, 2000.

Thacker, W. Ridley. *Ballymuckbeg: A Tale of Eighty Years Hence.* Dublin: William McGee, 1884.

Todorov, Tzvetan. *The Fantastic: a Structural Approach to a Literary Genre.* 2nd ed. Ithaca, NY: Cornell University Press, 1975.

von Däniken, Erich. *Chariots of the Gods?: unsolved mysteries of the past.* 1968. Trans. Michael Heron. London: World Books, 1971.

Wallmann, Jeffrey M. "Evolutionary Machinery: Foreshadowings of Science Fiction in Bernard Shaw's Dramas." *SHAW – The Annual of Bernard Shaw Studies, Volume 17:Shaw and Science Fiction.* Ed. Milton T. Wolf. University Park, Pennsylvania: The Pennsylvania State University Press, 1997. 81–96.

Wegner, Phillip E. *Imaginary Communities: Utopia, the Nation, and the Spatial Histories of Modernity.* Berkeley, Los Angeles and London: University of California Press, 2002.

Welch, Robert. *Tearmann.* Dublin: Coiscéim, 1997.

Westfahl, Gary. *The Mechanics of Wonder: The Creation of the Idea of Science Fiction.* Liverpool: Liverpool University Press, 1998.

White, James. "Full Time Hobbyist: James White Interview, Locus March 1993." 2002. 22 October 2009. <http://www.sectorgeneral.com/articles-locusinterview.html>.

—. "Hospital Station." *Beginning Operations: A Sector General Omnibus.* 1962. New York: Tom Doherty Associates, LLC, 2001. 13–199.

—. "Major Operation." *Beginning Operations: A Sector General Omnibus.* 1971. New York: Tom Doherty Associates, LLC, 2001. 365–511.

—. *Mind Changer.* New York: Tor, 1998.

—. *Monsters and Medics.* London: Corgi Books, 1977.

—. "Star Surgeon." *Beginning Operations: A Sector General Omnibus.* 1963. New York: Tom Doherty Associates, LLC, 2001. 201–364.

—. *Underkill.* London: Corgi Books, 1979.

Williams, Raymond. *Culture and Society: 1780–1950.* 1958. New York: Anchor Books, 1960.

—. *Marxism and Literature.* Marxist Introductions. Ed. Steven Lukes. Oxford and New York: Oxford University Press, 1977.

Wills, Clair. *That Neutral Island: A Cultural History of Ireland During the Second World War.* London: Faber and Faber Limited, 2007.

Windholz, Anne M. "An Emigrant and a Gentleman: Imperial Masculinity, British Magazines, and the Colony That Got Away." *Victorian Studies* 42: 4 (1999): 631–58.

Wise, Herbert A., and Phyllis Fraser, eds. *Great Tales of Terror and the Supernatural.* 1947. 5th ed. London: Hammond, Hammond & Co., 1969.

Wisenthal, J.L. "Shaw's Utopias." *SHAW – The Annual of Bernard Shaw Studies, Volume 17:Shaw and Science Fiction.* Ed. Milton T. Wolf. University Park, Pennsylvania: The Pennsylvania State University Press, 1997. 53–64.

Wolfe, Gary K. *The Known and the Unknown: The Iconography of Science Fiction.* Kent, OH: Kent State University Press, 1979.

Wyndham Bourke, Dermot Robert. *The War Cruise of the 'Aries' (A tale).* Dublin: Edward Ponsonby, 1894.

Yamano, Kôichi. "Japanese SF, Its Originality and Orientation (1969)." *Science Fiction Studies* 21: 1 (1994): 67–80. Trans. Kazuko Behrens.

Yeats, W.B., ed. *Fairy and Folk Tales of Ireland.* 1888. London: Pan Books Ltd., 1979.

Index